Tales of the

THIEFTAKER

Other Thieftaker books by D.B. Jackson:

Thieftaker (Tor Books, 2012)
Thieves' Quarry (Tor Books, 2013)
A Plunder of Souls (Tor Books, 2014)
Dead Man's Reach (Tor Books, 2015)

Tales of the

THIEFTAKER

D.B. JACKSON

To Emily,
I hope you enjoy this!
Very nice
meeting you.
All the best,

LORE
SEEKERS
PRESS

TAILS OF THE THIEFTAKER
ISBN 978-1-62268-131-0

Copyright © 2017 D.B. Jackson

"The Cully," previously published in *Big Bad II*, Dark Oak Press, 2015. "The Tavern Fire," previously published in *After Hours: Tales from the Ur-Bar*, Daw Books, 2011. "A Memory of Freedom," previously published at *Orson Scott Card's Intergalactic Medicine Show*, 2012. "The Price of Doing Business," previously published at *Tor.com*, 2014. "A Spell of Vengeance," previously published at *Tor.com*, 2012. "The Spelled Blade," previously published in *Realms of Imagination: An Urban Fantasy Anthology*, Dark Oak Press, 2014. "A Passing Storm," previously published at *Faithhunter.net*, 2014. "A Walking Tour of Boston, Narrated by Ethan Kaille," previously published at *AllThingsUrbanFantasy.com*, 2013. "An Encounter With Sephira Pryce," previously published at *ISmellSheep.com*, 2015.

Library of Congress Control Number: 2017961455

Also available in e-book form: ISBN 978-1-62268-132-7

Cover illustration by Chris McGrath.

Map reproduction courtesy of the Norman B. Leventhal Map Center at the Boston Public Library.

Printed in the United States of America on acid-free paper.

Lore Seekers Press is an imprint of Bella Rosa Books.
Lore Seekers Press and logo are trademarks of Bella Rosa Books.

10   9   8   7   6   5   4   3   2   1

For Bill

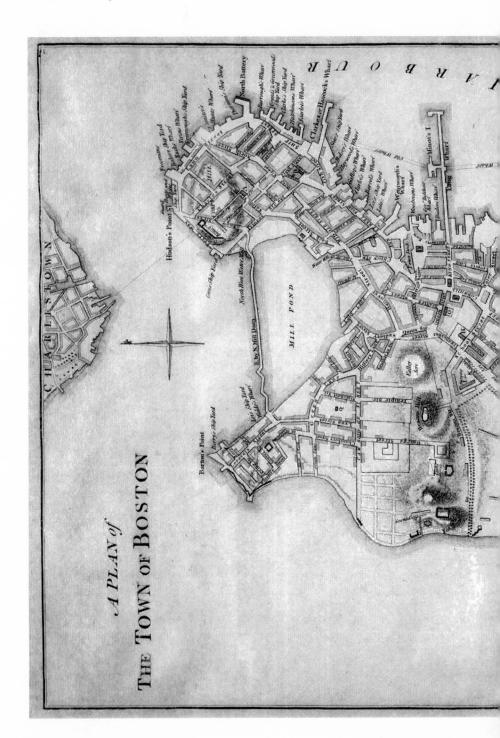

A PLAN of THE TOWN OF BOSTON

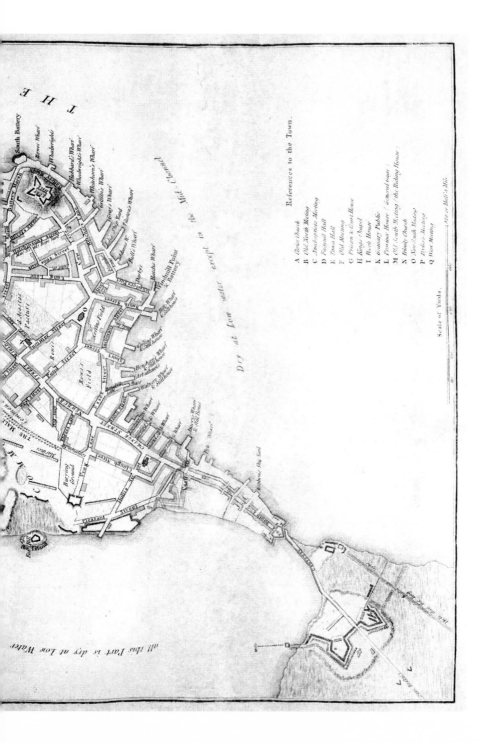

References to the Town.

A Tower Church.
B Old North Meeting.
C Brattle-street Meeting.
D Faneuil Hall.
E Town Hall.
F Old Meeting.
G Prison & Court House.
H Kings Chapel.
I Work House.
K Granary Public.
L Province House (a new one).
M Old South Meeting (the Riding House).
N Trinity Church.
O New South Meeting.
P Hollows Meeting.
Q New Meeting.

Table of Contents

Author's Forward

This collection of Thieftaker short fiction has been a long time in the making. I started writing Thieftaker stories long before *Thieftaker*, volume I in the Thieftaker Chronicles, was released in 2012, and I kept turning them out as the series progressed. The stories appeared in anthologies, in online short story markets, and in some cases at the websites of friends, colleagues, and online reviewers. I have continued to generate new Thieftaker fiction since I finished the fourth and final Thieftaker novel, *Dead Man's Reach.*

This collection includes a few pieces that were never actually published. "The Witch of Dedham" was available for a time on my website as a free download either in .pdf or .mp3 format (the latter with me doing the reading), but I never submitted it anywhere for publication. Three shorter pieces—"A Walking Tour of Boston," "An Encounter with Sephira Pryce," and "A Passing Storm"—were written originally for the blog tours I did to promote the various Thieftaker novels. "A Passing Storm" is actually as close to a piece of Thieftaker flash fiction as I ever wrote. It appeared originally at the site of my dear friend, Faith Hunter.

And, of course, the final piece in the collection, "The *Ruby Blade*" is a novella that I wrote in the last year as the capstone for this project. This is the first time it has appeared anywhere in any format.

Fans of the Thieftaker novels will find much here that is familiar—Ethan's rivalry with Sephira Pryce, his romance with Kannice Lester, his silently contentious partnership with Uncle Reg, his friendships with Diver Jervis, Henry Dall, and Kelf Fingarin. Ethan doesn't appear at all in one story, but Janna Windcatcher is featured. Naturally, there is magic and history aplenty in all the tales collected here. Where history and fiction have intersected, I have, as always, attempted to be as accurate as possible in portraying 1760s/'70s Boston, while also doing my best to write engaging fiction that will speak to a twenty-first century audience.

Those readers who are already familiar with the published stories reprinted here, might, upon close examination, notice a few small changes to xii

the texts. I have taken the liberty of doing some editing and polishing. These revisions are in wording only. I've done nothing to plot or character arc.

I wish to thank the Norman B. Leventhal Map Center at the Boston Public Library, in particular Catherine T. Wood, the Center's office manager, for allowing us to use the map of Boston that appears at the front of the book. I am also grateful to all the editors with whom I worked on these various stories: Edmund S. Schubert, Joshua Palmatier, Patricia Bray, John G. Hartness, Emily Lavin Leverett, and Kimberly Richardson, as well as the good folks at Tor.com, who originally published two of these pieces. Their work contributed immensely to the quality of the writing and storytelling here. Without their input, none of these stories would be as successful. Faith Hunter's edit of the manuscript, and most notably "The *Ruby Blade*," was thorough, insightful, and enormously helpful. My thanks as well to the folks at AllThingsUrbanFantasy.com and ISmellSheep.com, for their willingness to host me at their sites. Many thanks to Lore Seekers Press for publishing this collection. And, finally, my deepest appreciation and love go to my wife, Nancy, and my daughters, Alex and Erin, who make everything I do more fun and more meaningful.

Tales of the
THIEFTAKER

I wrote this story for the Big Bad II *anthology, which came out in 2015. The concept of both Big Bad anthologies was that the stories had to be written from the point of view of "the villain." At the time, I was working on* Dead Man's Reach *(Tor Books, 2015), the fourth Thieftaker novel, and so writing from Sephira's viewpoint seemed the logical choice. But I didn't want to create a typical Thieftaker story; I wanted to do something a little different. The result is, in essence, her "origin" story.*

"The Cully"
D.B. Jackson

Boston, Province of Massachusetts Bay, 18 July 1746

Sephira peered from between the shops, her body pressed against the side of one building the way Whittler had shown her. The byway stank of rotting greens, rancid meat, and horse piss; flies buzzed around her face, making her flinch and blink. But she stayed still, and she watched.

Whittler had left her there some minutes before, following the alley away from the waterfront so that he could circle back toward her from Faneuil Hall and give her a proper view. She saw him now, threading his way along the crowded lane, past merchants and wharfmen, his waistcoat and shirt stained, his breeches with holes at the knees. Others on the street looked as shabby as he, but none wore that beatific smile; he appeared to have not a care in the world. Spotting her, he winked. Sephira smiled in return. An instant later, his expression hardened, and he sidled toward a cluster of well-dressed men deep in conversation.

He was jostled as he walked; everyone was, including the merchants. Whittler, she knew, had been counting on that.

"Crowded street like this one," he had said before leaving her in the alley, "ev'ryone's bouncing up against ev'ryone else. Tha's what you want, get it?"

She had nodded, drinking in every word.

Now, as he stepped around the men, he allowed himself to be shoved into them. Sephira saw his hand dart into one gentleman's coat and emerge a moment later, but she could make out no more than that. And she had been looking for it. He was good; at sixteen, he was already better than anyone she had ever seen.

He continued past the men and toward her, his hands in his pockets now, his face relaxed. He didn't join her in the alley, didn't so much as glance her way as he walked by. But he turned at the next corner. Sephira eyed the wealthy men for a few seconds more. They still talked and laughed like fools, oblivious. Proud of Whittler, and of herself for being his friend, she retreated into the shadows and crept to the far end of the byway.

Whittler waited for her there, beaming.

"Did ya see?"

"Hardly," she said. "I saw your hand go in, bu' that was all."

"Aye, the fat cull never felt a thing."

He pulled a leather pouch from his pocket and held it in his palm, hefting it, satisfaction in his grin. Sephira heard the muffled clink of coins from within.

"Let's see what we've got, shall we?"

She nodded, eyes fixed on the purse.

He loosened the drawstrings and poured the coins into his other hand.

"Not bad," he whispered. "Not bad at all. One, two . . . there must be four pounds here, maybe four an' ten." He plucked three shillings from his bounty and held them out to Sephira. "There's your share."

She searched his face for some sign that he was joking. "But I didn't do anythin'."

"You was my watcher, my lookout. You'd have told me if th' sheriff was behind me, wouldn' ya?"

"'Course!"

"Then ya earned it. Come on: Put out your hand."

She held her hand under his, and he dropped the shillings. They rang like bells and kissed her skin, cool and comforting.

"I want to try," she said, curling her fingers over them.

"Try what?"

"Pinchin' a purse, of course!"

He scowled. "Ya're not ready." He returned his remaining coins to the purse and shoved it into his pocket.

"Sure I am! You've been teachin' me. You said I've been doin' good."

"Yeah, well doin' good ain' the same as bein' ready, is it?" When she didn't answer, he repeated, "Is it?" barking the words like a cur.

"No," Sephira whispered. She blinked hard against a sudden stinging in her eyes.

Whittler rubbed the back of his head, his mouth twisting. "Look, Seph, with some time I think you could be good. But ya're just a kid, an' there's other ways for a girl like you to make some coin in th' lanes. Safer ways.

Ways that won't wind up with you in th' town gaol or hanging from a gallows."

She shook her head.

"Don't go tellin' me 'no,'" he said, his tone growing stony again. "Ya're good-lookin'. And there's coves that don't mind a girl's body, if you take my meaning."

She ground her teeth, tears spilling down her cheeks. "I'm not whorin'. Tha's what my Ma did, an' . . . an' I'd rather take my chances with the sheriff."

"Well, then take it to the North End. I won't have ya gettin' caught here and ruinin' things for the rest of us. One diver gets caught with a hand in a pocket, and the rest of us has it twice as hard for a month."

"But we work together! You said so!"

"Only if you follow my rules." He started away from her.

Sephira ran after him, threw herself in front of him, and grabbed his arms to make him stop. He was two hands taller than she if he was an inch, and he was stronger, too, though for a girl of twelve years, she was strong enough. "But, you promised me—" She made no effort to stop her tears.

He pulled his arms from her grip and put his hands on her shoulders none too gently. "My rules, Seph. Follow them, or go spend your shillin's without me."

He pushed past her, and she let him go, although not without trying a dive of her own.

"Not ready, eh?" she called, just as he reached the end of the alley.

He turned. She could barely keep from laughing as she held up the rich man's coin purse and gave it a little shake. Its contents jangled.

Whittler's expression didn't change. He walked back to where she stood, his steps slow, deliberate. Upon reaching her, he took the purse from her hand and stared at it for what seemed an eternity. Then, without warning, he smacked her across the cheek with the back of his hand. Sephira staggered and fell on her rear.

He leveled a rigid finger at her like it was a bayonet. "Don' ever try a dive on me again," he said, the words thick with fury.

He turned and left her there. Sephira made no effort to stop him. Her skin blazed where he had struck her; pain throbbed with every heartbeat. She was crying again, sobs sticking in her throat, snot running into her mouth, mingling with blood.

Men had hit her before. Her uncle, who lived with Sephira and her mother before Sephira ran away, used to drink himself into terrible rages, and often beat both of them. And one man, who thought to use her as he had used Sephira's mother, struck her when she resisted. Only her mother's intervention kept the brute from doing worse.

But she never thought that Whittler would hurt her. They'd been together for nearly a year now, him teaching her to pick pockets and slip merchants' wares under her shirt without being spotted, and her finding them what food she could, even when it meant begging like a pauper. Sure, he got angry with her sometimes, when she didn't listen to him or got sloppy with her dives.

This was different, though. She'd used him as a cully, diving for his purse. And he had been none the wiser. If she hadn't called to him, he would have left her there, and the four pounds ten would have been hers.

She swallowed the last of her sobs and wiped her tears with the dirty cuff of her shirt sleeve.

She'd bested Whittler. That was why he hit her. She had done nothing wrong; just the opposite: she had been too good.

Sephira managed a shaky smile at that and climbed to her feet. Her face hurt. She could feel the skin tightening over the bruise and she knew that she would look a mess for several days. But there was nothing she could do about that. She might even use it to her advantage.

I'm ready, she told herself.

She left the alley and walked down to the South End waterfront, near Long Wharf. The streets here were nearly as crowded as they had been up at Faneuil Hall, though mostly with laborers, shipwrights, and wharfmen. She saw few men of means.

Take it to the North End, Whittler had said.

"All right, Whit," she said under her breath. "That's what I'll do."

She followed Mill Street over the creek into the North End, and angled north and east toward the wealthy homes around Copp's Hill. Now that she had it mind to steal from someone—someone other than Whittler—her heart had begun to labor and her mouth had gone dry. The streets here were not nearly as crowded as those near the markets of Faneuil Hall, and the men and women abroad in the lanes all were well-dressed. The men wore silk suits of green and blue, beige and red. The women were dressed in luxurious gowns, also silk, with matching petticoats and stomachers. Many wore straw hats, trimmed in satin.

Never in her life had Sephira been more aware of the roughness of her own garb: the stains on her ill-fitting shirt, the frayed length of rope that held up her torn breeches in lieu of a proper belt, the very fact that she wore no coat or waistcoat or hat.

Whittler had looked no better than she, but in the teeming streets of the South End, he had blended in. She did not; not here.

She thought about retreating to Cornhill, but she heard again his warning, his dismissal. *I won't have ya gettin' caught here and ruinin' things for the rest of us.* Those lanes were his; they had been long before he started teaching her. And he had as much as banished her.

She continued along Salem Street, holding herself the way he had taught her: not so proud that she drew attention to herself, but not so furtive that she appeared to be skulking. *Look like ya belong,* he had told her once, not so long ago, *and look like ya're goin' somewhere.* Her cheek throbbed at the memory.

A cluster of men caught her eye: six of them, gathered at the corner of Hull Street, near the base of the hill. They were talking—rich men always seemed to be talking. Two of them gestured pointedly at each other while the rest of their group smiled and laughed, as if the source of their argument were of little consequence. All of them wore silk ditto suits; several carried brass-tipped canes.

She approached them, marking their positions, their postures, where they held their hands, whether their coats were buttoned or open—the things Whittler had told her were important. When she was within five strides of them, she chose her cully. Her hands trembled, but she kept them loose at her sides. Casual. Unassuming. As she passed the cully, she darted a hand in, just the way Whittler had taught her.

Except for one thing.

Ya gotta watch a cully first. Ya can't just dive without knowin' the waters. Ya've got to know where your cully keeps his purse.

The pocket she chose for her dive was empty. And as she extracted her hand, she felt powerful fingers close around her wrist. She tried to bolt, but the man's hand held her like irons in a gaol.

"What have you caught there, Caleb?"

The gentleman holding fast to Sephira's wrist gave her an appraising look from uncovered head to poorly shod foot, his gaze lingering for a moment on her bruised cheek. He wasn't much taller than she, but he was round and double-chinned; his stubby fingers ground together the bones of her wrist.

"You're hurtin' me," she said, struggling once more to break free.

He peered at her through the small lenses of his spectacles, his pale blue eyes overlarge behind the circles of glass, his nose small, almost delicate, and utterly out of place on such a homely visage. Wisps of red hair poked out from beneath his powdered, plaited wig.

"I believe I've captured a brigand," he said, sounding amused.

Several of his companions laughed, though not the man who had asked the initial question. He regarded Sephira with unconcealed disgust.

"The sheriff will know what to do with her."

Sephira's captor frowned. "I'm not certain we need involve the sheriff. Her hand is empty; there's no harm done."

"She's a miscreant. Let her go, and she'll make the attempt again; perhaps next time she'll be successful. Give her to the sheriff, and no one need worry further about her."

Still gripping her wrist, the one named Caleb bent down to look her in the eye.

Sephira tried yet again to pull away, but to no avail. Her wrist was growing sore, and she feared the men would indeed turn her over to the sheriff. Did they hang pickpockets in Boston? Tears welled in her eyes.

"What's your name child?" Caleb asked.

"Let me go!" Tears coursed down her cheeks again—she couldn't remember the last time she had cried so much in one day.

"You're wasting your breath, Caleb."

The man glanced up at his friend. "It's mine to waste." To Sephira he said, "I just want to know your name, so that I can see you returned to your parents, where you belong."

She said nothing, but merely glared at him.

"I fear Benjamin may be right," another man said. "She's not worth your trouble."

Caleb straightened, and for a moment Sephira thought that he would follow the counsel of his friends and seek out the sheriff. Instead, his grip on her wrist relaxing somewhat though not so much that she could escape his grasp, he tipped his hat to his companions, bid them good day, and led Sephira up the lane on a steep incline toward the top of Copp's Hill.

"Where are you taking me?" she said, fighting in vain to free herself.

"To my home, so that I might decide what to do with you next. And if, while we're there, you happen to eat a bit of poultry and bread, and perhaps a pastry or two . . . Well, I don't suppose I'll mind that too much."

Sephira stopped struggling. The corners of the man's mouth quirked upward.

"What's your name?" he asked again, as they neared the top of the hill.

He sounded somewhat winded. Sephira breathed hard, too, and her legs had started to ache.

"Mary," she said. "My name is Mary Parker."

Caleb gave her a sidelong glance that bespoke more than a little skepticism. "Mary is it?"

She nodded.

"Where are your parents, Mary?"

"I don't know where my Da is. I don't remember the last time I saw him. My Ma . . . she doesn' live in Boston."

"Where does she live?"

Sephira shook her head. Aside from her name, she had told Caleb the truth; she wasn't sure she could get away with a second lie. "I'm not tellin' you that."

Caleb frowned. "Why not?"

"Because she's a whore. And I won't go back there."

He winced at her words, but after a few seconds he nodded. "Very well." He considered her again over the tops of his glasses. "Where did you get that bruise?"

"I'm not tellin' you that, either."

They crested the hill, and Caleb turned onto a curved drive that led to a large brick house. Sephira slowed, her wrist still in the man's grip. He halted glancing back at her.

"You live here?" she asked, gazing at the house.

"Yes, I do. Come along; I'll show you."

They walked to the portico and entered through a massive oaken door. The first room had a marble floor. A large spiderlike chandelier hung from the high ceiling. Sephira stared up at it, open-mouthed.

"How do you light those?" Sephira asked, pointing at the candles.

"The men and women who work for me use a stepladder."

The men and women who work for me . . . The phrase echoed in her mind. She might have allowed herself to be captured, but even Whittler would have to admit that she had chosen the right cully. Caleb had to be the richest man she'd ever met.

"There's more to the house than just the foyer," Caleb said, amusement in his eyes. "Come in and I'll show you."

Whit would have laughed at her. Here she was in a house with more treasure than she had ever seen, and all she could do was gawk like a child. Her cheeks burned as she followed Caleb into the next room, an enormous space filled with furniture and art, a dazzling array of colors that made her feel plain and ungainly. Wonderful aromas reached her—savory meat, fresh bread. Her stomach grumbled as if in answer, and her gaze strayed to the next doorway which appeared to lead to the dining room.

"Are you hungry?" Caleb asked.

Before she could answer, a woman joined them in the grand chamber.

"Good afternoon, Mister Moore. Are you ready to—" Spotting Sephira, she fell silent, her mouth open, her brow creased. She regarded Sephira much as Caleb's friends had on the street, her expression curdling as she took in the state of Sephira's garb. "A guest?" she finally asked.

"Yes, Sarah. Please set another place at the table. We'll dine immediately."

"Of course."

She stared at Sephira for another moment before hurrying back into what Sephira took to be the kitchen.

The woman returned soon after, her color still high. But she gestured Caleb and Sephira into the dining room, and even went so far as to pull out Sephira's chair for her. Sephira couldn't remember anyone doing that for her before.

"Has Missus Moore already supped?" Caleb asked.

"Aye, sir. But I can tell her you're here."

"That won't be necessary." A wry smile sprung to his lips. "I daresay she wouldn't know what to make of our guest any more than you do."

Sarah didn't answer.

"I'll have a cup of Madeira with my meal," Caleb said. "And for the child as well—generously watered, I think."

Sarah nodded and left them there.

Sephira surveyed the feast that had been laid before her—roasted fowl, a round of bread, a bowl filled with blackberries and blueberries, a wedge of cheese. She reached for the fowl, but Caleb cleared his throat loudly.

She stopped, her hand hovering over the food, and saw that he had his eyes closed and his hands folded in front of him. He mumbled something, a prayer no doubt. Sephira waited, watching him. When at last he muttered an "Amen," she grabbed a piece of fowl from the platter and began to tear at it.

She had eaten just that morning: a piece of stale bread and a morsel of bacon. But she didn't know when she would have a chance to sup like this ever again, and she resolved to gorge herself.

Sarah emerged from the kitchen once more bearing two cups, one of which she placed in front of Sephira. It held a liquid that was pale pink. Sephira finished chewing another mouthful of meat and swallowed. Then she lifted the cup to her lips and took a small sip.

She nearly spat it out.

"What is that?" she asked, pulling a face and setting her cup down as far from her plate as she could reach.

"Watered wine," Caleb said. "What do you usually drink?"

Sephira shrugged. "What I can find. Water usually. Sometimes ale or mead. I like ale."

"Ale isn't an appropriate beverage for a girl your age."

"Why not?"

"How is your food?"

She took another bite of fowl, nodding as she chewed. "It's good."

Caleb took a bite as well, and washed it down with a sip of his wine. "Did someone send you to steal my purse?"

Sephira gaped back at him, unsure of what to say.

"It's all right. I'm not going to take you to the sheriff, and I'm not trying to get your friends in trouble. I just want to understand what happened."

"No one sent me," she said. "And I wasn't workin' with someone either. I work alone. I saw you and your friends, and I figured you was rich."

"You were right. We're all men of means. But as for the rest, I'm not sure I believe you. If what I saw today is any indication, you wouldn't last very long on the streets if you were truly working alone."

"I do just fine," Sephira said, her voice rising. "You keep your purse in a different pocket is all. If not for that, I'd have pinched it and been on my way before you knew what happened."

He frowned again, taking a bite of cheese. Sephira shoved a piece of bread in her mouth, all the while glaring at him.

"You strike me as an intelligent girl. You have some spirit. You're pretty. You could do far better for yourself."

"I won't try whorin'!"

Caleb's cheeks turned pink, but he held her gaze. "I wasn't suggesting that you should. I was trying to say that you could do better than to live in the streets, stealing from innocents and running afoul of the law. You're still young. You don't have to remain on this path."

"I do just fine," she said again, knowing she sounded sullen and childish. She didn't like the way he watched her, or the cloying note of kindness she heard in his voice. She bit off one last mouthful of fowl, wiped her hands on the linen napkin beside her plate, and pushed back from the table.

"You were going to show me the rest of your house. You promised."

Caleb's smile was thin. "I suppose I did. Come along, then."

He stood and led her out of the dining room, back through the grand room she had already seen, and down a corridor. They stopped first in a study, its walls lined with bookshelves, its wood floors adorned with a colorful woven rug. A pair of ivory-handled dueling pistols were mounted on the wall near the door, and a portrait of Caleb and a woman Sephira assumed was his wife hung over the hearth.

Next he took her to a small sitting room with maroon satin drapes over the windows, and a pair of matching upholstered chairs facing an empty hearth.

Finally, he showed her a plain room at the back of the house. It was not nearly as ornate as the other chambers had been. Two small beds sat along opposite walls, and a simple wood bureau stood between them.

"This is Sarah's room," Caleb said, watching her.

Sephira nodded absently. She liked the other rooms better.

"There was another girl who worked for us, but she left not long ago. We've been looking for someone to take her place."

Sephira turned to look at him. "Are you sayin' I could live here? Work here?"

"Would you like that?" When she didn't answer, he went on. "You would earn a small wage at first—a few shillings each week. But your room and board would be free. And as you learned your work, and gained our trust, your wage would rise. Best of all, you would no longer be running wild in the street, stealing, getting beaten; instead, you would be living as a respectable girl should."

"Why would you want me?"

A faint smile flitted across his homely features. "I told you before: I believe you to be intelligent, and I think that with some prodding, you could do better for yourself. I would like to help in that regard."

"I tried to pinch your purse."

"Yes." The smile returned. "You would need to stop doing that if this arrangement is going to work."

A vision flashed like lightning in Sephira's mind. She saw herself wearing a simple black dress with a white lace collar, much like the one Sarah had on. She was serving dinner to Caleb and the woman in the portrait, clearing empty plates and bowls from the table, carrying a bucket of water from the pump on Hull Street to the kitchen. She barely recognized the girl she saw—she looked neat, well-kept, perhaps even happy. Mostly, she looked soft.

Sephira jerked her mind away from the vision, stifling a shudder.

Caleb still watched her, expectant, a self-satisfied smile on his lips.

She threw the punch without thinking, without knowing why she did it. Her fist caught Caleb square in the mouth. He staggered back a step, blood pouring from a split in his lip. Sephira closed the distance between them and hit him a second time, and then a third. With her fourth blow, this one to his temple, he collapsed to the floor.

She kicked him hard in the side. Caleb retched, drawing his knees up to his chest. She aimed a second kick at his forehead, opening a ragged, bloody gash.

He groaned, but he didn't seem capable of more than that. Sephira knelt beside him and searched his pockets for the elusive purse. When at last she found it, she grinned at its weight. This pouch held more coin by far than the one Whittler stole. She stowed the purse in one of her pockets.

Caleb stirred as she climbed back to her feet.

"Why?" he asked, the word thick in his bloodied mouth.

She kicked him again and left him in the back room. On her way to the foyer, she stopped in his study, took the dueling pistols from the wall, and tucked them into her pockets as well. Then she returned to the dining room and piled as much bread, cheese, and fowl into a napkin as she could fit. As an afterthought, she drank what was left in Caleb's cup of undiluted Madeira. She decided that she liked it much better than the watered wine he had given her.

She strode to the door. Before she reached it, though, she heard a light footfall behind her. She turned just enough to be able to look behind her, all the while taking care to keep the napkin hidden.

"Leaving already?" Sarah asked.

"Aye. Ca— Mister Moore said I should go. It was very nice of him to feed me."

Sarah glanced toward the dining room. "Where is he?"

"In his study, I think." Sephira smiled. "Goodbye."

She didn't wait for an answer, but let herself out of the house and walked back to the street, trying to appear unhurried. Only when she reached the lane did she break into a run that carried her down the steep slope of Copp's Hill. The pistols and purse bounced awkwardly in her pockets, and twice she nearly fell. But she kept her balance as she turned onto Salem Street and wound her way to the crowded lanes near the waterfront. Before long, she had crossed back into the South End.

She was breathing hard, grimacing at a stitch in her side. But she kept running, making her way to the small square within a cluster of old warehouses near Woodman's Wharf, where she and Whittler went when trying to get away from men of the night watch. Whittler was there now, with two of his friends: Bartie and Simon.

Sephira halted at the mouth of the space.

Bartie spotted her first, and hit Whittler's shoulder lightly with the back of his hand. "Looks like your shadow's here."

Simon and Whittler fell silent. Sephira remained where she was, panting, heat rising in her cheeks. Whittler eyed her for a moment and then waved her forward.

"Where you been?" he asked as she approached.

"North End, like you told me."

He indicated the napkin with a nod. "Wha's that?"

"Supper, if you want any." She tried to keep her tone light, as if she brought them meals all the time.

The three boys exchanged looks. She squatted down, placed the napkin on the ground, and opened it, revealing the food she had stolen.

Bartie whistled.

Whittler smiled and nodded again. "That looks fine," he said. "Where'd it come from?"

"Same place as these." She pulled the pistols from her pockets and held them out to Whittler. "Cully I found."

He stared at them, wide-eyed, making no move to take them from her. "Will ya look at those," he said, breathing the words.

"You'll get two pounds for them," Simon said, watching Whittler. "Easy."

"He's right," Whittler said, raising his gaze to hers. "Must have been some cully. That blood on your shirt?"

Sephira looked down. Her shirt was splattered with blood stains. "Aye."

"Any of it yours?"

"No."

"What else did you get?" Simon said, eyeing her hungrily.

Sephira glanced back at Whittler and gave a single, tiny shake of her head.

"What difference does it make to you?" Whittler said, rounding on the boy. "She brought supper an' a couple of pistols. Tha's more'n I've seen from you in the past week."

"I was just askin'," Simon said, flinching away. His mouth twisted sourly, but he looked Sephira in the eye as he said, "You done good, Seph. Real good."

"Let's have us a feast," Whittler said. "In fact, I've got just the thing." He walked to the back of their retreat, and pulled a dusty bottle from a small recess.

"What's that?" Bartie asked.

"Bottle of Madeira. Pinched it a few nights back from a crib on King Street."

He knelt beside the food-laden napkin, and the others did the same.

"You ever have Madeira, Seph?" Whittler asked.

"Aye. I like it."

"You should. It's a rich man's drink. A rich lady's, too."

He took a swig, wiped his mouth with his sleeve, and handed the bottle to Sephira. She tipped her head back and drank before handing the bottle on to Simon.

She ate a few bites more of the fowl and bread, but mostly she drank, and listened as the boys told stories of cullies they'd fleeced in the lanes. Caleb's purse remained in her pocket, hidden from Whittler's friends, its heft balanced on her thigh, reassuring. Maybe later she would tell the tale of how she had come by it, along with the pistols and the food. Whittler would believe her. The others might, too. With the blood on her shirt, and the treasure she carried, they could hardly doubt her.

But for now, she was content to enjoy their feast, and the fact that she was one of them, welcomed, accepted.

The bottle came around once again; it was mostly empty, but a few sips remained. She took it from Whittler, and drank a silent toast to Caleb, her first cully.

"The Tavern Fire" was the first piece of historical fiction I published. Though, like every other Thieftaker story, it takes place in pre-Revolutionary Boston, it differs from the Ethan Kaille novels and the other tales in this collection in certain ways. First, Ethan himself does not appear in the story. At the time the events chronicled here took place, Ethan was still a laboring prisoner on the sugar plantation in Barbados. Sephira Pryce doesn't appear in this story either, but Janna Windcatcher, a character familiar to those who have read the Thieftaker novels, does. In this story, she runs her bar, the Fat Spider, with a partner. His name is Gil, short for Gilgamesh.

The story first appeared in After Hours: Tales from the Ur-Bar, *an anthology from Daw Books (2011) that was edited by Joshua Palmatier and Patricia Bray. The rules for the anthology were simple: Every story had to take place in a bar or tavern, and Gilgamesh and his magical tablet had to play a role in each plot. I was still working on the first Thieftaker novel at the time, and, in my research, had come across multiple references to the Great Boston Fire of 1760, which started at the Brazen Head tavern, owned by Mary Jackson. The cause of the fire was never determined, leaving me plenty of room to play with possible explanations.*

"The Tavern Fire"
D.B. Jackson

Boston, Province of Massachusetts Bay, 19 March 1760

There was no fire when he woke. The room had gone cold and a bleak gray light seeped around the old cloth that hung over his window. He heard no wind, which was good. Tiller didn't like the wind; not this time of year. But he wanted to see gold at the window edges, and there was none.

He sighed and rolled out of bed, the ropes beneath his mattress groaning. He relieved himself and left the pot by his door, so that he wouldn't forget to empty it. He did that sometimes.

He dressed, donning a frock over his shirt for warmth, shrugging on his coat over that, and pulling his Monmouth cap onto his head. He stepped to the door, pausing as always at the small portrait of his mother and father. He touched his fingers to his lips and then to the drawing.

"Bye, Mama, Papa. I'll be back later."

He opened the door, emptied the pot into the yard, and, after checking to see that the key hung around his neck, pulled the door shut.

A leaden sky; still, icy air. Just as he had known.

He heard Crumbs before he saw him; a coarse *cawing* and the rustle of silken feathers as the crow glided down from the roof to Tiller's shoulder.

"Good morning, Crumbs," Tiller said. "Looks like we got a cold one today." He fished into his coat pocket and found a morsel of stale bread, which he fed to the bird. Crumbs ate it greedily.

"We'll find more later. I'm hungry, too."

He started toward the cart, but before he reached it, he heard a door scrape behind him.

"Thomas!"

Tiller turned, but kept his gaze fixed on the ground. "Good morning, Peter," he said quietly. "I'm sorry if we woke you."

"That's not—you didn't. It's time for rent, Thomas."

Tiller knew that. Just as Peter knew that he didn't like to be called Thomas. He hadn't been Thomas since he was a boy. But it angered Peter when Tiller reminded him, and since Peter leased him the room, Tiller tried not to make him mad. A cousin should have known what to call another cousin. Tiller should have been allowed to remind Peter of that, at least. But he rented the room and he kept his mouth shut. He had heard bad stories about the almshouse.

"Do you have the money?"

Tiller shook his head. "Not yet. But I will."

"Today is Wednesday. You know that, right?"

He nodded slowly. Wednesday sounded right.

"And rent—"

"A shilling by Friday," Tiller said. "Yes, I know."

Peter exhaled the way Papa used to. "All right then. Good day, Thomas."

"Good day, Peter."

He waited until Peter had gone back into the house and closed the door before walking to the cart and pushing it out of the yard onto Leverett's Lane. It rattled loudly on the cobbles, pots and pans swinging on their hooks and clanging together, old blades and rusted tools bouncing in their wooden compartments, the empty bottles he had carefully arranged the previous evening falling over one another like drunken sailors.

There had been seven pence in his pocket when he counted just before going to bed. He could get the other five today or tomorrow. Peter wouldn't have to put him out. That's what he told himself, anyway. But he pushed the cart down to the wharves, his eyes raking the streets, searching for anything that he might find and clean and sell. It always amazed him, the things people lost. Books, jewelry, coins sometimes. Once, a few years ago, he had found a half-crown in the North End on Charter Street. He often went back to the same spot, hoping to find money again, but so far there hadn't been any more. That wouldn't keep him from checking later.

He didn't see much today, at least not right off. A scrap of metal here, another bottle there. Once he crossed over into the North End, he found more: a knife with a broken blade, which might fetch a few pence; a full copy of Monday's *Gazette*—someone would pay a penny for that, if they hadn't read it yet; and a lady's linen kerchief that was almost clean. He tied the kerchief to the top of the cart beside the pans so that people could see it. It was sure to sell.

Crumbs rode on his shoulder for a short while, but then flew down to the harbor's edge to scavenge for food. The water was calm, but dark as ink. Tiller could smell salt and dead fish in the air. The wharf workers shouted at him and laughed; he wasn't sure what the men said, but he could tell that it wasn't kind, and he tried to ignore them. After a few minutes he made his way up from the docks.

He stopped first at the foundry on Foster Lane. Paul, who worked there, was always kind to him, and often bought an item or two. Tiller had started seeking out goods that would interest him, and earlier in the week he had found a small hammer, its head only slightly rusted, that he thought Paul would like.

He rummaged through the cart until he found it, and entered the smithy. He found Paul at the forge, his round face ruddy with the heat, his sleeves rolled up, revealing powerful forearms. Seeing Tiller, he raised a hand and stepped away from the fire.

"Good morning, Tiller."

"Good day, Paul." Belatedly, Tiller snatched the cap off his head.

"Where's your bird today?"

Tiller shrugged. "Eating somewhere. He'll find me later. I have something for you. Found it in Cornhill." He held out the hammer.

The smith's forehead creased and he crossed to where Tiller stood. "This is very nice," he said, taking the hammer from him and turning it over in his hands. "Very nice, indeed." He rubbed his thumb over a patch of rust. "A bit of polishing and this will be good as new." Paul looked up at him. "How much?"

Tiller gazed up at the ceiling, as if considering this, though he had already decided. "I dunno," he said, his gaze meeting Paul's for an instant before darting away. "Five pence maybe?"

The smith smiled. "Five pence seems more than fair." He dug into his pocket and took out a sixpence. "I don't have it exactly. How about we settle on six and call it even?"

"I have a penny," Tiller said, reaching into his own pocket.

"It's all right, Tiller. Six is a good price."

Tiller took the coin, a grin on his face. "I found a good one, didn't I?"

"Yes, you did."

He hesitated a moment, wondering if he should say more. At last he put his cap back on. "Well, thanks, Paul. I'll see you again in a few days."

"Good day, Tiller. May the Lord keep you."

Tiller left the shop and immediately Crumbs fluttered down to his shoulder.

"Got rent, Crumbs," he said, holding up the sixpence.

The crow bent toward it, his beak open.

"No, you don't. I need that for Peter."

He slid the coin into his pocket and pushed his cart onward. He stopped at a few other shops, but didn't sell anything more. By midday, he was back in Cornhill, and he made his way to the public houses, hoping to trade for a meal. He stopped first at the Bunch of Grapes and when the innkeeper there refused to look at his wares, he went on to the Light House. That proved no more fruitful. Against his better judgement, he then made his way to the Brazen Head, on Cornhill Street.

Mary Jackson, who owned the tavern, had never liked him. She called Crumbs "that filthy bird" and insisted that the crow stay outside. And she talked to Tiller as if he were a little boy.

He knew he wasn't as smart as some people, but he had gotten by on his own for a long time now. He didn't need Miss Jackson telling him how to take care of himself.

Occasionally, though, he had something she liked, and she gave him a free meal in exchange. He hoped the kerchief might catch her eye.

She stood behind the bar when he walked in, and she greeted him with a frown. Her hair—black, streaked with silver—was drawn up in a bun, and she wore a pale blue gown with a stomacher of white linen. Tiller noticed that her stomacher was a perfect match for the kerchief he had found.

"What do you want?" Miss Jackson asked, the lines around her mouth and eyes making her appear angry. Tiller had seen her smile now and again, and each time he was surprised by how pretty a smile made her look. He thought she should smile more. "I've told you I'm not interested in buying the rubbish you find in the streets."

"Yes, ma'am," Tiller said, stopping just inside her door and removing his cap. The tavern was crowded, and many of the people craned their necks to see him. Tiller tried hard to ignore them. "But I have something I think you'll like." He held up the kerchief for her to see.

She stared at it briefly, wrinkling her nose. "What is that?"

"A kerchief, ma'am. A nice one. Linen it is. With some cleaning—"

Miss Jackson began to laugh. It didn't make her look pretty. She glanced back at the others and they laughed as well. "You think I want to buy someone's dirty kerchief? You're mad!"

Tiller slowly lowered the hand holding the kerchief. "I have some other . . ." He stopped. Their laughter only grew louder. He turned to leave.

"Wait."

He faced Miss Jackson again.

"You spend some time at that other pub, don't you? The Fat Spider?"

"Yes." That was where Tiller intended to go next. It was a long walk, but Janna and Gil—who ran the tavern—they were his friends. They always fed him, even when he didn't have something on his cart that they wanted.

She beckoned him toward the bar. "Come here. Are you hungry . . . Tiller, is it?"

"Yes, ma'am," he said quietly, still standing by the door.

"It's all right, Tiller." She indicated a stool with an open hand. "You can sit right here." She glanced at her barman, a tall thin man with a high forehead and long plaited hair. "Johnny, fetch some chowder and bread for Tiller, will you?"

"Yeah, sure," Johnny said, and went back to the kitchen.

Tiller crossed to the bar. Most of her patrons had gone back to their conversations, but a few still watched him. None of them were laughing now. He halted by Miss Jackson, who nodded encouragement.

"That's it. Sit down."

He sat on the stool beside her.

Miss Jackson narrowed her eyes, which were the same color as her gown. "What can you tell me about that woman at the Fat Spider? Janna, right? What can you tell me about her?"

"Um . . . well . . . she's very nice. She . . . she gives me food sometimes and—"

"Where's she from? Do you know that?"

"An island somewhere, I think. Her skin's dark, and she speaks with an accent."

"I know that." She sounded the way Peter sometimes did when Tiller couldn't figure things out. But then she blew out a slow breath. "Tiller, have you ever seen her do strange things?"

"You mean magickal things?"

Her face brightened, and she smiled at him, a pretty, friendly smile. "Yes, that's exactly what I mean. How smart you are."

"I've seen her do that," Tiller said, pleased with himself. "I've—" He stopped, his cheeks burning. He had been about to say that he had felt her magick, too. That it made the ground hum beneath his feet. But Janna had warned him about telling anyone that, and while Miss Jackson was being nice to him right now, he was smart enough to know it wouldn't last, and then he would be sorry he had told her. He wondered if he had been wrong to say that Janna did magick. He knew that men and women were still hanged as witches in New England. He didn't think that Miss Jackson wanted to get Janna in trouble, but he regretted saying as much as he had. "I've heard that some people do it," he said, keeping his eyes fixed on the bar. "It might not have been Janna. I don't know who it was."

"It's all right, Tiller. She won't mind that you told me. I want her to do magick for me. I'll pay her for it. She'll be glad that we had this little talk."

Tiller wasn't so sure. But before he could say anything, Johnny emerged from the kitchen with his chowder and bread.

"You want ale with that?" Johnny asked.

Tiller looked at Miss Jackson.

"Of course he does," she said. She smiled at Tiller again. "Janna doesn't like me very much, Tiller. Did you know that?"

"No," he said. A lie. Janna didn't like anyone very much. She liked Gil, and she was nice to Tiller, but he had never seen her show any sign of liking other people. And she sometimes said bad things about Miss Jackson. Like that she was a lying snake, and that she couldn't be trusted to care for her own Mama, much less anyone else.

"Well, she doesn't," Miss Jackson went on. "And so I need your help. I need you to convince her to do a little magick for me. Can you do that?"

"I don't know," Tiller said. "It might not have been Janna."

"Of course. But if it was Janna, what kind of magick did she do? Can you remember that?"

He didn't know what to say. None of this had gone the way he wanted.

"I've heard people say that she does love spells," Miss Jackson said, her voice dropping to a whisper. "Is that what you've seen?"

Tiller stared back at her, too afraid to speak.

"Do you know how much people pay her for the charms?"

When he still didn't answer, her expression turned hard. "That's my food sitting in front of you, Tiller. I want answers. Now tell me: Does she do love spells?"

Tiller nodded. "Yes, ma'am," he whispered. "I don't know how much money she gets for them."

"Do they work?" Miss Jackson asked, hunger in her eyes and in her voice. "Is the magick real?"

"I think so," he said. "I've . . . I've heard people thank her."

She smiled like someone who had just won at cards. "That's what I needed to know. Thank you, Tiller."

Johnny put a cup of ale in front of him.

Miss Jackson stood. "Make sure he gets whatever he wants," she told Johnny. "He's our guest. You understand?"

"Yes, ma'am," Johnny said.

"You go to the Fat Spider when you're done, Tiller." Miss Jackson bent toward him, forcing Tiller to look her in the eye. "You tell Janna that I'm coming, all right?"

Tiller nodded, taking a spoonful of the chowder, which was very good. "Yesh, ma'am," he said through the food.

She patted his arm and walked away. Johnny moved to the far end of the bar to talk to the men sitting there. They left Tiller alone, didn't say another word to him. He didn't mind. He ate and he drank, and when he finished, he got up and left the Brazen Head. No one seemed to notice.

His cart still stood outside the tavern where he had left it, with Crumbs perched on the edge. The bird *cawed* crossly at Tiller.

"I didn't forget you," Tiller said, taking a piece of fresh bread from his pocket. "Here you go."

Crumbs took the bread, hopped to the far end of the cart, and began to tear at his food with his thick, black beak.

Tiller pushed the cart down Cornhill and onto Marlborough, passing the lofty spire of the Old South Church and the solid brick façade of the Province House. Soon, the closely packed houses and shops of the South End gave way to more open ground—pastures and fields, country homes and rolling lawns. Still Tiller pushed the cart, sweating now, despite the cold.

The Fat Spider sat by itself on a lonely stretch of Orange Street on the Boston Neck. It didn't look like much from the outside. It was made of old, graying wood, and it seemed to lean to one side, as if too tired to stand

straight. Its shingle roof sagged in the middle, and the sign out front—
which showed a fat, smiling spider crawling across its web toward a fly—
had been bleached of color by years of rain and snow and sun.

Inside, though, it smelled of roasted fowl and fresh bread, pipe smoke
and musty ale. Aside from his own room, it smelled more like home than
any place Tiller had ever been. A fire burned in the hearth, and spermaceti
candles glowed in iron sconces around the great room, casting flickering
shadows on the walls.

There were never many people in the tavern, and today there were
fewer than usual—just a pair of old men sitting in the back, talking quietly.
Tiller recognized them both; they came here often.

Crumbs flew to his usual perch over the hearth. Tiller went to the bar,
his cap in hand. Janna was polishing the ancient wood with a dirty white
rag, her back bent, her head tipped to the side.

"Good day, Janna," Tiller said.

Janna didn't look up. "Afternoon, Tiller. You hungry, darlin'?"

"No, I ate."

At that, she stopped and raised her head, her eyes hawklike—dark and
fierce. He had seen men twice her size flinch under that gaze. She was small
and bone thin, with white hair so short he could see through it to her
brown scalp. Her face was bony, wrinkled, and forbidding, even when she
wasn't angry. For a long time, Tiller had been afraid of her. He wasn't
anymore, now that he knew her.

Janna had been a slave once when she was a little girl. She had told him
that. She and her family had worked on one of the islands. But when she
sailed with her master to the colonies, their ship encountered a storm.
Everyone was killed except Janna. Tiller didn't know any more. He had
heard people say it was a miracle she hadn't been taken by another slave
owner. Others said that she had been, but had eventually bought her freedom. Tiller didn't know which was true. He knew only that she and Gil
owned the Fat Spider together, and that Janna didn't like to answer questions about her past.

"Did you sell somethin'?" she asked Tiller, starting to polish again.

"I did, but that's not how I got food."

"Who'd you sell to?"

"Paul, up in the North End," Tiller said.

"He's a good man. An' where'd you ge' th' food?"

"From Miss Jackson."

Janna scowled. "What'd she want?"

Tiller opened his mouth to answer, but then closed it again. The more he thought about what had happened back in the Brazen Head, the more he realized that he had done wrong. He didn't know how to tell Janna. Maybe he was still a little bit afraid of her after all.

Janna straightened, resting her hands on her hips. "Tiller, what'd she want?"

"She asked me questions about you," he said, speaking to her belly. "She wanted to know if you could do magick. She wants you to do a spell for her, so she told me to talk to you. She knows you don't like her."

"She's right abou' that last," Janna muttered. "An' she wanted you t' arrange it for her."

He shook his head. "Mostly she wanted to know if you really did magick. And . . . and she asked me to talk to you. I'm sorry, Janna."

"Look at me, Tiller."

Tiller raised his eyes to hers. His gaze kept sliding away, but each time it did, he forced it back.

"I ain' angry with you. You didn' do nothin' wrong. You understand me?"

He stared back at her, wanting to believe her, but convinced that he had done a bad thing.

"Wha' kind of magick she want? She say?"

"Love spell, I think," Tiller said. "She's coming here to talk to you."

"Who is coming here?"

Janna turned. Tiller stayed utterly still. Gil stood in the rear doorway, a cask of wine resting on his shoulder, anchored there by a large, powerful hand.

"Don' worry about it, Gil," Janna said. She returned to polishing the bar, but she cast a quick look Tiller's way and gave a small shake of her head.

Gil walked behind the bar and put down the cask. He extended a hand to Tiller, as he did whenever they met. Tiller gripped it, watching as Gil's hand appeared to swallow his own.

"How are you today, my friend?" Gil asked, his accent more subtle than Janna's, and harder to place. He had the dark curls of a Spaniard, the pale grayish green eyes of a Scotsman, and a black beard and mustache, with long, thin braids hanging from either side of his chin, that was unlike anything Tiller had seen on any man.

"I'm fine, Gil. How are you?"

The barman frowned. "I would be better if I had an answer to the question I asked a moment ago. Someone is coming to my bar, and Janna is unhappy about it. I would like to know why."

Janna rolled her eyes. "Tiller, would you like an ale?"

"Yes, all right."

She filled a tankard and handed it to him. "Why don' you take a seat over there near th' fire."

He did as he was told, knowing why she was sending him away. He sat with his back to the bar and stared into the hearth. But he listened.

"It's Mary Jackson," Janna said, her voice low. "She sent tha' boy here t' get me t' do magick for her."

"Mary Jackson. She owns a tavern, does she not?"

"Th' Brazen Head."

"Do you know what kind of magick she wants?" Gil asked.

"Uh huh. She been chasin' tha' merchant o' hers for more than a year now. She wants me t' spell him. Make him see her different, or somethin'."

"So cast your spell, make her pay a lot of money, and send her on her way."

"Yeah, I know," Janna said. "But I don' like her usin' Tiller tha' way. He's barely more than a child."

"I'm not a child," Tiller said, loud enough for both of them to hear.

Janna sighed. A moment later he heard her walk out from behind the bar.

"You weren' supposed t' be listenin'," she said, sitting down across from him, a small smile on her lips.

"I'm not a child," Tiller said.

Her expression sobered. "I know you're not. I'm sorry for sayin' that."

"I might not be smart like you and Gil, but I get by all right."

"Yes, you do. Bu' tha' don' give her th' right t' use you as a way of talkin' t' me."

"Maybe I used her," Tiller said. "I'm the one who got free food."

Janna stared at him for a moment and then burst out laughing. "Well, tha's true enough, isn' it?" She eyed him a moment longer, shaking her head, her grin easy and broad. Then she patted his arm, stood, and walked back to the bar.

Tiller sipped his ale, pleased with himself. It wasn't every day that he managed to make Janna laugh.

The feeling didn't last long. A few minutes after Janna left him, the door to the tavern opened, flooding the great room with silver light. Tiller twisted in his chair and saw that Miss Jackson had come.

She stood at the entrance to the tavern for a moment, squinting. Her gaze passed over Tiller as if he wasn't there and settled on the bar where Janna stood, a scowl on her lean face.

"There you are, Janna," Miss Jackson said, as if she and Janna were old friends. She walked to the bar, pulling off her mitts and unbuttoning her coat. "What a lovely aroma. What are you cooking?"

"Chowder," Janna said, a chill in the word.

"Would you mind spooning me a bowl? I must try it."

Janna eyed the woman, her tongue pushing out her cheek. But then she stalked into the kitchen, returning a few seconds later with a bowl and spoon, which she placed on the bar. "That's a shilling," she said, which was more than Tiller had ever heard her charge for a bowl of anything.

"Yes, of course," Miss Jackson said. But she didn't pull out her purse. Instead, she took up her spoon and tasted the chowder.

"Oh, that's very good. Even better than my own."

Janna frowned, picked up her polishing rag, and started to make her way to the far end of the bar.

"Hold on there, Janna. I'd like to talk to you about something."

Janna stopped and faced her again. "Yes, Mary, what is it?"

A cold smile flitted across Miss Jackson's face. She glanced briefly in Tiller's direction. "There's something else I'd like you to do for me," she said, her voice dropping. "I'll pay whatever you normally charge, but I want it done today."

"Uh huh. And wha' would tha' be?"

"I think you know," Miss Jackson said, still speaking quietly.

Janna walked back to where Miss Jackson sat. "No," she said.

"You don't know?"

"I won' do it."

"Won't do what?"

"I won' be castin' a spell for you. I don' care how much money you have."

Miss Jackson glanced around, as if she thought lots of people might be listening. Tiller was. But the two old men in the back didn't seem to care what she said.

"You don't even know what kind of magick I want," she told Janna, whispering now.

Janna grinned, her teeth sharp and pale yellow. "You wan' a love spell. You want that man you fancy t' leave his missus and come 'roun' to—"

Miss Jackson stood abruptly, spilling her chowder onto Janna's bar.

"How dare you!"

"I don't like you usin' my friends to get to me. I don' like you comin' 'roun' my place an' pretendin' you an' me got anythin' in common." Janna crossed her arms over her chest and raised her chin. "I don't like you."

"I will not be spoken to in that way! Certainly not by a Negro! I don't hold with slavery, but I believe a lashing would do you some good!"

Janna laughed. "My Mama always though' so, too. Turns out she was wrong." She started to mop up the spilled chowder. "I think it's time you were leavin', Mary."

Miss Jackson didn't move. "I need this done."

"You'll have t' find someone else t' do it."

"Ten pounds."

Tiller's mouth fell open. Ten pounds! He couldn't remember even seeing that much money.

Janna didn't look up. "No."

"Fifteen."

Janna picked up the bowl and spoon, and started toward the kitchen. "Goodbye, Mary."

Miss Jackson leaned forward, her hands on the bar. "There are those in Boston who would be quite alarmed to learn that a witch lives here in the city," she said, her whisper sounding harsh, like a spitting cat.

Janna halted.

"There are clergy—men I know—who would relish the chance to hang a servant of Satan."

"You can' prove anythin'."

"I don't have to. I'm a Christian woman and you're a Negro, a former slave. My word against yours. Be smart, woman. Who do you think people will believe?"

Janna walked back to the bar and carefully put down the bowl. Gil loomed in the doorway behind her, but he hung back and kept silent.

"All I want is one spell," Miss Jackson said, whispering again. "Cast it, and you have nothing to fear from me. You can have the money, and you can keep your tavern." She surveyed the room, her lip curling. "Such as it is."

Janna took a long, weary breath. "One spell, you say?"

Miss Jackson smiled, opening her hands. "That's all."

"An' otherwise you'll tell everyone that I'm a witch."

"You leave me no choice."

Janna shrugged. "My answer is still no." Her expression went stony.

"Now get out o' my place."

Miss Jackson looked like she had been slapped. Her eyes had gone wide, her cheeks had paled. She held her mouth open in a small 'o.' At last she drew herself up and said, "Fine, then! You'll be in prison by nightfall."

She was halfway to the door when a booming voice said, "Wait!"

Miss Jackson stopped.

"I will do this magick you want," Gil said, stepping to the bar.

"Gil, no!"

"Forgive, Janna," Gil said, his gaze never leaving Miss Jackson's face. "She forgets herself sometimes. Just as she forgets that I do not work for her or follow her commands."

Miss Jackson walked slowly back to the bar. "You can do magick, too?" she asked, her voice dropping once more.

A sly smile lifted the corners of his mouth. "I have some skill, yes." He tapped the bar with his hand. "Put your money here, and I will cast for you."

"Gil—"

"Get the tablet," he said to Janna.

She shook her head. "Don' do this. Jus' let her go."

"Get the tablet."

Tiller had never seen such fear in Janna's eyes. She walked out from behind the bar and over to the hearth. She dragged a chair over, and stood on it so that she could reach a large square slab that hung over the fireplace. Tiller had seen it on the wall before, but had never paid much attention to it. It was made of clay, and similar in color to the bricks used to build Faneuil Hall, and it was covered with strange lines and symbols. Given how Janna cradled it in her thin arms, Tiller guessed it must be heavy.

"Do you want me to carry that, Janna?" he asked.

She shook her head, saying nothing, and carried it back to the bar.

Miss Jackson had placed several coins on the wood.

"Good," Gil said, when Janna placed the tablet before him. "Now, fill a cup with ale."

"Gil—"

"Ale, Janna."

She filled a cup. Gil reached below the bar and produced a stoppered bottle that could have been just as old as that clay tablet. The glass was clouded and stained, and the cork was as black as pitch. Gil placed the cup of ale on the tablet. Then he unstoppered the bottle and held it over the cup. Muttering to himself, he allowed three drops of clear pink liquid to drop into Miss Jackson's ale.

Tiller found that he was on his feet, straining to see what happened when the two liquids mixed. He saw nothing unusual, but he felt that same vibration in the floor that he felt when Janna cast her spells. Only stronger. Much stronger, as if the bar was a giant violin, and Gil had just dragged a bow across its strings.

"What now?" Miss Jackson asked, sounding a little nervous.

"Now, you drink," Gil said. "Drink it all. And when you are done, go back to your home, and wait."

"That's all?"

"That is all."

She picked up her ale, hesitated for an instant, and then drank. It took her several minutes to finish the cup, and in all that time, no one spoke. When at last she finished, she looked expectantly at Gil.

"Now he'll come to me?"

"I swear that he will," Gil said. "Go home and wait."

"Yes, all right. Thank you." Miss Jackson stood, pausing to eye Janna. Tiller thought she might say something, but in the end she merely turned and hurried from the tavern.

"What'd you do t' her?" Janna asked, when the woman was gone.

"I sent the man to her, just as she wanted."

Janna shook her head. "Tha's not all you did. There's always more with your magick."

"Tiller," Gil said. "I am going to roast venison tonight. Will you stay and eat with us?"

Tiller beamed. "Sure I will, Gil. Thank you."

"Good. In the meantime, have another ale."

Gil walked back to the kitchen, Janna staring after him. After a few seconds she seemed to remember that Tiller was still there.

She filled a new cup with ale, and brought it to him.

"Here you go, Tiller," she said, sounding more kind than usual.

"I'm sorry, Janna. I shouldn't have said anything to Miss Jackson."

"Don' worry 'bout it," she said. "Gil took care of it."

Tiller drank that second ale and two more, enjoying the warmth of the fire and the feeling of having his rent in his pocket. As the day wore on, and the sky outside the tavern began to darken, the great room filled with the scent of roasting meat, so that Tiller's mouth watered and his stomach growled.

More and more people came to the Fat Spider. By the time Gil emerged from the back bearing a huge platter of food, the tavern was as crowded as Tiller had ever seen it. Somehow, men and women from all over Boston knew to come. Maybe the smell of Gil's venison had drifted through the streets. Maybe word of his feast had spread from home to home. Whatever the reason, it was a night unlike any Tiller could remember.

He ate and he drank until he'd had his fill, and then he had more. Eventually he must have dozed off at his table by the hearth. When he woke, sometime later, most of the people were gone. Gil stood beside his chair, firelight dancing across his features and gleaming in his eyes.

"I want you to stay here tonight, my friend. It is late for you to be walking home."

"But my cart. And Crumbs."

"They will be fine. You have my word." Gil smiled. "Crumbs has eaten well." He draped a blanket over Tiller and pulled over another chair so that Tiller could rest his legs. "Is there anything at your home that you need?" Gil asked. "Anything dear to you, that you must have?"

"Just the picture of my Mama and Papa."

"A painting?" Gil asked.

"A drawing."

"How big?"

Tiller held his hands a few inches apart. "Like this."

Gil nodded. He strode back to the bar and spoke in low tones with Janna. She cast a quick glance Tiller's way, but then nodded, drawing a small knife from a pocket of her dress. Tiller recognized the blade. It was the one Janna used when she drew blood from her arm for a conjuring.

Tiller saw her step back into the kitchen. Moments later, he felt another pulse of magick. It was weaker than what he felt when Gil made Miss Jackson her drink, but it made the tavern floor hum.

Janna reemerged from the kitchen, stepped out from behind the bar, and walked to Tiller's makeshift bed carrying the portrait.

"Here you go, darlin'," she said. "Sleep well."

"Thank you, Janna," Tiller whispered. He studied the drawing, front and back. It was his. He touched his fingers to his lips and then to the image of his parents. "Goodnight, Mama, Papa."

He propped the picture against the back of the second chair, settled back down, and was soon sleeping once more.

He woke again several hours later. The tavern smelled strongly of smoke, and he could hear Janna and Gil speaking at the doorway, their voices lowered.

"What've you done?" Janna asked him.

"I have done nothing. I granted her wish. The rest she brought to the casting herself."

"Tha's not—"

"You said it yourself," Gil told her. "Her merchant has a wife. Did she not expect that when the man came to her, the wife would follow? Mary was foolish."

"But your spell—"

"Did nothing more or less than I promised it would. Her man came to her. That he did so clumsily, making no attempt to hide his destination . . . That is not my fault."

"His wife started th' fire?"

"I know nothing for certain."

"Yes, you do," Janna said, a smile in her voice.

"If I were to guess, I would say that the fire started upstairs, in Mary's bedchamber. And that many items were thrown in anger, including a candle or two, or perhaps an oil lamp."

"You're a dangerous man, Gil."

Gil said nothing.

"It looks like th' whole city's burnin'," Janna said, sounding worried.

"It is not. Only a portion of it."

"Still, look at it. Who knows how many're dead?"

"I know. None."

"Gil—"

"None are dead, Janna. You have my word. You also have my word on this: She will not be back, and she will not threaten you again."

"Gil?" Tiller called. "What's happened?"

"Go back to sleep, my friend."

"What time is it?"

"After midnight, but still several hours before dawn. You should be sleeping."

Tiller got up from his chair and crossed to the tavern entrance. "What's happened?"

Gil didn't answer right away. "There is a fire."

"Where?"

"Near your home. There was a great wind, and it pushed the flames all the way to the water's edge."

Tiller peered out into the night. Janna was right. It did look like the whole city was ablaze. The sky over Boston glowed a baleful inconstant orange, and dark smoke billowed over the spires and rooftops.

"I am sorry, Tiller," the barman said, looking down at him.

"That's all right." Tiller sensed that he was pardoning Gil for more than sad tidings. "Pushed them from where?"

"What?"

"Pushed the flames from where to the water?" But Tiller already knew the answer.

Gil glanced at Janna, who still stared out toward the city. "From th' Brazen Head," she said in a low voice. "That's where this started."

"You say that Miss Jackson isn't dead?" Tiller asked.

"She is not," Gil told him. "I swear it."

Tiller nodded. "Good. She gives me food sometimes."

Historical Note: Early in the morning on March 20, 1760, a fire started at Boston's Brazen Head Tavern, which was owned by Mary Jackson. Driven by powerful winds, the fire consumed three hundred forty-nine buildings and homes, left more than a thousand people homeless, and destroyed more than one hundred thousand pounds worth of property. Miraculously, no one was killed. To this day, the cause of the fire remains unknown.

"A Memory of Freedom" first appeared at Orson Scott Card's Intergalactic Medicine Show *(http://www.intergalacticmedicineshow.com/) in March 2012, about four months before the release of* Thieftaker *(Tor Books, 2012), the first novel in the* Thieftaker Chronicles. *"The Tavern Fire," had come out in an anthology the year before, but this was the first published piece of fiction to feature Ethan Kaille. I suppose in a sense this is Ethan's "origin story," the tale of how he went from being little more than a broken man, an ex-convict without much of a future, to becoming a successful thieftaker and a conjurer willing to use his powers to solve crimes.*

"A Memory of Freedom"
D.B. Jackson

Boston, Province of Massachusetts Bay, 7 August 1760

Ethan Kaille was halfway through this week's issue of the *Boston Gazette* when he finally took note of the date on the front page. Monday, 4 August 1760. That made this the seventh. He had been a free man for exactly three months.

A quarter of a year gone. The days had flown by too fast. He should have been able to account for each one, and he couldn't. They were a blur—wasted and forgotten, gray and indistinguishable. For fourteen years he had wished away the hours, desperately coaxed the scorching sun across tropical skies, endured days of unending labor and nights of unbearable longing. Fourteen years. They might as well have been fourteen lifetimes. And now he had squandered three months of precious freedom.

Doing what?

For a panicked moment, he could remember accomplishing nothing of note—it seemed he had slept the months away. But no, he had made his way on foot from the plantation to port, where the ship to Charleston, South Carolina waited. That took two days. The voyage from Barbados to Charleston took closer to two weeks, as did the second voyage up the coast to Boston, where he had lived before prison, before the *Ruby Blade* mutiny. In between, he spent nearly a month working the wharves in Charleston trying to earn money for the second voyage. Then there were nights spent in Boston's Almshouse, days when he limped through the cobbled streets of the city, making his way from wharf to wharf, warehouse to shipyard, seeking employment. And finally, weeks of tedium working at the Silver

Key, serving food and drink, clearing tables, mopping floors, rolling and hefting barrels of ale, repairing tables and chairs damaged by the tavern's patrons during nights of drunken revelry.

It wasn't that time had slipped by, Ethan realized, but rather that, thus far, freedom, at least as he had imagined it during his incarceration, had eluded him.

"Kaille!"

Ethan lowered the paper. William Keyes, owner of the Silver Key, stood in the doorway to the small alcove where Ethan reclined on his rope bed.

"Yes, sir?"

"You can laze around on your own time. When you're workin' for me, you'll do just that: work."

Ethan had sailed in His Majesty's fleet and served as second mate aboard the *Ruby Blade*, a twenty-eight gun privateering vessel of some repute. Back in his native Bristol, his family had been known and respected. This man, Keyes, on the other hand, his breeches stained and ill-fitting, his linen shirt threadbare, was a brute who ran his tavern the way the plantation foreman had overseen labor in the cane fields. Except that rather than relying on fear of the whip to intimidate others, he used the threat of dismissal, and an underlying suggestion of physical violence.

Ethan had encountered too many men of this sort throughout his life. In the navy, on the wharves of Bristol and Boston, and again and again during his years of forced labor. He despised them, but he had learned that he was best off keeping his head down and staying out of their way.

Keyes stood half a head taller than Ethan; he towered over Simon, the Silver Key's mouse-like chef, and Sarah and Della, the two serving girls. His features were blunt, homely, except for his eyes, which were small and brown and watchful, like those of a street cur. Though his hair was silver—hence the name of the tavern—he couldn't have been much past his fortieth year.

Ethan thought him shrewd; he had seen him bargain with brewmasters and bread peddlers, butchers and rum distillers, and more often than not Keyes seemed to come out ahead. But Ethan wasn't entirely convinced that the man could read the newspaper he held, or even the bill of fare posted on the wall beside the bar.

He also knew for a fact that these few late afternoon hours belonged to him, not to the barkeep. Still, that wouldn't stop Keyes from throwing him out on the street if he refused to work. He didn't make much working in the tavern. Nor did it help that Keyes extracted from Ethan's wages the full price of every meal he ate and every ale he drank. But at least he had a place to sleep; he couldn't afford to lose that.

He laid the newspaper aside and stood. "What is it you need me to do?"

"You need t' ask?" Keyes gestured back toward the great room. "The place needs moppin'; the tables need wipin', as does the bar. And I want the brass polished before the regular night crowd shows up."

Ethan had cleaned the floors and tables earlier, but he kept this to himself. "Yes, sir," was all he said.

Keyes remained in the doorway. As Ethan tried to walk past, the barkeep put a hand on his chest, stopping him.

"I don't normally hire convicts, Kaille. Don't give me a reason t' put you back on the street."

Ethan held Keyes's gaze, saying nothing. He had put larger men on the floor with a single blow, without ever resorting to a conjuring. He had survived fourteen years in a living hell that would have broken a man like Keyes in a fraction of that time. The barkeep couldn't intimidate him.

Perhaps Keyes realized this. He moved his hand and let Ethan pass.

Ethan started on the floors, keeping his gaze lowered, his expression flat, dead. He would have preferred a job on the waterfront, but work was harder to find in Boston than it had been in Charleston. Had he not been drawn back to Boston by his vain hope of reconciling with Marielle—Elli— who had been his betrothed before the mutiny, he might have stayed in South Carolina. But here jobs were scarce.

Surely his limp made matters worse—who would want to hire a lame ex-convict? Nor did it help that so many of the wharf owners remembered the *Ruby Blade* mutiny and the tales of the male witch who had thrown in with the mutineers. If he could have told them that he hadn't cast a spell in fourteen years, he might have convinced Boston's merchants to hire him. For it was true: Having entered into a devil's pact with the men who led the *Blade* insurrection, men who had wanted him on their side solely because he could conjure, he had vowed never to cast another spell. His powers had cost him his youth and his love; they had left him scarred and half-crippled.

Once in prison, however, he became desperate to break this oath. Conjurings might have won him his freedom. Certainly healing spells could have cured the infection that left him lame. But surrounded by prisoners who looked for any opportunity to improve their lot, even if at the expense of one of their brethren, and watched constantly by vicious overseers, Ethan hadn't dared cast at all. Even one spell would have led him to the hangman's gallows, or to a public burning. Fear of witchcraft ran as deep in the Caribbean as it did here in New England.

For that self-same reason, Ethan knew he couldn't offer any reas-
surances to Boston's merchants. As long as his powers remained a rumor,
he was safe. But a promise that he would not conjure was tantamount to an
admission that he could if he chose to, and would lead to his execution.

So he mopped William Keyes' tavern, and when the floor was clean he
set to work on the tables and then the bar.

By the time he finished polishing the brass, the Key had begun to fill
with the usual evening crowd. Wharf men and day laborers clustered
around the bar ordering ales and oysters. A few craftsmen—mostly smiths
and ships' carpenters—sat at tables in pairs and in small groups, some
drinking Madeira wine. Others drank flips, their cups frothy with egg
whites, the concoctions redolent of warm rum and cinnamon. Most ate fish
chowder and bread. Ethan slipped into the kitchen, tied on an apron and
joined the girls in serving.

When Simon finished preparing a second pot of chowder, Ethan helped
the cook carry it to the bar and the two of them ladled out fresh bowls.

While they worked, the door opened and three hulking men walked in.
Immediately conversation ceased. The three took positions near the bar and
the door, their gazes sweeping over the tavern's patrons. A moment later a
fourth man entered.

John Gray.

People in the South End knew him as Hawker Gray, in part because he
was said to run a profitable trade in stolen goods, and in part because in his
youth he had earned a reputation as a skilled street fighter with a blade as
quick and deadly as a hawk's talons.

He was shorter than his three toughs, thick around the middle, with
long powerful arms. Silver streaked his black hair, which he wore tied back
in a plait. The years had etched lines into the corners of his eyes and mouth,
but otherwise his face remained boyish. Unlike the three toughs, he was
dressed neatly in a white silk shirt, black breeches, and a matching waistcoat. As he crossed to the bar, workmen fell over themselves getting out of
his way.

"I'll take a bowl of that," he said, waving a hand at the chowder. "And a
whiskey."

Simon nodded and filled a bowl, his hands trembling slightly. Ethan
poured out a dram of Scotch whiskey.

Both of them knew better than to ask for payment. Hawker was a
regular in the Key, but Ethan had never seen him pay for anything. He and

Keyes seemed to have some sort of arrangement. Hawker ate and drank what he pleased, and conducted his business in the tavern as he saw fit. The bar's owner, Ethan assumed, took a share of Gray's earnings.

One of Hawker's toughs shooed two men away from a nearby table. Gray positioned his chair so that he had his back to a wall and a clear view of the door.

Ethan and Simon returned to serving chowder. Gradually the voices that had been silenced by Hawker's arrival rose once more, until the din in the tavern returned more or less to its normal level. Ethan wiped up a few spilled ales, cleared tables and helped Simon with yet another huge pot of stew. The crowd in the great room swelled.

Near to eight o'clock, another man entered the tavern, pausing in the doorway to survey the throng. Bald, with a grizzled face and thick, muscular forearms, and he stood nearly a full head shorter than Ethan. He lingered near the door, his mouth hanging open, exposing a large gap where his front teeth should have been. He wore the clothes of a laborer, his breeches and shirt stained and tattered.

Spotting Hawker Gray at his table, the man stalked toward him, fists clenched. Before he had covered half the distance, two of Hawker's toughs intercepted him. They towered over the man making him appear as a mere child beside them.

Unable to get any closer, the stranger pointed a bony finger Hawker's way.

"Where are my toolth, Gray?" he demanded with a pronounced lisp. "I know you've got 'em, and I want 'em back!"

The tavern went quiet again. All eyes turned to Hawker and this bold stranger.

Hawker's expression remained mild. "And you are . . . ?"

"You know who I am, you bathtard! Now where are my toolth?"

Hawker glanced at one of his toughs, raised an eyebrow almost imperceptibly. That was enough.

The tough dug a fist into the stranger's belly, doubling him over. The man fell to his knees and retched.

"I remember you now," Hawker said, standing with a scrape of his chair on the wood floor. He stepped away from the table and walked to where the stranger knelt, his hands braced on the floor. "You're the cooper, the one who talkth funny."

He grinned briefly; his men laughed.

Otherwise, the tavern remained so quiet Ethan could hear Simon breathing beside him.

"You need to learn some manners, old man," Hawker went on, deadly serious now. "No one comes in here and calls me names. I think you owe me an apology."

The cooper didn't look up. "I want my toolth back."

Hawker glanced around at those watching him, a smile fixed on his face. He opened his hands, as if to say *What could I do?* Before anyone could speak, he raised his foot and stomped on the cooper's hand with the heel of his boot. Ethan heard bones crack. The cooper howled like a wild creature, clutched his hand to his chest, and toppled onto his side. Several patrons groaned; one of the serving girls began to cry.

Hawker nodded to his toughs again. One of them hoisted the cooper to his feet, pinning his arms at his sides. Another man pummeled him. In mere seconds the poor cooper was a bloody mess, his lip split, his nose probably broken, his eyes starting to swell.

At a word from Hawker, the toughs broke off their assault and threw the man out the door.

"I doubt he'll be back here making accusations," Hawker said, loud enough for all to hear. *And I doubt any of you will ever think to cross me.* This last hung in the tavern air, unsaid, but as pungent as pipe smoke.

Ethan strode toward the door only to feel someone grab his arm. Whirling, he found himself face-to-face with Keyes.

"Where d'you think you're goin'?" the barkeep asked. "You got work t' do."

Ethan shook off his hand and glared back at him. "The old man needs help."

"It's no bus'ness of yours."

Hawker had stolen the cooper's tools and Keyes stood to profit from the theft. Ethan was sure of it. In that moment, it was all he could do not to incinerate the man with a fire spell.

"If he dies on your doorstep," Ethan said, reining in his rage, "it'll be bad for business."

Keyes eyed him a moment longer before dismissing him with a wave of his hand and turning away. "Ten minutes. And it comes out of your wages."

Ethan shoved the door open and strode out into the warm night air. Whip-poor-wills sang overhead, and the stink of fish and tidal mud soured the city air.

The cooper lay in a heap at the mouth of an alley that ran between the tavern and a milliner's shop next door. He didn't move as Ethan knelt beside him, and for a moment Ethan feared that he was dead. Then he saw the shallow rise and fall of the man's chest and allowed himself to exhale.

"Nearly got yourself killed, you old fool," he whispered.

No response.

The cooper looked a mess, but Ethan knew that his hand needed healing most. Left to mend on its own, it would be mangled and useless for the rest of the cooper's life; he would never set another hoop, or plane another stave. Even a doctor might not be able to set it properly.

Which left conjuring.

What of his oath? What of all that he had endured because of the spells he had cast? Imprisonment, estrangement from his family and friends, the loss of Elli, his one love, who had made it clear that she wanted nothing to do with a mutineer and conjurer. This man was a stranger, a reckless fool who had brought these injuries on himself. After fourteen years without casting, why should he risk conjuring again for him?

So you'll leave him to live the rest of his life maimed, unable to work, just to uphold a promise made in your youth, when you, too, were a reckless fool?

Susannah's voice. Of his two sisters, she was the one who also conjured, who would understand the choice he faced.

Not long after Ethan was convicted and transported to Barbados to toil in the sun-baked cane fields, an older man, a fellow prisoner, sliced his foot open with a cane knife. It was an accident; the man apologized again and again, no doubt fearing that Ethan would repay him in kind, or simply kill him and be done with it. But accident or not, the wound quickly worsened. It oozed foul ichor and grew hot to the touch.

Within a couple of days Ethan's entire leg had grown bloated and tender. In the end, the plantation surgeons removed three of his toes and so managed to save his leg. Ever since, Ethan had walked with a pronounced limp.

He could have spared himself great suffering had he healed his foot with a conjuring before the wound became infected. He never made the attempt. And now, years later, faced with a choice of casting or leaving another man to live the rest of his life as a cripple, he had to admit that it wasn't his vow to foreswear conjuring that had stopped him so long ago. It had been his fear of being marked as a witch; it had been the very fact that he was a prisoner, watched at every moment and subject to the whims of cruel, narrow-minded men.

He could do nothing now to make his foot whole again. But he could heal the cooper. He knew how to speak the conjuring; and he was a free man. For too long he had struggled to divine just what that meant. Perhaps the answer lay hidden in the simple act of casting a spell.

He reached for his knife, then, glancing about, thought better of it. The alley was empty save for the two of them, and they were both in shadow. But how would he explain if someone happened upon them after he cut himself? Better to use the blood on the cooper's face. God knew there was enough.

His own hands shaking, he gently took hold of the cooper's shattered hand.

"*Remedium ex . . . ex cruore evocatum,*" he whispered. Healing, conjured from blood.

His Latin sounded ragged; it had been too many years since last a spell had crossed his lips. And yet the sensation was as familiar as the sound of his own name. Power thrummed like a bow string, humming in the cobblestones beneath him, in the walls of the buildings around him. At the same time, a spectral figure appeared at his shoulder, a ghostly form glowing with a deep russet hue. The shade was tall, lean, dressed in a coat of mail and a tabard bearing the three lions of the ancient kings. His beard and close-cropped hair might have been white had it not been for the radiance clinging to him.

This figure, too, Ethan remembered. The power necessary to cast spells dwelled at the boundary between the living world and the realm of the dead, the ephemeral plane of spirit and soul. Every conjurer relied on a spectral guide to access magick, and this old warrior with his bright, glowing eyes had appeared with every spell Ethan had ever cast. He might have been an ancestor; he reminded Ethan of his mother's prickly brother, Reginald. So Ethan had taken to calling the specter Uncle Reg.

The ghost glowered at him, a parent scowling at a wayward child.

"It's been a long time," Ethan said. "It's good to see you."

Reg didn't answer. In all the years Ethan had conjured, he had never known the ghost to say a word.

He felt power flow through his own hands into the cooper's shattered bones. After a few seconds, the bones started to reform beneath his touch, knitting themselves. The fractures were severe, and before he was done Ethan had to cast the spell a second time, drawing on the fresh blood that appeared on the cooper's face after his first conjuring. But at last he sat back on his heels, wiped the sweat from his forehead and took a long breath. The cooper's hand would be sore for days, perhaps longer. It might continue to bother him occasionally in the years to come, in the cold and damp, and after long days at his workbench. But soon enough he would have use of it again.

The rest of the man's injuries were less serious; they would heal on their own. Ethan had made up his mind to go back inside the tavern when the cooper let out a low groan. His swollen eyes fluttered open, though only to narrow slits.

The old man tried to get up, bracing himself on the cobblestones with his bad hand. Hissing sharply through his teeth, he collapsed back to the ground.

"Easy there, friend," Ethan said. "You won't be using that hand for a little while. And you won't be luring any lasses to your bed with that handsome face, either."

The cooper chuckled, winced.

"Who are you?" he asked, the words thick.

"Ethan Kaille. I work in the Silver Key. I saw what Hawker did to you; you're lucky to be alive."

The cooper stared at his hand and cautiously flexed his fingers. "I thought he'd broken it. I didn't think it would ever be any good again."

Ethan looked away. "I guess it wasn't as bad as you thought."

"Aye, I gueth," he said, the lisp more pronounced with his lip swollen.

"You might not be so lucky next time. You should go home."

The cooper stared at the tavern door. "I want my toolth back."

"You're not going to get them," Ethan said. "Look at me."

The cooper shifted his gaze to Ethan.

"You're not going to get them back. If you go in there again, Hawker will kill you. Go home, old man."

"Henry," the cooper said, sullen, eyes downcast.

"What?"

"My name'th Henry Dall, and I'm not all that old. The toolth cotht me everything I had. Without them, I might ath well give up my shop."

"You have old tools, right?"

Henry shrugged.

"Use them until you can afford another set of new ones. But don't go back in there. It's not worth it."

Ethan stood, extended a hand to the man. Henry eyed it for a moment, then grasped it with his good hand. Ethan pulled him to his feet.

"Goodnight, Henry Dall."

"Goodnight," Henry said, starting away. "Thank you."

Ethan watched him go before entering the tavern once more. Conversations had resumed. Everyone appeared content to drink, eat and exchange stories and news of the day. Hawker sat with his men, laughing about something. No one seemed to spare a thought for the cooper, except Simon and the girls, who asked if he was all right.

"Aye," Ethan told them, watching Hawker from the bar. "He'll be fine."

Hours later, after the tavern had closed and Ethan and the girls had wiped down the tables and chairs, Ethan retired to his alcove, bone weary.

But he didn't sleep well. He dreamed of the tavern and the beating he had witnessed, and though he managed to force himself awake, each time he dozed off again he fell back into the dream.

He arose with first light, and mopped and cleaned the tavern floors and tables before mid-morning. As he worked, his thoughts churned, as did his anger at what had been done to the cooper.

With his hand crushed, Henry would have been unable to make a living. Hawker had abandoned him to the street, maimed and bloody. He couldn't have cared less whether the cooper lived or died. And though Ethan had healed the man, his conjuring could only fix so much. How much better off was the old cooper, even with his hand healed, if he hadn't decent tools with which to ply his trade? The bruises and cuts and broken hand were only the most visible of the injuries Hawker and his men had inflicted; Hawker had crippled him simply by stealing from him. What was more, while Hawker had been incensed by Henry's accusations, the bastard had never denied them.

Ethan had no doubt as to his guilt. He was a brute and nothing more, like Keyes, like the plantation overseers in Barbados. But Ethan didn't depend on Hawker for a job or the roof over his head. And, as the healing spell he had cast the night before had reminded him, he wasn't a prisoner anymore.

Once he finished cleaning, he left the Silver Key and walked to Cooper's Alley, a narrow lane just off the South End's waterfront, where he assumed he would find Henry Dall's shop. Halfway down the lane, he spotted a sign above one of the storefronts: "Dall's Barrels and Crates." Another sign on the door read "Open. Entr."

Ethan pushed the door open and walked in. Henry sat at the back of the shop beside a half-completed barrel, cradling his injured hand, gazing morosely at his empty workbench. Seeing Ethan, he stood and took a step back. Ethan thought he might actually flee the shop. His face still looked terrible: dark bruises around his eyes, his lip swollen and scabbed.

He frowned, pointing a trembling finger Ethan's way. "You're the fella from latht night," he lisped. "Kaille, right?"

"Why are you so sure that it was Hawker who stole your tools?" Ethan asked, crossing the shop and stopping just in front of him. "This city is filled with thieves. What makes you think it was him?"

"I jutht know," the cooper said, though he sounded unsure of himself.

Ethan shook his head. "That's not good enough. I need more than that if I'm going to get your tools back."

Henry's eyes narrowed. "What? Get my— Why would you even try? You a thieftaker?"

"Are there thieftakers here in Boston?"

"There'th one. Her name ith Prythe."

Ethan nodded at the name. Sephira Pryce. He had heard men in the tavern speak of her. "Have you gone to her about this?"

"I can't afford her," Henry said. "And she doethn't work for men like me. She workth for wealthy men, influential men."

"Then I'll work for you," Ethan said. "I'm neither wealthy nor influential. But I'm good with a blade and with my fists, and I've half a brain. So to answer your question, yes, I'm a thieftaker."

"How much do you charge?"

"How much will you pay?"

Henry shrugged. "I can't offer you a lot. Fifteen shillingth maybe, but I'll have to thell a few thingth."

"Done," Ethan said. "Now, why do you think it was Hawker?"

The cooper frowned again, sat back down on the stool by his workbench. Ethan sensed that events were moving too fast for him.

"I thaw him the day I bought the toolth. He even thaid thomething to me about them—about how fine they were. I don't remember what exactly, but he definitely notithed them. And for a long time people have been thaying that he hireth men to thteal for him. That'th how he maketh money."

"Do you know where he lives?"

"Not far from here. He hath a big brick house at the north end of Joliffe'th Lane."

"All right. Then that's where I'll start."

"Do I need to pay you now?" the cooper asked, sounding wary.

"Do you have your tools back yet?"

"No."

"Then you don't pay me yet."

Henry grinned, then gingerly put a hand to his split lip.

"Tell me about the tools."

The cooper rattled off the items that had been stolen: a variety of planes, mallets, and knives, as well an adze, a borer, and a rounded shave for hollowing.

"What did all this cost you?" Ethan asked.

Henry shifted, clearly unnerved by the question. "More than fifteen shillingth," he said, his voice low.

Ethan smiled. "That's all right. You shouldn't have to pay for them twice. Three pounds? More?"

"Clother to five," Henry said.

"Good. Thank you."

"I bought them on credit," the cooper went on, as if he hadn't heard. "They're not even paid for yet."

"I'll find them," Ethan said. He crossed back to the shop entrance. "Take care of yourself, Henry," he said, pulling the door open. "I'll see you soon."

"All right." The cooper raised a hand, still seemingly perplexed by their conversation. "My thankth."

Ethan struck out westward on Milk Street toward Joliffe's Lane. As he drew near, he slipped into a narrow alley between two houses and pulled out his knife. He wasn't at all eager to conjure again, but he didn't see any other way to do what he had in mind. He pushed up his shirt sleeve revealing a forearm laced with old white scars—reminders of a time when he had conjured freely. After a moment's hesitation, he cut himself and watched as blood welled from the wound.

"*Velamentum ex cruore evocatum*," he said softly. Concealment, conjured from blood.

Power hummed in the street and in the walls of the two houses. Any conjurers in the area would feel it, and might even guess at what kind of spell Ethan had cast. But conjurers were rare, and those who didn't possess the ability to conjure wouldn't be aware of the spell. Nor would they be able to see Uncle Reg, who winked into view beside him, glowing brightly in the shadows. The shade smiled fiercely and even nodded his approval. Ethan wondered if Reg had missed these spells and his opportunities to tap into the power that dwelled in his realm. If he was honest with himself Ethan had to admit that he had missed them. It felt good to be casting again. As much as he had tried to deny it over the past fourteen years, conjuring was as much a part of him as his family name and the years he had spent at sea.

"Stay with me," Ethan said to the ghost. "I might need to cast again before long."

Reg's smile deepened.

Together they continued to Joliffe's Lane. With the spell in place, the people around them couldn't see Ethan, though they could hear him if he spoke or scuffed his feet. He and Reg crept along the street, keeping out of the way of men and women who walked with grim purpose to and from the waterfront. Horse drawn carriages rattled past, unshod hooves clopping drily on the cobblestones.

Hawker Gray's house proved easy enough to spot. As Henry had said, it was larger than its neighbors; it was also the only brick house at the north end of the lane.

Stepping with care so as not to give himself away, Ethan walked into the small yard and circled the house until he found a side entrance. He put his ear to the door, but heard nothing. He tried the door handle. Locked.

He pulled some grass from the ground at his feet, and said "*Discuti ex gramine evocatum.*" Shatter, conjured from grass. The spell hummed in the ground and the faint chiming of breaking iron sounded from the lock. Ethan pulled the door open and flashed a quick grin at Uncle Reg.

The doorway led into the kitchen, which smelled of freshly cooked eggs and bacon, but appeared to be empty, at least for the moment. With Reg at his back, Ethan padded silently to the nearest door, listened for voices or movement. After a moment, he heard the clink of silverware on china. He backed away from that door and retraced his steps to a narrow stone stairway that led down to a cellar.

If Hawker kept stolen goods in the house, chances were he wouldn't keep them in the living quarters. A cellar, on the other hand, might afford him ample space for storing items he hadn't yet sold.

Ethan eased his way down the stairs into the gloom. Once more, he pulled his knife from its sheath and cut his forearm. "*Lux ex cruore evocatus,*" he whispered. Light, conjured from blood.

A golden light appeared above his head, illuminating the cellar and casting dark, shifting shadows on the far walls.

He breathed hard, sweat dampening his brow and temples. In his youth, he had been able to cast many spells without tiring; not only was he older, he was also out of practice. He needed to find the stolen goods and return to the Key, where he could rest.

A wooden rack holding a collection of dusty wine bottles loomed on his right. To the left were several tables covered with tools and wood shavings and a few crude boxes and wooden bowls. None of the tools looked new, however. Forced to guess, Ethan would have said that Hawker or someone else in the household fancied himself a woodworker.

Footsteps overhead made him freeze. He heard voices as well, and thought he recognized Hawker as one of the speakers. He backed toward a corner. Before he reached it, though, he bumped one of the tables and knocked a wood bowl to the floor. It clattered, rolled back and forth, and came to rest against a table leg. The footsteps above him stopped; the voices went silent.

Then he heard the quick tread of several pairs of feet, all of them converging on the stairway.

Ethan slashed his arm again. "*Fini lux ex cruore evocatus!*" End light, conjured from blood!

The golden glow vanished, plunging the cellar into darkness. Ethan crept backward more cautiously this time, trying to reach the farthest corner of the cellar. Before he got there, the three toughs from the tavern reached the bottom of the stairs. Two of them held flintlock pistols, the third a knife. Hawker loomed just behind them, holding a lit candle.

"Out of my way," he said, pushing past his men.

He edged forward, raising the candle high and peering into the shadows. His gaze flicked over Ethan and Reg, but he gave no sign that he could see them through Ethan's spell.

After several moments, he lowered the candle and stooped to retrieve the fallen bowl.

"Probably a rat," he said. "Still, I want the three of you to go check the doors. I'll stay here and watch for our rodent."

The toughs grunted their agreement and started back up the stairs. Ethan and Reg exchanged looks.

Mere seconds later, one of the toughs came back down to the cellar.

"Th' lock on th' side door's been broke," he said.

Hawker gave a slow nod. "Well, isn't that interesting? Give me your weapon, then go get the others. And bring oil lamps. I can't see a damn thing down here."

The brute handed his pistol to Hawker and hurried back up to the kitchen.

Hawker raised the candle again, the pistol held ready in his other hand. "If you come out now," he said, pitching his voice to carry, "I might not shoot you, though I'd be in my rights to do so."

Slowly, noiselessly, Ethan dragged his blade over his arm, drawing fresh blood. He thought of a spell he had relied upon more than once in his youth . . . The memory brought a smile.

"*Dormite*," he whispered to himself. "*Ex cruore evocatum*." Slumber, conjured from blood.

Power pulsed in the stone floor of the basement, but Hawker didn't appear to notice. After a few seconds, his face went slack, his eyes rolled back into his head, and he pitched forward, smacking his forehead on the nearest table and then flopping onto the floor.

Footsteps overhead told Ethan that at least one of the toughs had heard. The man hurtled down the stairs, pistol in hand.

Ethan had no choice but to cut himself once more. Without hesitating, he cast another sleep spell. Moments later, the tough toppled to the floor, landing beside his boss. Ethan stepped over them and tiptoed up the stairs. He found the side door unguarded—probably that had been the sleeping tough's post.

He slipped from the house and hurried away, following the lanes back toward the Silver Key. He considered stopping to remove the concealment spell, but something occurred to him—another spot he needed to search for Henry's tools and the rest of Hawker's plunder.

Reaching the tavern, he turned into the same alley in which he had found the unconscious cooper the night before and entered the Key through the back, near the kitchen.

The stairway leading to the tavern cellar was broader than the stairway in Hawker's house; the cellar itself was illuminated by candles. The bitter smell of spermaceti hung in the air. Cured meats, wine bottles, and casks of ale, whiskey, and rum crowded the cellar's main chamber. But in the course of working for Keyes, Ethan had noticed a door at the back of the room. He wove his way through the clutter and tried the door handle. Locked.

He pulled his knife out and made another cut on his arm, which was growing red and tender. Back when he conjured more frequently, that had never been a problem.

He broke the lock with another shatter spell and pushed the door open. The faint candlelight from behind him spilled into the room and gleamed dully on what appeared to be a table laden with goods.

"*Lux ex cruore evocatus*."

His conjured glow filled this smaller room, revealing all that Ethan had expected to find at Hawker's house and more. Crystal glasses, shining new blades, and silver tableware; ivory-handled hair brushes and leather-bound books; a pair of dueling pistols with polished wooden stocks and several bottles of what appeared to be French wine. And, of course, a set of fine tools including blades, mallets, and planes.

Ethan didn't know where the other items had come from, but he was sure the tools were Henry's. He bundled them in a burlap sack that he found on the floor near the table, extinguished the light he had conjured, and climbed the stairs to the tavern.

When Ethan emerged from the kitchen, Keyes sat at the bar, eating a plate of oysters.

"Where th' hell have you been?" the barkeep demanded, pushing his plate aside and standing.

"Around," Ethan said striding past him.

"There's work t' be done. You seem t' forget that, Kaille."

"I cleaned up before I left."

He swung the burlap sack onto one of the tables.

Keyes nodded toward it. "What's that?"

Ethan pulled out two of the planes and the curved shave. "You tell me," he said. "As far as I can tell these are the tools of a cooper. Why would they be in your cellar?"

The barman's face reddened. He pulled himself up to his full height and balled his fists. "You're meddlin' where you shouldn't," he said, his voice low and hard. "A man can get himself killed doin' that."

Ethan stared back at him. "You watched Hawker's men beat that cooper within an inch of his life, and you didn't say a thing. You're the hireling of a thief and a brute, and that makes you no better than a thief yourself, and a cowardly one at that."

Keyes pulled a knife from his belt and advanced on him, a sneer contorting his face. Ethan stood his ground, drawing his own blade. He didn't move as well as he had in his youth—the plantation surgeons had seen to that. But against a man as big and clumsy as the barman, he was more than quick enough.

Keyes slashed at him. Ethan jumped back out of reach, the shining steel flashing past harmlessly.

Della, the younger of the serving girls, appeared in the kitchen doorway and seeing the two of them facing each other in the middle of the tavern, knives drawn, let out a small cry. Ethan's eyes flicked in her direction.

"Go back in the kitchen!" he said.

Sensing an opening, Keyes lunged at him again, thrusting his blade straight at Ethan's chest. Ethan shifted his weight, eluding the attack, and drove the heel of his left hand up into the barman's nose. He heard cartilage snap, felt blood splatter on his arm, neck, and face.

Keyes staggered back. Ethan closed the distance between them with a single stride and hammered a fist into the man's side. The barman gasped. Ethan hit him a second time, and Keyes collapsed to the floor. Standing over him, Ethan drew back his foot to kick the man.

"Ethan, don't!" Della cried out.

She looked terrified, her eyes wide, her cheeks pale.

He pivoted and when he did kick out it was only to knock the knife from Keyes's hand. The blade skittered across the tavern floor.

"If you ever come near me again, you'll get worse," Ethan said, glaring down at the barman, breathing hard. "And if you or Hawker or his men ever touch Henry Dall again, or take so much as a scrap of wood from his shop, I'll kill you. Do you understand?"

Keyes had his eyes closed and was panting as well, but he nodded once.

"You also might want to get rid of that wine downstairs. The customs boys don't look kindly on fat barmen who traffic in goods from enemies of the Crown. And I'll be sending them to your door straight away."

He packed up Henry's tools, then ducked into the alcove where he slept to retrieve his meager belongings: a change of clothes, a spare blade, a coat, and a thin bundle of letters he had received from his sister since his arrival in Boston. By the time he crossed back through the great room, Keyes was sitting up. Blood still flowed freely from his nose down over his lips and chin, and he glowered at Ethan as if girding himself for another fight.

"By the way, I quit," Ethan said, walking past him with barely a glance. "In case that wasn't clear."

"Don't ever show your face in here again!"

Ethan laughed. "I don't think there's any danger of that." Turning to the serving girl, he said, "Take care of yourself, Della. Say goodbye to Simon and Sarah for me."

She nodded

Ethan laughed once more, pulled the door open, and stepped out into the street.

When Ethan entered the cooperage again, Henry was straightening up his workbench, humming to himself.

He turned at the sound of the door opening and then gaped as Ethan opened the sack and began to remove the recovered tools one by one.

"How did you find them?"

"They were at the Silver Key, in the cellar. I'm sorry, Henry. If I had known that Keyes was storing the goods Hawker stole, I would have stopped working for him long ago."

"And if you'd done that, I wouldn't have my toolth back." Henry grinned, exposing the gap in his teeth.

Ethan smiled in turn. "True."

"It gueth I owe you fifteen shillingth."

"Maybe."

Henry frowned. "That wath what we agreed, right?"

"Yes," Ethan said. "But there are other things to consider. Thanks to you, I have a new profession: Ethan Kaille, thieftaker. But I no longer have a place to live and I couldn't help noticing that there's a spare room over your shop, and another one out back."

"The one out back ith mine," Henry said. "The one upstairth . . ." He shrugged, gave a toothless smile. "I could rent it to you."

"How many weeks would ten of those shillings buy me?"

The cooper shrugged again. "A lot. Three monthth, I would think."

"You should know that I was a convict. Almost fifteen years ago I took part in a mutiny aboard a privateering ship. If you don't want a man like me living over your shop, I'll understand. No hard feelings."

"You gonna thteal from me?" the cooper asked.

"No."

"You gonna come down here in the middle of the night and cut my throat?"

Ethan smiled, shook his head. "No."

"You gonna pay rent and get my toolth back when Hawker thtealth them again?"

"Yes."

"Then you're welcome here."

Ethan put out his hand, and Henry gripped it. "Thank you," Ethan said.

"I think I thtill owe you five shillingth."

"You can pay me later." Ethan put down his small bundle of belongings. "Can I leave these things here for a while?"

"Of coursth," Henry said. "Where are you going?"

"I don't know. I'm just going to walk."

"All right. I'll thee you later, then."

Ethan nodded and stepped back out into Cooper's Alley. He inhaled deeply, taking in the familiar smells of the city: fish and saltwater, hay and horse manure, smoke and hewn wood. His forearm still throbbed from the spells he had cast, but he didn't mind. There was something familiar about that as well. He looked in both directions, and then struck out southward, toward Fort Hill.

It felt odd to do nothing but walk. And yet Ethan remembered this feeling, too, from before the cane fields and the *Ruby Blade*. From when he last had been free.

In "The Price of Doing Business," we find Ethan navigating his first encounter with the lovely Sephira Pryce, his arch nemesis and rival in thieftaking. The idea for Sephira came from the true life history of Jonathan Wild, London's most famous thieftaker who, reminiscent of Sephira, made a name for himself by commissioning crimes against London's monied class and then "solving" those crimes for a handsome fee. Upon reading about Wild, in a footnote in Robert Hughes's wonderful history of Australia, The Fatal Shore, *I knew that I wanted to write about thieftakers with a "Wild" character as the chief competition for my honest thieftaking hero. Villainous though Sephira is, she is also just about my favorite character in the Thieftaker universe. This story originally appeared at* Tor.com *on February 19, 2014.*

"The Price of Doing Business"
D.B. Jackson

Boston, Province of Massachusetts Bay, 8 April 1761

Ethan Kaille eyed the tavern door, his fingers drumming an impatient rhythm on the worn wood of the table at which he sat. He had arrived early at the Crane's Roost, a publick house on North Street in Boston's North End, but he felt certain that by now the appointed time for his meeting had come and gone. Knowing how important this job could be for him, Ethan had put on his cleanest linen shirt and his finest waistcoat and matching breeches. But the shirt had fit him better in the days just after his release from prison, when he was so emaciated that he feared the parchment-thin skin over his ribs might tear. And though the waistcoat and breeches might have looked better than his usual clothes, wearing them made him feel like a fop.

The man he was waiting for, a merchant named Aubrey Heap, lived nearby on Princes Street and had a small warehouse on Verin's Wharf. Whether he had been home or at his place of business, he wouldn't have needed to travel far to reach the Roost.

But Ethan had yet to see anyone who looked like a merchant enter the tavern. Several wharfmen and a few joiners, their shirts still covered with sawdust, had straggled in since his arrival, most of them congregating at the bar to eat oysters and drink ales. A short while before, several craftsmen— shipwrights probably, given the proximity to the tavern of so many of Boston's largest shipyards—had entered the Roost and taken a table near his. They were now eating stew and drinking flips; they ignored him.

No one would have counted Heap among the most successful or influential of Boston's merchants; next to men like Thomas Hancock and Abner Berson, Heap seemed of little consequence. But while Ethan had plied his trade as a thieftaker for the better part of a year, he had so far worked only for men of middling means, like Henry Dall, the cooper from whom he rented his room. If Heap—Mr. Heap—decided to hire Ethan, he would be far and away the wealthiest client for whom Ethan had worked in his new profession.

Feeling uneasy, he shifted in his seat and considered buying himself an ale. He immediately thought better of it. Mr. Heap would want to see that he was sober and responsible. He smoothed his waistcoat, and settled back once more, still eyeing the door.

The message delivered to Ethan at his room on Cooper's Alley had been quite specific about the time and place of their meeting, but vague on the particulars of the inquiry Mr. Heap wanted Ethan to conduct. As a thieftaker, Ethan recovered stolen items and returned them to their rightful owners for a fee. It could be dangerous work, but after nearly fourteen years as a convict, toiling under a blazing sun on a sugar plantation in Barbados, few other lines of work remained open to him. He had some skill with a blade and with his fists, and though few knew it, he was also a conjurer who could cast spells that made thieftaking a bit easier and less risky.

He knew of no spells, though, that could speed a man to an appointment for which he was late.

He had just made up his mind to buy himself an ale—sobriety be damned!—when the door opened again and a wisp of a man, half a head shorter than Ethan and as slight as a child, entered the tavern. He paused at the door, surveyed the great room. Spotting Ethan, he faltered, glanced around one last time, and then started toward the table. Ethan stood.

"Mister Heap?" Ethan said.

"Mister Kaille." The man smiled and extended a hand. Despite his diminutive stature, he possessed a firm grip.

They both sat. Heap leaned forward resting his hands on the table, palms down. His beige silk suit and his powdered wig, plaited in back, marked him as a man of some means. His face was youthful, his brow smooth, his eyes a clear bright blue. Forced to guess the man's age, Ethan would have placed him in his late thirties.

"Thank you for meeting me, Mister Kaille. I apologize for being late."

"Not at all, sir. Your message indicated that you've recently had property pinched from your home."

The merchant frowned, though the corners of his mouth quirked up-ward. "Pinched? Is that a term used in the streets?"

"Aye. Forgive me."

"You needn't apologize, Mister Kaille. It sounds rather more exciting than simply saying that we were robbed."

"Yes, sir. Can you tell me what was taken?"

"Mostly items of a personal nature. A gold watch that had belonged to my wife's father, two brooches made with small diamonds and emeralds, a set of hair combs made of ivory and gold, and . . ." The merchant's cheeks shaded to red. "Well, several bottles of . . . of French wine."

Ethan schooled his features. War still raged between France and the British Empire, making the sale of any French products, including wines, illegal in the colonies. Unless those bottles dated from before the war's start, chances were they had been smuggled into Boston. Judging from Mister Heap's apparent discomfort, Ethan assumed he had acquired them recently.

"The wine is nothing," Heap said. "The bottles were rather dear, but they're of little importance. The other items, however, are a different mat-ter. The watch especially is of great sentimental value to my wife."

"Yes, sir. Do you have any idea who might have stolen these treasures from you?"

"As it happens, I do. I've no proof, mind you. But there was a man—a laborer who did some work for us this past autumn. Our home was built originally by my grandfather, and after all these years, the hearths in two of our bed chambers had fallen into disrepair. This man represented himself as a trained mason, although I'm now convinced that this was a ruse. His work-manship was poor, and he spent far too much time lavishing his attentions on my elder daughter, who of course did all she could to spurn his advances."

"Do you remember the man's name?"

"Edwin Randle," Heap said. "He called himself 'Ned.' I don't know where he lives, but he's a tall man, red hair, ruddy complexion. He has a scar on his chin." Heap placed a finger just to the right of the shallow cleft in his own chin. "Right here."

"Thank you, sir. That should be quite helpful."

"So, do you think you might be able to retrieve what we've lost? I approached another thieftaker about this, but was told that the jewelry was probably already beyond our reach, sold to one who deals in pilfered goods."

Ethan frowned at this. "Who told you that?"

"A thieftaker of some renown—a woman. Sephira Pryce."

"Sephira Pryce told you your property couldn't be retrieved?"

"Yes. Do you know her?"

Ethan sat back in his chair. "By reputation," he said. Perhaps he should have told Mister Heap more, but the man's revelation had left him too bewildered.

Sephira Pryce, the so-called Empress of the South End, was the most notorious and successful thieftaker in Boston, perhaps in all the colonies. Rumor spoke of her comeliness, her charm, and her uncompromising ruthlessness. Some said—though always in whispers—that while she managed to find most every stolen item she sought, this was only because the men who worked for her were responsible for the lion's share of the thefts. She stole with one hand, returned property with the other and reaped handsome rewards for her efforts. That she had judged Heap's property irretrievable struck Ethan as peculiar, to say the least. He wondered if she'd had some other reason for refusing to take on this inquiry.

"So, do you think you can help me, Mister Kaille?" Heap asked once more, pulling Ethan from his musings.

"Aye, sir, I believe I can."

Heap smiled with obvious relief. "I'm glad to hear it." The man's smile turned brittle. "Would that I could see to this matter myself. Understand, I'm no coward. But Randle is a brute, and as you can see"—he gestured at himself—"I am anything but."

"Of course, sir. I understand."

The merchant faltered. "I've never done this before—actually hired a thieftaker, I mean. Do I pay you now?"

"You pay me a retainer, sir. I receive the balance of my fee upon returning your property."

"And what do you charge for your . . . your services?"

"Different people pay me different amounts, in proportion to their means and the value they place on those items they've lost."

Heap still looked uncertain.

"I'll take a pound and ten as a retainer," Ethan said, wondering if the merchant would balk at such a large amount. "And three pounds, ten upon returning your property."

Heap appeared to consider this. At last he nodded. "Five pounds sounds reasonable." He pulled out a leather purse that rang with coins when he placed it on the table. With great care, he counted out one pound and ten shillings and handed the coins to Ethan. "There you are."

"Thank you, sir," Ethan said, pocketing the money. "I'll be in touch as soon as I have tidings to share. Would you prefer that I contact you at your home or at the warehouse?"

"I believe the warehouse would be best."

"Very well." Ethan stood. "I'll start my inquiry immediately."

Heap climbed to his feet as well and shook Ethan's hand again with great vigor. "Thank you, Mister Kaille. I look forward to our next encounter."

"Yes, sir." He watched the merchant leave the tavern, and then crossed to the bar.

At first, the barkeep, a tall, narrow-shouldered man with lank brown hair, barely spared him a glance. But when Ethan placed a shilling on the dull, dark wood, the man walked over and reached for the coin. Before his fingers touched it, Ethan covered the shilling with his hand.

"I'd like an ale," he said. "Kent Pale, if you have it. And I'm wondering if you know a man named Ned Randle."

The barkeep met Ethan's gaze for but a moment before looking down at his hand once more.

"That man paid you more than a shillin'," the barkeep said.

"Aye, he did. And last I checked, an ale should only be costing me a penny and a half. Do you want the shilling or not?"

The barkeep licked his lips. "We haven' got the Kent. Just a local small beer. Cider's pretty good though."

"All right," Ethan said. "And Randle?"

"He comes in now an' again. He's not a regular, but I know him."

"Do you know where I might find him when he's not here?"

The barkeep shook his head. "There must be a dozen pubs between here and the wharves. He could be in any one of them."

"He works the wharves?"

The man shrugged. "Most scrubs do when times are hard. And when was the last time they wasn' hard?"

"Do you trust him?"

"Do I trust him?" the barkeep repeated, chuckling. "I trust him as much as I trust any of the coves who show up here, and a fair bit more than I trust you."

Ethan could hardly fault him for this. He removed his hand from the coin. The barkeep pocketed the shilling, then reached for a tankard.

"Cider then?" he asked.

Ethan started toward the door. "Another time," he said over his shoulder. He stepped out of the tavern into the chill air of an early spring day. The sun shone down on Boston Harbor, her wind-riffled waters sparkling as if strewn with diamonds. Gulls circled overhead, their plaintive cries echoing across the harbor and through the lanes of the North End, and cormorants preened atop the roofs of nearby warehouses.

Ethan weighed his options, then struck out westward, skirting the base of Copp's Hill and making his way to Gee's Shipyard. Mr. Heap had known a good deal about the man who robbed him; few of Ethan's clients provided so much information. But still, Ethan didn't know where to begin his search. Thus, he thought it best to follow the counsel of the Roost's barkeep and look for Randle first on the wharves and in the North End shipyards.

He followed Charles Street to Salem Street and walked past the old Christ Church, with its brick façade and soaring white spire. Taking a right onto Shease, he checked to see that no one was watching and slipped into a narrow alley between a pair of buildings. There, he pulled his knife from the sheath on his belt, pushed up his coat and shirt sleeves, and cut his forearm.

Blood welled from the wound. "*Velamentum ex cruore evocatum*," he whispered. Concealment conjured from blood.

Power thrummed in the cobblestones beneath his feet and in the brick walls on either side of him. At the same time, a glowing russet figure winked into view beside Ethan. He appeared to be an older man, lean, with closely shorn white hair and a trim beard. He wore chain mail and a tabard bearing the lions of the ancient Plantagenet kings. A long sword hung from his belt.

"Good day, Reg," Ethan said.

The spirit frowned, his eyes glowing brightly in the shadows of the alley. Ethan did not actually know the old man's name. He was the shade of an ancient ancestor, a specter who allowed Ethan to access the power that dwelt between the living world and the realm of the dead. Without him, Ethan's conjurings would have no effect. But his appearance and perpetual scowl reminded Ethan of his mother's splenetic brother, Reginald, and so Ethan had long ago taken to calling him Uncle Reg.

Ethan's concealment spell rendered him invisible to those around him, at least those who weren't also conjurers. He could search the wharves and shipyards freely, without drawing attention to himself or to his inquiry, and, he hoped, without scaring Randle away before he had a chance to question the man.

He left the alley, Reg stalking beside him, and soon reached Princes Street, near Aubrey Heap's house. He turned northwestward in the direction of Gee's Shipyard and fell in step with men and women making their way to the Charlestown Ferry, using their footfalls to mask his own.

Once Ethan reached the shipyard and its dock on the Charles River, he had to take greater care not to make noise. Those around him might not be able to see him, but they could hear every sound he made and they might even notice signs of his footsteps on the dirt fill of the wharf.

One ship, its hull mostly complete, sat on blocks near the end of a pier at the west end of the shipyard. Shipwrights and mechanics scrambled over the vessel, like beetles on a carcass, but otherwise there was little activity in the yard.

Back in 1744, before Ethan's imprisonment, when he first came to Boston, the shipyards of the North End had bustled with activity, and had been among the most productive in all of North America. But with the onset of war with the French, hard times had come to New England, and today, while shipbuilders in Philadelphia and New York continued to do a good business, many of Boston's yards had fallen idle.

Ethan walked the length and breadth of the yard, but saw no one who matched Heap's description of Ned Randle. He returned to the street and followed Ferry Way past the Charlestown Ferry dock and Hudson's Point checking each yard as he went. Still, he saw no sign of Randle.

But as he searched Greenough's Shipyard, he did spot a familiar face. Young Devren Jervis—Diver, for short—had been but a boy when Ethan first reached Boston. But even then, separated in age by nearly ten years, Ethan and Diver had become fast friends. They had seen each other a few times since Ethan's return to the city from prison, and of all the people Ethan had known before his court-martial as a conspirator in the *Ruby Blade* mutiny, Diver was the only one who had treated him as a friend rather than as an embarrassment. He was also one of the few people in Boston who knew that Ethan could conjure.

Diver was perched near the top of a ladder, caulking the hull of a ship with strips of oakum, and setting them in place with irons. Other men worked nearby, but none of them was so close to Diver that they noticed as Ethan walked to the base of his friend's ladder and gave it a small shake.

Diver paused in his work, looking down. After a moment he turned his attention back to the caulking. Ethan shook the ladder a second time.

Frowning, Diver descended the ladder, the irons and his bucket of oakum in hand.

As he reached the bottom of the hull, Ethan edged closer to him and whispered, "Diver."

His friend jumped and glanced around, his eyes wide.

"It's me," Ethan said. "I've cast a concealment spell."

Diver scowled. "Ethan?"

"Meet me at the water's edge."

Ethan stepped out of the unfinished hull and walked to the edge of the wharf. Along the way he bent to pick up a rusted nail that he spotted lying in the dirt. When Diver emerged from the hull and paused to survey the pier, Ethan tossed the nail into the water.

At the sound of the splash, Diver strode in his direction.

"Sorry about that," Ethan said, as his friend approached.

"You nearly scared me to death," Diver said with quiet intensity, gazing out over the harbor. "What are you doing here anyway?"

"I'm looking for someone, and I thought you might know him."

"And you figured that making me piss myself was a good way to convince me to help you?"

"It wasn't that bad," Ethan said. He smiled, though he knew his friend couldn't see. "You should have seen your face."

Diver grinned. He was good-looking: tall, dark-eyed, with black curly hair and a winning smile. Every week or two he had a new girl on his arm. And just as he was incapable of holding on to a pound or a sovereign, he was never able to keep any of the girls for long. Ethan had assumed that at some point Diver would grow up, find steady work, and marry. But so far his friend had shown no interest in either a lasting job or a wife.

"Who is it you're after?" the younger man asked.

"His name is Edwin Randle, though you may know him as Ned."

Diver turned toward Ethan at that, his expression darkening. "Ned Randle? Are you serious?"

"You do know him."

His friend stared out at the harbor again, his gaze following a flock of cormorants flying low over the water, ebon against aqua. "Aye, I know him. He's a cheat and a liar, and if he wasn't the size of a seventy-gun ship I'd have broken his nose a long time ago."

"What did he do to you?"

Diver shook his head. "It doesn't matter. You won't find him in the shipyards or on a wharf. Not anymore. He makes a pretty decent living cracking the houses of rich men." Glancing again in Ethan's direction, he added, "That's probably why you're asking me about him in the first place."

"Aye," Ethan said. "Do you know where I can find him?"

"I've heard some say that he spends time in a tavern on Union Street— the Three Elms, I think it's called. He lives not far from there, in a room above a smithy on Cold Lane."

"For a man you seem to hate, you certainly know a lot about him."

Diver's cheeks reddened. He had worked in the shipyards for some time, but he had also been known to dabble in business ventures of a less savory nature.

"We haven't had any dealings recently," Diver said, an admission in the words. "But I had some business with him last summer."

He volunteered no more than that, and Ethan didn't ask.

"Jervis!"

They both turned. A man stood near the ship Diver had been working on, glaring in their direction.

"My foreman," Diver said under his breath. "Yes, sir!" he called. "Just needed a moment."

"You're not being paid to stare off at the gulls!"

"No, sir!" He started back toward he ship. "Good luck, Ethan," he muttered.

"Thanks, Diver. I'm in your debt."

"Aye. Two ales, at least."

Ethan smiled, walked back to Lynn Street, and then crossed through the North End toward Union Street. Along the way, he paused on a deserted lane to cut himself a second time and whisper, "*Fini velamentum ex cruore evocatum.*" End concealment, conjured from blood. The spell would have faded on its own eventually, but it would have taken hours, and Ethan couldn't wait.

Visible once more, he walked on to the Three Elms. He didn't find Randle there, but slipping into his old Bristol accent, he pretended to be a friend of Ned's, fresh off a ship from England, and thus confirmed with the barkeep that Randle still lived on Cold Lane. The barkeep even described the building for him.

Leaving the pub, Ethan strode through the streets to the narrow lane. The wind still swept in off the harbor, keening like a wild creature as it whipped through the narrow passages between buildings. As Ethan neared the smithy, he drew his knife. He preferred not to conjure in front of Randle, and had no reason to believe that the thief was a conjurer himself. But both Aubrey Heap and Diver had spoken of the man's size; Ethan felt better with his blade in hand.

A narrow wooden stairway at the far corner of the building led to a second floor room. Ethan took the stairs with care, but still the wood creaked loudly with every step. As he reached the door, someone from within bellowed, "Who's there?"

"I'm looking for Ned Randle," Ethan called back.

"Well you've found him! Now begone, or his pistol'll find you!"

Ethan pushed up his sleeve. It seemed he might have to conjure after all.

"I just want to talk to you, Ned," Ethan said.

"I've got nothin' t' say t' no one!"

"Then just listen. My name's Ethan Kaille. I'm a thieftaker and I've been hired by a man named Aubrey Heap to retrieve some goods that were taken—"

The entire building shook with what sounded like the lumbering of a grizzly bear. An instant later, the door flew open, revealing a giant of a man. He was at least half a head taller than Ethan and as brawny as a quarryman. He held a flintlock pistol in his right hand, which he leveled at Ethan's forehead.

Ethan took a quick step back, and bumped up against the wooden railing of the stairway, which creaked ominously. He bit down hard on the inside of his cheek, tasting blood. *Conflare ex cruore evocatum*, he recited silently. Heat, conjured from blood. Power hummed in the wood of the stairs, and Uncle Reg appeared beside Ethan, baring his teeth at Randle like a street cur.

Randle didn't appear to feel the spell as Ethan did, nor did he see Uncle Reg; only another conjurer could have done either. But an instant later, he started violently, dropping his pistol onto the stairway landing. Ethan kicked it down the stairs out of reach.

Randle stared wide-eyed at Ethan, rubbing his hand. "How'd you do that? How'd you make my pistol go all hot that way?"

"I just want to talk to you, Ned," Ethan said again, ignoring the question. "Mister Heap mentioned to me that . . ." He stopped, staring at the man's face.

Both of Randle's eyes had been blackened. His lip was split, and he bore cuts and bruises on his cheeks and temples. Ethan had been too concerned with Randle's weapon and his size to notice straight away. But for all the man's brawn, it seemed that someone had bested him in a fight.

Randle glared back at him, his mouth set in a thin, hard line. After a moment, he turned his back on Ethan and stomped back into the room.

But he left the door open. Ethan hesitated before following him inside, Reg a stride behind him. A single candle burned on a table, the smell of spermaceti bittering the air.

"What happened to you?" Ethan asked.

Randle dropped himself into a chair; Ethan couldn't imagine how it didn't collapse under his weight.

"I should never have gone near Heap's place," the big man said, staring at the floor, forlorn. "I should've known better."

"What does Heap—?"

"You steal from the poor an' no one cares a whit. But as soon as you rob the rich . . ." He shook his head.

"I don't understand," Ethan said. "Who did this to you?"

"Pryce's men." Randle met Ethan's gaze. "She showed up here last night with four of them. They beat me nearly senseless, found the jewels an stuff that I'd taken, an' left. But not before leavin' a message for you."

Ethan blinked. "What? How did they know I'd be coming?"

"You'll have to ask Miss Pryce about that. But she knew. She said to tell you that she'd be waitin' for you at the Crow's Nest. You're to go there t'night."

At first Ethan didn't believe him. He wondered if Ned worked for Pryce. This might have been a ruse intended to keep Ethan from finding Mr. Heap's jewels. As quickly as the idea came to him, he dismissed it. Those bruises on Randle's face were real, and Ethan sensed no deception in his words. How had Pryce known he would come here? Heap had tried to hire her, and she had refused. Had this been her intention all along: to lure Ethan to the Crow's Nest?

"They took everything?" Ethan asked.

Randle nodded. "Even the damn wine."

Ethan exhaled and turned to leave the room, wondering what Sephira Pryce could want with him.

"It used to be easier," Randle said, before he could go. "Nowadays, Boston's lousy with thieftakers. When did that happen?"

It would have been rude to laugh at the man, even though he was a thief. "I don't know," Ethan said, without looking back. "Stay out of trouble, Ned."

The Crow's Nest was a rundown tavern located in the North End on Paddy's Alley, almost directly across Ann Street from Wentworth's Wharf.

Ethan had spent little time within its shabby walls, but he knew of its reputation as a place frequented by thieves, whores, and other low types, including those looking to buy stolen and smuggled goods.

Upon entering the tavern he was assaulted by the din of a dozen conversations and the smells of pipe smoke and stale beer. He paused by the doorway, scanning the crowded great room for Sephira Pryce. He needn't have bothered.

He hadn't been inside half a minute when two men approached him. They were huge; they made Ned Randle look like a mere pup. Ethan guessed that they were also skilled with either blade or pistol. Sephira Pryce would have demanded no less of anyone working for her. One of the men had pale yellow hair that he wore in a plait, and a long horse-like face; the other was dark-haired, with crooked yellow teeth, and small, widely spaced eyes.

"You Kaille?" the yellow-haired man asked, drawling the words.

"Aye. Who are you?"

"Miss Pryce is waiting for you."

"All right," Ethan said.

Neither of the brutes moved.

"I'll need your knife," the yellow-haired man said. "And any other weapons you're carrying."

Ethan shook his head. "I'm not in the habit of walking into a bar like this one unarmed."

"And Miss Pryce ain't in the habit of negotiating with the likes of you. Now give me the knife, or me and Gordon here will take it from you."

It seemed he didn't have much choice in the matter, at least not if he wanted to speak with Miss Pryce. The truth was, even without his knife he could conjure, and even with it he wouldn't have much chance in a physical fight against these two. He pulled the blade from its sheath and handed it hilt-first to Yellow-hair.

"That all?" the man asked.

"Aye."

"This way."

The two brutes led him through the tavern to a table near the back of the room, the crowd parting before them.

Ethan had seen Sephira Pryce before, although only from a distance on a street in the South End. He had heard some wax poetic about her beauty, but even so, he wasn't prepared for what awaited him at the back of the tavern.

He noticed her eyes first: Large and sapphire blue, they found his immediately and then raked over him head to toe, appraising him in the span of a heartbeat, and finally meeting his gaze once more. Shining black curls cascaded down over her shoulders and back, framing a face that was at once feminine and shrewd and hard. She had high cheekbones and a sharp chin, but otherwise her features were delicate, womanly. She wore a white silk blouse, open at the neck, black breeches, and a matching waistcoat that fit her snugly, accentuating her curves. Even in the dim candlelight of the tavern, he couldn't help but notice several small white scars on her cheek, temple, and brow, and one long one that traced her jawline. But somehow these only served to add to her allure. She hadn't yet said a word to him, and already Ethan thought her the most fascinating woman he had ever seen.

"Mister Kaille," she said, her voice low, gravelly, like the purring of some jungle cat. "I've heard a good deal about you. I'm glad we finally get to meet." She indicated the chair opposite her own with a slender hand, also scarred. "Please sit." Glancing at the two brutes, she nodded once. They melted into the crowd, though Ethan felt certain that they wouldn't go far.

He lowered himself into the chair. Pryce had barely moved, but he felt as if there was a gun aimed at his heart.

"It's an honor to meet you, Miss Pryce," he said. "I'm sure that whatever you've heard about me is nothing compared to the legend of Sephira Pryce."

Her smile was thin and fleeting. "Yes, well we know what legends are worth, don't we? And I think you understate your own reputation." She leaned forward, her fingers laced, her forearms resting on the table. "After all," she said softly, "it's not every day that one meets a thieftaker who's also a witch."

Ethan tensed. Conjurers had long been called witches, not only in England, but here in the New World as well. And the Province of Massachusetts Bay had seen many so-called witches hanged or burned at the stake in the past century.

Clearly, Sephira saw the effect her words had on him. She smiled again, exposing perfect teeth. "You've nothing to fear from me, Mister Kaille. At least not right now. I believe we can reach an understanding, you and I, one that will make me happy and keep you alive."

"Why did you refuse to work for Aubrey Heap?" Ethan asked, struggling to regain his composure.

She straightened, lifted her hand perhaps six inches off the table. In mere seconds, Yellow-hair was at her side once more. "Madeira for me," she said. "Ethan? May I call you Ethan?"

"An ale," Ethan said.

She nodded her approval. Yellow-hair pushed through the crowd to the bar.

"I refused to work for Heap because he wasn't worth my time," she said. "What is he paying you? Seven pounds? Eight?"

Ethan stared back at her, embarrassed to reveal that he had asked for less than that. "Your point?"

"I don't work for men like Heap," she said. "I don't need to. And that's the first thing you should remember about me, about us. Heap and men like him: They're yours. The Beacon Hill types belong to me, and I don't like to share."

"If Heap wasn't worth your time, why did you send your men to Randle's place?"

This time her smile was radiant. "I wanted to meet you, of course. This seemed the best way to get your attention. And also because I want you to understand a second thing about me: I can always find you. I can always retrieve property more quickly than you can. I always know what you're doing and who you're doing it for."

"Boasts don't become you."

He held her gaze, watching as her smile faded.

"You doubt me?" she asked. Her eyes glittered in the candlelight. "Before Heap you worked for a man named Arthur Crane, retrieving a set of crystal goblets that had been stolen from his home. Before Crane, you searched for a set of tools stolen from a smith in Cornhill—I believe his name was Grayson." She quirked an eyebrow. "Need I go on?"

Ethan gaped at her. Yellow-hair returned with the wine and ale, but even after he had placed them on the table and walked away again, Ethan still didn't know what to say.

"Did you honestly think that I would ignore another thieftaker?" she asked. "I know everything about you, Ethan. You're from Bristol. You sailed in His Majesty's fleet during King George's War and were at Toulon aboard the *Stirling Castle*. You were second mate aboard the *Ruby Blade* and took part in a mutiny that led to your imprisonment and forced labor in Barbados. That's where you lost three toes on your left foot and acquired that limp." She sipped her wine. "How am I doing so far?"

He lifted the tankard to his lips with a steady hand and took a long pull of ale.

"You said something about an understanding," he said, setting the tankard back on the table. "What did you mean?"

"I've already told you. You can have the small jobs, but you're to leave the more lucrative ones to me. And on those occasions when witchery is involved, I'll send clients your way. I have no desire to take on inquiries that are bound to end in failure. That would be bad for business."

"And what if such an inquiry comes from Beacon Hill?" Ethan asked. "What if Thomas Hancock himself has need of a thieftaker who also happens to be a conjurer?"

"Then so be it," she said, her expression souring.

Ethan weighed her offer. He had no desire to make an enemy of Sephira Pryce, but neither did he wish to cede to her every wealthy client in Boston. "If I refuse?"

She studied him, ice in her gaze. "I find it convenient having you around to take on those jobs that are more suited to your . . . talents. But that won't stop me from having you killed should you become a nuisance."

So much for not making an enemy.

"What did you do with Heap's property?" Ethan asked.

"I returned it to him, of course. And I collected your three pounds ten." She smirked.

Ethan felt his cheeks redden. She had already known how little Heap was paying him. She had been toying with him.

"You have some skill as a thieftaker, Ethan. You can make a fine wage working for the Heaps of the world, better even than you know, apparently. Don't make the mistake of challenging me. You'll lose."

He took another sip of ale and pushed back from the table.

"Is there anything else?" he asked.

She eyed him, enchanting and dangerous. "I'd like an answer to my proposal."

"You've made no proposal. Threats, yes, but that's all. You want me to promise that I won't work for any of the city's richest families, and in return you say that you'll allow me to have those clients who were going to be mine anyway. I'd be a fool to accept those terms. So here's my proposal: You see to your business, I'll see to mine, and we can allow the families of Boston to decide who they want to hire."

He stood.

"Don't cross me, Kaille," she said. "You won't survive the night."

Ethan stared back at her refusing to be intimidated. He had fought in a war, endured prison and years of back-breaking labor in conditions that would have destroyed most men. He had lost his youth, his only love, his dreams, not to mention part of his foot. He knew better than to group Pryce with common men of the street, and he was not so foolish as to dismiss her threats as idle; but there was little that he feared anymore.

"I'll take my chances," he said. "Please tell your man that I'd like my knife back."

She grinned. "Tell him yourself."

Ethan shrugged and left the tavern.

He knew Pryce wouldn't allow him to end their encounter like this, unscathed and unbowed. Even as he walked away from the Crow's Nest, his boot heels clicking on the cobblestone street, he heard the tavern door open and the scuffle of footsteps. He halted, turned.

Three men stalked toward him: the two brutes who had met him at the door, and a smaller, dark-haired man—about Ethan's height and build—who despite his size looked every bit as menacing as the other two.

"Have you come to return my knife?" Ethan asked.

The men stopped a few paces short of where he stood. Yellow-hair shook his head slowly. "You're not very smart, are you, Kaille?"

"I suppose that depends," Ethan said. "In comparison to whom?"

He hated having to bite his cheek to draw blood—he carried a knife just so that it would be easy for him to conjure. And his mouth was still sore from the spell he had cast earlier in the day, when Randle had his pistol trained on him. But he bit his cheek again and said in his mind *Dormite omnes, ex cruore evocatum.* Slumber, all of them, conjured from blood.

Power pulsed in the stone beneath his feet. Uncle Reg appeared once more, glowing like the newly risen moon. Yellow-hair staggered, braced himself against the nearest wall. An instant later, the small man slumped to his knees and toppled to his side.

"Hey . . ." Yellow-hair said, the word thick in his mouth. Before he could say more, he and the other brute dropped to the ground. In moments, all three of them were snoring.

Ethan stepped forward, bent over Yellow-hair, and searched the man's pockets for his blade.

Just as he found it, he heard another footfall, light and surprisingly close. He looked up in time to see Pryce standing over him, a blade already in hand.

Silver flashed, a blur in the moonlight. Ethan flinched, felt a sudden sharp pain in his shoulder. He stumbled backward, righted himself.

Pryce advanced on him, as graceful and lithe as a dancer. "What did you do to my men?"

"I put them to sleep." Ethan said, dropping into a fighter's crouch, his knife held ready. "Shall I do the same to you?"

His shoulder burned.

"Or perhaps I should do this," he said. "*Discuti ex cruore evocatum.*" Shatter, conjured from blood.

Power hummed again; the blood vanished from his shoulder. Pryce's blade fractured with a sound like the chiming of a small bell, and the shards fell to the cobbles at her feet. She gaped, first at the useless hilt in her hand and then at Ethan.

"You shouldn't have done that, Kaille," she said, her voice shaking. "If you think you can humiliate me and—"

"I haven't humiliated you. Look around. Your men are dreaming, and there's no one else here to see. I give you my word that I won't speak of this to anyone. I have no quarrel with you, Miss Pryce. All I wish to do is ply my trade. You're Boston's leading thieftaker, the Empress of the South End. I'm just an ex-convict trying to earn a bit of coin."

Pryce straightened. After a moment she let the knife hilt drop from her hand. It clattered on the cobblestones.

"You might want to consider whether it's wise to use your witchery so brazenly. They still hang witches in Boston, you know. Or at least they would if given the chance."

"I don't know what you're talking about," Ethan said, looking her in the eye. "Your men simply fell into a slumber; I wonder if you're not working them too hard. And as for your knife . . ." He shrugged. "I'd say it was shoddy workmanship."

Sephira actually laughed. It was a good laugh, throaty, sensuous. But she quickly grew serious again. "If ever I hear anyone breathe a word of what's happened here tonight, even you—especially you—you're a dead man. Do you understand me?"

"Of course I do."

"You're right, you know," she said. "I am the leading thieftaker in Boston. You may flatter yourself to think that you're in competition with me, but you're not. You're nothing."

Ethan didn't respond.

After glaring at him for a few seconds more, Pryce glanced back at her men.

"How long will they be like that?" she asked.

"Not very long," he said. He allowed himself a faint smile. "And I don't want to be here when they wake."

"No, I imagine not."

Ethan started to back away, his knife still in hand. "Good evening, Miss Pryce,"

"You'd best have a care, Kaille. This isn't over between us."

"Then I'll look forward to our next meeting."

He continued to back away from her until at last he reached the nearest corner. With one last glance Pryce's way, he turned onto the next street and hurried toward his home on Cooper's Alley. Her men would wake eventually—not so soon as he had led her to believe, but soon enough—and he didn't doubt for an instant that she would send them after him at the first opportunity.

Upon reaching his room, he locked the door and retrieved from his night stand a small pouch of mullein, a powerful herb for conjuring. Taking out several leaves, he whispered, "*Tegimen ex verbasco evocatum.*" Warding, conjured from mullein.

Uncle Reg appeared by the door, an amused expression on his lined face.

"That will keep them out, right?" Ethan asked.

The old ghost nodded before starting to fade from view.

"Not so fast." Ethan began to unbutton his shirt. "My shoulder needs healing."

Ethan slept poorly, his slumber haunted by Pryce and her men, who seemed to chase him from one dream to the next.

Upon waking he made his way to Verin's Wharf and Aubrey Heap's small warehouse. He found the merchant standing at his desk in a cramped office at the back of the building, reading through some papers.

Ethan knocked on the open door.

Heap turned, removing his reading glasses. "Mister Kaille," he said, clearly surprised to see Ethan there.

"Good morning, sir."

"What can I do for you? Surely you've heard by now that Miss Pryce managed to find my property after all. I'm afraid she claimed the balance of your fee."

"Yes, sir, I understand. I came to return your retainer."

The merchant frowned. "Whatever for?"

"Well, as you say, Miss Pryce found your wife's jewels and the watch. I didn't. I don't deserve the money."

"Nonsense, Mister Kaille. I'm sure you did your best. As far as I'm concerned, I paid five pounds and got back all that I had lost. I couldn't have asked for more than that. The pound and ten is yours to keep." He started to raise his glasses to his face once more. "Was there anything else?"

"No, sir," Ethan said. "Thank you."

"Of course."

Heap reached for the papers, but before Ethan could leave, the merchant faced him again.

"You know, Mister Kaille, you and Miss Pryce might consider if you wouldn't both be better off as partners rather than rivals. She's obviously quite good at what she does, and I have no doubt that you have skills she would find useful." He nodded, seeming to ponder the idea himself. "Yes, a partnership might be just the thing."

It was all Ethan could do not to laugh out loud. "Thank you, sir. I'll give that some thought. Good day."

"Good day, Mister Kaille."

Ethan left the warehouse and after a moment's indecision started toward a tavern on Sudbury Street—the Dowsing Rod—where he had of late been spending some time.

As he walked, he couldn't keep from glancing back over his shoulder, expecting at any moment to see Pryce's toughs bearing down on him.

A partnership with Sephira Pryce.

Alone on the street, he did laugh, though with little mirth. He walked with his hands buried in his pockets, casting a wary eye at every alley, every doorway.

He had made an enemy last night, though he hadn't meant to. Intentionally or not, by choosing to become a thieftaker, he had declared himself her rival. Here now was the cost of that choice, the price of doing business.

For as long as he worked these streets, he would be watching for her, anticipating the bite of her blade. He felt a twinge in his shoulder at the thought, the remembered pain of the previous night's encounter. *This isn't over*, she had told him. Ethan didn't need to hear her words echoing in his head to know it was true.

"A Spell of Vengeance" first appeared at Tor.com *on June 13, 2012. It's an important story in the Thieftaker chronology for a number of reasons. In it we meet Nate Ramsey, who will go on to play a crucial role in the Thieftaker Chronicles, beginning with* A Plunder of Souls *(Tor Books, 2014). And in this tale we also see Ethan and Kannice Lester, the owner of the Dowsing Rod tavern, begin their romance.*

The first mention of Nate Ramsey comes in Thieftaker *(Tor Books, 2012), when Ethan reflects on his encounter with the captain, who was "as potent a speller as any [Ethan] had known." At the time I wrote the novel, I had little sense of how this encounter unfolded, and so, between the writing of* Thieftaker *and its sequel,* Thieves' Quarry *(Tor Books, 2013) I decided to write this story, mostly as a way of figuring out what had happened. Only as I wrote the story, and came to love Nate Ramsey as a villain, did it occur to me to bring him back later in the series.*

"A Spell of Vengeance"
D.B. Jackson

Boston, Province of Massachusetts Bay, 9 December 1763

Ethan Kaille could count on one hand the number of times in recent years he had refused an ale in favor of some stronger spirit. He rarely had enough coin for anything more than the cheap ales that came out of Boston's local breweries, and even when he did, he usually preferred the pale ales of Kent to whiskey or rum. But December had brought to the New England colonies gray skies and frigid winds, and even the fine fish chowder served here in the Dowsing Rod, a tavern on Sudbury Street, wasn't enough to ward off the chill.

With a cup of hot rum warming his hands, however, and several sips of the toddy already heating his belly, Ethan could convince himself that winter's advance had been slowed, at least for the evening.

Many of the tavern's patrons sat or stood in a tight arc around the hearth, where a bright fire blazed, smoke drifting among the rafters and the candle fixtures overhead. They laughed and told stories; a few sang songs like "Ye Good Fellows All" and "Preach Not to Me Your Musty Rules." Ethan, though, kept to himself. A small number of the others might have welcomed him, but most knew him to be a convict and thought of him as a troublemaker and an unrepentant mutineer. A handful might even have known that he was a conjurer.

On the other hand, the tavern's owner, a young widow named Kannice Lester, had lately taken an interest in him, and he in her. As he sat watching the men by the fire and chuckling to himself at their poor singing, Kannice brought him a second bowl of chowder, the rising steam redolent of bay and fresh cream. He hadn't asked for it.

"I thought you might enjoy another helping," she said, placing it in front of him. "What with the others hogging the fire and all."

"Thank you."

She tucked a strand of auburn hair behind her ear, smoothed her green linen gown with an open hand, and gestured at the empty chair opposite his. "May I sit for a moment?"

"I believe it's your tavern, isn't it?"

"Aye, it is." She sat, rested an elbow on the table and her chin in her palm. "You're an odd man, Ethan Kaille."

"Am I?"

She nodded. "You keep apart from the others, as if you don't want company. Yet you come in here night after night, when you could just as easily be alone, which is what you seem to prefer."

He leaned forward, his gaze holding hers. Her eyes were periwinkle blue, and when she smiled a small crease dimpled her cheek, just to the right of her lips.

"Maybe I don't want their company," he said, nodding toward the fire. "But that doesn't mean I don't want any company at all."

Her smile deepened, but her cheeks didn't color, nor did her gaze waver. Thinking about it, he wasn't sure he had ever seen her blush. It was just one of the many things about her he found intriguing.

"Well, if I hear of anyone who's also looking for company, I'll be sure to point them in your direction."

Ethan laughed. "Thank you."

She pushed back from his table and stood. "Let me know when you're ready for another rum."

Before she could turn away, the tavern door opened, and three men entered, their woolen greatcoats and tricorn hats coated with a fine dusting of snow. Ethan didn't recognize two of the men. The third he would have known anywhere: Stephen Greenleaf, sheriff of Suffolk County.

Greenleaf was an imposing man, tall, solidly built. He commanded no army, no militia, no constabulary force of any kind. Yet he managed to keep some semblance of peace here in Boston. Usually such an achievement would have been enough to earn Ethan's respect, perhaps even his friendship. But in the two years since Ethan had established himself as one of the city's leading thieftakers, the sheriff had made it clear to anyone else who would listen that he neither trusted Ethan nor saw him as a legitimate rival to Sephira Pryce, Boston's most famous and successful thieftaker. In private, Greenleaf had told Ethan that he remembered all too well the *Ruby Blade* mutiny and Ethan's role in it. He also recalled the rumors of "witchery" that circulated at the time of Ethan's conviction.

"I think what they say about you is true, Kaille," the sheriff had told him one night this past spring, after Ethan managed to retrieve gems stolen from the wife of one of Boston's prominent shipbuilders. "I think you are a witch. I can't prove it, yet. But at the first hint of devilry, I'll have you in shackles so fast you won't even know what happened."

That night, Ethan had walked away from the man, but not before asking Greenleaf, in as light a tone as he could muster, "But, Sheriff, if I am a witch, what makes you think that shackles can hold me?"

Ethan had enjoyed the moment, but his remark served only to make the sheriff more suspicious of him. He had enough trouble trying to compete with Pryce and her toughs, who always seemed to be dogging his investigations; the last thing he needed was Greenleaf dogging his every step. The truth was, Ethan relied on his spellmaking—his "witchery" —to help him recover stolen goods that other thieftakers couldn't.

He regarded the sheriff's appearance here in the Dowsing Rod as an ill omen.

Still standing by the door, Greenleaf spotted Ethan, muttered something to his companions, and strode toward Ethan's table. Kannice glanced quickly at Ethan before placing herself directly in the sheriff's path, a hand on her hip, her head canted to the side.

Small and willowy, she looked like a child beside the man. Still, her voice remained steady as she said, "Good evening, Sheriff Greenleaf. Care for a bowl of chowder? Or perhaps a flip and some oysters?"

"No," he said, sounding impatient. "I've come for a word with Kaille."

"He's a guest of the Dowser, he's paid for his meal, and he's eating."

Ethan tried to conceal his amusement.

"Fine then. Chowder and an ale."

"And you gentlemen?" Kannice asked the sheriff's companions.

Both men had unbuttoned their coats, revealing silk shirts and woolen suits with matching jackets, waistcoats, and breeches—ditto suits, as many in Boston called them. Ethan guessed that they were merchants.

One of the men shook his head in response to Kannice's question. "Nothing for me."

Kannice narrowed her gaze, standing her ground.

The other man, the more portly of the two, said, "I think I'll have a brandy, and some of that stew might warm me up."

"Yes, sir." Kannice cast another quick look Ethan's way, winked once, then walked behind the bar and into the Dowser's kitchen.

Greenleaf approached Ethan's table, the merchants in tow. "May we join you, Mister Kaille?"

"Of course," Ethan said without enthusiasm.

The portly man lowered himself into the chair in which Kannice had been sitting and leaned his walking cane against the table. Greenleaf and the other man pulled over chairs from a nearby table and sat as well.

"This is Deron Forrs," Greenleaf said, indicating the portly man. "And this is Isaac Keller." The sheriff nodded toward Ethan. "Ethan Kaille, gentlemen."

Ethan shook hands with both men.

"Mister Kaille is the thieftaker I've been telling you about. I believe he may be able to help you with your . . . your problem."

Forrs and Keller shared a look. After a brief silence, Forrs regarded Ethan.

"I'm a merchant, Mister Kaille. Both of us are. I'm not a wealthy man —nor is Mister Keller—but neither of us wants for much. I trade in coal from Louisburg and Newcastle, and in wood from Penobscot. As you can imagine, this time of year I'm reasonably busy. Mister Keller deals in iron-ware from Norfolk and Plymouth—axes, tools, locks, that sort of thing."

He started to say more, then broke off as Kannice and Kelf Fingarin, her massive barman, brought them their food and drinks. Once they had returned to the bar, Forrs continued.

"For some time we did business with a merchant captain named Nathaniel Ramsey. He owned a vessel, the *Muirenn*, and made a good living for himself sailing the waters of New England."

"You say you 'did business' with him," Ethan said. "You don't anymore?"

The merchant's eyes flicked toward Keller.

"Ramsey died several months ago," Keller said. "His son, Nate Ramsey, now captains the *Muirenn*."

"He's not the sailor his father was," Forrs added. "Nor the businessman."

Ethan shifted in his chair. "Forgive me for interrupting, gentlemen, but I know little about commerce. I'm a thieftaker; I recover stolen items for a fee. Has one of you been robbed?"

"No," Forrs said. "Nothing like that. But I do believe that you can help us. You see, before Nathaniel died, he accused Mister Keller and me of stealing from him, a charge that his son has repeated in the months since. Indeed, he has gone so far as to threaten us if we don't make restitution."

"What do they believe you stole?"

"Money," Keller said. "Nathaniel believed that we owed him money for several transactions. We, of course, know that we didn't. But he insisted that we had cheated him, and after his death his son repeated these slanders. Now, as Mister Forrs has said, he has made threats against us."

Ethan looked at Greenleaf and found that the sheriff was already watching him, his spoon poised over the bowl before him.

"I'm afraid I still don't see how I can help you," Ethan told the merchants. "Your dispute with the Ramseys is over a matter of trade. I concern myself with theft and crimes of the street, not transactions on the wharves."

Forrs frowned. "Sheriff Greenleaf, you led us to—"

"Tell him the rest," Greenleaf said.

Neither of the merchants said a word.

"The rest of what?" Ethan asked.

Forrs removed a handkerchief from his pocket and dabbed at his upper lip. "There were rumors about Nathaniel. Some said that he could . . . do things. A few went so far as to say that he engaged in witchcraft."

Ethan sat back in his chair and looked once more at the sheriff. Greenleaf returned his gaze steadily. Of course. This matter had nothing to do thieftaking and everything to do with the fact that Ethan was a conjurer.

"I take it the son is a speller as well," Ethan said.

Keller nodded. "He's never admitted it in so many words, but his threats to us have hinted at such things. He speaks of burning us alive, of killing us in our sleep, of inflicting all manner of violence upon us. And he claims there is nothing we can do to save ourselves. 'No distance is too great,' he says. 'No lock is too strong, no walls too thick. No matter where you hide, I can reach you.'" Keller shuddered visibly. "I'm not easily cowed, Mister Kaille. But I'm not above admitting that this man frightens me."

Ethan faced Greenleaf once more. "And what made you think that I could help these men?"

Greenleaf hesitated. "I've heard tales about *you*, as well, Kaille," he finally said, talking around the chunk of fish he'd been chewing. "There are those who say you know something of the dark arts, and of those who dabble in them. I thought that perhaps you could make some inquiries."

Ethan had half a mind to refuse. After two years of harrying him, of threatening again and again to have him hanged as a witch, the sheriff now had the nerve to come here, hat in hand, asking for help of this sort? He wanted to laugh at the man, drink the rest of his rum, and leave.

It occurred to him, though, that by helping the merchants he would be putting the sheriff in his debt. Plus, he would be paid. As much as he disliked Greenleaf, he was able to recognize a profitable business opportunity when it presented itself.

"I, of course, know nothing of these dark arts of which you speak. But I know of a few here in Boston who are reputed to do so. I might be forced to consort with them, strictly on the merchants' behalf, of course, and I would hate to be tarred with the same brush of witchery. I take it, Sheriff, that no one involved in this inquiry will have anything to fear from you."

Greenleaf's mouth twitched with ire, but he nodded. "I give you my word."

Ethan tried not to let his satisfaction show, lest he anger the man further. The merchants must have paid Greenleaf for his trouble, but still, Ethan could see that it galled the sheriff to come to him in this way. All the more reason to take the job.

"As I've told you," Ethan said to the merchants, "this isn't the sort of work in which I usually engage. But under the circumstances, I might be of service. Exactly what is it you would like me to do?"

"Find out what he wants from us," Forrs said. "We've asked the pup how we can settle this matter to our mutual satisfaction, but he simply responds with more threats. We want you to convince him that we are now under your protection, and that any attempt to do us harm will not only fail, but will also result in injury to himself." The merchant paused, his brow creasing. "Nathaniel was not a well man at the end. I believe he imagined wrongs and twisted common business practices into foul offenses. In his conversations with his son, he must have portrayed Mister Keller and me as the worst sort of villains."

"Yes, sir."

"I won't allow myself to be held hostage to the delusions of an ill man, but I'm also not insensitive to the young man's loss. I'm willing to pay a reasonable sum if doing so will end this ugliness."

"And you'd like me to convey this message to Captain Ramsey as well."

"Precisely. You are authorized to negotiate on our behalf, in consultation with the two of us, of course."

"Do you know if Ramsey is currently in Boston?" Ethan asked.

Forrs wet his lips. "The *Muirenn* docked at Wentworth's Wharf this afternoon." He produced a leather pouch from his coat pocket and placed it on the table in front of Ethan. The pouch's contents jangled softly. "That is five pounds. When this matter is concluded and the younger Ramsey has forsworn his misplaced vengeance, you'll receive five more. Is that satisfactory?"

Ethan picked up the pouch, heard the muffled ring of the coins, felt their heft. After a few seconds he slipped the pouch into his pocket. "Yes, it is," he said. "I'll speak with Captain Ramsey tomorrow morning."

For the first time since their conversation began, Forrs smiled. Keller merely nodded, but he looked relieved as well.

The two merchants pushed back from the table, their chairs scraping on the wooden floor. Standing, Forrs extended his hand to Ethan.

"Thank you, Mister Kaille."

Ethan shook hands with each of the men in turn. "I'll let you know as soon as I have news. Where can I find you?"

"We both have warehouses on Tileston's Wharf," Forrs said. "We're there most days."

"Very well. I expect you'll hear from me soon."

Greenleaf had stood as well, but he gave no indication that he intended to leave. Both men nodded to him.

"Gentlemen," he said, nodding in return.

Forrs and Keller left the tavern.

Ethan eyed the sheriff briefly before sitting once more. Greenleaf lowered himself into his chair and took another spoonful of chowder.

"So you'll threaten to have me hanged as a witch," Ethan said. "But when it suits your needs you'll have me use whatever resources I have at my disposal to give comfort to your wealthy friends."

The sheriff considered this for a moment, then nodded. "Yes," he said, and spooned more stew into his mouth.

Ethan couldn't help but laugh. "Well, at least you're honest about it." Sobering, he asked, "Do you believe Nate Ramsey is a speller?"

"I don't know. If I could determine such things for certain, you probably would have swung years ago." Greenleaf flashed a wicked smile. "How's that for honesty?"

Ethan's laugh this time was drier. He finished his toddy and stood. "I think I'd best be going."

"If he is a speller," Greenleaf said, looking up at him, "will you do as Forrs and Keller have asked?"

"Why wouldn't I?"

The sheriff shrugged. "I'm just wondering if perhaps your loyalty lies more with your own kind than with a couple of merchants."

"I'm loyal to my family and friends," Ethan said. "As for the rest, I'm a businessman, just like Forrs and Keller. They paid me to do a job, so that's what I'll do. And just so you know, if I were a witch, I'd offer the same reply. Goodnight, Sheriff."

Greenleaf said nothing, but reached for his ale.

Ethan took his greatcoat off the back of his chair and strode toward the door. As he passed the bar, he noticed Kannice watching him from the entrance to the kitchen. He slowed and sketched a small bow, drawing a dimpled smile. Shrugging on his coat, he pulled the door open and stepped out into the wintry air.

The distance from the Dowsing Rod, on the edge of the West End, to his room above Dall's Cooperage on Cooper's Alley, in the heart of the South End, was barely more than a half mile. But with a hard wind whipping through the streets of Boston and scything through his coat and clothing, it seemed much farther. For more than ten years, Ethan had walked with a limp, the result of an injury he suffered during his imprisonment and forced labor on a sugar plantation in Barbados. These raw New England nights always made the pain in his leg worse.

Upon reaching his room, he found that the fire in his stove had long since burned itself out, and the water sitting in a cast-iron pot atop the stove had frozen solid. Being a conjurer had its advantages, though, not least among them the ease with which he could start a fire on a cold night in December. Ethan piled fresh wood in the stove. Then he pulled his knife from the sheath on his belt, pushed up his sleeve, and cut his forearm.

"*Ignis ex cruore evocatus*," he said in Latin. Fire, conjured from blood.

Power thrummed in the floor and walls as if God himself had plucked a harp string. At the same time, a ghostly figure appeared in the room just beside the stove. He was tall, dour, and he wore chain mail and a tabard bearing the three lions of Britain's medieval kings. His short hair and trim beard might have been white had he not glowed with a deep russet hue, the color of a rising autumn moon. Ethan thought it likely that this was the shade of one of his ancient ancestors on his mother's side. The spirit, who appeared each time Ethan conjured, enabling him to draw upon the power dwelling between the living world and the realm of the dead, had always reminded Ethan of Reginald, his mother's splenetic brother. So, Ethan called him Uncle Reg.

The ghost gave him a disapproving look, as if offended at being disturbed for the mere lighting of a stove.

"It's cold," Ethan said, trying not to sound defensive, knowing that he failed.

Reg continued to scowl as he faded from view.

The room was small, but it warmed slowly, and even with two woolen blankets wrapped around him, Ethan lay awake for a long time.

He didn't know of many conjurers living here in Boston: Janna Windcatcher ran a small tavern on the Neck; Old Gavin Black lived in the North End and claimed to have given up spellmaking years ago. Aside from them, however, and one or two others whom he didn't know by name, he was alone, a rare conjurer in a city filled with frightened men and women who had long since given in to superstition and the extravagant fictions of Sunday sermons.

He didn't necessarily believe that Ramsey's son could cast; false rumors of witchery were as old as the Province of Massachusetts Bay itself. But a part of him hoped that in this case the whispers would prove true, and that he would convince Ramsey to cease making threats against the merchants. Perhaps, if the man proved reasonable, they might forge a friendship. He hadn't been able to speak of spellmaking with another conjurer since leaving his mother and sister in Bristol.

Ethan slept poorly, rousing himself several times to put more wood in the stove. When at last daylight began to seep into his room around the edges of the shuttered windows, he climbed out of bed, washed his face with the water on his stove, and dressed.

After a quick breakfast—hard cheese and the last of the bread he had bought at Faneuil Hall the day before—he set out for Wentworth's Wharf. Already wharfmen and laborers crowded the cobblestone lanes along the South End waterfront, all of them bundled in coats and wearing woolen Monmouth caps. The wind had died down and the skies had cleared to a crisp, bright blue, but the air remained frigid. As Ethan walked, his breath billowed before him in swirling clouds of vapor.

Wentworth's Wharf jutted into the calm waters of Boston Harbor just north of the Town Dock. It was shorter by far than Long Wharf and even Hancock's Wharf, but it was one of the longer piers on the waterfront.

Ethan walked the length of it and then nearly all the way back to Ann Street before finally spotting the *Muirenn* tied to a pair of bollards between two larger ships. She was a pink, small but well cared for. Her gangplank was up and she sat heavy in the water, no doubt still laden with cargo. Ethan approached the vessel, which at first glance appeared to be deserted.

"Ahoy, the *Muirenn*!" he called.

At first, no one answered, and he wondered if perhaps all the crew, including her captain, had spent the night in the city. But then he heard someone moving belowdecks and a faint call of "Ahoy!"

A moment later, a man appeared at the rails amidships. He was tall and spear thin, with a long face darkened by an unkempt beard. He wore only a silk shirt and breeches, but appeared unaffected by the cold.

"What can I do for you, friend?" he asked.

"I'm looking for Captain Ramsey."

The man grinned, exposing crooked, yellow teeth. "That would be me. And you are?"

"My name is Ethan Kaille. I'm a thieftaker."

Ramsey's grin faded and the look in his pale eyes turned flinty. "I don't peddle stolen goods, thieftaker. I never have. Anyone who says different is lying."

"I believe you," Ethan said.

"An' yet you're here."

"I'm wondering if I can have a word with you in private, Captain."

Ramsey regarded him briefly, then glanced up and down the wharf, opening his arms wide. "My crew's below, most of them asleep. An' those who aren't I trust. I see no one on the dock. I think this is private enough."

"Very well. I was hired by two men who claim to know you. Merchants. They say you've been threatening them."

This time, the captain's smile was forced and sour. "I should've known," he said. "Forrs an' Keller."

"Yes, sir."

"Why would they hire a thieftaker? I didn't steal from them."

"No, but as I say, you've been making threats."

"You're damn right I have! I'll be following through on them before long." He paused, staring at Ethan again. "Kaille was it?"

"Yes, sir. Ethan Kaille."

"You should go, Mister Kaille. This don't concern you. An' there's nothing you can do to stop me."

He walked away from the rails.

"Are you a speller, Captain Ramsey?" Ethan called after him.

Ramsey stopped, turned to face him again.

"I think you know I am," he said. "An' I'll wager every shilling I've got left that you're one, too. That's why they hired you, isn't it? They're afraid of what I'll do to them, so they've hired a speller for protection. Isn't that right?"

"They hired me on a rumor; word of my abilities reached them through an unlikely source. But yes, that's essentially what they've done."

"Well, this is another matter then," Ramsey said, "you being a conjurer an' all." He crossed back to the rails and lowered the gangplank. Ethan took hold of it from below and together they set it in place.

"You can board, Kaille," Ramsey said before disappearing from view.

Ethan ascended the plank and stepped onto the ship, only to find the decks empty. Wary, he pulled his knife from his belt and pushed up his sleeve. A moment later, though, Ramsey emerged from the hold bearing a bottle of what appeared to be Madeira wine and two pewter cups.

"I haven't much to eat," he said. "But I can at least offer you a dram of wine." He eyed Ethan's knife. "Put that away before someone gets hurt." He perched on the rail and waved Ethan over.

Ethan sat beside him and took an offered cup. Ramsey poured a bit of wine into it and then poured substantially more into his own.

"What shall we drink to?" he asked. Before Ethan could respond, he said, "How about my father?"

"Of course," Ethan said.

The captain raised his cup. "To Captain Nathaniel Ramsey. May a steady wind ever fill his sails."

"To Nathaniel Ramsey," Ethan repeated, and sipped his wine.

"I don't imagine Forrs an' Keller told you much about him," Ramsey said, after nearly draining his cup. "They would've said that he accused them of stealing from him, a charge they deny, of course. It seems they also told you he was a speller. An' I would hazard a guess that they made him sound more than a little mad. Probably they say the same about me."

Ethan gazed into his cup. "They never said that he was mad. They do feel that he might have mistaken their motives at the end and led you to believe—"

"Did they tell ya how he died?" Ramsey asked.

"No."

"He hanged himself." Ramsey pointed up at the starboard side of the main yard. "Right there."

Ethan said nothing.

"He probably was mad at the end. My mum died fourteen years ago, an' he never really got over that. But he was all right as long as he could sail an' turn some profit from his runs up an' down the coast. Forrs an' Keller had him trading with the French, buying molasses from Martinique an' selling it to them at a cut rate so they could turn around an' sell it at a handsome profit to rum distillers here in Boston an' over in Medford. They paid him less an' less, an' when he complained, they threatened to turn him over to the customs boys. By the end, he was barely making enough to cover his costs an' pay his crew."

"Why didn't he just stop doing business with them?"

Ramsay's smile was fleeting, bitter. "He did. That's why he killed himself. He told them he wouldn't run the route anymore, an' that if they wanted to go to customs, they could. He'd tell the custom boys everything. So Forrs an' Keller told him that they knew he was a witch, an' that I was, too. An' they said that unless he wanted both of us to swing, he'd 'get back on his damned ship an' get his arse down to Martinique.'" He looked at Ethan and their eyes locked. "Their words," he said. "Not mine."

Ethan didn't know what to say. He tore his gaze away and stared out over the sunlit waters of the harbor.

"You don't believe me."

Actually, Ethan did believe him. Every word. But he had taken the merchants' money. He had promised them that he would convince Ramsey to renounce his claim to vengeance, or, failing that, that he would guard them from his spells.

"It's not a matter of what I believe," he said. "I told Forrs and Keller that I'd protect them, and in return for that promise they gave me a good bit of coin."

"Do you do that often, Kaille? Take money in exchange for promises you can't keep?"

Ethan heard the goad in Ramsey's question and chose to ignore it.

"You've frightened them," he said instead. "They're terrified of what you might do. I know it's small compensation, but maybe you can take some satisfaction in that."

Ramsey poured himself more wine. "I can. I like the idea of them two being scared. I'm just not willing to stop there."

"They'll pay you. They sent me to negotiate in their stead. You can name your price."

"You mean I can take the money that should have been my father's in the first place?"

Ethan frowned. "I have no interest in fighting for these men, Ramsey. But to be absolutely clear, my mistake was taking money from men who couldn't be trusted. I made no promises that I couldn't keep."

The captain had raised his cup to his lips once more, but he hesitated now, then lowered it, all the while staring hard at Ethan. "You think you're good enough with spells to stop me from killing them?"

"I don't want it to come to that."

"Then you should return their money, 'cause it's going to."

Ethan drank the rest of his wine, set the cup on the gunwale, and stood. He held out his hand to Ramsey. After a moment, the young man gripped it.

"You have my deepest condolences, Captain."

"Thank you."

"I live on Cooper's Alley, above Dall's Cooperage, and if I'm not there, you can leave word for me at the Dowsing Rod on Sudbury Street. Just in case you change your mind."

Ethan stepped onto the gangplank and walked back down to the wharf.

"Kaille!"

He turned. Ramsey stood at the rails again.

"You should ask yourself if men like Forrs an' Keller are really worth dying for."

"And you should do the same," Ethan said.

A faint smile touched the captain's lips. He raised his cup once more, as if in salute. Then he drained it, walked back to his quarters on the aft deck, and shut the door behind him.

Reluctantly, Ethan walked back to Ann Street and followed the waterfront southward past Fort Hill and the South Battery, to Tileston's Wharf. There, a wharfman who was loading barrels of wine onto a cart pointed him to Keller's warehouse.

Ethan found the merchant in a small office at the back of the building, standing before a writing desk and poring over a ledger.

At the scrape of Ethan's shoe on the office floor, Keller glanced back over his shoulder.

"Yes, what is it?" An instant later, his eyes widened in recognition. "Mister Kaille! Come in, come in!" His tone was welcoming, but he quickly closed the ledger and shut and locked the desk.

"Good morning, sir."

"You have news for us?" the man asked. Before Ethan could say anything, the merchant's brow creased. "Deron should be here." He stepped past Ethan to the office doorway and beckoned to a worker. "Go get Mister Forrs. Tell him Kaille is here."

The laborer hurried off.

Turning back to Ethan, Keller offered a weak smile. "He shouldn't be long."

"Yes, sir."

"Did you find him? Have you spoken to Nathaniel's son?"

"Yes, sir, I have."

"And has he agreed to put an end to these threats?"

Ethan weighed the question briefly. "I think you're right, sir. We should wait for Mister Forrs."

"Yes, of course." Keller smiled again, but he seemed not to know what to do with himself.

"Don't let me keep you from your work, sir," Ethan said.

"Yes. Thank you."

The merchant walked stiffly back to his desk, opened it, and pulled out the ledger he had been studying when Ethan arrived. Ethan lingered by the doorway, watching for the laborer and Forrs. Sooner than he might have expected, he spotted them striding toward the office, the merchant leaning on his cane but keeping pace with the laborer.

Reaching Keller's office, Forrs strode past Ethan to the middle of the room, looked first at Keller, then at Ethan, and said, "Well, what's happened?"

"He talked to Nathaniel's boy," Keller said.

"And?" Forrs asked. "Out with it, Mister Kaille."

"Why didn't you tell me how Captain Ramsey the elder died?" Ethan asked, eyeing both men. "That was a pertinent bit of information, don't you think?"

"We told you Nathaniel hadn't been well," Forrs said, "that he was imagining things."

Ethan shook his head. "That was no imaginary rope around his neck, was it?"

Forrs waved his hand impatiently. "Fine. We should have told you. Now, what did the boy say? Did you tell him we'd pay to end this matter?"

"He doesn't want your money," Ethan said. "And he remains determined to have his revenge."

The color fled Keller's cheeks.

Forrs rapped his cane on the floor and muttered, "Damn." Glaring at

Ethan he said, "We expected more of you, Mister Kaille. You explained to him that you would be guarding us, that his witchery would be met by yours?"

"I told him that the two of you were under my protection." Ethan smiled faintly, much as Ramsey had aboard the *Muirenn*. "He didn't seem to be impressed."

"So, he is a witch," Keller said. "You're certain of this?"

It was all Ethan could do not to laugh at the man. Witches were the stuff of legend, of nightmare. Witchery was a word used by preachers to frighten their flocks. "He admitted that he's a *conjurer*," Ethan said, using the word spellers preferred. "And he's confident in his abilities."

"So what do we do now?" Keller asked, his voice unsteady.

Ethan thought back to his encounter with Ramsey. "He still has cargo in his hold. I expect he'll spend the day offloading his goods and preparing to sail. I'll keep an eye on him and his ship, and I won't let him get near you."

"See that you don't," Forrs said.

Ethan nodded to both men, left the warehouse, and started back toward Wentworth's Wharf. His leg had started to hurt, his limp growing more pronounced with every step. Before reaching the wharf, he turned into a narrow lane and, after making certain that no one could see him, drew his blade and bared his forearm. Ramsey would sense a conjuring, but at this distance he wouldn't know what kind of spell Ethan had cast.

Cutting himself, he whispered, "*Velamentum ex cruore evocatum.*" Concealment, conjured from blood. Power pulsed in the cobblestones and the walls of nearby buildings. Reg winked into view beside him, eyeing him avidly. It sometimes seemed to Ethan that the old ghost could sense a coming battle the way a sea captain might smell a storm riding a freshening breeze.

"Can you feel Ramsey's power?" Ethan asked the shade.

Reg nodded.

"Is he as skilled as I am?"

The old warrior hesitated, then nodded again.

"As I feared," Ethan said.

Reg expression remained grim as he faded from view.

Ethan left the alley and resumed his walk to the wharf. His concealment spell rendered him essentially invisible to the men and women walking the streets of Boston. A truly powerful conjurer might see through the charm, but Ethan didn't believe that Ramsey could.

As he neared the wharf, he slowed, searching for a vantage point from

which he could see the *Muirenn*. With the vessel moored where it was, however, Ethan had little choice but to position himself beside a bollard un-
comfortably close to Ramsey's ship. He could see the young captain clearly,
could hear him shouting orders to his men. Ethan settled in for what
promised to be a long, cold day.

Oddly, Ramsey remained above decks for the rest of the morning and
into the afternoon. At times he leaned against the rails, appearing to banter
with his men. Occasionally he walked the deck, as if inspecting his crew's
work. But at no point did Ethan lose sight of him. It almost seemed that
Ramsey knew he was being watched, and that he wished to make himself as
easy to find as possible. Ethan wondered if the captain, upon sensing
Ethan's conjuring earlier in the day, had guessed correctly at what sort of
spell he had cast and knew he was near.

By late afternoon, Ethan could see that most of the *Muirenn*'s cargo had
been offloaded. The ship rode much higher in the harbor waters, and most
of her crew had settled themselves on the rails. Ramsey still stood in plain
view and now he said something to his men that drew a cheer.

An instant later, Ethan felt a pulse of conjuring power. A spinning
wheel of light appeared directly above the ship, throwing off sparks of gold
and blue, orange and green, silver and red. At the same time, a ghostly
figure appeared beside Ramsey. He was stooped, a man even older than
Uncle Reg. Like Ethan's spirit guide, this figure glowed, though with a
shade of deep aqua that reminded Ethan of the sea on a calm summer
morning.

Ramsey's crew paid no attention to the ghost; unless they too were conjurers, they couldn't see him. But they cheered and whistled at the wheel of
light. Apparently they knew their captain was a speller, and minded not at
all.

The captain left the rail and walked to the center of the deck. Ethan
could barely see him, though he did see someone brandish a knife and hold
it high overhead so that the blade gleamed in the late afternoon sun. Then
the blade descended and Ethan felt the thrum of a second spell in the
ground beneath his feet. Jets of fire burst from the ship, drawing frightened
stares from men and women walking on the street near the wharf. The first
conjuring had been an illusion spell, a weak casting conjured from the air or
from water. But even from a distance, Ethan felt the heat of these flames
and knew that this had been a blood conjuring.

Two more spells surged through the ground in quick succession; the air
around Ethan seemed alive with the power of Ramsey's spells. Bright

flames arced across the bow of the *Muirenn*, and another brilliant spinning light appeared over the ship, grander and more magnificent than the first.

The *Muirenn*'s crew let out shouts of approval and began to sing "Row Well Ye Mariners," their voices loud and jovial, if somewhat off key.

They were halfway through the second verse when Ethan realized that he no longer saw any sign of Ramsey.

Ethan took a step toward the ship, rose onto his tiptoes. He could see several members of the crew, but not the captain.

"Damn!" he said, louder than he should have given that he remained concealed. Fortunately the wharf was nearly deserted.

Too late he realized that the spells the captain had cast for his crew's amusement might also have served to mask a concealment spell of his own. Several spells had resonated through the wharf—how many had there been? And how many flames had he seen? Ramsey couldn't have gone far. Of that much Ethan was sure.

He ran up the dock to Ann Street and again threaded his way through the lanes and avenues of Cornhill and the South End, desperate now to reach Tileston's Wharf. Ramsey had a head start on him, and he wasn't hobbled by a bad leg.

Ethan had just turned onto Flounder Lane when the first pulse of conjuring power reached him. Fearing that he was already too late, he sprinted onto the wharf and toward Keller's warehouse, gritting his teeth against the agony in his leg, cold sweat on his face.

Nearing the warehouse, he saw laborers streaming out the door, all of them wild-eyed, frantic.

Ethan shoved past them, not caring that they couldn't see him, that they wouldn't know who or what had touched them. Once inside, he raced toward Keller's office. Well before he reached it, he halted. Ramsey's spirit guide glowed brightly in the shadows. The old ghost looked Ethan's way, seeming to see right through his concealment spell.

Power hummed in the floors and walls. Ramsey materialized just beside his ghost, knife in hand, his sleeve still pushed up to reveal his scarred forearm.

Ethan saw no sign of Keller.

"Are you going to show yourself, Kaille, or do you just plan to watch, the way you watched my ship all day?"

Ethan hesitated, then pulled out his knife and cut himself. *Fini velamentum ex cruore evocatum*, he recited to himself. End concealment, conjured from blood.

Power pulsed. Reg appeared beside him and immediately bared his teeth at the other ghost. Ethan held his knife ready and eased forward, his gaze fixed on the young captain. When he reached the door to Keller's office, he chanced a quick glance inside. The merchant lived still. He stood at his writing desk, hands at his side, sweat shining on his pallid face.

"I haven't killed him yet, if that's what you're wondering."

"You were supposed to keep him away from me, Kaille!" Keller said. "Not chase him right into my warehouse."

Ramsey glowered at the man. "Shut your mouth." To Ethan he said, "You shouldn't have come. I know they've paid you, but this isn't your concern."

"I told you that I wouldn't let you kill them," Ethan said, positioning himself directly in front of Keller's door. "I understand that you want vengeance. I would too, if I was in your place. But you won't be killing anyone this evening."

The captain smiled and gave a small shake of his head. For the span of a single heartbeat neither he nor Ethan moved. Then, at the same time, they slashed at their forearms and shouted spells.

"*Tegimen! Ex cruore evocatum!*" Ethan said. Warding! Conjured from blood!

The building trembled with the power of their conjurings.

Ethan didn't hear what Ramsey said, but there could be no mistaking the effect. Fire. It flew from the captain's hand, hissing like some nightmare beast, and hammered at Ethan, staggering him, seeming to sear his flesh.

Fire spread to the walls of the warehouse, but left Ethan unscathed. For the moment, the merchant remained unharmed as well. Ethan's warding had held.

Ramsey drew blood again. Ethan did the same and warded himself a second time. But the captain didn't direct his next fire spell at him or at Keller. Instead he threw it at those walls that weren't yet ablaze.

"I don't care how he dies!" the captain shouted over the growing roar of the flames. "And I don't care if I die with him!"

Smoke hazed the air in the building. The heat grew unbearable.

Ethan cut himself again. "*Discuti ex cruore evocatus!*" Shatter, conjured from blood!

Ramsey howled and collapsed to the floor, clutching his leg. Ethan hadn't wanted to hurt him, but he wasn't about to let the fool bring down the building around them.

"Come on!" he called to Keller.

He strode to where the captain lay and stooped to lift him. Ramsey had already cut himself again.

"*Ignis ex cruore evocatus*," he heard the man say through gritted teeth. Fire, conjured from blood.

The spell lit Ethan's coat ablaze. Flames licked at his face and neck. He dropped to the floor, rolled from side to side, desperate to put out the fire.

He heard the captain say something else, felt power in the warehouse floor. But by the time he had extinguished the flames on his coat, it was too late for him to save Keller. Whatever spell Ramsey had used—a shattering spell perhaps, directed at the merchant's neck—appeared to have killed the man instantly. Ethan climbed to his feet, his eyes watering, his lungs burning. Ramsey stared up at him, his knife held ready. Ethan sheathed his own blade, lifted the captain to his feet, and then slung the man over his shoulder.

Seconds after they emerged from the warehouse, a section of the roof collapsed. A bucket brigade had already formed, with men scooping water out of the harbor. But they made no attempt to quell the blaze, choosing instead to douse the adjacent buildings and keep the fire from spreading.

"Was there anyone else inside?" a man asked, as Ethan lowered Ramsey to the ground.

"Isaac Keller," Ethan said. "We tried to reach him, but it was too late."

The man nodded, his expression grim. He went back to helping with the buckets.

"Forrs would've told you to let me die," Ramsey said, his voice low.

"Aye, but five pounds and a promise of more only buys so much."

Ramsey nodded and bared his teeth. "I like you, Kaille. I think we could've been friends. I'm sorry that won't be possible."

Ethan opened his mouth to respond; he never got the chance. With the fire raging inside the warehouse and Keller dead, it never occurred to Ethan to wonder what had become of Ramsey's blade. As it turned out, the captain still held it in his hand.

Ramsey slashed at his own forearm, the steel flashing in the golden light of the setting sun. Ethan's hand flew to the hilt of his knife, but he knew he couldn't possibly ward himself in time.

"*Dormite ex cruore evocatum*," he heard Ramsey say. Slumber, conjured from blood.

"Ramsey, no . . ." But already he was falling, sleep taking him.

"Kaille. Kaille, get up."

The voice seemed to reach Ethan from far off. The hard toe of the boot digging insistently into his side felt decidedly closer.

He opened his eyes to a sky filled with bright stars. A bulky figure loomed over him. Sitting up, he felt his world pitch and roll, as if he were at sea in the midst of a storm. He squeezed his eyes shut for several seconds. When he opened them again, he felt marginally better.

"What happened?"

He squinted up at the man standing beside him.

"Is that you, Sheriff?"

"Aye," Greenleaf said. "Tell me what happened."

Ethan climbed to his feet, swayed even as he surveyed his surroundings. They stood at the mouth of a narrow alley, just off Tileston Wharf. "Ramsey put me to sleep with a spell. He had already killed Keller and burnt his warehouse to the ground."

"Well, he managed to kill Forrs, too. It looks like he snapped the man's neck."

Ethan closed his eyes again, exhaled through his teeth. "I made an utter mess of this."

"That you did."

"Where is Ramsey now?"

The sheriff appeared as little more than a shadow against the night sky, but Ethan saw him nod toward the harbor.

"He's put out to sea. By the time I knew enough to look for him, the *Muirenn* had left Wentworth's Wharf. I doubt we'll see him in Boston again." He rounded on Ethan. "And that leaves me with a problem. Two merchants are dead, and I have no one to hold accountable."

"Except me."

"My guess is that both of them were killed with witchery. And you're a witch."

"I've told you before: I'm not a witch. And you gave me your word that I'd have nothing to fear from you."

"And you swore to protect Forrs and Keller!" Greenleaf said, his voice rising. "Do you really think their families care what I promised you?"

"Probably not."

Greenleaf couldn't subdue Ethan on his own; despite Ethan's protestations, they both knew it. The sheriff might have been bigger and stronger, but Ethan could conjure. Still, Ethan had no desire to flee Boston and live the rest of his life as an outlaw.

"Did you know that Ramsey's father killed himself?" he asked. "Forrs and Keller had him running French molasses, which they then sold to the local distillers. They kept lowering the price they paid him, and when he complained they threatened to have him and his son hanged as witches. They paid us both with blood money."

"The pup tell you that?"

"Yes. And I believe him."

The sheriff sighed. "To be honest, I believe it, too."

"You can try to arrest me, Sheriff. But if all you believe you know about me is true, I won't be taken easily."

Greenleaf shook his head slowly. "Damnable witches. I hate every last one of you."

"I'm not a witch," he said again, though even to his own ears the denial lacked conviction.

"You can call yourself what you will," Greenleaf said, seeing through Ethan's denial. "It's all the same to me."

They lapsed into a lengthy silence. Ethan stomped his feet against the cold. Acrid smoke still rose from the burned warehouse out on the wharf, making his eyes water.

"So what are you going to do?" he asked after some time.

The sheriff shrugged. "There isn't much I can do. You know as well as I do, Kaille: Smugglers like Forrs and Keller get killed all the time without a murderer being found. It's the risk they take."

Ethan released a breath he hadn't known he held. Yes, he could have fought off Greenleaf if it came to a confrontation, but he was relieved that he didn't have to. "Thank you," he said.

"I don't expect we'll ever have need to speak of this again."

"No, sir."

"Good. Go home, Kaille."

Ethan walked slowly from the wharf, still dazed from Ramsey's sleeping spell. The burns on his neck and jaw ached. After walking only a block or so, he stopped in an empty lane, cut himself, and healed the raw, blistered skin as best he could. Then he continued on, though not toward home. Instead, he made his way to the Dowsing Rod.

The tavern was crowded and boisterous when he arrived, the air inside warm and heavy with welcoming scents: sweet pipe smoke and musty ale, fresh-baked bread and savory stew. It was true he lived on Cooper's Alley, but in recent weeks the Dowser had come to feel like home. Men clustered around the bar, speaking loudly, laughing, many of them with arms draped around one another's shoulders. Most of the tables near the back of the tavern's great room sat empty.

A few of the conversations broke off as Ethan pushed his way to the bar. Belatedly, he realized that his coat had been burned and that he must look a mess. Abruptly self-conscious, he thought about leaving. Before he could, Kannice appeared before him, grinning and holding out a tankard.

"Have you heard?" she asked, shouting over the din.

"Heard what?"

"News from London! The war's over. We've signed a treaty with the French."

A man beside Ethan called out, "God save the king!" Immediately the rest of the throng launched into a chorus of the song of the same title, which in recent years had become an anthem of sorts for subjects of the Crown on both sides of the Atlantic.

"That's good news," Ethan said, taking the offered tankard. But already his mind had turned to Nate Ramsey and his father, to embargoes among warring nations and contraband French molasses. Seven years of warfare finished now because of a piece of paper signed three thousand miles away. How many lives might have been spared had peace come six months earlier? Or a year? Tens of thousands of soldiers might still be alive. And perhaps as well an old captain and two Boston merchants.

"You don't seem pleased," Kannice said, her brow creasing.

"I am. Thank you for the ale." He dug into his pocket.

"You can pay later, after you eat."

She motioned for him to follow and then walked out from behind the bar to the far end of the tavern. It was quieter here; they could speak without being overheard.

"You're hurt," she said, eyeing his neck and jaw. "And your coat has seen better days."

"It was . . . there was an accident."

She arched an eyebrow. "An accident," she repeated, skepticism in the words.

"Aye."

"And do all your accidents leave your coat burned and the hair on the back of your head singed?"

Ethan reached back and touched his hair, strands of which felt brittle. His fingers came away with the bitter scent of burned hair. She touched his blackened sleeve, ran her hand from his wrist to his elbow.

"It seems a most unusual accident." Her eyes met his for a more moment before dropping again to his coat.

He didn't know Kannice well, but from all he had seen, and all he had heard about her, he knew her to be intelligent and keenly observant. She missed nothing that happened within these walls. If people had been whispering about the convict, the mutineer who was also a witch, she would know it. Chances were, she wouldn't want such a person frequenting her establishment.

He sipped his ale, placed the tankard on the nearest table. "Perhaps I should go," he said.

"Is it true then?" she asked in a whisper. "Are you a witch?"

He had been deflecting questions like this one for most of his life, choosing his words with great care, resorting to half-truths, even lying outright when left with no choice. But this time, speaking to this woman, after all that had happened this day, he didn't want to evade or deceive. Still, after so many years, candor came grudgingly.

"Why? Do you allow witches in your tavern?"

"I allow anyone in the Dowser, as long as they pay for their food and drink, and don't cause trouble. I'm asking because I'm curious."

He smiled. "About witches?"

"About you."

Ethan glanced down at the table, but then forced himself to meet her gaze again. "We don't call ourselves witches. We're conjurers, spellmakers, spellers even. Preachers rail against witchery as a tool of the devil. I don't believe there's evil in what I do."

"And did another speller do that to your coat, or did you light yourself on fire?"

He laughed. "That was someone else."

"What happened to him?"

Ethan sobered, looked down again. "He killed two men I was supposed to be protecting, and he got away."

"The two who were here last night? With the sheriff?"

Had it just been last night? "Yes," he said.

"I'm sorry."

His throat felt thick, and he knew it would be some time before he forgave himself for failing the merchants, even with all they had done to Nathaniel Ramsey. But he couldn't deny that he took some solace in being able to speak of it openly, without worrying that he might reveal too much.

"It was my fault," he said.

"Well, that's always the worst, isn't it? It wouldn't be so hard if you could blame someone else."

"No, I don't suppose it would."

"Sit," she said, tapping one of the chairs. "I'll have Kelf bring you some stew."

"All right."

She started to walk away, but Ethan reached out and caught her hand in his own. Her skin felt cool, smooth. Kannice stopped, looked at their fingers, raised her eyes to his.

"Thank you," he said.

She smiled, her cheeks coloring this one time.

"The Witch of Dedham" may well be my favorite of the Thieftaker short stories. I wrote it in 2012, not for an anthology or a website. Not even to sell. I wrote it because the story of Mary Crenshaw presented itself to me, and the opening line below echoed in my head until I had no choice but to build a tale around it. For some time, the story appeared on the D.B. Jackson website as a freebie—a downloadable .pdf and an .mp3 file of me reading the story. And it is a story I have used again and again at convention readings, precisely because I love it so much.

In the Thieftaker novels, Ethan tends to succeed in what he sets out to do. Readers have certain expectations when they read a novel, and as authors we don't wish to disappoint our audience. But short stories are different. They offer us writers a bit more freedom; they give us the leeway to take chances and, on occasion, allow our heroes to "lose." Because sometimes those "losses" are far more meaningful than the triumphs.

"The Witch of Dedham"
D.B. Jackson

Boston, Province of Massachusetts Bay, 16 April 1764

Ethan Kaille first heard people speak of the Dedham witch early in the spring of 1764. By then, of course, it was too late for him to save her life.

April found Boston in the midst of an early thaw. Already bright sunshine and warm winds off the harbor had coaxed crocuses from the soil. Fork-tailed swallows had returned to the skies over the city, darting and swooping like winged sprites, and eagles, handsome in white and chestnut, constructed great nests along the water's edge.

The smallpox epidemic that had paralyzed the city for much of the winter seemed at last to be abating. Ethan had managed to avoid the dreaded disease, as had most of the people he knew. But across the city, many hundreds had taken ill; nearly two hundred had died. Talk in the Dowsing Rod, the tavern Ethan frequented, had centered on the epidemic for so long, he could hardly remember people there speaking of anything else.

And so the night he overheard two men talking about a woman in the small town of Dedham, to the south and west of Boston, Ethan assumed that the disease had spread to the countryside. The more he heard, however, the more he realized that these men weren't speaking of smallpox.

"She's just a young thing," one of the men said, speaking around a mouthful of bread. "But she's old enough to do her mischief."

"And old enough to swing, I'd wager," said the man's companion.

"Aye. Certainly that, after what she's said to have done."

Ethan had become a regular in the Dowsing Rod in large part because he and the tavern's widowed owner, Kannice Lester, had been lovers for several months. Her usual patrons, though, were far less accepting of Ethan than she. They thought him untrustworthy; some believed him dangerous, and had told Kannice as much. Ethan could hardly fault them for their judgment of his character. He had spent the better part of fourteen years laboring as a prisoner on a sugar plantation in the Caribbean, punishment for his part in the infamous *Ruby Blade* mutiny. Moreover, he had been the subject of rumor ever since his return to Boston. Some said that he was a conjurer, that he communed with the shade of an ancient spellmaker, and that it was only a matter of time before he himself was hanged as a witch. Ethan didn't relish the idea of people talking about him, but he couldn't deny any of it. The first two points were true, and the third seemed likely.

Whether they believed these rumors, or merely thought him an unrepentant mutineer, Kannice's patrons almost never spoke to him; they rarely dared to make eye contact. Which may explain why the two men at the adjacent table started so violently when Ethan turned to look at them.

"Who are you talking about?" he asked, his tone more severe than he had intended.

The men stared at him, eyes wide, mouths agape. They shared a glance; one of them wet his lips.

"There's a woman," this one finally said, his gaze meeting Ethan's for just an instant before sliding away. "In Dedham."

"Yes, I heard that much. What of her?"

"She's a witch," said the other man. He appeared to have recovered from his initial fright. Ethan heard a note of challenge in his voice. His hard glare didn't waver. "At least, that's what some are saying."

"A witch," Ethan repeated. "What makes people think she's a witch?"

"From what I hear, she admits as much," said the bold one, reaching with a steady hand for his flip.

"And what mischief is she supposed to have done?"

"Near to killed a man. Least aways, that's what they say."

"Is that what you heard, too?" Ethan asked the other one.

This man also reached for his drink, but then stopped himself. Ethan could see the tremor in his hand. "All I know is that she worked her devilry, and got caught at it. I never heard what it was she did."

"She's a witch," the bold one said. "That's all that matters. She admits as much. And two days from now, she'll swing."

Ethan felt his body sag, as if he had taken a fist to the gut. "Two days?"

"Aye."

"Do you know her?" the timid man asked.

"No," Ethan said.

"I thought maybe—"

The man's companion laid a hand on his arm, silencing him.

A thin smile tugged at the corners of Ethan's mouth and vanished as quickly as it had come. *I thought maybe all of you witches knew each other.* Likely, the man had intended to say something of the sort.

"Allow me to buy you a round of ales, gentlemen," Ethan said, forcing himself to smile again.

Another glance passed between them. After a moment, the bold one nodded. "All right."

Ethan raised a hand, catching the eye of Kelf Fingarin, Kannice's mountain of a barkeep. He raised two fingers and then pointed to the men. Kelf nodded and began to fill a pair of tankards.

The men resumed their conversation in low voices, their heads lowered and close together.

"Do you know how old she is?" Ethan asked, drawing their attention once more. "One of you said she was young. How young?"

"Fifteen," said the bold man, as Kelf arrived at their table bearing their ales.

"Anythin' for you, Ethan?" the barkeep asked.

"I'll have another, as well. Thanks."

He leaned back in his chair and watched Kelf lumber to the bar. His thoughts churned.

Fifteen. And she had confessed to being a witch. She might as well have thrown herself off a bridge, or taken a blade to her breast. What of her parents, or her husband if she had already married? Had they allowed her confession? Or had they shunned her, casting her from her home, siding with those who had no doubt accused her of consorting with the devil?

Kelf returned to the table carrying a full tankard, which he placed in front of Ethan. The two men seemed to have moved on to some other topic of conversation; they paid no more attention to him. That suited Ethan. He drank his ale, and he brooded.

Conjurers in the New World and also in England, had for centuries been condemned as witches by small-minded people who didn't understand the workings of spells. Men and women in Boston still spoke of the witch trials that took place in Salem late in the previous century, but though those condemnations had since come to be seen as a travesty, accusations of "witchery" still occurred with some frequency in the Province of Massachusetts Bay. Stephen Greenleaf, the sheriff of Suffolk County, had long accused Ethan of dabbling in black magick and had threatened to have him hanged, though thus far he had been unable to prove anything. But while Ethan had been fortunate, he and other conjurers lived in constant fear of being the next "witch" to die with a noose around his neck, or at the hands of a mob whipped to a frenzy by an overzealous preacher or sheriff.

And now came word from Dedham that a woman—a girl, really—had chosen such an end for herself.

After some time, Kannice emerged from the tavern kitchen and, seeing Ethan, stepped out from behind the bar and walked to his table.

"When did you come in?" she asked, smiling. She bent down and brushed his lips with hers. Her auburn hair smelled of lavender, and her breath carried the scent of whiskey.

"I've been here for a while," he said.

"What's wrong?"

"What makes you think that anything is wrong?" he asked, trying to keep his tone light.

She pulled a chair around from the far side of the table and sat beside him. "What's wrong?" she asked again, her eyes, periwinkle blue, locked on his.

He contemplated his ale. "Have you heard about the woman in Dedham?"

"Aye," Kannice said, sighing the word. "Kelf told me earlier today. A couple of boys from Roxbury mentioned it to him."

"She's fifteen. They're going to hang her, and she's fifteen years old."

"I know."

"I'm going to Dedham," he said, making up his mind in that moment. "I'm going to speak with her. If I leave early enough in the morning, I can walk there and be back before nightfall."

"Ethan—"

"Maybe I can help her."

"Or maybe you can get yourself hanged alongside her!"

Conversations around them faltered. The men at the next table sent furtive glances their way.

"I'm sorry," Kannice said, lowering her voice once more. "But don't you think that by going to see her you'll be announcing to everyone in Dedham who and what you are?"

"Well, if I take you along, you can do it for me."

He grinned and so did she, though she sobered quickly.

"I'm serious," she said. "It's too dangerous. You shouldn't go."

"I'll tell anyone who asks that I'm just a friend who wants to visit with her before she dies."

"And that will work right up until the moment you . . ." She glanced around the tavern before going on in a whisper. "You break her out of the prison."

"Is that what you think I intend to do?"

"I have no idea what you intend," Kannice said, sounding exasperated. "I don't believe you do, either. And so yes, I think it's possible that you could wind up doing something you'll regret."

He looked away. "Why shouldn't I help her? A girl that age . . ." He broke off, shaking his head.

She reached across the table and took his hand in both of hers.

"Why would you do this? What do you think you can do for her?"

"Honestly, Kannice, I don't know. But I do know that I need to see her, to hear from her why she would confess to being a witch." Ethan faced her again. "I won't do anything stupid. I promise you. But I am going."

Kannice lifted her shoulders slightly. "All right."

"All right?" Ethan repeated. "You have nothing more to say?"

"You've made up your mind. I've no interest in pounding my head against a wall." She lifted his hand to her lips and kissed the back of it. Then she stood. "Will you be staying the night?"

"That depends. Are you willing to share your bed with a man as foolish as me?"

She shrugged again. "I was last night, and the night before that. I suppose I still am." She kissed the top of his head before returning to the bar.

Early the following morning, Ethan woke to the sound of a chaise rattling past on the cobblestone lane outside the Dowsing Rod. The first murky light of dawn glimmered around the shutters covering Kannice's bedroom window, barely illuminating the chamber. Ethan slipped out of bed; Kannice stirred but didn't wake. He dressed, let himself out of her chamber, descended the stairs to the tavern's great room, and stepped into the cool morning light.

A thin mist hung over the city, the air heavy with the smells of fish and brine. The strident cries of gulls echoed from the harbor and a dog barked somewhere up toward the West End. Ethan struck out southward, following Sudbury Street to Treamount and then cutting east to Marlborough and following that toward Boston's Neck, the narrow strand of marshy grassland that led eventually to the Town Gate.

A man of the watch opened the gate at Ethan's approach and watched wordlessly as he walked out of the city and onto the causeway that crossed the Roxbury Flats. With the tide low, the sour stink of the mudflats made Ethan's eyes water. Herons stood motionless in the foul ooze, warily eyeing a pair of clammers digging nearby.

Once over the causeway, Ethan followed the lane across the Salt Marshes to Roxbury and then took what was commonly called the Middle Road toward Dedham. He would have preferred to hire a carriage for the journey. He walked with a pronounced limp, the result of a severe injury to his left foot suffered during his years as a prisoner, and already he could feel the strain of this walk on his bad leg. But while he had enjoyed some small success as a thieftaker in Boston, he was not a man of means. And even if he had been, arriving at Dedham's prison in a carriage might well have drawn unwanted attention to his visit. Walking the nearly ten miles struck him as the more prudent choice.

As the sun climbed into the morning sky, the air warmed. Before long, Ethan removed his coat and slung it over his shoulder. The pain in his leg worsened steadily, until his face was damp with sweat and he grimaced with every step.

Still he made good progress, coming to the village well before the sun reached its zenith. Though Dedham was small, its lanes bustled with artisans and merchants, with women carrying small children or leading them by the hand, or both. He passed a farrier's shop and a smithy, saw at the far end of the town a small church with a white spire that gleamed in the sun. He halted at the sight of a solid looking courthouse and after a moment's hesitation entered Fisher's Inn, which stood directly across the main street.

As Ethan stepped to the bar, the barkeep nodded a greeting.

"We've just had a meat pie out of the oven," the man said. "That and an ale?"

"Thank you," Ethan said. He dug a shilling out of his pocket and placed it on the bar.

The barkeep grinned. "You must be from the city. Around here, that will buy you at least another ale or two."

"That's all right. Maybe you can answer a question for me and keep the extra pence."

He might as well have asked the man to consent to Ethan marrying his sister. The smile fled the barkeep's face, leaving his expression stony. He reached for a tankard and began to fill it, but he didn't so much as glance Ethan's way as he said, "I've nothing to say to strangers."

"You don't even know what I was going to ask."

The barkeep set the tankard down smartly in front of Ethan, slopping some ale onto the bar.

"It doesn't matter," he said, and stepped into the kitchen.

He emerged again moments later bearing a plate of food. But after placing this beside Ethan's tankard, he retreated to the far end of the bar and began to polish the wood, steadfastly avoiding Ethan's gaze.

Ethan ate in silence. The pie was good, although not nearly as fine as anything Kannice served in her tavern. When he finished, he stood and glanced once more at the barkeep. The man still refused to look his way. At last Ethan walked out, leaving the shilling on the bar.

Out on the lane once more, he glanced northward, back the way he had come, but then set out toward the church at the south end of the village. Upon entering the sanctuary, Ethan spotted a minister sitting in the chancel beyond a simple wooden pulpit.

"My pardon, Reverend sir," Ethan called to the man.

The minister set aside his bible and stood. He was a young man, slight and pale. He appeared quite frail, despite his youth. "Who is that?" he called, squinting slightly.

"My name is Ethan Kaille," Ethan said, walking past the dark wooden pews toward the pulpit. "I've come from Boston. I wish to speak with the young woman accused of being a witch."

"Not accused," the minister said. "Confessed."

"Aye. So I had heard."

"Are you a friend? A relation?"

Ethan thought about lying, as he had promised Kannice he would. But though he wasn't a religious man, he couldn't bring himself to lie to a minister inside the man's own church. He shook his head. "I don't even know her name."

"And yet, you've come from Boston to see her," the minister said, his voice as grave as his manner.

"Aye."

"Why would you do that? Why would a witch in Dedham draw the notice of a man of the city?"

"You're the second person to ask me that, Reverend sir. I have no answer for you. But I rose with the sun this morning, and I walked all the way here. I would ask that you allow me to speak with her."

"She's in the gaol," the minister said, "at the rear of the courthouse. But even so, it is not my place to give you leave to speak with her. If she chooses to speak, she may. If she refuses, you'll have no recourse through me."

"Very well." Ethan hesitated. "Can you tell me what happened to make her confess such a thing?"

The young man shook his head. "That's not my tale. Either she'll tell you or she won't." He paused, rubbing his brow. "I will say this, though. I must root out evil in my congregation, no matter the form it takes. I'm sworn to do so. But this . . . this is a dark business."

"What do you mean?"

The minister shook his head again. "I probably should not have said as much as I have. Ask her. I hope she chooses to speak with you, Mister Kaille. Truly, I do."

He sat and took up his bible once more, and he didn't look at Ethan again. After a few moments, Ethan walked up the aisle toward the sanctuary's entryway.

Just as Ethan reached the door, however, the minister said, "Her name is Mary Crenshaw."

Ethan turned. The minister's voice had been so low that for an instant he wondered if the man had actually spoken at all, or if he had imagined it. As far as Ethan could tell, the minister remained engrossed in his reading. At last he turned once more and let himself out of the church.

He made his way to the courthouse and walked around the structure to a small, stone building in back. It had no windows on its front façade, just an oaken door with a heavy cast-iron lock. He knocked once.

After a few seconds the door behind him, the rear door of the courthouse, was pulled open from within. Ethan turned to find a burly man in black breeches, a black coat, and a white linen shirt looking him over through narrowed eyes.

"Who are you?"

"I'm here to see Mary Crenshaw."

"You a friend of hers?"

"I've walked many miles to see her," Ethan said, approaching the man. "I would be crazy to do such a thing if I weren't her friend. Wouldn't you agree?"

The burly man scowled and closed the door, leaving Ethan to wonder if he had been dismissed. A few seconds later, though, he heard the muffled jangle of keys. The door opened again and the man stepped past him, muttering "This way."

Ethan followed the keeper to the austere oaken door, and waited as he found the correct key. The man opened the door and gestured Ethan inside.

"Knock when you're done," he said, and pulled the door shut.

The hollow echo of the door's close jarred Ethan like a blow to the head, bringing back memories of his own imprisonment. It had been eighteen years since first he heard that sound from this side of the door, and yet he found himself trembling, a trickle of sweat on his brow.

"Do I know you?"

There was only the one cell in the gaol: a tiny square set off by stone and iron and another heavy wooden door, this one with a small barred window at eye level. The face that peered out at him was that of a child, not a woman. She was plain—round cheeks, blue eyes, a small, upturned nose, and a generous sprinkling of freckles.

"Are you a prisoner, like me?"

"No," Ethan said, finding his voice. "At least not anymore. I was a prisoner once."

He eyed the door, the lock, the hinges. If she could conjure, and if she wanted to escape, there was nothing holding her here that a spell or two couldn't overmaster.

"Are you a messenger, then?"

"What?"

"A messenger. I prayed to God to send me guidance, and I'm wondering if He sent you."

Ethan considered lying to her. *Yes, God sent me to command you to protest your innocence, to fight for your freedom!* It would have been so easy to say. But again he couldn't bring himself to speak the words. Not about this. He had lost his own faith long ago, in the hell of his prison labor; he would not use this girl's faith to mislead her.

"I'm no messenger," he said. "I'm a conjurer. I would assume that you are, too."

She opened her mouth, closed it again.

"*Veni ad me,*" he said in Latin. Come to me.

The glowing figure who winked into view beside him wore chain mail and a tabard bearing the insignia of the Plantagenet kings. He was tall, lean, dour; his hair and beard were closely shorn. This ghost, whom Ethan had named Uncle Reg, after his mother's splenetic brother, helped him to access the power that dwelt between the living world and the realm of the dead. He was a guide of sorts for Ethan's spellmaking and as such he appeared whenever Ethan used his conjuring powers. Every living conjurer communed with a specter like Reg, though not all the ghosts were as glum as Ethan's.

The girl staring out at him from the small cell glanced briefly in Reg's direction, but she didn't start or gasp. Only someone with conjurer's blood in her veins could have seen the old ghost, and only someone accustomed to spellmaking would have shown so little surprise at his sudden appearance.

"So you are a messenger," she said, her tone icy. "You were sent here by the devil."

"I was not sent by anyone, or anything. I came to see you because . . . because you can't do this. You can't allow them to hang you."

She regarded the shade again, then said to Ethan. "You shouldn't have come." She turned and walked away from the door.

Ethan and Reg shared a quick look.

"*Dimmitto te*," Ethan said, his voice soft. I release you. As the ghost started to fade from view, Ethan whispered, "I'm sorry to have summoned you."

Reg said nothing. Ethan had never known him to speak. But as he vanished, his glowing eyes, which could be so expressive, remained fixed on the cell door.

Ethan walked to the door and look through the small window. Mary sat on a straw pallet in the far corner. There was a single brown woolen blanket bunched up beside her. A waste bucket sat at the foot of the bed. Otherwise, the cell was empty.

She wore a plain linen dress and a shawl, which she pulled tight around her shoulders upon seeing Ethan at the door. Her wheaten hair was pulled back in a plait; her feet were bare.

"It's a sin, you know," the girl said, her tone matter-of-fact. "Even just magicking that spirit here the way you did. You could hang, just as I will."

Ethan shook his head. "I don't believe it is a sin."

"Mister Haven says it is."

"Mister Haven?"

"The rector of our church."

"Ah," Ethan said. "Yes, I'm sure he does say that. But I believe he's wrong. I live in Boston, where I work as a thieftaker. My spells help me find property that has been stolen, so that I can return the items to their rightful owner. How can that be a sin?"

She dropped her gaze.

"I can heal with a spell," Ethan said, his voice low and gentle, as if he were speaking to a small child. "I've saved people's lives with my conjuring. Is that a sin?"

"If I could save one life by taking another," she said, "then I might do some good, but I would still be committing a sin."

He frowned. "I don't take a life when I conjure."

"I know that. What I mean, though, is that even if we do some good, a sin is still a sin."

"What have you done with your conjurings, Mary? Surely you've cast spells that helped others."

She shook her head, looking away again. "I've done terrible things," she whispered. "You should go."

"What terrible things? Is this why you told them you were a witch? Is this why you want to hang?"

A tear rolled down her cheek, and then another. "Please go."

"Not until I understand."

"Why did you come here? Why should you care if I live or die? You live in the city. You don't know me; you don't care about me."

"I came because when one conjurer is executed, we all suffer. The hanging of one accused witch raises fears everywhere. If you hang, it will be more dangerous for conjurers in Roxbury and Newton and Dorchester, and yes, even Boston."

"So, you came to save yourself," the girl said.

He started to respond, but stopped himself. He had given her the first answer that came to mind, an answer that wasn't true.

Why had he come here? Three times he had been asked, by three different people: First Kannice, then the minister, and now Mary. And though he knew that there was as much myth and superstition surrounding spell-making and so-called witchery as there was fact, he couldn't deny the power of certain numbers, of certain patterns. Having been asked three times, Ethan felt compelled to answer. More, having heard the question for a third time, he finally understood his own mind.

"No," Ethan said. "I didn't come to save myself. I'm not even sure that I came to save you."

"Good. I don't want to be saved."

"Why not?" Ethan asked.

"Because living with this evil inside of me, is worse by far than what awaits me on the hangman's gallows."

He nodded. "I understand that. I understand hating your powers so much that you would rather deny they exist. When I was a younger man, I used spells in a mutiny aboard a privateering ship. The mutiny failed and I was put in prison."

"Why weren't you executed?"

"During the mutiny, I actually changed my mind, and just barely in time. The man who led the mutiny took control of the ship briefly, and he proved to be worse by far than our captain. He was cruel and merciless and reckless. When I saw this, I freed the captain and helped him retake his ship. When we returned to port, I was court-martialed, but my life was spared.

"After my trial, I swore that I would never conjure again. I despised myself. I had been foolish, and I blamed my spellmaking, since my powers were what made the mutineers recruit me in the first place. I'd lost my freedom, I'd lost the one love I had ever known. It seemed to me that I had lost everything that mattered." Ethan paused, leaning against the door. Mary watched him from her pallet, unmoving, unblinking. "For fourteen years I denied who and what I was. I refused to conjure; I saw my ability to cast spells as something black and evil. It was like living with a cancer on my soul."

"What made you start casting again?" Mary asked in a whisper.

"I watched as a man was beaten, and I knew that no one could heal him but me." He paused, searching for the right words. "I decided to come here when I heard that you had confessed to being a witch. I had a feeling that no one else could help you."

"I told you: I don't want help. I don't need saving."

"Don't you?" Before she could answer, he asked, "What terrible things have you done?"

All the color drained from her cheeks. "Why won't you just leave?"

"I believe actions are evil only when we intend them as such," Ethan said. "I don't believe you've done anything evil. I think maybe you did something you hadn't meant to do, and someone got hurt."

She was crying again, staring at him as if unable to look away.

"Is that what happened, Mary?"

The girl mouthed the word "Go," but she didn't move, not even to break eye contact.

"Did you try a spell, and it didn't work the way you thought it would?" Ethan asked. "That happens to all of us, more often than you might think. Once when I was—"

"No," she said, her voice echoing like a hammer blow. "The spell did exactly what I wanted it to do." She stood, her glare still fixed on him. Then she began to pace the small cell, wringing her hands. "Sarah—that's my younger sister—she's twelve now, and fair as can be. Not like me and Heather, my older sister. We're the plain ones, like our brothers. But Sarah . . . well, I suppose some would call her simple. She's kind and generous. She wouldn't hurt a soul. But even at twelve, she can't take care of herself. She has her garden, and she sews during the cold months. But she doesn't understand the world. She is too trusting, too good in a way. I fear that she'll never be able to leave home. She needs Mother too much."

Mary halted, glaring toward the door. "She's not stupid. And she would never lie."

"I believe you," Ethan said.

"Papa loved her very much. She might have been his favorite." A smile flickered across her features. "None of us begrudged her his attentions. We all dote on her a little bit. Except Daniel, that is." Her voice went cold at her mention of the name.

"Who is Daniel?"

"When Papa died, he left my mother the house, and a good deal of land. And barely six months later, Daniel began coming by, claiming that he had done business with Papa. We all knew, though, that he was courting Mother, hoping to marry his way onto our land.

"All of us, that is, except Mother. Daniel is handsome and three years younger than she. I think she was flattered. She never doubted his motives. And she didn't notice when Sarah started to shy away whenever the brute came near."

Ethan felt his stomach clench.

"I noticed," Mary said. "So did James and Thomas, my brothers. They don't have my . . . my talents. And so it fell to me to stop him."

"Lord have mercy," Ethan whispered, though he wasn't a praying man.

"No mercy," the girl said. "None at all."

"What did you do?"

She shrugged and crossed her arms over her chest. "I cast a spell. I put it on Sarah. That seemed to be the safest way. It did nothing to the rest of us, but if Daniel touched her again . . ." Another smile flickered, grim this time. "It burned him," she said.

"His hands?"

She shook her head. "All of him. The rest of us were working the field, planting. He said he was going to get firewood, but he went searching for Sarah instead. And when he came staggering around from the back of the house, with his hair and clothes and skin burning like the fires of Hell, we knew. Even Mother knew."

"Is he dead?" Ethan asked, barely managing to speak the words.

"No. Hideously scarred, but very much alive."

Ethan shook his head. "No one can blame you for this, Mary. You were protecting your sister. Surely others can see that."

"At first no one did blame me. Daniel said it was Sarah who did it to him. He said that she was a witch, that all this time she hadn't been simple at all; it was just that the Devil had put his mark on her mind. They were going to hang her. So, I told them the truth: that it was me all along." She took a long, ragged breath, fresh tears rolling down her cheeks. "Don't you see? I did this to protect her, and in the end it almost got her killed. That's why I confessed. I couldn't bear the thought of saving her just so that she could be put to death."

"But you did what you had to do," Ethan said. "You shouldn't be punished at all."

She regarded him as if he were the simple one.

Ethan understood why. What he had said was hopelessly naïve. Conjurers were feared throughout the New World, and with Daniel having been burned so severely, people in this village would be terrified. Someone had to bear the blame.

"You could conjure yourself out of here," he said, his voice dropping once more. "Shatter the locks; break the hinges. Destroy the walls if you have to."

"To what end? If I flee, blame will fall on my family, most likely on my sister. That's precisely what I've hoped to avoid." She smiled. It had to be forced, and yet it brightened her face, making her look rather pretty, and even younger than she was. "I've chosen my fate. I'm at peace. Let me be, mister thieftaker. Please."

"My name is Ethan," he said.

"I'm grateful to you for coming, Ethan. I mean that. But there is nothing you can do for me. That is, unless you would care to pray for me."

He almost told her that he didn't believe in God, that it had been years since he had prayed for himself, much less for anyone else. But this had been a strange day, and her tale had moved him. In end he merely nodded and said, "Yes, of course I will."

"Thank you."

She seated herself on the pallet once more. She appeared more composed now. Her eyes were dry, her hands folded in her lap.

"Farewell, Mary Crenshaw."

The girl gazed at him, but offered no answer. After another moment, Ethan turned and knocked on the prison door. Almost immediately he heard the jangle of keys and the creak of hinges as the door swung open to reveal the burly gaol keeper.

Ethan blinked against the glare, glanced one last time at the door to Mary's cell. He had thought—hoped—that she might come to the window again. She hadn't.

"She say much to you?" the keeper asked as he led Ethan around toward the front of the courthouse.

"No."

"She don't say much to anyone. But she's a witch all right. Saw what she did to Daniel Bard—the aftermath anyway. There's no denying she's a witch." He shook his head. "Never thought I'd see the day, not here in Dedham."

"Thank you," Ethan said as they reached the street. He started northward toward the city. He had a long walk ahead of him.

"Aren't you going to stay for the hanging? It's just tomorrow, you know."

"I can't stay," Ethan said over his shoulder. "I've got to be getting back to Boston."

"Boston!" the man repeated. "Long way to come for a few minutes conversation."

Ethan said no more, but raised a hand in farewell. He walked slowly, his bad leg still aching from the journey to Dedham, his feet sore. A part of him wanted to return to the village and rail at the girl until she changed her mind and tried somehow to win her freedom. A part of him was tempted to tear the gaol apart, stone by stone. But of course he did neither.

He walked toward his home. And along the way, for the first time in so many years, he whispered a prayer.

"The Spelled Blade," was something I wrote on a lark. The idea came to me, and I spent a few days writing it, assuming I would find a home for it eventually. It sat on my hard drive for a year or more, gathering virtual dust. But then a friend of mine, the wonderful Kimberly Richardson, approached me about an urban fantasy anthology she was editing: Realms of Imagination. *She wanted to know if I had anything that might fit in with the other stories she'd found. I remembered this one and offered it to her. The anthology was released by Dark Oak Press in 2014.*

"The Spelled Blade"
D.B. Jackson

Boston, Province of Massachusetts Bay, 29 May 1766

For the second time in as many weeks, men and a few intrepid women had crowded onto Boston's Neck to watch the racing of horses. The lea fronting the Roxbury Flats had been cleared of cows, though evidence of their presence remained underfoot, and stakes had been placed in the fertile ground to mark out a race course.

Ethan Kaille had heard men speak with great enthusiasm of the first races held on the Neck the previous week. So, too, had Kannice Lester, the widowed owner of a tavern called the Dowsing Rod, who also happened to be Ethan's lover. More often than not, women were discouraged from attending horse races, as well as cockfights, dogfights, and other boisterous affairs deemed more suitable for the hardy dispositions of men. But Kannice insisted that she wanted to come, arguing that she had seen worse behavior in her own tavern than she was likely to see on the Neck in broad daylight.

"I never go anywhere, Ethan," she had said the night before, as they lay in bed. "I work all day, every day running this tavern. And I promise you that watching a handful of fools swear themselves blue in the face over a few lost shillings and pounds isn't about to shock me."

With all that he had seen in her tavern over the years, Ethan couldn't bring himself to argue.

She had put on a satin gown—periwinkle blue to match her eyes—with a white satin stomacher and white petticoats. Ethan wore his best breeches and coat, with a white silk shirt and black cravat. He felt like a fop, but Kannice seemed to appreciate the effort he had made. She walked with her arm hooked in his, her head held high, sunlight gleaming in her auburn hair. He had never seen her look more lovely.

All around them, men wagered their hard-earned cash, confident that the laws prohibiting such activity would not be enforced on this day, just as they hadn't been during the previous event.

The first race of the morning pitted four horses against one another. Two were from Narragansett—a bay and a white; the third was another bay out of Newport; and the fourth was a black from nearby Dorchester. At the sound of the starter's pistol Ethan and Kannice shouted encouragement to the local animal and his rider, and groaned with the rest of the crowd as the beast ran a distant fourth.

Some time after this first race had been run, four more horses were positioned for the second contest. But already talk had turned to what would be the fifth and final race of the day, a test of six horses, including two from Newport and one from a small town outside of Hartford. These three animals were considered champions, and that final race promised to be swift and hard-fought.

As Ethan and Kannice pressed forward, trying to improve their view of the course, they heard voices raised at the far end of the track, near where the races would conclude. Kannice craned her neck to see what was happening. Ethan didn't bother. Arguments, even fist fights, were commonplace at horse races throughout New England. He didn't see any reason why Boston's contests should be any different. Instead he chose to keep an eye out for pickpockets, who often sought to take advantage of such commotions to ply their ignominious trade.

But as the disturbance continued and seemed to intensify, Kannice took hold of his arm.

"I think something's happened," she said, a frown creasing her brow. "I think maybe someone's hurt."

Staring toward the tumult, Ethan had to agree that this seemed to be something more than just a routine disagreement. He took her hand, and they threaded their way through the crowd, following the sound of those raised voices. They hadn't gotten far when they heard the single report of what sounded like a pistol.

"Is the race starting?" someone asked from nearby.

But Ethan knew better. The sound had come from ahead of them, not back where the races commenced.

He halted and turned to Kannice. "You should stay here."

"And let you go ahead alone to get yourself shot? I don't think so."

"I'm not planning to get myself shot."

"Of course not," she said. "Nor do you ever plan to get yourself cut or beaten or burned. And yet you do, all the time." She waved a disdainful hand in the direction they had been going. "Lead on. I'm coming with you."

Ethan sighed. Taking her hand once more, he pushed on toward the din. The crowd grew more dense with every step Ethan and Kannice took, but Ethan could tell that they were drawing close to the center of whatever had happened. Men stood on their toes, rocking from side to side, trying to get a view. Many gave the pair filthy looks as they shouldered past, but no one stopped them until they had emerged at last from the crowd to find themselves confronted with an odd spectacle.

The crowd had formed an open circle about ten paces wide. Within the ring, two men sat on the grass. One of them appeared to be a worker—a wharfman, perhaps, or maybe a member of a ship's crew. He wore loose-fitting breeches that were stained and torn, and a plain linen shirt. Judging from the lines on his face and the flecks of gray in his mussed hair, Ethan guessed that he was the older of the two men. The second man wore a silk suit of beige over a white silk shirt and cravat. He had on a powdered wig, which had been knocked askew, revealing dark plaited hair beneath. He also sported a bloodied nose and a split lip; drops of blood stained his shirt and coat.

The well-dressed man stared at the ground in front of him, his eyes red-rimmed, almost as if he had shed tears. The other man glared in his direction, his dark-eyes smoldering.

Between the two men stood a third figure, the sole one of the three whom Ethan recognized. Stephen Greenleaf, Sheriff of Suffolk County, cut an imposing figure: Tall, broad shouldered, he stood with his feet wide and braced firmly on the lush grass, his mien grim, the gaze from his pale, penetrating eyes roaming the crowd. He held a flintlock pistol at his side. Ethan assumed that his was the weapon he and Kannice had heard.

Ethan and the Sheriff saw eye-to-eye about as often as did the kings of France and England. True, the man had been tasked with a job that was nigh impossible: He was expected to keep the peace in Boston and her surrounding countryside despite having no officers or soldiers in his employ. But Greenleaf had spent the past several years threatening to have Ethan hanged as a "witch," as those who didn't know better called conjurers. He knew that Ethan was an ex-convict who had served close to fourteen years laboring on a sugar plantation in the Caribbean as punishment for his role in the *Ruby Blade* mutiny. He seemed to assume that it was but a matter of time before Ethan fell afoul of the law once more. Greenleaf also went out of his way to hinder Ethan's inquiries as a thieftaker, in particular on those occasions when Ethan found himself working in competition with his rival, Sephira Pryce. And usually the sheriff made clear that he resented Ethan's involvement in any investigation he himself conducted.

On the other hand, if ever the sheriff found himself baffled by the evidence before him, or if he had any reason at all to believe that spellmaking had a role in one of his inquiries, he did not hesitate to seek out Ethan's help.

So Ethan was not entirely surprised when Greenleaf spotted him in the crowd and said, "Kaille! Just the man I was hoping to see."

Every man in the throng turned to stare at him.

"Aye, I'm sure," Kannice muttered under her breath. "Perhaps this wasn't such a fine idea after all."

"Well, we're here now," Ethan whispered back to her. He stepped forward, fixing a smile on his lips. "Well met, Sheriff. How can I be of service?"

Greenleaf waved his pistol at the two men sitting on the grass. "I'm hoping you can help me determine what these two have been on about."

"I told ye already!" said the sailor. "That feller there tried to rob me!"

Ethan blinked once before turning back to the sheriff, who had quirked an eyebrow.

"Not what you were expecting, eh?" Greenleaf said.

"What does this one say?" Ethan asked, nodding toward the man in the silk suit.

Greenleaf walked to where the bloodied man sat and squatted down before him. "This one hasn't said a thing."

The man continued to stare at the ground, refusing to meet the sheriff's gaze, or Ethan's for that matter.

"What did he steal from you?" Ethan asked the other man.

The sailor grinned. "Nothin'. See what I done to his face? Does he look like a man who got away with anythin' at all?"

"All right. What did he *try* to steal?"

The man's expression turned guarded. "That's between me and him."

Ethan glanced at the sheriff, who had straightened once more.

"You see my problem," Greenleaf said. He waved his pistol at the man in the suit. "This one says not a word, and the other will say only so much."

Ethan eyed the crowd around them before meeting Greenleaf's gaze again. The sheriff seemed to catch his meaning.

"The rest of you can go about your business," the sheriff said, pitching his voice to carry. "There's nothing more to see here, and the next race will be starting soon."

No one moved.

"Go on, I say! This is none of your concern!"

Mumbles greeted these words, but no one challenged him. The crowd began to move off, back toward the race course. It took some time for the men to disperse, during which Ethan, Kannice, the sheriff and the two men remained silent. Eventually they found themselves alone, or at least as alone as five people could be in the midst of horse races on Boston's Neck.

As the crowd dispersed, Ethan had tried to think of questions he might ask the men to get them to reveal what had happened. Before he could ask any of them, however, Kannice knelt down beside the bloodied man, pulled out a kerchief, and began to dab at the blood on his chin.

"You look a mess," she said, sympathy in her voice and visage.

The sailor scowled. "He deserved what he got."

Ethan, though, understood what she had in mind. Perhaps her ministrations and kind words would serve to loosen the wealthy man's tongue.

"A physician should minister to that lip," she went, on acting as though she hadn't heard the sailor. "It must hurt."

"Not so much," the second man said, his voice so soft that Ethan had trouble making out the words.

The sheriff caught Ethan's eye, eyebrows raised once more.

"Sheriff, might you find us something to put on this cut?" Kannice asked. "Surely some gentleman here on the neck must have a dram of rum."

Ethan thought that Greenleaf would refuse. He wasn't accustomed to being ordered about by anyone, except maybe Sephira Pryce. But perhaps he grasped Kannice's purpose as well. He regarded Ethan for another moment, then nodded and started off. After taking no more than a step or two, he halted.

"You come with me," he said to the sailor.

"Why?"

"Because I don't trust Kaille to keep an eye on you." Greenleaf turned just long enough for Ethan to see the corners of his mouth twitch upward.

The sheriff led the sailor off, leaving Ethan and Kannice with the man in the suit.

"I have to go," the young man said.

"You're not going anywhere," Ethan said, planting himself just behind Kannice, so that he stood over both of them. "She'll see to your injuries, but until you tell us what this is about, you'll be staying right here."

"Are you hurt anywhere else?" Kannice asked, giving the man no opportunity to argue.

"Naught but my pride," he said. A bitter smile touched his lips and was gone. "He needed but two blows to put me on the ground."

"Some men aren't meant to fight," Kannice said. "I'm sure you have other talents that are just as valuable."

"I'm grateful for your kindness, even if it is feigned."

Kannice sat back on her heels and glanced up at Ethan.

"I heard the sheriff refer to you as Kaille," the man went on. "Am I to assume that you are Ethan Kaille, the thieftaker?"

"Aye, I am."

"I've heard other things about you as well, Mister Kaille."

"Is that right?"

The man whispered something under his breath that Ethan couldn't make out. In the next instant, though, he saw the effect. A faint, glowing figure appeared by the man's side—an old woman with plaited hair wearing a fine gown and gems on her hands and at her neck. She shone with a pale green hue, the color of new spring leaves.

Ethan could have summoned a similar figure: a man instead of a woman, russet in color, dressed in battle mail and a tabard bearding the mark of England's ancient kings, but ghostly like this one. Every conjurer communed with a such a spirit. They were the shades of ancient spellmakers, ancestors of the living conjurers, Ethan assumed, who helped them cast spells by drawing on the power that dwelt between the living world and the realm of the dead. None but conjurers could see them, much less call them forth.

"You see?" the man said. "You and I are natural allies."

"What's happening?" Kannice asked, climbing to her feet.

"He's a conjurer," Ethan said, keeping his voice low. "You know Uncle Reg?" he asked, referring to the shade who appeared whenever he conjured.

"Of course."

"This man has a lady friend for him."

"Uncle Reg?" the man asked, actually managing a grin.

"My guide has always reminded me of my mother's brother, a rather unpleasant man named Reginald Jerill. I call him Uncle Reg."

The man nodded, his expression sobering. "I need your help, Mister

Kaille."

"The mere fact that you're a conjurer doesn't make us allies," Ethan said, still speaking in a whisper. "Nor does it make me inclined to help you. Is the other man telling the truth? Did you try to steal something from him?"

The man took a steadying breath. "Yes."

"What was it?"

"I'm not prepared to tell you that just yet."

"All right. Why don't we start with your name, then?"

"Stewart Dorr," he said. He stood and proffered a hand, which Ethan shook. Dorr had a firm grip and was taller than Ethan had expected— several inches taller than Ethan himself. "I live in Newport. I came over for the races."

Ethan frowned. "You live in Newport and you know my name? You know I'm a conjurer?"

"You helped an acquaintance of mine," Dorr said. "Jeremiah Hood. He mentioned to me that you were rumored to be a speller."

"Hood," Ethan repeated. "The shipbuilder."

"That's right."

Ethan remembered the inquiry. Two years before he had retrieved some jewelry that had been stolen from Hood's home, and in the process he had nearly gotten himself killed by Sephira Pryce's toughs. Still, he didn't like the idea of people discussing his conjuring abilities. The more people who knew, the greater the likelihood that, in time, word would reach someone with the power to have him hanged or burned as a witch. And he was troubled to learn that people beyond the bounds of Boston were speaking of him.

It seemed the Dorr read his thoughts. "I've mentioned you to no one. You have my word on that."

"I'm grateful," Ethan said, eager to return to the subject of Dorr's confrontation with the sailor. "So you came to Boston for the races. Did you know that you would run into the other man—"

"His name is Christopher Channing."

"Did you know that you would find Mister Channing here?"

"I had no idea."

"But you and he had met previously."

Dorr hesitated before conceding the point with lift of his shoulder. "We've had dealings, yes."

"What kind of dealings would a man of your station have with someone like Mister Channing?"

He didn't answer, leading Ethan to assume that their previous meeting had direct bearing on whatever it was Dorr had attempted to steal.

"Mister Channing is a conjurer, too," Kannice said, drawing Ethan's gaze as well as Dorr's. "Isn't he?"

The young man answered with a tight smile. "And are you also a thieftaker, Miss . . . ?"

"*Missus* Lester," she said. "No, I'm not."

"Perhaps you should be. You're right: Channing is a conjurer."

Ethan glared at the man. "And you let him leave with the sheriff?"

"What choice did I have? You of all people wouldn't expect me to do anything that would reveal to the sheriff of Suffolk County that I'm a speller. Channing is no fool. He won't harm the sheriff."

"He may not be a fool, but I believe you must be. He doesn't have to harm Greenleaf to make his escape."

As if to prove Ethan's point, in the next moment power rippled through the earth beneath their feet, humming in the ground like a plucked string on a great harp. Ethan and Dorr shared a look.

"Damn!" the younger man said.

"What is it?" Kannice asked.

"A spell," Ethan said. "Not a particularly strong one, but no doubt strong enough."

He took her hand, and headed in the direction the sheriff had gone with Channing. Dorr followed.

They hadn't walked far when they happened upon Greenleaf. He appeared confused and stood very much alone.

"He vanished!" the sheriff said. "He was here, and then he simply wasn't!" He leveled a thick finger at Ethan. "Is this your doing, Kaille? Are you using your foul witchery again?"

"I did nothing, Sheriff. But according to Mister Dorr here, the man you were with is a conjurer." *One who has mastered concealment spells.* This Ethan kept to himself; the last thing he needed to do was confirm the sheriff's suspicions by demonstrating his expertise in conjurings.

Greenleaf stared hard at Dorr, his eyes narrowed. "And how would Mister Dorr know that?"

"That doesn't matter right now," Ethan said. He asked Dorr, "Where would he go?"

"Back to the South End wharves, I would think."

"Then we should seek him there."

"Hold it, Kaille," Greenleaf said. He still had his glare fixed on Dorr, and now he produced his pistol once again. "According to Channing, this man tried to rob him. I don't have to chase shadows all over the city. I have my man right here. And I have a feeling this one's a witch, too."

"Sheriff—"

"If you want to find the other man, you should," the sheriff told him. He flashed a hard grin. "For once, you're free to go. But I'm not letting this one out of my sight."

Dorr eyed Greenleaf's weapon.

"Go on," Kannice said, her voice low as she gave Ethan's hand a quick squeeze. "I'll stay with them."

"You're sure?"

She nodded, eyes dancing. "I might even get to see another race."

Reluctant though he was to leave her there, Ethan didn't believe that Dorr meant to harm her, or anyone for that matter. To his surprise, he even found that he trusted Greenleaf to keep her safe.

"I'll return as soon as I can," he said, and strode off toward the South End.

The advantage of leaving the sheriff behind was that once he put some distance between himself and the Neck, as well as the crowd gathered there, he could cast a spell. He found a sheltered spot between a pair of dilapidated buildings and drew his knife. Making certain that no one could see him, he pushed up the coat and shirt sleeve on his left arm, revealing a lattice of old scars, and dragged the blade across his skin. Blood welled from the wound.

"*Locus magi ex cruore evocatus*," he said in Latin. Location of conjurer, conjured from blood.

Uncle Reg appeared beside him, the customary scowl on his lean, bearded face. Power thrummed in the street and in the fragile walls on either side of him, spreading out through the city like ripples in a still pond. Seconds later, the conjuring echoed back toward him from two directions. One of the echoes came from the Neck—Dorr, he assumed. The second came from the South End, though not from the waterfront. Rather, it seemed to bounce back at him from somewhere closer, perhaps near the New South Meeting House on Summer Street. Channing—if that's who this was—hadn't yet reached the wharves.

"Can you tell where he is?" Ethan asked the ghost.

Reg shook his head, then faded from view.

Ethan hurried on, knowing that the sailor would have felt his spell, but hoping that he would think it had been cast by Dorr. Channing would expect the younger man to come after him, but maybe he wouldn't expect to see Ethan on the South End lanes.

During his time as a prisoner, Ethan had suffered a wound to his foot that left him partially lame. Walking at a quick pace through Boston's cobbled streets, it didn't take long for the pain of that old injury to return. By the time Ethan reached the first wharves near the South Battery, he was limping, sweat running down his temples.

Finding a deserted lane, he cut himself a second time and cast another finding spell. He didn't relish the idea of alerting Channing to his pursuit, but neither did he wish to lose the man to the tangle of streets in Cornhill and the South End. With the conjuring, Reg reappeared. He watched Ethan, silent as ever.

Dorr still seemed to be on the Neck, but Channing was closer this time, a short distance north of where Ethan stood. He guessed that the man was on Long Wharf, off of King Street. He continued in that direction, moving with as much speed as his awkward gait would allow.

As Ethan neared the wharf, he scanned it for any sign of the sailor. That is, until he remembered that Channing had used a concealment spell to escape the sheriff. Perhaps he remained hidden. In which case the man might have been watching Ethan at that moment. He didn't dare pull out his dagger again. Instead, he bit down hard on the inside of his cheek drawing blood.

"*Aufer carmen, ex cruore evocatum,*" he muttered to himself. Remove spell, conjured from blood.

Power pulsed in the street, and an instant later Channing winked into view on the edge of the wharf, just across a narrow strip of water from where Ethan walked. His eyes were wide as he scanned the lanes, no doubt still searching for Dorr.

Ethan kept his head lowered, watching the man out of the corner of his eye, but not allowing his features to be seen. As he stepped onto the wharf, another spell rumbled through the ground. This one seemed to come from a distance. Dorr perhaps, trying to locate them. Or casting some other sort of spell, something less benign. He thought of Kannice, apprehension rising in his chest. He had to resist the urge to hurry back to the Neck.

But he had almost reached Channing, and the touch of that last conjuring from farther away appeared to have alerted the sailor to his error.

Ethan saw him bite down, guessed that he had bloodied the inside of his own cheek, as Ethan had moments before.

Power hummed in the wharf beneath Ethan's feet. The glowing figure of a young man materialized beside Channing. And a finding spell lashed out at Ethan like a coachman's whip. Channing's gaze snapped to his face.

"I don't want to fight you," Ethan said, halting and raising his hands in a placating gesture. "I just want to talk."

"I've got nothin' to say to you."

"You're going to have to talk to someone, especially after what you did to get away from the Neck."

Channing wet his lips. "Where's th' sheriff? Where's Dorr?"

"I left them at the races. I came alone."

A few men stood nearby, watching them, puzzlement etched on their faces.

Ethan eased forward again. "My name is Ethan Kaille, Mister Channing. I might be able to help you, if you'll let me."

"What did Dorr tell you?" Channing asked. "Whatever it was, he lied. I promise you tha' much."

Ethan took another step; Channing retreated a pace and pulled a knife from his belt. The blade was tarnished, the hilt worn and discolored. But he held it ready, to fight or to conjure. "That's close enough," he said.

Ethan halted, fearing the man would flee, or attack him with a spell. Without knowing how skilled Channing was with either a blade or his magick, Ethan thought his best hope might be to win the man's trust. "Dorr admitted that he tried to pinch something from you," he said. He kept his voice low, so that none but the sailor could hear. "He said that the two of you were previously acquainted, but he wouldn't tell me more than that. I think your past encounters with him are connected to whatever it was he tried to take, as is the fact that both of you are conjurers."

"Did he tell you all that?"

"No. I'm a thieftaker, and I have some skill at piecing together tales like this one."

Channing eyed him, his brow creased. "All right then, what'll you do if I tell you what I know?"

"That depends on what you have to say. But I'm not the sheriff, and no one has hired me to retrieve anything. At this point, I'm trying to keep Greenleaf from hanging all three of us as witches."

Channing stared at him, saying nothing. At last, with obvious reluctance, he made a small gesture with his blade. "You see this knife?" he said. "I got if from my Da. He told me . . ." Channing shook his head. "I didn' believe him at the time, but he told me it once belonged to another speller;

a pirate, if you want to know. The blade itself is supposed to be spelled. It makes conjurin's stronger. At least that's what my Da told me."

"And that blade is what Dorr was trying to steal."

"Aye," Channing said. "I was a landsman on a privateerin' ship that put in at Newport late last year. I got careless, cast a spell when I thought I was alone on the dock. Dorr felt it. At first I thought he was goin' to get me hanged, but then I realized that he couldn't do nothin' without lettin' people know he could cast, too. So we started talkin'. At some point I mentioned my Da's knife." The landsman shrugged. "We wound up drinkin' half the night—he was buyin' and was sparin' no expense, if you know what I mean. I probably should have suspected somethin' then, but I didn't. After a bunch of ales, he tried to spell me to sleep, but he'd had too much, and the spell didn't work. I hit him, ran out of the pub and back to my ship, and didn't see him again until today."

"Do you think he came to Boston hoping to find you?"

"I don't know. Wouldn't surprise me if he had. I spotted him today before he got close enough to use a spell on me, and I warded myself. So then he offered me money—twenty pounds. And when I refused to sell, he pulled his own knife and threatened me." Channing lifted a shoulder. "That's when I bloodied him."

"Why did you come back here?"

Channing pointed at a nearby vessel. "That's my ship. We're not sailin' until late today, but I thought I'd be safer here than on the Neck."

"You may well be right," Ethan said. "Before, when I removed your concealment spell, did you feel another conjuring?"

"Aye," Channing said. "It was far off. You think it was Dorr?"

"Aye. And I think I'd better be getting back—"

He didn't have time to say more.

Another spell sang in the ground beneath them, powerful and very close. Power twined about Ethan's legs, like vines reaching up through the wharf. A finding spell.

Both of them turned in time to see a chaise come to an abrupt stop on King Street, at the head of Long Wharf.

Dorr vaulted out of the carriage, accompanied by his glowing ghost, and started in their direction. Ethan pulled out his knife, but then thought better of cutting himself. He and Channing were beyond the hearing of the nearest wharfmen, but they were in plain sight. Cutting themselves to conjure would have been tantamount to shouting at the top of their voices that they were spellers.

Ethan bit down on his cheek again, the pain of this second bite far worse than the first. He hoped that Channing had done the same.

Tegimen ex cruore evocatum, Ethan said to himself. Warding, conjured from blood.

Uncle Reg reappeared as Ethan's spell hummed in the ground. Channing's ghost winked into view as well.

Dorr faltered at the sight of the two ghosts, but then continued forward, cautious now. As he drew near, he acknowledged Ethan with a tip of his tricorn.

"I knew you'd find him for me. Well done, Mister Kaille."

"What did you do to Kannice?"

"Your friend and the sheriff are quite well. They'll be asleep for some time, but when they wake they should be fine." To Channing he said, "I take it you've told him what this is about."

"You planned this all along, didn't you?" Channing said.

Dorr shook his head. "To be honest, no. I had hoped to have you carted off to the Boston gaol by Sheriff Greenleaf. But when Mister Kaille showed up, I realized that there might be a better way." He put his hand in his coat pocket and took hold of what appeared to be a pistol. "This is the sheriff's," he said, with a nod toward the concealed weapon. "And I assure you it's been reloaded since he fired that shot on the Neck."

"You won't use that," Ethan said. "You would draw too much attention to yourself."

"You might have been right had you not drawn your knife when you saw me. Now I can shoot and claim that I was protecting myself. That should at least allow me to get out of Boston before Greenleaf arrives."

Ethan set his knife on the ground, drawing a thin smile from Dorr.

"There are still two of you threatening to harm me," the young man said. "Besides, that's the knife I want." He turned his gaze, and the shrouded barrel of the pistol, on Channing. "Give it to me."

As soon as Dorr turned his attention to the other man, Ethan bit down on his cheek once more—his mouth was going to be sore for days.

Tasting warm blood on his tongue, he spoke another spell in his mind, directing it at the pistol. *Conflare ex cruore evocatum*. Heat, conjured from blood.

Dorr cried out. He tried to pull his hand from his coat pocket, but somehow got it stuck instead. The report of the weapon echoed across the waterfront. The bullet glanced off the ground, but smoke and flames burst from Dorr's coat pocket, setting the man's clothes ablaze.

Dorr flailed at the fire with his free hand, spinning frantically until he fell to his knees. He managed to extract his other hand from the coat pocket—his flesh was blackened—and now he tore at his burning coat and shirt, desperate to remove them.

Ethan leapt forward, pulling off his own coat and using it to smother the flames. By the time he and Dorr had put out the fire, much of the young man's shirt had burned away. The bared skin on his chest and arms was livid and blistered, and he lay on the ground, panting, whimpering in pain.

Ethan turned to tell Channing to find a physician, but the sailor was nowhere to be seen.

"Where did he go?" Ethan muttered.

Dorr didn't even open his eyes. "We won't see him again," he whispered. "I made a mess of this, I'm afraid."

"Yes, you did."

Several of the wharfmen came to see if Dorr was still alive. Ethan sent one of them in search of a doctor.

"Are you going to hand me over to Greenleaf?" Dorr asked, opening one eye.

"Not if you promise to leave Boston, and stay far away."

Dorr closed his eye again, his aspect curdling. A moment later though, he said, "Yes, all right."

Ethan said no more, but he remained by Dorr's side until a surgeon arrived. As the doctor began to treat the man's burns, Ethan stood, intending to head back to the Neck to find Kannice.

Seeing Dorr's discarded, burned coat, he stooped and pulled out the blackened remains of the sheriff's pistol. With one last glance back at Dorr and the doctor, he made his way off the wharf and toward the Neck.

After a brief search, he found Kannice and the sheriff in the middle of a knot of people. The two of them sat on the grass, appearing somewhat dazed. Kannice had stalks of grass in her hair, and her fine gown was rumpled. Seeing Ethan, she clambered to her feet and threw herself into his arms.

"Are you all right?" Ethan asked.

"Aye. You?"

"Yes, fine."

"Oh, look at your coat," Kannice said, seeing the burns in the fabric. "I always liked that one."

"Where are they, Kaille?" Greenleaf demanded struggling to his feet as well. "Where is the witch who vanished? And for that matter, where is the other villain who put us to sleep?"

"I don't know where Channing is," Ethan said. He kept his arm around Kannice's shoulders, but he faced the sheriff. "He's gone. The one who used a sleeping spell on the two of you, Stewart Dorr, is on Long Wharf, being attended to by a physician."

Greenleaf frowned. "What happened to him?"

Ethan drew out the remains of the sheriff's pistol and held it for Greenleaf to take. "He had this in his pocket and he tried to shoot us. He wound up setting himself on fire. And I'm afraid he ruined your weapon."

Greenleaf took the pistol and stared at it, wide-eyed and open-mouthed. "You say he's on Long Wharf?"

"He was when I left. I don't know if he's still there."

The sheriff raised his eyes to Ethan's. "They're both witches, aren't they?"

"You would have to ask them, Sheriff."

The sheriff scowled. "Well, maybe I will." He stalked off, shouldering his way past the men who had gathered around them.

"Are the races done?" Kannice asked.

"I don't know," Ethan said. "I would have thought you'd be ready to head home."

Kannice smiled. "Not at all! This is more excitement than I've had in a long time. Why would I want to go home?"

Ethan grinned. "Perhaps Dorr was right. You would make a good thief-taker."

"Perhaps. I hear that Boston has a pretty good one already."

"Sephira Pryce, you mean," Ethan said.

She arched an eyebrow, and together they started back toward the race course.

In the summer of 2014, I embarked on what had, by then, become something of a tradition: a summer blog tour promoting my latest Thieftaker novel. A Plunder of Souls (Tor Books, 2014), the third book in the Thieftaker Chronicles, had been released right around the July 4th holiday, and I was writing posts and responding to interview requests at various sites. My wonderful friend, Faith Hunter, invited me to her blog as well (http://faithhunter.net), but we agreed that I should do something more elaborate for the occasion. The result was this story, "A Passing Storm." It is too long a piece to be considered flash fiction, but it's close. Whatever you call it, it was fun to write.

"A Passing Storm"
D.B. Jackson

Boston, Province of Massachusetts Bay, 14 July 1767

Ethan and Kannice were but a few strides from the door of the confectionery when the skies opened.

Thunder had been rumbling across Boston for the better part of the day, and clouds like boulders had piled high into the hazy summer sky throughout the afternoon. In a city desperate for rain, the sights and sounds of the imminent storm were welcome. Still, Ethan had hoped that the deluge might hold off for a few minutes more, while he escorted Kannice to Cannon's shop.

But though his conjuring talents enabled him to cast all manner of magick spells, he could do little to influence the heavens. Not that Kannice seemed to care. In moments her gown—one of his favorites; periwinkle blue to match her eyes—and petticoats were soaked, as was her auburn hair. She merely laughed and pulled him the rest of the way to the shop door.

"This is your fault," he said over the rush of rainfall.

"Aye, because I control the weather."

He grinned and pushed open the door, motioning her inside. Once she was safely within the shop, he removed his tricorn hat and shook it off. "I suppose it could have been worse. We might have—"

"Ethan."

He heard in her utterance of his name a warning, and a hint of fear. Looking past her, he saw why. Sephira Pryce stood by the store counter, with Nap, one of her toughs.

Sephira was Boston's foremost thieftaker. Lovely, cruel, dangerous as an unsheathed blade, she considered Ethan an unworthy rival. But not so unworthy that she didn't remind him at every opportunity that his life, and the lives of every friend he had in the city, were forfeit should she choose to rid herself of him.

She watched him now, her pale eyes appraising and cold. Nap had gone still, like a wolf that has caught the scent of prey. Thunder rolled through the streets, rattling the door and windows of the shop. Rain pounded the roof with a dull roar.

"Good day, Sephira," Ethan said, breaking a lengthy silence.

"Ethan." She purred his name. "How lovely to see you." Her gaze flicked toward Kannice. "And your little friend, as well."

Kannice stiffened. "Little friend?"

He laid a hand on her arm.

"Forgive me. What would you prefer? Wife? Fiancée? Really, Ethan: When are you going to make an honest woman of the poor dear?"

Kannice's cheeks blazed.

Ethan reached for the door handle. "We should go."

Kannice shook her head. "I came for a sweet, and I'll not let this ha'penny whore keep me from it."

Sephira's glare turned icy. "Have a care, sweetling. I don't take that from anyone, not even a woman who shares her bed with a witch."

Ethan glanced outside. Rain came down in windswept sheets, flooding the cobblestone lane and thickening the air so that he could barely make out the shops across the street. For the moment, none of them was going anywhere.

Facing forward again, Ethan noticed the store clerk for the first time. He was a short, round, bespectacled man who stood behind the counter, looking perplexed and more than little frightened. "How are you today, Mister Cannon?"

"W-well, thank you."

Ethan nodded.

A small box, half-filled with chocolates, sat on the counter between Sephira and the hapless storekeeper.

Sephira glanced at the box and then eyed the confectioner. "Get on with it, Cannon. I haven't all day."

He let out a squeak of assent and began to pile candies into the container, seeming to select them from his case at random.

For his part, Ethan found it hard to imagine Sephira enjoying sweets.

Then again, he found it hard to imagine her eating anything other than iron nails and raw meat.

Kannice stepped to the counter, halting just beside Sephira and eyeing Mister Cannon's wares. She was several inches shorter than Sephira, and so willowy as to appear waiflike by comparison. But she stood straight-backed, her head held high, and she at least pretended to ignore the other woman.

Sephira glanced her way, but then turned to face Ethan once more. Nap remained wary, one hand in a coat pocket where, Ethan assumed, he carried his flintlock.

"Who are you working for right now, Ethan?"

"No one at the moment."

She bared her teeth. "Good. Perhaps this would be a good time for you to consider some other line of work. I tire of sharing my clients with you, of having to clean up your messes, and of having to explain again and again why I tolerate competition from a neophyte like you."

Ethan saw Kannice bristle, but before she could do or say more, he laughed.

"You think I'm joking?" Sephira demanded.

"I know you're not. But I find you amusing nevertheless."

Lightning flashed, brightening the shop for an instant, and another clap of thunder shook the building.

"You're taking an awful risk, Ethan," she said, her voice low, menacing, her gaze shifting in Kannice's direction.

Ethan bit down on the inside of his cheek, tasting blood. With it he could conjure, either to protect Kannice, or to lash out at Sephira and her man.

"No, I'm not," he whispered. "You're the one at risk. Do you understand?"

He saw from the glimmer of alarm in her eyes that she did. He glanced Nap's way. "Keep your hands where I can see them, or I'll light her hair on fire."

They stood thus for several moments, none of them saying a word. Perhaps realizing belatedly that she was in peril, Kannice backed away from the counter so that she stood once more with Ethan. Mister Cannon watched Sephira the way a child might a rabid dog.

At last, though, Sephira laughed, full-throated, her head thrown back. Despite himself, Ethan had always liked her laugh.

At the sound, Nap appeared to exhale, and Mister Cannon nearly collapsed in a relieved heap.

"Who would have thought that buying a few confections would bring such excitement?" Sephira said. "This is why I continue to let you live and work in my city, Ethan. You can make an otherwise dreary day so much fun."

Kannice raised an eyebrow, but had the good sense to keep her thoughts to herself.

Sephira looked past Ethan to the window. "Ah, it's let up."

He turned. Indeed, the rainfall had slackened and the skies were marginally brighter.

"Just a passing storm," Sephira said. "Nothing worth getting agitated about." To Nap, she added, "Retrieve the chaise and bring it to the door. I'll be all right. Won't I, Ethan?"

"Of course. We've just come for a sweet."

Nap regarded Ethan for another moment before slipping out of the shop.

Sephira smiled and pulled a small purse from the pocket of her coat. She plucked a shilling from the purse and set it on the counter. "There you go, Mister Cannon. So good to see you again."

"A-and you, Miss Pryce."

A chaise, pulled by a large bay, rolled up out front.

"Goodbye, Ethan." Sephira turned to Kannice. "My dear. I so look forward to our next encounter. I like fiery women. Almost as much as I like the men who love them."

She took her box of chocolates and left the shop. Cannon sagged against the counter.

Ethan exhaled.

Kannice stared after Sephira. "I hope she chokes on one of those candies."

"I wouldn't count on it," Ethan said. "You might want to reconsider calling her a ha'penny whore. That's twice you've done it. She might not tolerate a third time."

Kannice shrugged. "I'll think about it. In the meantime, I want my chocolates."

"Of course you do," Ethan said with a grin. "Mister Cannon, what are your specialties today?"

A smile broke over the shopkeeper's face and he began to catalog the items in his case. Ethan took Kannice's hand, listening with her. He heard one more rumble of thunder to the east, out over the harbor. It sounded distant now, no longer a threat. But he knew there would be other storms. With Sephira in Boston, there always were.

In the summer of 2013, I put together a blog tour to help with promotion of the second Thieftaker novel, Thieves' Quarry *(Tor Books, 2013). One of my stops on the tour was at AllThingsUrbanFantasy.com. At the time, ATUF was doing a "Deadly Destinations" promotion and asking authors to write tours of their settings written from the point of view of their lead characters. Hence this short piece, a walking tour of Boston narrated by Ethan Kaille. It was a great promotion, and a really fun post to write. I hope you enjoy it.*

"A Walking Tour of Boston, Narrated by Ethan Kaille"
D.B. Jackson

Boston, Province of Massachusetts Bay, 1 October 1768

You're here at last. Good. We haven't much time. Under most circumstances, I would not consent even to this brief encounter, but Janna Windcatcher indicated that all of you could be trusted, and Janna is not only a good friend, but also the most accomplished conjurer here in Boston. If she says that you are people of honor, then I believe her. My name is Ethan Kaille. I am a thieftaker of some small renown. And since you are friends of Janna's I will confide that I am also, like Janna, a conjurer. But please, speak not a word of this to anyone we meet; in this time, conjurers are still hanged as "witches."

Janna mentioned that you might not be entirely aware of the date. I know not what manner of spell she used to bring you to this place, but it must have been powerful indeed.

Very well. Today is the first of October in the year of our Lord seventeen hundred and sixty-eight. You are in the city of Boston, in what is known as Cornhill, near the Old Meeting House and the Town Hall. Just to the north and east of us can be found Peter Faneuil's grand new hall and market.

I do not know what cities look like in your place and time, but once, not so long ago, Boston was the finest city in all of British North America. She shone like the sun and bustled with commerce and culture and a virtuous and hearty citizenry. Sadly, this is no longer the case. Since the early days of the war with the French, which concluded more than five years ago, she has been in decline. Commerce has fled these shores for the wharves of New York and Philadelphia. The city has fallen upon hard times, and has become instead a haven for the most unsavory sort of men. It has also garnered a well-earned reputation as a center for unrest, for conflict between His Majesty King George III, and those who would question the Crown's authority in this new land. And yet still I call this town my home, and hope that some day it will shine as once it did.

Close your eyes for a moment. Breathe deep of the air. This is as cool and clear a day as we have had this autumn, but still the scents of brine, of fish, and of tar from the shipyards lay heavy on our city. This is, and shall always be, a city tied to the harbor and the sea. Closer by, you might catch as well the scent of cooking fires from nearby publick houses, of freshly cut timber and dried, fallen leaves, and perhaps the less pleasant odors of horses. You can hear the dry clop of unshod horse hooves on cobblestone and the rattle of wagons, carriages, and chaises as they pass by. Men and women shout to each other in the lanes, hoping to strike deals in the streets before merchants add to the price of goods at market. And if you strain your ears, you might also hear the distant strains of fifes blowing in the late afternoon sun, of drums beating, and of regiments of soldiers marching in unison.

Walk with me. It's not far. Just to the edge of King Street where it meets Long Wharf. There. Do you see those ships? More than a dozen of them remain anchored near the wharf, bobbing on the gentle swells, looking like shadows against the glittering waters. They are British war vessels: frigates, sloops, post ships. Though they are mostly empty now, only hours ago their decks were crowded with men in the bright red uniforms of His Majesty's army. They appeared in the harbor not so many days ago, bearing from Halifax a force of British soldiers, more than a thousand strong. All through the summer, as rioters took to the streets and agents of the Crown attempted in vain to impose order on the city, Francis Bernard, Governor of the Province of Massachusetts Bay, pleaded with his superiors in London to send troops to pacify the city. At last his pleas have been answered.

Today, just within the past few hours, the occupation of Boston has begun. For the first time, we are a garrisoned town. I am British, born and raised. I served in His Majesty's fleet during the War of the Austrian Succession, and I have long considered myself a supporter of Parliament and its authority. I have stood opposed to the rabble-rousing of men like Samuel Adams and James Otis. But this . . . I never thought I'd see the day when my city was occupied, as if we were a foreign enemy at war with the King and his men. I fear this is a day that we may all long regret.

And yet, I cannot join with others in the taverns, as they speak of these matters over ales and plates piled high with oysters. I have an inquiry to conduct. Once again, I must ask that you keep this in strictest confidence. In the last day or two, events both terrible and mysterious have been brought to my attention. One ship among the British fleet, the *HMS Graystone*, has suffered a dark fate. All the men aboard the vessel—sailors, soldiers, officers; nearly a hundred in all—are dead, killed, it seems, by a single spell of unthinkable power.

Because I am a thieftaker, and because rumors of my spellmaking abilities have followed me for many years, I have been asked by officials in the employ of the Crown to investigate these murders. To be honest, I know not where to begin my inquiry. A spell as strong as this one had to have been cast by a conjurer far more powerful than I, or even than Janna. I know of no such conjurers in Boston. Which means that a force of magick hitherto unknown to my friends and me is now abroad in the streets of Boston.

For this reason, I must end our visit now. I am sorry for this. Had you come some other day, perhaps I could have introduced you to my friend Kannice Lester, a woman dear to me, who is proprietor of a tavern called the Dowsing Rod. She makes as fine a fish stew—a chowder, as such dishes have come to be called here in recent years—as any served in the city. I could have shown you the impressive estates of Beacon Hill, and the open leas of Boston's fine Common. But alas, murder and foul conjurings have come once more to our fair city, and it falls to me to find the villains responsible.

Farewell, my friends. Keep safe, and please reveal to no one the confidences I have shared with you.

This interview with Sephira Pryce appeared at the genre/book review website ISmellSheep.com in July 2015, as I was promoting Dead Man's Reach *(Tor Books, 2015) and* His Father's Eyes *(Baen Books, 2015), the second Justis Fearsson novel, which I wrote as David B. Coe. It is one of a number of Sephira interviews I posted during my various Thieftaker blog tours. She is so much fun to write, especially in these mock interview settings, because she is so insufferable, so full of herself, so dismissive of everyone else, and so clueless about all of this. This interview was probably my favorite, in large part because it is so silly, and because in this case she turns her ire on me. I hope you enjoy it.*

"An Encounter with Sephira Pryce"
David B. Coe/D.B. Jackson

Boston, Province of Massachusetts Bay, 2 February 1770

I'm delighted to be here for this installment in my virtual tour. My name is David B. Coe, and I'm currently promoting two books. The first, DEAD MAN'S REACH, is the fourth novel in my Thieftaker Chronicles, a historical urban fantasy, set in pre-Revolutionary Boston, which I write for Tor Books under the name D.B. Jackson. It came out last week. The second, HIS FATHER'S EYES, is the second volume in The Case Files of Justis Fearsson, a contemporary urban fantasy that I write for Baen Books under my own name. It will be released next week on August 4th. I wanted to talk to you today about—

Sephira Pryce: Boring!

DBC: *Excuse me?*

SP: I said, boring. As in, you are boring these poor people to tears. It's hard to believe that you could have such a powerfully soporific effect on these unfortunate souls. You've barely started, and already they're nodding off. A few more paragraphs and you might actually kill someone.

DBC: *You're Sephira Pryce, the villain from the Thieftaker novels.*

SP: Villain! You have some nerve! I'm the heroine of the series.

DBC: *No, Ethan Kaille is the hero. You're his nemesis.*

SP: Potato, po-tah-to.

DBC: *Well, no—*

SP: Your little fairy tales would be nothing without me. The scenes I'm in sparkle, like sunlight on the waters on Boston Harbor. Even when I'm not actually in a particular passage, the mere mention of my name, a hint at my possible ire, the threat of my retribution, infuses all that you write. Without me, your novels would be as flat and dull as this essay would have been had I left you to your devices. It's hard to believe, really. I mean, you created me, so apparently you have some small capacity for writing words of interest. And yet the rest of what you do is so . . . lacking.

DBC: *I'm not certain that's true.*

SP: I'm reasonably certain I didn't ask. I came to rescue you from yourself. You want to sell books, don't you? Of course you do. So you have two choices: You can pick up where you left off and hope that putting these people to sleep somehow translates to sales. Or you can take advantage of my fortuitous arrival and rely upon my charm, my wit, my intellect, and, of course, my stunning physical beauty, to help you interest readers in that nonsense you write about Ethan and me. Choose. Quickly. I'm a busy woman. If you don't wish to avail yourself of my services, I am sure there are others who will.

DBC: *Fine. Why don't you tell our audience a bit about yourself.*

SP: Is that really necessary? Haven't they all heard of me already?

DBC: *It's possible that some have not.*

SP: Oh! The poor dears! Well then, yes. By all means. [Clearing throat] My name is Sephira Pryce, and I am the foremost thieftaker in the city of Boston. Some know me as the Empress of the South End, but you and our guests here today may call me Miss Pryce.

DBC: *You are a contemporary of Samuel Adams, are you not?*

SP: Yes, I am. But he is hardly someone of interest to those reading this piece. He solves no crimes, he has not fought his way up through the streets of this town to a position of power and respect. He is the son of a politician who has not managed to rise above his father's middling station.

DBC: *But his actions on behalf of liberty, and his role in forming the Sons of Liberty—*

SP: Yes, yes, yes. He has his little cause. What is it they call themselves? Patriots? [Laughs] Really, I don't think their actions will ever amount to much. Their movement is a trifle and little more. I hardly expect that the king fears this rabble. Ask me something else.

DBC: *All right. Tell me about your rivalry with Ethan Kaille.*

SP: I have no rivals. Kaille is a nuisance, but I hardly think he warrants consideration as a rival to me.

DBC: *He has survived in Boston as a . . . competitor for some time now.*

SP: He has been fortunate, and I have allowed him to survive. Thus far. I am too filled with the milk of human kindness for my own good. I could have rid the city of him years ago, but I have tolerated his presence here out of charity. And let's not forget his confounding witchery, which has saved him from his own carelessness more often than I care to say. If not for his spells, and his luck, no one would ever think to compare him to me.

DBC: *And yet, he has solved mysteries that you could not.*

SP: Only by dint of his magick! I have nothing more to say on the matter! I do not wish to speak of Kaille, nor do I wish to have his name spoken again in my presence!

DBC: *All right. Tell us what you think of the British occupation of Boston, which has been in effect now for well more than a year.*

SP: It is a necessity. Adams and his rabble may be naifs and fools, but they have been responsible for too much mischief to be ignored. They have destroyed property, disrupted commerce, harassed merchants of unimpeachable character simply because the men refuse to go along with Adams' non-importation agreements. These rebels like to complain about the military presence, but they have no one to blame for it but themselves. Your questions grow tiresome. Don't you wish to know more about me?

DBC: *I do believe my readers would be interested to know how you have enjoyed so much success in a city—and an era—so dominated by men.*

SP: Ah! At last, a fine question! The answer is quite simple, really. Men are fools. Don't get me wrong. I enjoy the company of some. And I'll admit that Kaille, despite his annoying habit of getting in my way time and again, is a most compelling specimen. But generally speaking, men expect women to behave a certain way, and when we don't they become quite flummoxed. I confound their expectations. With my beauty and my charm, I distract and disarm them, and with my brilliance and ruthlessness I surprise and ultimately overwhelm them. Most don't stand a chance against me. Kaille is more clever than the vast majority, and he is not easily intimidated. But he is the exception, and I told you already I didn't wish to speak of him anymore.

DBC: *I didn't bring him up. You did.*

SP: Well, you tricked me into it. All this talk of men and their predilections. You knew it would lead back to Kaille eventually.

DBC: *Actually I didn't—*

SP: I am done here. You had your chance. I could have helped you, but you would rather write your stories about Kaille. So be it. Farewell.

DBC: *That was Sephira Pryce, the rival and nemesis of Ethan Kaille, my thieftaking, conjuring hero in the Thieftaker Chronicles. Thank you for joining us!*

Since the publication of Thieftaker *(Tor Books, 2012), people have asked me when I would write the story of the* Ruby Blade *mutiny. Probably because of the central role the mutiny and its aftermath plays in Ethan's backstory, the events of that period in his life have held a certain fascination for fans of the series. I have long intended to write the story—I knew all along that I would need to eventually—but I didn't think its telling would be enough to fill an entire novel. When I hit upon the idea for this collection, though, I realized that at last the time had come.*

I didn't want to limit this story—it's a novella actually—to just the events of 1745, and so I decided to bring in a new element to the tale: a mystery that picks up sort of where Dead Man's Reach *(Tor Books, 2015), the fourth* Thieftaker *book, left off. And, of course, I had to involve Sephira, because, you know, Sephira . . .*

In any case, here at last is the story of the mutiny aboard the privateering vessel, Ruby Blade. *I hope you have as much fun reading it as I had writing it.*

"The *Ruby Blade*"
D.B. Jackson

Boston, Province of Massachusetts Bay, January 8, 1771

I

A fire crackled and danced in the hearth of the Dowsing Rod, warming the tavern against the howling winds and scratching snow of yet another New England blizzard. Ethan Kaille, conjurer, former thieftaker, now bar-hand under the kindly if tasking eye of his beloved wife, Kannice, sat near the blaze, his feet—clad only in woolen hose—propped on a second chair, a cup of barely-watered Madeira by his side.

It was a rare luxury for Ethan and Kannice to have the Dowser very nearly to themselves on a Tuesday night. On most nights the tavern was filled to bursting with her usual patrons, who frequented the establishment for her savory stews and chowders, and the fine spiced-rum flips concocted by her hulking barman, Kelf Fingarin. Tonight, though, it was just the three of them.

Ethan might have felt guilty, reclined as he was, listening as Kelf and Kannice bustled in the kitchen behind the bar. They were, it seemed, doing some conjuring of their own, creating a feast from foodstuffs that might otherwise have gone to waste in the empty tavern. But for all his talents with woodwork and furniture repairs, not to mention his abilities with spell-making, he had no aptitude for cooking. Ethan didn't know what they were making, and they had all but ordered him out of their way.

That suited him. His back and shoulders ached from clearing nearly a foot of snow from the entry way to the tavern. Kelf had offered to do this, but Ethan had noticed in recent days the start of a paunch around his belly. It seemed the excellence of Kannice's fare, and the relatively staid life of a tavern worker, at least when compared to the rigors of thieftaking, had begun to catch up with him. He had welcomed the opportunity to exert himself, just as he now welcomed the opportunity to warm his frozen toes and sip his wine.

Kannice emerged from the kitchen and stepped around the bar, bearing a steaming bowl of stew in one hand and a small round of bread in the other. A few strands of auburn hair hung over her brow, and her cheeks were flushed, making her cornflower blue eyes appear even more vivid than usual.

"You look comfortable," she said, setting the food in front of him.

Ethan swung his feet to the cool floor and straightened. "I should be helping."

"You're helping by staying as far from my kitchen as possible."

He settled back in the chair. "Where's *your* food?"

"Kelf is bringing it out. In the meantime, try this."

Ethan inhaled the fragrant steam rising from the bowl, which was rich with fresh cream and bay leaf. "What is it?"

"Oyster chowder. There's roasted cod as well. While the rest of Boston hides from the storm, we'll be enjoying a feast that would make King George himself jealous."

"I think you're trying to fatten me up."

She stooped and kissed his cheek, smelling of lavender. "Aye," she whispered. "You'll fetch a better price at market. Eat up."

She spun away and returned to the kitchen. Ethan tasted his chowder, which somehow exceeded the promise of its aroma.

Kannice appeared again a moment later, Kelf in tow, both of them carrying platters and bowls filled with stew and fish, potatoes and bread.

They had just placed their burdens on the table, when the tavern door opened with a squeak of hinges and a blast of cold air.

Kannice and Kelf turned. Ethan stood.

Two men entered the tavern. One was slight, about Ethan's height, with dark, watchful eyes and dark hair. The other was a mountain of a man—at least as big as Kelf—his dark hair straggly, his face broad and homely. Nap and Afton.

Behind them, sauntering with the self-assurance of the queen consort, came their employer, Sephira Pryce, Empress of the South End, the most notorious and feared thieftaker in all of Boston. Dark curls fell over her shoulders and down her back, sparkling with snowflakes. She wore a black cloak, also dusted with snow, and clasped at the neck with a golden brooch. Halting just inside the doorway, she glanced about the tavern, cool appraisal in her icy blue eyes, an insolent grin on her lovely face.

Wind whistled at her back, and flakes swept in onto the wooden floor.

"Would you mind closing the door?" Ethan said.

Sephira made the smallest of gestures. Afton shut the door, silencing the wind.

Ethan stepped in front of Kannice. "I should have been clearer. I meant with you on the other side of it."

Her laugh was throaty, unrestrained. Ethan had always thought it her best quality.

She removed her cloak, revealing her usual raiment: black breeches, a white shirt, and a velvet waistcoat that hugged her form with unnerving snugness. Nap took the cloak and draped it over an arm.

"I see we're just in time for supper. How lovely."

"They're not welcome here," Kannice said, pointing at Sephira's toughs. "For that matter, neither are you."

Afton's meaty hand disappeared into a pocket of his overcoat. Ethan guessed he carried a flintlock.

Ethan drew his blade and pushed up his sleeve exposing his forearm and the lattice of scars there from a lifetime of blood conjurings.

"Is that how it is, Ethan?" Sephira asked, seemingly unperturbed by Kannice's declaration and the threat implied by his blade. "Now that you're married, you're forbidden from visiting with your old friends?"

"Not at all. As soon as an old friend arrives, I'll be more than happy to visit. In the meantime, I believe Kannice instructed your men to leave her tavern."

Sephira gave a small pout. "Now that wasn't very nice."

"Sephira—"

"I need to speak with you," she said, all pretense vanishing, "and it's cold outside. Neither Nap nor Afton will do anything to anyone. They will sit in this corner" —she pointed to a table near the door—"and be as quiet as mice. You have my word."

"Your word," Kannice repeated, voice dripping with sarcasm.

Sephira went still, like a hunting cat. "Tread lightly, Missus Kaille," she said, a silken chill to her tone. "It's one thing to be rude, and quite another to question my honor."

Ethan laid a hand on Kannice's shoulder. "It's all right." To Sephira he said, "What is it we need to discuss that couldn't wait for daylight and an end to this storm?"

She smiled, exposing perfect teeth. "A fine question. Shall we sit?"

Sephira's toughs watched her, as if unsure of what they should do. Kannice cast a glance Ethan's way.

"It *is* cold out," he said, swayed, despite himself, by Sephira's hints.

Kannice rolled her eyes. "Fine. But not a word out of them. And if they so much as shuffle their feet, they're to leave. Understood?"

"Yes, ma'am." Ethan said.

She frowned.

Sephira crossed to their table, tossed two shillings onto the worn wood, and sat. "Whatever you're having smells quite good. I'd love some."

Kannice glared at the coins the way she would at vermin in her larder. It was more than she charged for a meal, but after a moment she swept the shillings off the table and into her pocket, and stalked off to the kitchen for another bowl.

Kelf hovered nearby, massive arms crossed over his chest, his glower shifting from the toughs to Sephira and back again.

"Sit down, Ethan," the empress said, mistress of any room she entered. "We have matters to discuss. And your chowder grows cold."

He had long resisted taking commands from her, even when the consequences of his defiance were far more dire than cold stew and sore feet, but he didn't bother to argue. He returned to his chair and lowered himself into it, setting his knife on the table within easy reach. After a moment's hesitation, he took another spoonful of chowder.

Sephira watched him across the table, mocking amusement on her lips.

"You look well enough," she said. "The soft life agrees with you, though you might want to curb your appetite a touch." She patted the underside of her own perfect chin with the back of her hand. "You've added a pound or two."

"What are you doing here, Sephira?"

"Yes, why have you come?" Kannice echoed, returning from behind the bar with Sephira's chowder. Ethan wondered if she had added anything to it. Dishwater? Spittle? Arsenic?

Apparently Sephira had the same thought. She eyed the bowl, and then looked up at Kannice. At last she shrugged and took a taste.

"Not bad," she said, raising her eyebrows. "You're a lucky man, Ethan, in so many ways."

He stared back at her, waiting.

She frowned. "You used to be more fun."

Ethan opened his mouth, intending to ask again why she had shown up at the Dowser on this of all nights, braving cold and wind and snow. But she raised a hand, forestalling him. She set her spoon on the table.

"Some months ago, when first you were tamed by your lovely bride, I said that on certain occasions, when I was presented with jobs that might lie within the purview of your meager talents and limited intelligence, I would offer you the chance to work for me, in exchange for one quarter of the fee paid by my employer."

"It was for one half," Kannice said. "And what makes you think he's interested in working with someone who does nothing but insult him?"

Sephira thinned a smile. "Are you his representative on top of everything else?"

"It *was* one half," Ethan said.

"Fine. Half, then."

"And what of Mariz?" Ethan went on. "Can't he help you with whatever work has come your way? You've been so happy to have a conjurer of your own. And now you need me?"

"This is about more than witchery." She canted her head, considering him. Her eyes glinted with candlelight. "In fact, I can honestly say that no one else in this world can help with this matter. I need you, Ethan," she purred, "as I never have before."

Ethan sensed Kannice bristling beside him, but he was used to this sort of goading from Sephira. So though he was, he had to admit, intrigued by what she'd said, he made every effort to mask his interest.

"Yes, I'm sure you do," he said, his tone dry. "Perhaps you'd like me to defeat a lock for you."

She remained unperturbed. "Nothing like that, no. Perhaps I should tell you something of my inquiry. I trust its significance for you will become apparent soon enough."

"By all means," he said, affecting indifference. The truth was, however, she had his attention.

She gave a low, gravelly chuckle; Ethan had the feeling he wasn't fooling her at all.

"What do you know about Edward and Lydia Fowls?" she asked, and took a mouthful of chowder. Her eyebrows rose and she turned a look of pure innocence Kannice's way. "This really is quite good."

Kannice stared back at her, saying nothing.

Ethan pondered the question. Edward Fowls and his wife were not, by any measure, counted among Boston's most famous personages. A relatively young couple—he might have been in his late twenties, or perhaps thirty, and she was several years younger—they lived in a brick house with marble colonnades on Garden Court Street near North Square, a lane known for its impressive homes. Theirs was neither the largest nor the smallest of those structures, though it was larger than they needed, as they had no children. Mister Fowls worked as a customs commissioner, which was one reason Ethan knew as much as he did about the man. He was a colleague of Geoffrey Brower, who was husband to Ethan's sister, Bett.

The Fowls were also neighbors to Thomas Hutchinson, acting governor of the province, whose home had been ransacked during the riots that followed implementation of the Stamp Tax back in 1765. Their home, which at the time belonged to Fowls's father, was spared by the rabble, but the events of that August night brought attention, largely unwanted, to all who lived on that usually quiet street.

And Edward Fowls had drawn Ethan's attention for one last reason. Despite their obvious wealth—Garden Court Street was not an address for those of modest means—Ethan could not have said with any confidence what it was Mister Fowls had done to earn his status or wealth. His appointment as a customs agent had come only in the last eighteen months, several years after he and his wife had moved into their home and established themselves in Boston's wealthy society. Some said that their money came largely from Lydia's family, but beyond that Ethan had heard few details.

He related all of this to Sephira as she ate.

"Very good," she said when he had finished. "I knew nearly as much— or perhaps I should say nearly as little—although not about dear Geoffrey. All that changed when I received a message from Mister Fowles a week ago today. It seems that on the night of December thirty-first, as the Fowls were visiting with friends on Beacon Street, celebrating the turn of the year, they were the victims of a most despicable crime."

"A crime you had nothing to do with?"

Her grin ossified. "Watch yourself, Ethan. I may need you, but I'll only brook so much."

He glanced pointedly at his blade before meeting her gaze again. "Your threats don't carry much weight here. Tell me about the theft."

"Yes, well, this is where things start to get interesting. To be honest with you, it took some time before they would tell me precisely what was pinched. I went to their home Wednesday morning, the second of January. The back door had been kicked in and a chest had been taken from a wardrobe in their master bedroom. Missus Fowls told me that it was filled with 'valuables.'"

"'Valuables,'" Ethan repeated. "That was all she said?"

"At first, yes. I asked several questions, of course, but she remained evasive. I had the distinct impression that summoning me had been her husband's idea. But what was just as noteworthy as her reticence on the subject of the chest's contents, was her certainty that nothing else had been taken, or even disturbed. Their house is well-appointed. The thief or thieves would have forsaken artwork, silver, jewelry, even a collection of carved jade figures from the Orient in Mister Fowls' study, just to get to that chest. Which, of course, begs several questions. Who were they? What was in that chest? And how did the thieves know to look for it?"

Ethan leaned forward. "I assume you persisted in asking such questions of Missus Fowls."

"I did, but still she wouldn't tell me much. Eventually I did get her to admit that the chest contained a certain amount of gold."

Even Kannice straightened at this.

"Gold jewelry?" Ethan asked. "Gold coins?"

"She wouldn't say."

"Then how are you supposed to retrieve what was taken?"

"A fine question," Sephira said. "One you may prove helpful in answering."

"So that's why—"

"No," she cut in. "Mariz might help me find the culprits. So might Sheriff Greenleaf. Patience, Ethan. Your connection to all of this lies a bit deeper."

He and Kannice exchanged glances. As they did, Afton stood and approached their table, as diffident as a school boy. Reaching Sephira, he hesitated, then bent close to her and whispered something. The more he said, the more her expression darkened, until she was scowling and he had straightened once more.

"Go sit down," she said.

The tough turned and shambled back to where he had been sitting.

"Is there something wrong?" Ethan asked.

Sephira seemed genuinely discomfited and wouldn't quite look at him. "He . . . he said that . . . that your stew smells quite delicious," she finally admitted, addressing Kannice. "And he and Nap were wondering if they might each have a small bowl." She stared daggers back at them. "At my expense, of course."

Kannice said nothing, but held out her hand. Sephira produced her purse and counted out four shillings. Again, Kannice did not bother correcting her as to the price of fare in the Dowser. Coin in hand, she nodded to Kelf, who appeared reluctant to give up standing watch over them. After a moment, he returned to the kitchen for two more bowls.

"You were saying that Missus Fowls refuses to reveal the exact contents of the stolen chest," Ethan prompted.

Sephira nodded with her usual crisp authority. "That's right. Fortunately, I'm more resourceful than she might have guessed. I made some inquiries with persons of authority here in Boston. I sent missives to London as well, but, of course, I don't expect a reply for some time, and I hope to have this matter resolved long before it arrives."

Against his will, Ethan found himself eager to hear what Sephira had learned. For her part, she took another spoonful of chowder, clearly relishing his impatience.

"You, there," Sephira said, obviously addressing Kelf, who had just emerged once more from the kitchen with food for her toughs. "They'll want bread as well."

The barman looked like he might refuse, but at a nod from Kannice he stomped back behind the bar.

"As far as anyone here can tell, Edward Fowls is no more or less than what he seems. The son of a middling family, a man of means but not wealth, of competence but not talent, of limited wit but certainly not intellect. In other words, he's the perfect customs agent."

"And what about Missus Fowls?"

Sephira turned coy. "Well, now we come to the heart of my tale. Unlike her husband, the charming Lydia is a good deal more than a first glance might suggest. She's clever, and, it turns out, willing to go to great lengths to conceal certain elements of her past."

"Such as?"

"Such as her true name."

Ethan narrowed his gaze. "Her true name?"

"She's Lydia Fowls now, of course. And before they were married, she was Lydia Sheed. Or so we were supposed to believe."

"An alias?"

"Yes. She claimed to have been born here in Boston, but we found only one record of anyone named Sheed, and that woman turned out to be her mother. The real Miss Sheed married and took her husband's name, but some time later, the daughter, Lydia, assumed her mother's family name. When I learned of this and confronted her, she admitted to changing her name to avoid the embarrassment of a series of scandals involving her father. By this time her parents were estranged, and the father had long since left Boston for . . . well, let's just say for warmer climes."

Ethan's pulse quickened at this, and warning bells pealed in his mind. He knew where all of this would lead. Impossible, and yet he knew.

"Care to guess at her true name, Ethan?" Sephira asked, enjoying herself far too much.

"I don't want any part of this," he said, his voice barely carrying.

Kannice covered his hand with her own slender fingers, which felt smooth and warmer than they should have been.

"Your hands are freezing," she whispered. She faced Sephira. "I think you should go."

Sephira's gaze never left Ethan's face. She held her lips parted in a sly smile, the knowledge in her sapphire eyes aimed like a weapon at the deepest secrets of his life.

"It's too late for that," she said. "Her name was Selker. Lydia Selker. But you knew that already, didn't you? Would you care to tell us her father's name?"

Kannice's eyes flicked between Sephira and Ethan, her brows bunched in concern.

"Rayne Selker," he said, the name coming out rough and low.

"The very same."

"Is that who I think it is?" Kannice asked. Because, of course, she knew from stories he had told her long ago.

But the rest—

"Who in God's name is Rayne Selker?" Kelf asked, returning from serving the toughs.

Who indeed?

II

Ethan first saw the *Ruby Blade* on a warm June morning in 1745. Boston's waterfront bustled with sailors and merchants, the smells of fish and ship's tar and sweat layered over salt and surf. Everywhere men shouted and laughed. A few sang. Gulls cried from atop masts and warehouse roofs.

The *Blade* was tied in at Wentworth's Wharf, her sails furled, the red lettering on her escutcheon gleaming in the sun.

Ethan had served in His Majesty's royal navy, aboard no less a ship than the *Stirling Castle*, a third-rate ship-of-the-line bearing seventy guns. A twenty-eight gun frigate like the *Blade* wasn't about to leave him overawed. But she was a handsome vessel, well-tended, and he knew with a glance that she would be far more agile than the *Castle*, an essential quality in privateering ships.

"She's a fine ship, isn't she?" said the boy beside him, looking up at Ethan with such pride one might have thought the lad captained the *Blade*. Derrey was tall for his age, fresh-faced, with dark eyes and a head of glossy black curls. His clothes fit him poorly, mostly because his uncle, a miserly, mean-spirited man, didn't care about the boy enough to buy him shirts and breeches that fit.

"Aye, she is."

Derrey beamed. "I told you."

"And you're sure they're looking for a hand?"

"Not just a hand," he said. "A second mate. And aye, I'm sure. Had it from one of the crew, who's a friend of the first mate himself."

Ethan couldn't help but grin at the boy's surety, and also at the racing of his own heart. This was the just the opportunity he needed. Elli might begrudge the time apart, but she would see the sense in seeking his fortune now, before they were married.

"Thanks, Derrey. This is perfect."

"I told you," the boy said, aggrieved, "it's Diver. All the lads have street names, and that's mine. You should get one, too."

"I'll stick with Ethan for now, thanks. It's served me well for a number of years."

Derrey shrugged with the condescending wisdom only a nine year-old could muster. "I guess you have to do what you think is best. But in the meantime, I'm Diver, all right?"

"Sure." He handed the lad sixpence, and started along the wharf toward the *Blade*.

Derrey followed. "If they hire you, will you tell them about me?"

"In time I will, certainly. But a privateering ship isn't likely to take on a lad your age. You're better off working the wharves."

"I'm tired of working the wharves. Ships are where the money is."

"Then a merchant ship, if you can convince them to take you on. But privateering can be risky work."

"So you'd rather I was on a merchant ship when it's boarded by French corsairs?"

Ethan halted and faced him, amused. "You've an argument for everything, don't you?"

Derrey lifted a shoulder again, looking pleased with himself. "Most things, at least."

"A merchant ship, Derrey. No privateering captain will bring you aboard at your age. Trust me."

His face fell. "Aye, all right."

Ethan gripped Derrey's shoulder a moment before continuing on to the ship.

"And it's Diver!" the lad called after him.

He raised a hand in acknowledgment, smiling to himself.

The *Blade* was tied to bollards on the pier, the ropes creaking as she shifted slightly in the gentle swells of the harbor. High overhead, an osprey circled with a flock of raucous gulls.

"Ahoy, the *Ruby Blade*," Ethan called.

A man appeared at the rails. "Ahoy. You, Kaille?"

"Aye, sir. Permission to come aboard?"

"Granted," the man said, waving Ethan toward the plank amidship.

Ethan walked the boards up to the rails and hopped onto the deck where the man waited for him. He was taller than Ethan, with pale gray eyes, and a handsome square face, browned by the sun. Thin lines crinkled at the corners of his eyes and mouth. A few strands of silver shone amid the wheaten hair at his temples, and in the plait that hung to the middle of his back. Ethan would have been hard-pressed to guess his age, but he thought the man had to be at least thirty-five years old. He wore red breeches, black boots, and a trim white linen shirt. The sailor proffered a hand and smiled a greeting.

"Allen Foster," he said, in an accent Ethan knew well. "First mate."

Ethan clasped his hand. The man had a grip like a vise.

"Ethan Kaille, sir. It's a pleasure to make your acquaintance."

"Your father is Ellis Kaille?"

He blinked his surprise. "He is. And your accent marks you as a Bristol man."

"As does yours."

Ethan schooled his features against burgeoning confidence. Whatever doubts he might have had with regard to his chances of being hired on the ship vanished in that moment.

"How do you know my father?"

"I've never actually met him," Foster said. "But most sailors out of Bristol know of Ellis Kaille. He has more medals than I have teeth."

Ethan looked away, taking the opportunity to survey the ship's decks, which were spotless.

He and his father had never been close, notwithstanding Ethan's decision to follow Ellis into the English navy. For he had long since followed his mother's example as well, and thus learned to harness the conjuring power that flowed in his veins. Ellis tolerated his wife's spellmaking, and that of his daughters, in particular Susannah, the older of Ethan's sisters. But he thought it an inappropriate diversion for any naval man, his son most of all.

No doubt Ellis had hoped that Ethan's enlistment would cure him of his "magickal tendencies." Instead, Ethan's brief service aboard the *Stirling Castle* cured him of his desire to sail with His Majesty's fleet.

He didn't mind being part of such a large crew—more than five hundred strong—nor had he shied from battle. The exigencies of naval combat intrigued him, even if they didn't fill him with the war lust he had seen in some of his fellow sailors.

But though the Battle of Toulon ended badly for the English fleet, and though the *Stirling Castle* was one of the lead vessels in that campaign, Ethan did not believe that his captain, Thomas Cooper, or the fleet commander, Thomas Matthews, deserved blame for the outcome. When both men were court-martialed, he was outraged, and he expressed his anger in a letter to his father.

"It is not your place to question the judgment of the naval high command," Ellis wrote in response. "Nor is it wise for you to commit such opinions to paper, lest you find yourself charged with treason. You are a sailor in His Majesty George II's navy. In that capacity you are expected to follow commands and acquit yourself in such a manner as will reflect best on your king, your country, your fleet, and your ship, not to mention your father and mother. Your duties amount to no more than that, and certainly no less."

Soon after receiving this missive, Ethan wrote to his father again, this time to ask that he use his influence within the navy to have Ethan excused from further service. He was sure Ellis would refuse, and so sent a second letter to his mother in Bristol, telling her of the request. He had no doubt that she prevailed upon her husband to honor Ethan's request, because somehow Ellis convinced those in authority to release Ethan from his commitment to the fleet.

Ethan left the *Stirling Castle* in July of 1744, returned to Bristol long enough to gather what few belongings he thought he would need in the New World, and sailed from his home city near the end of the summer. He arrived in Boston in September. By that time, it had been more than four months since he and his father had exchanged a word, by letter or in person.

"Allow me to show you rest of the ship," Foster said, after a brief silence, drawing Ethan's gaze again.

"I'd like that."

They walked toward the hatch leading down into the hold. "As you can see," the first mate said, "our captain expects us to keep a tidy ship. To his mind, a licensed vessel like ours is as much a part of the British fleet as any warship, and thus members of her crew should comport themselves by the standards of His Majesty's navy."

Ethan tried not to react to this, but he heard in the words a strong echo of his father's admonition. The crew members he could see were all dressed much the same way: red breeches, black boots, white shirts. Just as Foster wore.

"Well," Ethan began, feeling he ought to offer some comment, "there can be nothing wrong with discipline and order on a privateering ship."

Foster nodded, amusement tugging at the corners of his mouth. "Well, said." He kept his voice low. "You'll do just fine."

"I didn't mean—"

"Don't trouble yourself," the first mate went on, still speaking quietly as they reached the hatch. "There's a few of us know how to have fun, without violating any of the captain's rules of course. At least the spirit of them." He grinned again, and Ethan gave a grudging smile of his own.

They went below, into a hold that was as neat as any he had ever seen, including that of the *Stirling Castle*. Familiar smells soured the air—mold, sweat, urine, stale ale and old food—but they were more muted than on other ships. And the order of the space was unusual to say the least. Barrels were set in rows and crates were stacked in exact columns. Pyramids of cannon balls were set beside each of the guns. Even the rolled up hammocks of the crew were arranged with unnerving precision.

Ethan felt some of his enthusiasm for this position sluicing away.

"It's not quite as bad as it seems," Foster said in that same confidential tone. "The captain keeps to his quarters much of the time, and, for the most part, so long as we keep things clean the way he likes, he leaves us be. Not always, of course. But mostly."

"And the ship does well?" Ethan asked, facing him. "In its raids, I mean. I miss being at sea, but mostly I'm doing this because I need the money."

Foster lifted an eyebrow. "That's why we're all doing it, lad." He sobered. "She does all right. We generally keep to short runs. Captain doesn't like to be away from Boston for too long at any one time. That can limit our take a little. We're hoping to do better on this voyage than we did on the last." His grin this time appeared forced. "You'll help us with that, won't you? A navy man and all."

"I'll try, sir, of course. And our shares—"

"Captain will talk to you about that. Not my place."

"Right. I should have . . . Forgive me."

"This way then," Foster said, turning and starting back up the stairs.

Ethan followed, aware as they reached the deck once more that several of the crew were watching them. Him, really. He couldn't read much in their expressions beyond a sort of detached curiosity. They didn't appear welcoming, but neither were they overtly hostile. Ethan chanced a nod at one of the men, a swarthy, bald fellow, tall and lean. The man stared back at him, offering no response. Ethan looked away.

They walked to the stern of the *Blade*, pausing before the wooden door to the captain's quarters. With a glance at Ethan, Foster rapped on the door. At a summons from within, Foster opened the door and gestured Ethan inside.

Ethan hesitated. He had been aboard enough ships to know that one didn't simply enter the captain's quarters without leave from the man himself.

"At ease, sailor," the captain said in a deep baritone, pivoting at his desk to glance at Ethan. "You may enter."

"Thank you, sir," Ethan said, entering the quarters.

Foster left them, closing the door behind him.

The captain wore a powdered wig that ended in a plait, and accentuated his tanned features in the dim light of the chamber. He stood as tall as Ethan, his build average, his eyes dark and widely spaced, his mien youthful, bland, and impassive. Ethan doubted the captain was as old as his first mate. Selker extended a hand, which Ethan gripped. The man's handshake was mild compared with that of Foster.

"You're Mister Kaille?"

"Aye, sir. Ethan Kaille, originally of Bristol."

"Captain Rayne Selker."

"It's my pleasure, sir."

The captain sat in a narrow wooden chair and indicated with a lean, graceful hand that Ethan should do the same.

"Foster tells me you served in His Majesty's navy."

"Yes, sir."

"Aboard the *Stirling Castle*, no less."

"Yes, that's right."

"And why are you no longer under Captain Cooper's command?"

Ethan stared, wet his lips. "Well, after the court-martial—"

"Captain Cooper was reinstated to his command, even if Admiral Matthews was not."

"Yes, I know. But—"

"Perhaps you felt you knew better than those who saw fit to return the captain to his post."

"No, sir!" Ethan said, drawing himself up. "Just the opposite. I was infuriated and disillusioned by the courts-martial themselves. I wanted nothing more to do with the British navy."

"And so you quit."

Ethan frowned, feeling trapped by his own choices. No matter his reasons for leaving the navy, Captain Selker seemed inclined to judge him harshly.

"I felt I could no longer serve in good conscience, sir."

"And how did you manage to leave the king's service? The British navy seldom makes it easy for ordinary sailors to renege on such a commitment."

He felt certain the man knew the answer to this already; he wanted to hear Ethan admit to exploiting his father's influence. Ethan was many things, but a coward had never been one of them.

"My father is an officer in the navy, sir. I prevailed upon him to facilitate my . . . my resignation."

Selker's expression curdled. "I see."

For moments that stretched on and on, they sat in silence, refusing to look each other in the eye.

"You understand, Mister Kaille, that the *Ruby Blade* sails in service of His Majesty, just as does the *Stirling Castle* and other naval ships. We may be privateers, and we may concern ourselves at least in part with profit, but with each boarding we strike a blow at the French in support of the King's war."

"Yes, sir. Mister Foster told me as much."

"Did he?" Selker asked, his tone betraying skepticism.

"Yes, sir, he did. And if I may, I want you to understand that I remain a loyal subject of His Majesty and the Empire. It may be that some men are better suited than others to life on a warship. I was outraged by the treatment of my captain and Admiral Matthews. That's why I left. And now . . . now I need to make a living."

"So it's gold you're after."

"I seek employment, yes. Just like every other man on this vessel." He heard in his own words an echo of what Foster had said to him moments before. Still, he forged on. "But I assure you, Captain, I'm a skilled sailor. I've courage, strength, and good sense, and I'll bring all to bear in service to this vessel. I give you my word."

"I'd like to believe you, Mister Kaille. But I would assume that you swore a similar oath, and a more formal one at that, when you enlisted in His Majesty's navy. And so I'm forced to wonder what value to place on your word."

It was all Ethan could do to keep from lurching to his feet and storming from the chamber. Bad enough that the captain should demonstrate such disapproval of his decision to leave the navy, but to compound that by questioning Ethan's integrity . . . It was almost too much for Ethan to endure. But endure it he did. He stared back at the man, refusing to flinch from his glare.

"I hope, sir," he said, struggling to keep his voice level, "that you will give me the chance to prove the worth of my word."

Selker held his gaze, appearing unimpressed. "We shall see, Mister Kaille. We shall see. For now, you may go."

Ethan sat for the span of another heartbeat, Selker watching him, seeming to dare him to object to this dismissal.

"Thank you, sir," he finally said, standing and crossing to the door.

He cast one more look at the captain, but by that time Selker had turned his attention to a sheaf of paper on his desk. Ethan opened the door, slipped out into the daylight and briny air, and closed the door behind him, taking care to do so gently.

After the dark of the chamber, he had to blink several times before his eyes adjusted to the glare of sun and water.

Foster spotted him from near the mainmast and started in his direction. Ethan met him at the end of the quarterdeck.

"How did that go?" the man asked. His voice sounded falsely bright, giving Ethan the sense that he knew full well what had transpired in the captain's quarters.

"Well," Ethan said, "I don't think I'll be joining your crew after all."

Foster tucked his chin in surprise. "She's a fine ship, Kaille."

"Aye, she is. This isn't my choice. Your captain made it quite clear that he doesn't trust me, and isn't inclined to bring me aboard as a member of his crew."

The first mate chuckled at this, and waved a hand, dismissing his concerns. "Don't you worry about that. Our captain's young and as full of himself as most his age." He looked Ethan up and down, as if only just taking note of Ethan's youth. "Forgive me, but it's the truth. My point is, he relies on me for guidance in such matters, and I believe you'll be a fine addition to our crew."

As much as he appreciated the sentiment, Ethan didn't share the first mate's surety.

"Captain Selker and I will speak of this in the evening. Where can we find you?"

"I've let a room in a private home near Fort Hill. Missus Keighly's."

Foster nodded. "I know the place."

"And if you can't find me there, ask Derrey Jervis. He has an uncommon knack for tracking people down."

"He does at that," Foster said, his affection for the lad sounding genuine. He walked Ethan back to the gangplank. "Await my word, Mister Kaille. I have every confidence that you'll be a member of this crew before long, and that you'll be sailing with us when we leave this pier in two days' time."

Ethan thanked him, shook his hand, and descended the walkway to the wharf. He doubted Foster could change the captain's mind about him, but on the off chance that he was wrong, he needed to speak with Elli. He thought it likely that she would be even less pleased with him than Selker had been.

III

Sephira eyed Kelf in the candlelight, far more smug than she had any right to be.

"Ethan," she said in mock reproach. "Don't tell me you haven't shared this tale with your friends. Or, dare I hope it, with your wife."

"I think it's time you were leaving," Kannice said, a growl in her voice.

"You don't know, do you?"

"Of course I know," she said, contempt in her voice. "I've known for nearly as long as we've been together. And whether or not he tells others is entirely up to him. Now get out of my bar."

"It's all right, Kannice."

She rounded on him. "You keep telling me that. But it's not all right. She's a demon, and she doesn't deserve your help or your consideration. You certainly shouldn't be defending her."

"I'm not," he said, weary. "I want to know what this matter with the Fowls is about, and I want to share in her gold. The rest is . . ." He made a vague gesture. "I don't care anymore who hears the tale. Everyone in this tavern knows I'm a conjurer."

He and Kelf exchanged glances. The barman had only learned of Ethan's spellmaking talent last March, on the night of the shootings on King Street, when Ethan had used a healing spell, cast in love and desperation, to save Kannice's life. Pleased as he was that Kannice survived, Kelf hadn't approved then of Ethan's magicking. Perhaps he didn't still. But their friendship had survived the revelation, which was all that concerned Ethan.

"And," he went on, "if everyone here learns the truth of the *Ruby Blade* so be it. I've borne that secret for too many years."

"That's surprisingly mature of you, Ethan." The words were kind enough, but Sephira appeared disappointed.

"One less secret for you to lord over me," he said with a reflexive smile.

Kelf looked lost. "The *Ruby Blade*," he said with a furrowed brow. "I seem to remember hearin' somethin' about that when I was younger. Don't recall much of it now."

"It was quite the *cause célèbre* at the time," Sephira said, warming to the discussion. "Or so I've been told. I was far too young to have any clear memory of the events as they happened."

"Then why don't you allow me to relate them. That's what you've wanted all along, isn't it?"

"What I want is your help in finding that stolen chest. But we'll begin with this."

"You really don't have to," Kannice said, her head bent close to his. "Not tonight at least."

He started to say again that it was all right, but he stopped himself. "I know I don't. But I meant what I said. I'm tired of keeping this secret."

She took his hand and held it to her lips.

Sephira rolled her eyes. "Oh, please."

"Rayne Selker was the ship's captain." Ethan addressed Kelf. Somehow that seemed easier than telling Sephira. "And from the beginning, he was reluctant to trust me."

"Because of . . . you know." Kelf's cheeks reddened. "Your conjurin'?"

"No, he didn't yet know about that. It was because I'd left the navy after Toulon. And probably because Foster wanted me. They were at odds all along."

"Who's Foster?"

"Forgive me," Ethan said with a shake of his head. "I'm getting ahead of myself. The important things to know are that I left the navy after our loss at the Battle of Toulon, that I sailed to North America soon after, and that by the spring of 1745 I had my reasons for wanting to go back to sea."

Sephira slanted a frown at him. "For someone who speaks of wanting to shed secrecy, you're being awfully vague. 'I had my reasons'?"

Ethan colored, but kept his gaze on her rather than on Kannice.

"It's all right." Kannice laughed, as if surprised to hear herself saying it this time. "I know why you wanted to sail. You might as well tell them that as well."

"You're certain?" he asked her.

"Why not? You're married to me now, aren't you? And there's nothing Elli can do about that."

He grinned. "As if she'd dare even try."

IV

The Taylor family owned a grand marble house atop Copp's Hill, on Charles Street, in one of the most opulent neighborhoods of Boston's North End. Vernon "Van" Taylor, Marielle's father, was one of the city's foremost shipbuilders and a prominent member of Boston society.

So prominent, in fact, that others of a similar social status, who were acquainted with Mister Taylor and his family, had already taken notice of Ethan's affection for his daughter, and pronounced him an unfit match for the girl.

As Ethan made his way up Copp's Hill toward the Taylor mansion, he was aware of people watching him, marking with disapproval his intrusion upon their demesne.

At the waterfront, where men were more likely to know of Ethan's father and his military accomplishments, Ethan rarely felt out of place. Even now, after all that had happened to fray their relationship, mention of

Captain Ellis Kaille remained a powerful credential for him. Ethan's exchange with Allen Foster proved as much.

But here, among Boston's wealthiest, his clothes were too plain, his hair too unkempt, his speech and manners just a shade too rough.

Elli didn't seem to notice. Or if she did, she didn't care. In a way, perhaps, that might have been part of what had drawn her to him. He wasn't like other men she knew. He was respectable, but he didn't conform precisely to her father's expectations. Even at his tender age Ethan was wise enough to recognize the allure for an eighteen year-old girl of that combination.

Edith Taylor, Marielle's mother, always welcomed Ethan into her home with a kind mien and generous words, and Jane, Elli's younger sister, had already expressed her enthusiasm for their marriage, and for Elli's room, which she would take the moment Ethan and Elli moved to a house of their own.

Mister Taylor, taciturn on the best of days, remained cool toward Ethan and had thus far refrained from partaking in any conversation that touched on a possible betrothal. True, he was a creature of the wharves, just as was Ethan. In this instance, however, that connection did not help Ethan's cause. Of all men in Boston, Van Taylor would be most familiar with the circumstances of Ethan's family. He had been a navy man himself, so he knew how little Ellis had made from his captaincies. And he knew as well what it would have taken for Ethan to leave the service. Had he not been so devoted to his elder daughter, Mister Taylor might already have barred Ethan from their home. As it was, he barely tolerated the romance that had grown between Marielle and Ethan.

Ethan believed he had but one hope of winning the man over: He needed to make his fortune now, or at least be able to present to Mister Taylor a plausible path to a comfortable and respectable life, before he could ask for Elli's hand. He hoped that Mister Foster would succeed in convincing Captain Selker to make him second mate of the *Ruby Blade*.

Reaching the top of the hill, Ethan crossed Charles Street, followed the flagstone path to the Taylor's door, and tapped on it with the shining brass lion's head knocker. After a few moments, the door opened revealing Henry, the Taylor's African servant. He wore a suit of brown linen, and a white silk shirt beneath.

"Good afternoon, Mister Kaille."

"Good afternoon, Henry. Is Miss Taylor taking callers?"

"She is, sir. Come in."

Ethan followed Henry through the marble foyer into a sitting room with oaken floors and portraits of Edith, Marielle, and Jane adorning the walls. Henry left him there. Moments later, Marielle breezed into the room with a whisper of satin and the sweet scent of lilac. Her dark hair had been braided and coiled, revealing the gentle curve of her neck, the smooth slope of her shoulders. Her gown, emerald green, was a perfect match for her eyes, the bodice accenting her figure.

She hurried to him, brushed her lips across his cheek, and clasped him to her for an instant before breaking away. Jane followed her into the room an instant later. She wore satin as well, pale blue—the color of her eyes. The sisters resembled each other in certain ways—the olive complexions and flawless oval faces. But Jane remained lean and coltish, her limbs appearing slightly too long for her form. Marielle, on the other hand . . . well, she was the most beautiful woman Ethan had ever known. And somehow she loved him.

Selker had to hire him.

"We were hoping you'd visit," Jane said. "Weren't we, Elli?"

"Yes, we were." A warm alto, soft and strong both. A voice he often heard in his dreams. Her smile was a gift that made his heart dance.

"Perhaps we might take a stroll in your gardens," Ethan managed to say. "There are matters I very much wish to discuss with you."

"Can I come along?" Jane asked.

Elli's gaze lingered on his for a moment longer, a question in her shining eyes.

"I'd like to speak with your sister in private, Jane. If I may. And after, you're free to join us. I hear you've been working on a new song. I'd very much like to hear it."

Jane blushed. "If you hadn't asked so nicely, I'd have said no. Fine, then. Have your time alone. And then come back to me."

"Thank you, Janey," Elli said.

"Don't call me that."

Elli brushed a stray lock of hair from her sister's brow. "I think I will."

She led Ethan through the house to a rear door that opened onto an elaborate garden. Another stone path wound among beds of marigolds and lilies, lavender and peonies. The drone of honeybees filled the air, and a wren chattered from a cluster of woodbine.

"She really is quite fond of you," Elli said, lifting the hem of her gown so that it wouldn't drag along the grass and stone.

"She's a girl of uncommon good taste."

Elli arched an eyebrow. "She's young and gullible."

He laughed. Elli glanced up at the house. Following the line of her gaze, Ethan saw a lace curtain shift in an upstairs window. Her mother?

"What did you wish to discuss?"

"They don't yet trust me," Ethan said.

She hooked her arm through his. "Perhaps it's me they don't trust." She didn't look at him, but her color rose.

Ethan's heart beat a little faster.

"My mother is very fond of you," she went on. "You know that. And Father . . . well, he's slower to warm to everyone. He just needs some more time."

"I don't think so. He wants to know that I can provide for you, give you the life that you deserve. Until I can prove to him that I'm capable of doing so, he'll never allow us to marry."

"Of course he will. My father loves me, and I love you. Therefore, he'll grow to be as fond of you as Mother is." She eyed him through her lashes. "It's simple arithmetic."

She wasn't making this easy for him.

"I really don't believe it's that simple."

Elli halted, disengaged her arm from his. "What is it you're trying to say?" Her tone had hardened, as had her features. She was ever a beauty, but at times like these she put him in mind of starlight: glorious, but remote and chill.

"If you were my daughter—"

"I'm not. I'm the woman who wishes to be your wife."

"If you were my daughter," he began again, enunciating each word, "I would insist that any man who fancied himself an appropriate suitor have the means to care for you as you deserve. Or if not the means quite yet, at least a notion of how such a life might be provided. That, I believe, is what has prevented your father from viewing me as a suitable husband for you."

"And so now you claim to know my own father better than I do."

He didn't respond, but merely watched her, waiting as she reined in her pique.

"And so do you have one?" An admission in the question, acknowledgment that her father's reserve had bothered her as well. "A notion, I mean. Do you know how you might convince him?"

"There's a ship—"

"Ethan, no."

"It's called the *Ruby Blade*. It's a grand name, isn't it? Full of promise."

She scowled. "You could call it the '*Diamond Mine*,' and I still wouldn't approve."

"She's a privateering vessel."

"Privateering is dangerous work."

"No more so than serving in the king's navy."

"Barely less so."

"Elli—"

"You would be a member of the crew?"

"Second mate. It's not certain yet, but I spoke with the captain and first mate just before coming here. The first mate seems to think I'll be hired."

She scanned the garden, her lips thinned, but he could see she was considering the opportunity.

"Second mate at your age," she said. "Even Father would be impressed with that."

"As I said, I don't have the job yet. But if not this ship then another. Privateering is my best chance, Elli. This war won't last forever. I give it another two or three years at the most. And then the only jobs at sea will be on merchant ships. My share on a privateering vessel could be enough to start us out. And enough as well to earn your father's blessing."

Her brow creased. "Two years? Three? We'd be apart for that long?"

"No. I might serve on the ship for several years, but we'll be back in Boston every few months. I'm sure of it. The first mate mentioned that the captain prefers not to be away from his home for too long."

"Still, Ethan, months at a time, for so long."

He took both her hands, glanced up again at that curtained window. Seeing no one there, he leaned forward and kissed her lips. Despite everything, she smiled.

"I don't want to be away from you for even a day. You know that. But we have to plan for our future. I'd gladly endure some months apart if it means a lifetime together."

Her expression turned wry. "With a few silvered words like that, you'll have my father convinced in no time."

"That was my thinking."

She eyed him and sighed. "All right. Take the posting and earn your gold. But no mermaids for you, Mister Kaille. You're mine."

He kissed her again, his heart as full as it had ever been. "Aye, that I am."

Elli reclaimed his arm, and they resumed their circuit around the garden.

"How long have you been thinking about this?" she asked. "The privateering, I mean."

He winced at the question, knowing he should have mentioned it to her long ago. "For some time," he confessed. "Two or three months now."

"And you were afraid to tell me?"

"Aye. I knew you wouldn't like the idea of it: the uncertainty, the months apart, the danger."

"Well, you're right, I don't like any of those things. But I dislike secrets even more. So let's promise each other now: I'll try to be more amenable to your plans, and in return you're to share everything with me. *Everything*. No secrets."

"Of course." He heard the hesitation in his reply, and knew she did as well.

"I know you want to protect me, Ethan," she said misinterpreting his reluctance to agree, "but I'm a grown woman. By the time my mother was my age, she had already miscarried once and given birth to me. If I'm old enough to be your wife, I'm old enough to be your confidante as well. That's how a marriage ought to be. That's how ours *will* be."

"You're right," he said, forcing brightness into his voice, hoping this response had been more convincing.

But he cringed within, for he had one secret that he'd yet to share with her. And he didn't know how to broach the subject.

She and her family were, like so many high families in Boston, devoted Congregationalists. Her father often expressed his admiration for the writings of Cotton Mather and he defended the actions Mather had taken in Salem a half century before, as had the famed minister himself up until the day he died.

Elli worshipped her father, and often adopted his beliefs and opinions as her own.

So how was Ethan to confide in her that he was a conjurer, that his sisters were conjurers, that his mother, and her mother before her, and countless others going back through generations of Jerill women, were all conjurers? How could he tell her that he had cast more spells than he could count? He had spilled blood in order to cast. He had drawn upon herbs and tree leaves and grass, and had even summoned illusions from fire and from the vapor suspended in the very air they breathed.

Magick had been an essential element of his life for as long as could recall. His mother had healed his cuts and bruises with it when he was a boy. She had conjured flame to wick every evening of his childhood, and had used the same power to kindle cooking fires in the family hearth. Ethan and Susannah had vied with each other for their mother's praise, mastering the Latin needed to conjure, learning spell after spell. Of all the many thin white scars on his forearm—evidence of so many years of spellmaking—he could still point to the first, the origins of his initiation into blood magick.

Most gentlemen did not fold up their shirt sleeves in front of a lady, but Elli had seen Ethan split wood for the hearth. She had watched as her mother invited Ethan to help pull weeds from the Taylor family garden, an invitation Ethan had been happy to accept. But never once had he allowed Elli to see his forearms. His left forearm. Surely such an informality could have been forgiven under these circumstances. But to do so would have been to expose that web of scarring, to prompt questions he was not ready to answer, and might never be.

It comes from my family, he could have told her. *Like my blue eyes and my brown hair. Denying it would be like denying my name.*

Except that would have been a lie. He could just as easily have followed the example of Bett, his other sister, the one with whom he had so little in common, the one who favored his father over his mother. She had long since forsworn spellmaking, and instead had become as fierce as her rector in condemning conjurers as witches. Ethan could have done the same.

The truth, which he could hardly imagine ever sharing with her, was that he valued his spellmaking gift. He took comfort in knowing he could protect himself and those he loved, be it from wounds he could heal, or would-be attackers he could fend off with conjurings. More than that, he *enjoyed* casting spells, even knowing that with each expression of his magick he risked revealing to the world that he could conjure. He feared being hanged as a witch; he would be a fool not to. But though he concealed this part of who he was, he would not abandon it. He possessed but a fraction of the skill he had seen in his mother, but he took tremendous satisfaction in a casting well-executed, and he intended to hone further his abilities.

Loving Elli as he did, he wanted to share all of this with her. If only he could show her what a casting might do, perhaps he could make her understand and begin to overcome her fear of magick, her hatred of so-called witches. His affection for her, though, could not blind him to how stubborn she could be, how committed to her notions regardless of how wrong-headed he thought them. And so this secret he kept, though it was fraught with danger should she discover the truth.

"You're still reluctant," she said, regarding him, appearing pensive and unsettled. Even her frowns were lovely. "I can tell. You know, you're not that much older than I. And in spite of what all men seem to believe, women do not require coddling."

"Cuddling, did you say?" he asked, trying to turn the conversation. "You don't require cuddling?"

Her frown deepened. "At times you really are far too much a man."

He kept silent, chagrined, and they walked on. His small jest had served only to make her more cross with him. Perhaps she was right, and what he needed to do was confide in her fully. She loved him. She would understand. More, she would be grateful for his honesty.

But how to broach the subject.

"You're right," he said. "From this day forward, I shall tell you all. You have my word."

"Thank you." Her tone warmed slightly.

Ethan took a breath. "In fact there's something else I wish to discuss with you."

She looked his way again. "All right."

"I . . . I'm not quite sure where to begin." He paused, feeling her eyes still upon him. After a few moments he decided on an approach to the matter. "What did your rector talk about in his sermon this past Sunday?"

"That's an odd question, and one you should be able to answer yourself. I've been meaning to speak with you about this. Your absence from King's Chapel on Sunday was most conspicuous, as it has been for weeks now. Father asked Reverend Price if you could attend services as our guest, and the rector agreed. Each week, when you don't join us, it is an embarrassment for Father. And for me. You worry about having enough coin in your pocket to impress Father, but the truth is, he would be far more impressed with you if you proved yourself a man of faith, a man of God. As far as he is concerned, *that* is the true measure of my future husband. It is for me as well, Ethan. You should know that by now. Prove yourself in the eyes of the Lord, and the rest will be granted to you by Providence."

Ethan schooled his expression as she spoke, trying to appear contrite, trying to make it seem that he considered her every word. But within, he wilted. If his failure to attend Sunday's sermon disturbed her and her father so much, what would the confession he'd had in mind to give do to them?

He couldn't tell her. He realized that now. Perhaps someday, when they had been married for a time, when they had a home and a family, and all in their life together was settled and comfortable—perhaps he could tell her then. But not now. Which meant that he would have to forswear magick after all. He would never speak against conjurers as Bett did, but if he wanted Elli to be his wife—and he did, desperately—he would have to attend King's Chapel with her, whisper "Amen" to sermons that railed against practitioners of the "dark arts," listen with equanimity as others condemned him and his kind as witches, as servants of Satan, as devils on this earth.

"Forgive me," she said. "I interrupted you. What was it you wanted to discuss with me?"

He felt as though he was choking on ashes, so dry was his mouth. "Just that," he managed. "I've realized I must start to show my piety. In order to earn your father's respect and affection. And in order to deserve yours. I don't know how soon I'll be setting sail, but until then . . . and as often as I can while we're in port, I'll attend services with you."

She had halted to stare at him, astonishment and joy mingling with her tears. "Truly, Ethan?"

"Yes." He smiled, ashamed of his evasion, but elated by what his words had done to her.

Elli threw her arms around him, heedless of who might see. "This will mean more to him than gold," she said, breathless. "Just as it does to me."

She held him tight for another second before releasing him, taking his arm once more, and resuming their stroll.

He had come to win her approval for his posting aboard the *Blade*, or whatever privateering vessel might take him. And in this he had succeeded. This was a good day, and, at a good word from Mister Foster, it might be one of great moment. He had been poised to reach for too much. Telling Elli now of his abilities would have been rash, to say the least. Reason had prevailed. He had been fortunate, in spite of his reckless instincts.

So Ethan told himself.

But as they circled back to the house to hear Jane sing whatever song she had mastered most recently, he feared he had lost his integrity amid the twists and turns of their stroll.

V

Allen Foster proved true to his word. Despite Ethan's difficult exchange with Captain Selker, he received a missive at Missus Keighly's that very evening. The following morning, he returned to the *Ruby Blade*'s berth on Wentworth's Wharf, and at a welcoming word from the deck, boarded the ship.

There he was greeted by the first mate and captain. The latter seemed a changed man. He formally offered Ethan the post of second mate aboard the vessel, and shook Ethan's hand with enthusiasm when Ethan accepted.

"I must say, sir, I'm surprised by the offer."

Foster shot him a warning glance and gave a curt shake of his head.

"Why is that, Mister Kaille?" Selker asked.

"Well, I just thought . . . after our conversation, I mean—"

"Yes, yes. I know. I was brooding over other affairs and shouldn't have taken out my frustration on you. You left the navy. What does it matter? His Majesty's loss is our gain. Isn't that right, Mister Foster?"

"I believe it is, Captain."

"Well, thank you, sir," Ethan said. "I'm very excited to be sailing with you."

"Yes. Good. Carry on then." The captain turned on his heel and walked back toward his quarters.

Ethan and Foster watched him.

"Don't do that again," the first mate said, his voice low and hard.

Ethan blinked. "Do what?"

The man faced him. "It's no small thing convincing the captain to do those things he's not inclined to do. Like hiring you. I worked long and hard to get you this posting. Reminding him of what he said yesterday only puts doubt in his mind, and it risks undoing all my efforts on your behalf. Understand?"

Ethan nodded.

"When he makes a decision, especially a decision we want, something we've worked for, leave it be."

"I will. My apologies."

Foster waved this away. "No matter. We'd like to sail this evening. Can you be ready?"

"Of course, sir."

"Good." He walked to the bow of the ship, away from much of the crew, who brought stores aboard and loaded them into the hold in a steady stream, like ants carrying food to a colony. "As with most privateering vessels, we work on shares," he said, lowering his voice again. "After the king and his men collect their thirty per cent of our take, and the ship's owners take theirs, the rest is ours to divide. We've a complement of eighty-four men, plus the captain and the two of us. Most of the crew get a single share. A few—the bosun, the carpenter, ship's surgeon, the gunner, sail master—they get four each. I serve as quartermaster as well as first mate, so I get seven. Captain gets ten. You'll be getting four like those others I mentioned."

"Thank you, sir."

"I trust you'll earn it, Kaille. We've need of a man like you. As I told you yesterday, our take hasn't been what I'd hoped. But we're going to change that, you and I. And when we do, everyone will be happier."

"Yes, sir. I'll do my very best."

Foster remained sober. "I'm sure of it. We've some formalities to address, but those can wait until you return. Go on now. Settle your affairs and be back here when evening falls. The tide should be turning then."

Ethan grasped the man's proffered hand one last time before hurrying off the ship and back to his room at Fort Hill. When he had gathered his few belongings, he returned to the Taylor home to say his farewells.

Elli wept openly, as did Jane. Ethan shed a few tears of his own. Missus Taylor wished him Godspeed and appeared genuinely moved by the emotions she saw in Ethan and her daughter. Mister Taylor wasn't there.

His heart aching, Ethan plodded back to the waterfront oblivious of all that was around him. He nearly collided with Diver on Ann Street in front of the Wharf.

"You all right, Ethan?" the lad asked, peering at Ethan, his features scrunched. "You look like you've been through a war."

He tried to smile, failed. "Not a war, no. Just a goodbye. And yes, I'm fine."

Diver eyed the satchel Ethan had slung over his shoulder. "You leaving Boston?"

"Aye. Thanks to you, I'm second mate aboard the *Ruby Blade*. We sail tonight."

The boy's expression brightened. "I really did it!"

"You really did, and I'm indebted to you."

"Can you hire me onto the ship? I can leave tonight; I don't mind."

"I already told you, Diver. Not on this ship, not at your age. But this will lead to other postings to other ships, and when it does, I'll find a place for you in my crew. You have my word."

Diver didn't hide his disappointment, but he nodded and stuck out a slender hand. "Farewell then, Ethan," he said, solemn and earnest. "And safe return."

Ethan shook his hand and then reached into his bag for an old blade he'd first acquired in Bristol some years before.

"You know, Diver, I have a knife that I keep on my belt, but this one I've had forever. I wouldn't want it to get lost at sea. Can you keep it for me?"

His eyes lit up. "You mean it?"

"I do. You'll keep it safe, right?"

"'Course I will!"

Diver was still ogling the blade as Ethan strode down the wharf toward his ship.

Upon boarding the *Ruby Blade* this time, Ethan was greeted by Foster, who steered him to the middle of the deck, and in a ringing voice introduced him as the ship's new second mate. The crew's response to these tidings was more muted than Ethan might have hoped. A few men nodded his way. The bosun, a burly, red-haired man with a Scottish burr, gripped his hand and gave his name as Thaddeus Holme. But most of the sailors ignored him, continuing about their business.

Ethan tried not to take this tepid welcome to heart. The ship was moments from leaving port, he reminded himself. He hoped the men would be more receptive once they were underway.

Moments after Foster's announcement, Captain Selker emerged from his quarters, the scowl on his boyish face giving him a petulant mien.

Seeing Ethan, he muttered, "At last," loud enough for everyone on deck to hear. "I want us on sweeps, now," he said, this time pitching his voice to carry. "We've tarried here long enough."

"Aye, Captain," Foster called in reply.

But already Selker had spun away and was returning to his quarters.

"Stow your bag below," the first mate said. "For tonight, you'll accompany me. That should give you a chance to learn how things go on the *Blade*. Tomorrow you'll begin to learn your duties."

"Aye, sir."

He took his satchel below, set it in a corner out of the way, and rejoined Foster on deck.

Whatever the crew's response to Ethan's arrival, there could be no doubting their competence or the alacrity with which they followed orders. Within a few moments the ship's lines had been taken in and her oars dropped into the harbor waters. With a shouted order from Foster, and the first sharp pull of the starboard oars, the ship lurched away from the wharf. Soon she was running with the outgoing tide, cutting through the harbor swells, away from the city and southward toward Dorchester Point and Castle Island.

Once on open waters, the sweeps were shipped and the sails on all three masts unfurled and raised. The evening air was cool and calm, but there was breeze enough to billow the cloth and carry them as they tacked eastward past Hull and Nantasket Peninsula.

Stars spread across a darkening sky, and the gibbous moon rose ahead of them, blood red and huge. One of the sailors lit lanterns and set them in hooks on the quarterdeck and by the main mast.

As painful as it had been leaving Elli, Ethan couldn't deny that he had missed life on a ship, and nights on the water most of all. He could think of nothing more peaceful than gazing up at a star-speckled sky on the gentle swells of a calm sea.

"All right there, Kaille?"

Foster's voice.

Ethan turned and stepped away from the rail. "Aye, sir. Is there something you need me to do?"

"No." The first mate joined him, leaned against the rail himself to stare out over the water. "Though there'll be plenty in the days ahead. I'm about to go below. You can sleep up here if you like or in one of the hammocks in the hold. There are empty ones deeper in, away from the hatch."

"That'll be fine, sir."

"Captain prefers that his mates sleep and eat among the crew. Don't know what you were used to elsewhere, but that's how it is on the *Blade*."

Foster's tone implied that he didn't like this arrangement. Ethan thought it best not to comment.

"I think I'll sleep below," was all he said.

The first mate nodded and together they made their way into the hold.

Ethan crossed to the corner where he'd left his satchel, but even as he approached the bag in the dim lantern light he saw that it had been moved. Not a lot. He faltered only a moment. No doubt someone had kicked it by accident, or maybe stumbled on it.

He glanced at Foster, but the first mate busied himself with his hammock, which was nearest the hatch. The man paid no attention to Ethan.

Ethan reached for his satchel, intending to swing it on to his shoulder and carry it to one of the open hammocks. Instead, he knelt and opened the sack. His belongings had been moved as well. This time he had no doubt. Even if someone had kicked the bag, it wouldn't have changed his arrangement of his items so much. Nothing had been taken. His purse was still there, the coins within undisturbed. But he was certain: Someone had searched his bag, to what end he couldn't say. He glanced up, scanned the hold. No one looked his way or spoke a word to him. He straightened and carried his satchel to the first open hammock, eyeing the men around him, his entire body coiled like a spring.

He thought about reporting the occurrence to Foster, or perhaps to the captain.

What would you report?

The question brought him up short. Nothing had been taken, not even his money. Someone had been curious. That was all. Did he truly wish to create a fuss over a simple search of his satchel? Did he want to gain a reputation as a whiddler over a trifle such as this? It took him all of two seconds to decide he didn't. He was new to this ship, to this crew. For all he knew, some among the men were testing him, taking his measure. He wouldn't give them reason to mistrust him, not over this. He set the satchel beneath his hammock, and settled in to sleep.

VI

Over the weeks that followed, Ethan learned the rhythms and patterns of life aboard Rayne Selker's ship. The captain kept himself apart from the crew, spending much of his time either in his quarters or alone on the aft deck at the ship's helm.

Foster relayed his orders to the crew and saw personally to nearly every aspect of life and work aboard the *Blade*. No one, it seemed to Ethan, worked harder than the first mate.

Ethan's duties had him working most often with Mister Holme, the red-haired bosun. Together they supervised the maintenance of the vessel's rigging and gear. They also monitored the ship's stores, informing Mister Foster when shortages of one sort or another required that they put in at a port and replenish their supplies.

The *Blade* patrolled south to the warm waters in proximity to the Indies, watching for French ships making their way to or from the isles. For the first two months, however, the ship engaged not one vessel. Twice they spotted merchant ships that might have been easy prey, but both times the captain refused to give chase. The first ship he deemed too far ahead to be caught, though Foster seemed to believe otherwise. The second, a brigantine carrying twelve guns, he refused to engage, saying only that the perils outweighed the potential gains.

Ethan considered himself a cautious man; he had more of his father in him than he liked to admit. More, he understood that privateering captains answered to the owners of their ships. As reluctant as Selker would have been to put at risk a vessel of his own, he was doubly constrained where the *Blade* was concerned. But still, the captain's reluctance to engage these ships left Ethan frustrated and despairing of ever making the fortune he so desperately needed.

Yet, his disappointment paled beside the anger of Foster and several other members of the crew.

Almost since the night they sailed from Boston, Ethan had noticed that while the crew worked together with efficiency, they tended to break off into two groups during their moments of leisure. One group, its members younger and somewhat more wild, orbited the first mate. They laughed at his jokes, hung on his every word as if he were a sage.

The other group was older, more staid, and though they didn't have a particular leader, they did tend to gravitate toward the swarthy, bald man Ethan had seen his first day aboard the ship. He was the ship's master gunner, a Welshman named Trevor Pugh, and he had served with the captain longer than any other man on the *Blade*.

Foster and his group were most vocal in their expressions of displeasure with Selker's decisions, although even they took care not to utter any complaint in the captain's presence. Pugh and his allies didn't exactly defend Selker, but they spoke in sober tones about the responsibilities of a privateering captain, and the dangers to ship and crew of an unsuccessful raid on an armed merchant ship.

"We've no fleet behind us," Ethan heard Pugh say the evening after Selker refused to engage the brigantine. The men around him nodded their agreement, and he went on, his brogue roughening the words. "If we're crippled in a battle, we might as well take blades to our own throats. Captain needs to have a care."

Later, Ethan overheard several of Foster's men calling Pugh a coward and worse.

"What's the use of a master gunner who's afraid of his own weapons? The man doesn't have balls enough to fire his balls."

Uproarious laughter followed this, and the men repeated the line several times, each retelling punctuated by more hilarity.

Ethan saw no humor in the matter.

He felt as though he were the only man on board who had not aligned himself with one group or the other. He had no desire to involve himself in the crew's growing feud, but neither did he wish to be caught between the two factions without allies of his own. Though he tried to cultivate such alliances, most of the crew remained wary of him. The captain's supporters, he believed, saw him as Foster's man, but Foster kept his distance, making him suspect in the eyes of those who followed the first mate.

Most of the time, he kept to himself, saw to his duties, and occupied himself writing letters to Elli that he left at various ports for transport back to Boston. He told her of life at sea, of the places where they had stopped, of how much he missed her and how often he thought of her. Never did he mention their encounters with French ships, no matter how benign. He certainly told her nothing of the divisions he had observed among the crew.

Only a few days after they allowed the brigantine to pass, Selker ordered the crew to take a sloop one of the men had spotted from the rigging. The vessel was laughably small, a single-masted merchant ship, unarmed. But she flew French colors and appeared to be carrying goods between Guadeloupe and Martinique.

The crew of the sloop struck her sails and surrendered without the *Blade* having to fire its guns. Selker steered alongside her, and Foster, with Ethan just behind him, led a group of thirty armed men onto the smaller vessel.

The ship's crew numbered no more than two dozen, nearly half of them Africans. They had already piled their weapons on deck and placed their hands behind their heads when Ethan and the others boarded. Most of them were young; they looked frightened.

Their captain was French and claimed to speak not a word of English. Fortunately, Foster understood enough French to communicate with him. He questioned the man briefly before leading a dozen of the *Blade* sailors on a search of the captured ship. They found several barrels of rum, some fruit and cured pork, and a small amount of gold.

Returning to the deck, where Ethan and the rest of his men kept watch on their hostages, Foster approached the captain again, a small leather pouch in his hand, pale eyes smoldering.

"They're hiding the rest," Foster said, coins chiming within the purse he carried. "This can't be all."

Ethan regarded the ship's captain. "Are you certain? He could be telling—"

Foster cut him off with a sharp gesture. To the captain he said, "*C'est tout l'or que vous avez?*"

The captain licked his lips, appearing frightened. "*Oui, c'est tout.*"

"*Vous mentez?*"

Foster dug a fist into the man's gut, doubling him over. "*Où est le reste?*"

"*Nous n'avons plus,*" the man said, gasping the words.

"*Menteur!*"

The first mate hit him again. The jaw this time. The sloop's captain collapsed to the deck, blood pouring from his mouth. He spat out fragments of a tooth.

"Je veux le reste!"

"Il n'y a plus!"

Foster kicked him in the gut. The man retched. Ethan looked away, eyeing the other French sailors. Some glared at the mate, others cast murderous looks at the rest of the *Blade*'s men, including Ethan.

Foster pulled his flintlock from his belt and cocked the hammer.

"Mister Foster—"

"Shut up, Kaille."

The first mate squatted and set the barrel of his weapon against the captain's forehead. *"Où est le reste de votre or?"* he asked, pitching his voice to carry. *"Dis-moi ou je le tuerai."*

None of the French sailors said a word.

Foster scowled, shifted his weapon and fired at the captain's leg. The report was like cannon fire. Blood sprayed across the bleached wood, and the captain howled his agony. A gust of wind swept away a billow of white smoke.

Ethan's stomach turned an uneasy somersault.

Foster slipped his weapon back into his belt and held out a hand toward Ethan.

"Give me your pistol."

"Sir, I—"

"Give me the fucking pistol!"

Ethan drew his weapon and handed it to Foster, butt first. Foster cocked it as he had his own, and again pressed the barrel to the captain's head.

"Je veux l'or. Toute de suite!"

Tears streamed from the captain's eyes, and his blood continued to soak the weathered wood. Ethan averted his gaze, expecting Foster to pull the trigger at any moment.

"I know where it is," said one of the Africans, his words heavily accented. "I give it to you."

Ethan exhaled, sagging. Foster grinned, flipped the pistol and caught it by the grip, then handed it back to him.

"Go with him, Kaille. Get me that gold. If he troubles you at all, kill him."

"Yes, sir," Ethan said through gritted teeth.

He followed the man, the hand holding his pistol slick with sweat. The sailor was broad and muscular. Ethan kept his distance, fearing the man might try to overpower him, as afraid of having to kill him as of being killed himself.

The sailor led him into the hold, which only heightened Ethan's apprehension. No captain he knew would allow for something so valuable to be stored in the common areas belowdecks.

As if anticipating this, the man glanced back his way and said, "We hide it down here when we see your ship. Do not shoot."

Ethan nodded, said nothing.

The sailor picked his way among what little was left of the vessel's stores, as well as the personal items of the crew, which had been scattered across the hold. At the aft, starboard corner of the space, he knelt, shifted a plank of wood, and pulled out a small leather pouch, much like the one the ship's captain had already given to Foster. Straightening, he turned and tossed the pouch to Ethan, who caught it with his free hand.

Coins jangled within, but not many. The purse felt light in his hand.

"This is all?" he asked.

"*Oui.* Yes. That is all."

Ethan eyed the man a moment longer, trying to decide if he believed him. "All right, then," he said, waving his pistol toward the hatch. "You go first."

"You shoot me now?" the man asked.

"No, I'm not going to shoot you."

"The other man would. He . . . I don't know the word. *Il est fou.* He is . . . he is mad. That is what you would say."

"He's not," Ethan said, though the words lacked conviction. "He's . . . your captain lied to us. He risked all of your lives for a few gold coins. You tell me who the madman is."

The sailor shrugged, returned to the hatch, and climbed to the deck, Ethan behind him.

"What did you find?" Foster asked.

The ship's captain still lay at the first mate's feet, sweat dripping from his face, low moans escaping him every few seconds.

Ethan threw the pouch to Foster, who caught it and opened it.

The first mate frowned at what he saw within. "You're certain this is all?"

"Aye, sir."

"Fine, then." Foster glanced about the ship and then at the sailors. "If we had room, and were properly outfitted, I'd take them as slaves. Some of them might fetch a fair price. Shame to give up that gold."

Ethan tensed at the suggestion.

A moment later, to his vast relief, Foster shook his head. "But as things stand, we have enough mouths to feed, and we're already more cramped than I'd like . . ." He shrugged. "Take their sailcloth," he said, to the rest of the *Blade* sailors. "We might find a use for it. And anything else you think has value." He looked down at the captain. "Leave their oars."

He started back toward the *Blade*'s ratline. "Kaille, you're with me."

Ethan hadn't expected that. The other members of the Blade's crew watched him. "Aye, sir," he said. He returned his pistol to his belt and followed Foster back to their ship.

Once there, the first mate led Ethan into the hold. He motioned toward a nearby barrel. "Sit."

Ethan did as he was told. Foster kept his feet, remaining near the hatch.

"Not a very profitable raid," the first mate said, hefting the two pouches of coin. "Barely enough to have made it worthwhile."

"Aye, sir. Perhaps we'll be more fortunate next time."

"Maybe. We'll see. That's not why I brought you down here."

Ethan said nothing.

"Do you have any idea why I did?"

"I . . . I suppose—"

"Defying an order during an engagement with the enemy is a hanging offense, Kaille. You understand that, don't you?"

Ethan felt the blood drain from his face. "Aye, sir," he whispered.

"Every man on that ship heard me when I ordered you to hand over your pistol. And every man heard you start to argue, saw you hesitate. What am I supposed to do about that?"

He straightened, stared past Foster at the post behind him. "I believe your duty is clear, sir."

Silence. And then Foster began to laugh.

"You are still a navy man, aren't you?"

As quickly as the color had left Ethan's face, it returned, making his cheeks burn. "Sir?"

"I'm not going to have you hanged. It would be a waste of good rope."

He still laughed. Ethan didn't know what to make of any of this. *Il est fou*, he heard in his mind.

"Don't defy me again. I wouldn't have killed the man, but I wanted that gold. You wanted it, too. So did every man on the *Blade*. This may not be His Majesty's navy, but this is still a ship of war, and sometimes we have to get a bit of blood on our shirts to do what's necessary. Understand me?"

"Aye, sir. I apologize."

"Apology accepted."

Foster didn't move, nor did he dismiss Ethan. His gaze, though, flicked to the stairs leading to the ship's deck.

"What do you make of this ship, Kaille?"

"Sir?"

"You've been with us for close to ten weeks now. You've seen how the crew functions, how Captain leads. What are your impressions?"

"She's . . . a fine ship, sir. I'm proud to be a member of her crew."

"But?"

Ethan hadn't intended to say more. "I beg your pardon?"

"Come now. You can't tell me that you've no complaints, no concerns. We're not a perfect ship."

"Well . . . It . . . it has been somewhat less . . . profitable than I had hoped." It was his turn to glance toward the stairway. "I had thought we would have completed more raids by now."

Foster gave a sage nod. "Aye, that has been a problem."

"But I'm sure it's simply a matter of time. Eventually we'll . . ." He trailed off as the first mate winced and canted his head.

"I told you the first time we spoke: This has been a problem with the *Blade* for some months now. Or, not the *Blade* so much as . . ." He eyed the stairway once again. "Well, let's be honest," he went on in a whisper. "It's a problem with the captain, isn't it?"

Ethan stared at the man, afraid to make any reply, wishing he were anywhere else. The first mate had ventured into hazardous waters. The wrong person overhearing what he'd said might even accuse him of treason.

Foster smiled and laid a hand on his shoulder. "Don't trouble yourself, lad. It's an old argument between the captain and me. I don't mean anything by it."

"No, sir. Of course not."

Still the man didn't grant Ethan leave to end their conversation, though Ethan wanted nothing so much as to walk away.

"You didn't like what I did to that man, did you?"

One unanswerable remark after another. Ethan wondered if Foster meant to unbalance him, to keep him fearful and confused.

"You can speak. I asked a question. I've already told you that you're to follow orders, and I trust you will from this day forward. Now I'm asking what you think. No harm will come of whatever answer you give."

He didn't know how much stock to put in these assurances. And whether or not the man intended it, he did have Ethan discomposed.

"It worked, sir," he said.

"That's not what I asked."

"It's all that's relevant. You acted, and what you did achieved the purpose you had in mind. Who am I to question the means by which you succeeded?"

"You've a silver tongue, Kaille. That could serve you well as you move along in life."

Ethan remembered Elli saying something similar to him before he sailed from Boston. He thrust the memory away, unwilling, just then, to give in to that particular weakness.

"Yes, sir."

"I asked what I did because I believe you could have acted to save the brigantine's captain from all I did to him."

He blinked. "Sir?"

"What I mean is, you could have learned of that hidden gold using . . . methods of your own. Isn't that so?"

He went cold. "I don't know what you mean."

"No?" The first mate lifted a shoulder. "Perhaps I'm in error then, though I don't think I am. Consider it, Kaille." Foster patted his shoulder again. "You're dismissed."

But rather than waiting for Ethan to walk away, he turned and climbed the stairway to the deck, leaving Ethan alone in the hold.

He wanted to follow the man, to insist that he was mistaken and that Ethan had no idea what he could have meant.

But he did know.

Somehow, the first mate had learned that Ethan was a conjurer.

Ethan had said nothing about his abilities to anyone. He took great care with his shirt sleeves, lest any among the crew see the scars on his forearm from the blood spells he had cast. He had written letters only to Elli, and of course he would have said nothing to her about conjurings or spells. He had received no missives at all. If he was right, and Foster had learned of his spellmaking skills, he couldn't imagine how.

Unless the first mate had known all along.

Your father is Ellis Kaille.

Almost the first words Foster had spoken to him, in an accent that marked him as a Bristol man. Did the first mate know his family, his mother in particular? Or one of his sisters perhaps?

Had he known all along? Was that why he wanted Ethan on the ship?

He forced himself into motion, knowing he couldn't remain in the hold forever. Emerging onto the deck, he spotted Foster standing with the bosun and several of the other men in his circle. All of them glanced Ethan's way as he moved to the rail. He tried to ignore them.

The master gunner and others who supported the captain paid Ethan little heed.

Moments later Captain Selker stepped out of his quarters to the aft deck. He raised his hands to gain the attention of the crew, but at first many of the men didn't appear to notice. Finally, after a shrill whistle from Foster gained their attention, the Blade's sailors quieted.

Selker held up the two pouches of coins the first mate's party had taken from the brigantine.

"We had a fine morning," the captain said, a grin splitting his face.

A few of the men cheered this. Many others remained silent.

"Two or three more raids like this one," the captain went on, "and we will count this a successful voyage and head back to Boston. Well done, men."

The cheers that met this were even more muted than the first had been. Ethan couldn't bring himself to do more than clap his hands a few times. Two or three similar raids would do precious little for his purse. Five or six would barely be sufficient. Yes, they had taken more than just the gold: several barrels of rum, food, cloth. But even accounting for all of that, their takings had been meager. After the Crown and the ship's owners took their shares, and the remaining gains were divided among the crew, Ethan's earnings would be negligible.

He could tell that many of the men around him were thinking along similar lines, doing the discouraging calculations in their heads. The captain appeared oblivious.

"We took food from that ship today. We'll eat well tonight."

"And we'll have a tipple of rum!" a man called from the rigging.

This elicited the loudest cheers of the day.

Selker glanced up in the direction from which the voice had come, a frown furrowing his brow. "No, I'm afraid we won't," he said, hushing them again. "The food won't keep, but the rum is spoil from today's raid, and therefore belongs in substantial part to our sponsors. We will return with it to port, where it will be dealt with at the discretion of the ship's owners."

Silence.

Ethan chanced a quick look toward the first mate, and wished immediately that he hadn't. The man stared back at him, speculation in the glance.

VII

Ethan gazed into the fire, Kannice's fingers entwined with his. He knew the rest were watching him: Sephira, Kelf, even Afton and Nap. He didn't much care.

"Did you ever find out how he knew?" Kannice asked. "Foster, I mean."

"Not really, no. We discussed it again the following day, but I'm still not sure I believe the answer he gave. With all that followed, I never learned the truth, and it's not as though we had much time to speak of it after."

"Did he threaten to have you hanged?" Sephira asked, amusement in the words.

Ethan eyed her in the light of the blaze. "Not in so many words. And not right away."

"I would have, and I wouldn't have bothered with subtlety."

Kannice arched an eyebrow. "Imagine our surprise."

Ethan had turned back to the fire, memories swarming in his mind. With all that occurred in his first several weeks on the *Blade*, and with all the dark twists and turns of what followed the raid on the sloop, he had long been struck by the absurdity of the events of that night. Livelihoods were at stake, not to mention command of the vessel. Men died. The trajectory of his own life was forever altered. And it all started with the damned rum. At the time, the irony was too thick for him to swallow. Now, so many years later, he allowed himself a soft chuckle.

"What's funny?" Kannice asked.

"It was the rum that did it," he said.

Sephira slanted a look his way. "Did what?"

"Started the mutiny, of course. That is what you want to hear about, right? The *Ruby Blade* mutiny?"

"You mutinied over rum?"

"In a manner of speaking. The mutiny started that way, but it happened because Foster wanted it. He'd been planning it for months, I'm sure. He brought me aboard because he needed a conjurer to tip the balance within the crew, and he was confident he could win my trust." He turned back to the hearth. "He was right, at least at first."

"And what about Selker? What was his role in all of this? *That's* how this conversation began."

Ethan lifted a shoulder. "Selker was a mystery, to all of us. At the time, I thought him aloof and punctilious, too enamored of his rank and his own authority. Looking back, I've come to believe he was just young and unsure of himself."

"But what did he do?"

His smile this time felt forced. "Precisely what Foster hoped he would."

VIII

The sailors managed to keep their distance from the confiscated rum for a full six hours after the captain's remarks. Ethan heard grumbles as he saw to his duties, but he didn't think much would come of the men's discontent. He certainly could not have foreseen what occurred after nightfall.

He had hoped and expected that their supper—salted pork, watered rum, and a purple fruit he'd never seen before, which tasted like the sweetest grapes he'd ever had—would appease the men and make them forget the barrels of pure spirit in the hold.

It didn't.

With darkness spreading through the clear sky, and reflections of starlight and torch fire sparkling on the swells, a cluster of men gathered near the main mast. Several of them spoke loudly about the injustice of confiscating so much undiluted rum but being barred from partaking of even a small dram.

The more they talked, the more attention they drew, until a sizable portion of the crew had joined them on the deck. For once, supporters of the captain and the first mate mingled freely, shouting their approval as one man after another called on the captain to allow them to open a barrel or two.

Neither Foster or Selker appeared on the deck. Ethan wasn't surprised that the captain kept to his quarters, but he would have expected the first mate to make some attempt at calming the men. Their absence left Ethan, the bosun, and the master gunner as the highest ranking members of the crew present.

Mister Holme, the Bosun, stood on the fringe of the gathered mob, listening and watching. Judging from his expression, it seemed he was entertained by the growing commotion. He said nothing, and refrained from joining in with the cheers, but he certainly made no attempt to quiet the others. The gunner, Trevor Pugh, also observed, having positioned himself near the port rail, not so far from Holme. His expression remained grave, but it usually was. As Ethan eyed him, the man turned to meet his gaze and raised an eyebrow in inquiry.

Did he think it Ethan's responsibility to put a stop to this?

The man continued to stare his way, until at last Ethan felt he had no choice but to intervene.

He stepped forward, pushing through the throng until he reached the main mast and the men there. Only then did he realize how large the leaders were. All four of them were tall and broad. He had no hope of over-powering any one of them, much less all at once. It occurred to him that a spell might do what his limited physical strength could not, but he wasn't willing to reveal his abilities here, under these circumstances. Nor did he think it wise to produce his weapon.

Instead, he tried reason.

"Gentlemen, I appreciate your candor on this matter, and I'm sure your fellow crew men do as well. But this has gone on long enough. Some of you have duties to complete. The rest of you should make your way be-low."

"You gonna stop us talkin'?" one of the men asked, menace in his tone.

Ethan held his ground. "I'm ordering you to stop," he said, pleased to hear that his voice didn't waver. "Defy that order, and you'll face serious consequences."

The man exposed crooked, yellowed teeth. "You're too green and small to put much fear in me, lad. But I admire you for trying."

Ethan saw the blow coming, tried to raise an arm to block it. But for a large man, the sailor was deceptively quick. Or maybe Ethan wasn't as good in a fight as he thought.

By the time he came to, the deck was empty save for the bosun, who stood over him, a frown twisting his lips, amusement in his eyes. Voices and the rumble of many men moving many barrels of rum, echoed from the hold.

"Damn," Ethan said. He winced, holding a hand to his battered jaw. The skin felt tight and swollen and fevered.

Mister Holme extended a hand and, when Ethan gripped it, helped him to his feet.

"You're an idiot," the bosun said.

Ethan stared back at him, his legs unsteady beneath him. "I was doing my job."

"Your job isn't to get yourself killed. At least not over a few barrels of rum."

"So I shouldn't have said anything at all? I should have just stood there and watched as they took spirit that isn't theirs?"

The man shrugged, his gaze steady. *That's what I did*, his look seemed to say.

Apparently, the master gunner had done the same. Perhaps Ethan *was* an idiot.

"What's happening down there?" he asked.

"About what you'd expect. They've broken into several barrels—"

A cheer from below stopped him for a moment.

"And now one more. And they're in the process of drinking themselves blind."

"Still no sign of the captain or first mate?"

"The captain will wait until the men are calmer, or passed out, or both," Holme said, and Ethan couldn't miss the note of disdain in his voice.

"As to Mister Foster, make no mistake. You may not see him, but he's minding the situation. He won't allow it to get out of hand."

Again Ethan dabbed at his tender jaw with his fingertips. "Hasn't it already?"

"Not really." Holme scrutinized his face, narrowing his eyes for a moment. "You're all right. Doesn't look like he broke anything."

"If that's the measure—"

"It's not. Have a little faith, Kaille. Mister Foster knows what he's about."

He didn't find this reassuring in the least, but he decided he'd be wise to keep his lack of confidence to himself.

"What should we do then?"

"Well, I'm not sure what you're going to do, but I intend to have a dram or two of rum."

He started away toward the hatch. Ethan could do naught but stare after him. After confronting the sailors, he could hardly give in and partake of the rum himself. Or could he? The men didn't yet trust him. Humbling himself in this way might be the first step in ingratiating himself with the crew.

He followed Holme. The bosun glanced back at him and nodded his approval.

As they descended the stairway, the sailors quieted and watched them, clearly wary of their intentions. The usual smells of the hold had been overwhelmed by the sweet pungency of so much spirit. It was, Ethan had to admit, a vast improvement.

The men continued to eye him. Even Holme, ahead of him, had turned.

Ethan raised his eyebrows. "Someone told me once that rum was rather effective in soothing a sore jaw. I thought it time for me to test his advice."

The men released a collective breath and laughed, none more than the brute who had hit him and who now brought him his first draught of the rum. It was very good. The best he'd ever tasted, if he was honest with himself.

The bosun caught his eye and winked. Ethan scanned the rest of the hold. He saw a good many of the men whom he considered supporters of the captain, though far more of those who were drinking belonged to Foster's circle. The master gunner was nowhere to be seen.

The gathering had the feel of a celebration, acknowledgment of a raid gone well in the midst of a voyage that had been less than successful.

As the festivities continued, one of the ship's servants, a young man of perhaps fifteen years, whom Ethan knew only as Billy, squeezed through the throng, shouted, "Oi, look what I've got!" and held up a dark glass bottle for all to see.

"What's that, lad?" asked one of the men.

A broad smile lit the boy's face. "Captain's brandy," he said with pride.

"How'd you get it?"

He shrugged, clearly feeling important. "I seen where he hides things. Bottles, keys. Stuff like that."

The man questioning him turned to Ethan. So did several of the others.

"Whaddya say, Mister Kaille?" the crew man asked. "Is this off limits as well?"

The sailors watched him, an undercurrent of tension permeating the air again. Ethan had tried once to stand firm before the men, and surely the captain would have expected him to do the same now. But Selker had erred earlier this day. Anyone could see that. Certainly it seemed clear to Ethan, warmed now by the rum he'd imbibed. Better to let the men enjoy the day's spoils than worry about sponsors a thousand miles away. The loss of this bottle struck Ethan as just deserts for the captain's decision. Or rather, he considered the brandy a just dessert for these men. Pleased with himself for the play on words. He eyed Billy.

"Bring that bottle here, lad," he said, with as much severity as he could muster.

A hush fell over the hold. The boy glanced at the others, his joy, and much of the color, draining from his cheeks. But he did as Ethan instructed, and when Ethan put out his hand, Billy gave him the bottle.

Ethan looked around him at the silent, wary men.

"Someone has to taste it," he said, "to make sure it's fit for such delicate palates."

The men erupted with laughter, and cheered as Ethan unstoppered the bottle and took a long drink. It was fine brandy. This one bottle probably cost more than most of these men would earn for their entire voyage. He passed the bottle back to Billy, who raised it to his lips as well, eliciting more cheers. The boy handed the brandy to another sailor and Ethan soon lost track of it. But they had plenty of rum, to keep their celebration going.

Ethan moved among the men, suffering their critical scrutiny of his bruised jaw, speaking and laughing with many of them, learning their names and something of their histories—things he should have learned some time ago. Perhaps being struck had been a gift. For despite how the evening had begun, when he settled into his hammock sometime after midnight, Ethan felt more at home among his fellow sailors than he had at any time since leaving Boston.

Morning, however, brought a stern summons from the deck, not to mention a headache and a roiled stomach.

Ethan's jaw ached and he found he could barely move it to speak. He dreaded trying to chew, though, he realized, that wouldn't be a problem, since he couldn't imagine his appetite returning for several weeks. He plodded up the stairway to the deck, sailors ahead of him and behind, all of them muttering to themselves, many of them gray-faced and bleary-eyed.

Captain Selker awaited them on the aft deck, trim and neat in red and white. He held his hands behind his back, the downward curve of his mouth and the hard gleam in his dark eyes bespeaking his displeasure. Foster stood beside him and back a pace, arms at his side, his mien stolid. The two of them, and the master gunner, who stood on the captain's other side, might have been the only men aboard who weren't suffering from the previous night's excesses.

"What did I tell all of you yesterday about the confiscated rum in our hold?" the captain demanded.

No one said a word.

His gaze skipped over their faces, coming to rest at last on Ethan. The captain appeared to mark his injury, his scowl deepening further.

"Mister Kaille," he said. "What happened to your face?"

Ethan barely hesitated. "An accident, sir," he said, the words muddied by his injury. "Clumsiness on my part. I fell last night while trying to climb into my hammock."

Selker's brow creased in disapproval. Foster, on the other hand, gave the most subtle of nods. Wherever he might have been the previous evening, he knew something of what had transpired.

"You fell and landed on your jaw?" the captain asked, bristling with skepticism.

"As I said, clumsiness."

"Yes, well, your . . .'clumsiness' cannot explain the rest of last night's occurrences. I would be grateful, Mister Kaille, if you would return to the hold, and count for me the number of barrels of rum that remain intact and full." He smirked. "Taking extra care as you descend, of course. We wouldn't want you to have another spill, would we?"

"I should do this now, sir?"

"Of course now. Unless there is some reason you wish to wait?"

"No, sir."

Ethan flicked his gaze to Foster, but the man merely stared back at him. He could offer no help. Pivoting, Ethan returned to the hatch and descended into the hold, knowing already what he would find. The stench of spirit remained, but had soured with time so that his eyes watered as he moved into the shadows of the space. Empty barrels abounded. Fresh stains from spilled rum darkened the floor planks. He had some trouble locating full, undisturbed barrels. At last, in the farthest reaches of the hold, he found a cluster of six, preserved no doubt as an oversight, rather than as a result of any moderation on the part of the crew.

Six. Already he could imagine Selker's response. Or he thought he could. He also found, lying on its side, the empty bottle that had held the captain's brandy.

Ascending to the deck once more, and returning to where the others waited for him, Ethan found the tableau unchanged. He wondered if anyone had so much as spoken a word in his absence.

"Well?" Selker asked. "What did you find, Mister Kaille? It's all gone, isn't it?" he went on, giving Ethan no time to reply. "Every barrel. Despite my orders."

"No, sir. Not every barrel. I found six that were undisturbed."

"Six." The captain shook his head, a small mirthless laugh escaping. "And I suppose I should be pleased by this, grateful to all for your restraint in not quaffing down every last drop."

Foster eased forward a step. "Captain—"

"Silence!" Selker said, rounding on him. He faced the crew again. "Nineteen barrels we took in yesterday's raid. Nineteen. I thought my wishes with respect to the rum were quite clear. Were they not, Mister Foster?"

This time the captain did wait, half-turning to regard the first mate.

"They were, Captain," Foster said, the words wrung from him.

"Which begs the question, why did you not prevent this?"

"An inexcusable failure on my part, Captain. Mine alone. And I'm prepared to accept whatever punishment you deem appropriate."

It was a noble gesture, one Ethan didn't believe Selker would allow. He wondered if Foster knew as much.

"I think not. I want to know who was responsible for this . . . this defiance of my orders."

"We all were, Captain," Ethan said.

"Your bruise says otherwise. But I am willing to punish every man aboard, if the true culprits refuse to identify themselves." Again he turned. "Mister Pugh?"

The master gunner snapped his fingers, and a dozen men around the ship, some standing by the rails, others hanging in the rigging, produced pistols, all of them full-cocked and ready to fire. Pugh pulled from his belt a cat-o'-nine-tails.

"Every man with the smell of spirit on his breath will have his turn on the post," the captain said. "Six lashes each, I think. One for every barrel that remains. Unless the men responsible care to identify themselves. If you do, I give my word that only you will be so disciplined. You know who you are. It is your choice. Subject your fellow crew members to lashings, or admit your guilt and spare them."

For some seconds, no one spoke. A gust of wind rustled the sail cloth, and swells slapped at the ship's hull.

Then a man stepped forward. Peter Doyle, one of the brutes who had been by the main mast the previous night. Three others followed, including James Canfield, the man who struck Ethan.

Moments passed. No one else came forward.

"This is all?" Selker demanded.

Silence.

"Mister Kaille, is this all of them?"

Ethan glared back at the captain, unwilling to answer.

"It's all right, lad," Canfield told him in a low voice. "You've done well by all of us. Tell him now."

Ethan met the man's gaze and dipped his chin. Then he faced the captain. "Yes, sir," he said, biting off the words. "This is all."

"Fine then." Selker gestured to Pugh, who barked an order to the men holding the pistols.

Four of these men waded through the gathered crew, pressed their weapons into the backs of the sailors who had accepted blame, and steered them onto the raised deck. The other armed men followed them, walking backward, pistols aimed at the rest of the crew to hold them at bay.

The master gunner had two more of the crew strip off Doyle's shirt and tie him to the mizzenmast with his back exposed. Old scars lined the man's tanned skin. This wouldn't be the first lashing to which he had been subjected. Hardly a consolation.

"Thirteen lashes," Selker said, watching all of this.

Foster's gaze snapped to the captain's face. "You said six!"

"I promised six to every member of the crew if these men didn't come forward. They have. And for their crimes against this ship, against her crew, against me, and against our sponsors, I decree that they shall endure thirteen lashes each, one for every barrel taken last night. Do you question my authority to do so?"

There had been murmurs among the rest of the crew, expressions of outrage at the punishment being meted out by the captain, insults hurled at the men helping him. But at this, everyone went still. All watched the first mate, awaiting his reply.

"No, Captain," he said at last. "You are empowered to subject your crew to whatever discipline you see fit."

"Yes, I am." He turned to the master gunner and nodded once.

Ethan had seen men flogged before. It had happened aboard the *Stirling Castle*, and he had seen it on the piers in Bristol when he was younger. But it wasn't anything to which he would ever grow accustomed.

The crackle of a cat-o'-nine-tails striking flesh was like no other sound he had heard: concussive, raw, haunting. Boyle gasped with every lash, but he made no other sound, not even a whimper. Blood coursed from his lacerated skin. It splattered on his breeches and on the wood of the deck; it speckled the master gunner's shirt and hands and face.

Thirteen lashes seemed to take forever. Ethan thought the man's punishment would never end. When at last it did, the captain and master gunner allowed two men from the crew to come forward, untie Boyle and lead him away to be ministered to by the ship's surgeon.

But, of course, they weren't done.

Canfield was forced onto the aft deck next. They stripped him as well, bound his wrists on the far side of the mast. Mister Pugh dipped the cat-o'-nine-tails in a bucket of water, and renewed his bloody task. Canfield grunted with every impact. Near the end, he cried out. His blood mingling on the deck with that of Boyle.

The other two men, Gaine and Fillroy, endured their beatings as well, though Gaine passed out after the eleventh stroke.

The crew watched it all, grave, resentful, fearful. Foster looked on, his aspect devoid of emotion, his gaze wandering over the faces before him, as if he were gauging their reactions.

It didn't escape Ethan's notice that all four of the punished men bore the marks of earlier beatings. Was this random luck, or had the four been chosen somehow for just this reason? Had they been chosen at all? How much of what had happened was planned? Or was he mad even to think this way?

The last of the beatings ended, mercifully, and Ethan blew out a breath.

Selker, though, wasn't done. "I daresay I've made my point with those men," he said, watching as two more of the crew helped Fillroy off the deck and toward the hold. He wrinkled his nose at the blood glistening on the wood beside the aft mast. "But the rest of you should not go unpunished."

A murmur of anger rose from the sailors who remained above deck.

"You shouldn't act surprised," the captain said, "you all partook of the rum."

"So you're going to whip every one of us after all?" one man asked.

"No. Much as I would like to, I gave you my word I wouldn't. But I do believe that the value of the spirit you drank matches, and then some, the value of the gold and rum that remain. And so none of you shall profit from yesterday's raid on the sloop. His Majesty, our sponsors, and I will keep the gold, and the proceeds from the sale of what rum remains."

This elicited more cries of protest and rage.

"You brought this on yourselves," Selker told them. "In the future, I'd suggest you follow orders."

Ethan's gut knotted like wet rope. Their takings the day before had been meager at best, but at least he finally had something to show for these long weeks away from Boston, away from Elli. Now, the captain had taken even that.

And still, the man wasn't finished.

"Where is Mister Wakeford?"

Ethan didn't recognize the name, but the silence that met Selker's question chilled him like a storm wind.

"Where is he?" the captain repeated, his voice rising.

"Here, sir."

Hearing the voice—its youth, the apprehension in this simple acknowledgment—Ethan knew a moment of pure panic. He turned to see Billy thread his way through the crowd to stand before Selker. The lad's cheeks were the color of sailcloth, his eyes wide and fearful. He looked even younger than usual, a mere child.

"Perhaps you can explain to me, Mister Wakeford, why I appear to be missing a bottle of brandy from my private stock."

"I took it," Ethan said. "I broke into your cabin and stole it from you."

Selker's lips thinned in a smirk. "A wasted effort, Mister Kaille. You do the boy no good by protecting him. He needs to be taught the consequences of betraying a senior officer." He faced Billy again. "Well, boy?"

Billy said nothing.

"It lies within my power to have you cast overboard. Don't compound your crime with falsehood and cowardice. Tell me what happened to my brandy."

Billy swallowed. "I took it, sir," he whispered. "I—I shared it with the crew."

"It's my fault we drank it," Ethan said. "Not his!"

"Not another word!" The captain narrowed his gaze, still considering the lad. "Fifteen lashes, I think."

Billy's legs gave way, and he collapsed to the deck.

It was all Ethan could do not to leap at the captain and throttle him. "Fifteen? You'll kill him."

"Nonsense. He's young, healthy. But he needs to learn discipline. And I daresay, he'll remember this lesson a good long time." Selker nodded to the master gunner.

Pugh stepped forward to where Billy half lay, half sat. He extended a hand to the boy and gently spoke his name. Billy looked up at him. After a moment, he took Pugh's hand and allowed the master gunner to help him up and lead him to the blood-spattered mast. Ethan wasn't sure he had ever seen an act of such raw courage.

Billy pulled off his shirt, and closed his eyes. Pugh bound his wrists into an embrace of the mast.

The lad screamed with the first lash of the cat-o'-nine-tails. He passed out after the fourth. Pugh looked to the captain at that point, perhaps hoping Selker would call off the rest of the beating. But the captain stared straight ahead, his features betraying no emotion. In that moment, Ethan hated him more than he had any man he'd ever known. Pugh continued the lashings, though Ethan thought the snap of the whip might have been slightly less pronounced than the previous ones had been.

Still, when the punishment had been administered, and sailors rushed forward to untie and lad and take him below, the blood from his back left a crimson trail across the deck.

The captain waited until he was out of sight. Then, speaking not a word, he turned on his heel and withdrew to the solitude of his quarters. Foster remained where he was, though he did glare after Selker.

Much of the rest of the crew accompanied Billy into the hold, where the others were being treated.

Ethan didn't know where to go. He wanted to check on the men and the boy, but wasn't certain he would be welcomed below. At the same time, he feared being seen as callous if he remained on the deck and made no attempt to join the others. He certainly wanted nothing to do with the captain, nor, for that matter, with the first mate. He wandered forward to the railing near the ship's bow, staring across open ocean, the wind whipping at his hair and face. For the first time he could remember, he felt trapped aboard a ship, desperate to be anywhere but at sea on the *Ruby Blade*.

"Kaille."

He turned. Foster stalked in his direction. He straightened, forced himself to meet the man's gaze. "Yes, sir."

"Come with me." The first mate didn't wait for a response, but turned back the way he had come and led Ethan to the hatch and down into the hold. He didn't go to where the men were clustered around the wounded. Instead, he lingered near the stairway, out of sight of the others. Ethan joined him there.

"You can help them. I know you can."

Blood fled Ethan's face, leaving his cheeks icy, making him light-headed. "I don't—"

"Stop it. This is no time for fatuous denials. We both know of what I speak. Before—" He made a vague gesture that put Ethan in mind of their previous conversation in the hold. "We could afford your claims of innocence, and ignorance. Not anymore. Those men are in pain, and you can heal them."

Ethan was too stunned and too alarmed to respond. He gaped at the man, knowing he must look a fool.

"Do you deny it?" Foster asked in a fierce whisper, stepping closer to him.

He ought to. For all he knew, his life might be forfeit if the wrong person learned he was a conjurer. But just then, he couldn't bring himself to lie to the man. He shook his head, whispered, "How did you know?"

"A good first mate knows everything about his crew."

"But when did you—"

"Later, Kaille. The only question that matters now is what will you do for those poor men. And for Billy. They have been beaten bloody, for little cause. They bleed still, and who knows what might happen to their scars in these tropical waters. Men at sea die of infection. Surely you know that."

"The others—"

"The others are easily ordered back onto the deck. Only the surgeon need remain, and the two of us, of course."

"Conjurers are hanged, even at sea."

"Not on this ship," Foster said. "Not as long as I'm first mate. You have my word."

His assurances helped only a little. He remained afraid for himself. But how could he allow such fears to prevent him from healing men who had been so brutally and—yes, he would say it—*unjustly* punished?

"Aye, very well," he said, his voice wavering. "Send the others up, and I'll do what I can."

Foster gripped Ethan's shoulder. "There's a good man. I knew I could count on you."

Foster spun away from him and shouted for the men to go back above, his command echoing in the hold. Men looked his way and the first mate repeated himself. Slowly, their gazes shifting from Foster to Ethan, they headed to the stairway and up onto the deck. Within a few moments, the hold was empty save for Ethan and Foster, the ship's surgeon, and the five beaten men, including Billy, all of whom lay on blankets, face down. Two of the men were covered with poultices. The surgeon had yet to minister to the others. Their wounds still wept foully.

Ethan approached Billy, knowing the surgeon watched him with mistrust.

"Calm yourself, Doctor," Foster said. "Our young friend has come to help."

"Are you a surgeon as well," the man asked, his tone making it clear that he knew how Ethan would answer.

"No, he's not," Foster said. "Better than that. He's a conjurer."

The doctor rounded on the first mate. "You can't be serious."

"I am. Mister Kaille can close their wounds now, in a matter of moments. Can you do that? Can you guarantee these injuries won't become fevered?"

The surgeon scowled, but said nothing.

"I thought not. These men are part of my crew, and I'll do whatever I must—allow whatever I must—to ensure that they recuperate. Do you understand?"

"Yes, sir." The man eyed Ethan again. "Can you really do what he says?"

He wasn't as skilled a conjurer as he should have been. He wasn't even as good as his sister, Susannah, though he was several years her senior. His mother had urged him to hone his skills. But while aboard the *Stirling Castle*, he couldn't very well practice what others thought of as witchcraft, and since arriving in Boston and meeting Elli, he had shied from his spellmaking powers. Still, the first spells he had learned were healing spells. His mother had thought them the most vital.

And so it was with some confidence that he said, "Yes, sir, I can."

The surgeon gave a small shrug and stepped back, giving him ample room. Ethan knelt beside Billy and examined the wounds on his bony back. The cat-o'-nail-tails didn't bite particularly deep, but up and down the lad's torso the flesh had been torn to shreds, so that it resembled flag cloth left too long in a gale. Enough blood remained in the gashes made by the lashing to fuel his spell. He didn't have to cut himself.

He placed his hands on the boy's ravaged skin with utmost care, and still Billy stiffened and uttered a cry through clenched teeth. Tears leaked from his eyes.

Closing his own eyes, Ethan whispered, *"Remedium ex cruore evocatum."* Healing, conjured from blood. Power thrummed in the wood of the ship, as if some great bell had been struck below the ocean's surface. The healing spell buzzed like bumblebee wings in his open palms. The lad exhaled again, but then seemed to relax fractionally under Ethan's touch.

Ethan opened his eyes. The glowing spectral figure who always appeared to him when he conjured—a dour soldier bearing a tabard of the Plantagenet kings—loomed over him, glowering in a manner that reminded Ethan of his mother's splenetic brother.

Foster stood nearby, oblivious of the ghost, who could only be seen by those with spellmaking ability. But in his own way, the first mate watched Ethan just as keenly.

Ethan turned his attention back to Billy. Already he could feel the boy's skin mending beneath his hands. Despite his apprehension, his fears of being hanged as a witch, he was reminded again of the satisfaction he drew from conjuring, particularly when his powers enabled him to give aid.

Eventually he shifted his hands to another part of the lad's back and repeated his spell. When that swath of skin had healed, he moved his hands and conjured again, and again, and again. By the time he had finished with Billy, he was sweating and worn. But he moved on to the four sailors, healing each in turn.

He had no sense of the time when at last he finished. Foster and the surgeon remained with him in the hold, both of them watching. The surgeon appeared simultaneously disturbed and fascinated by all Ethan did. Ethan sensed that he wished to ask questions, but feared giving them voice, though whether because the man didn't wish to interrupt, or was reluctant to appear too interested, he couldn't say.

The first mate appeared fascinated as well, though Ethan thought he saw something rapacious in Foster's avid stare. For the time being, he chose to ignore this, concentrating instead on the men he'd healed and the surgeon's ministrations to their closed wounds.

"I never would have believed such a thing possible," the doctor said, the words seeming to come grudgingly. "Your . . . talent—what you did here—it really is quite remarkable."

"Thank you, doctor," Ethan said. He climbed to his feet, his legs cramped, his back and neck aching. He had sweated through his shirt and waistcoat. Dampened hair clung to his brow.

"Watching you, one wouldn't think you exerted yourself at all, and yet there you stand . . ." His gesture encompassed Ethan's sweat darkened clothes, the perspiration on his face.

"Aye, it's more taxing than it appears."

"And have you been trained? In medicine, I mean. Have you—"

Foster cleared his throat, cutting the man off. "Doctor, if you would see to the bandages for these men, I'd be grateful. They may be healed in part, but I'm sure you'll agree that their wounds shouldn't be exposed to the elements. Particularly in this clime."

"Yes, of course, Mister Foster. I'll take care of them immediately."

Foster's smile didn't fool Ethan at all. "Very good." He faced Ethan. "Mister Kaille, I'd have a word with you."

He walked to the stairway and climbed to the deck, leaving Ethan to follow.

"I hope to continue our conversation, Mister Kaille," the surgeon said, as Ethan turned to leave.

Though preoccupied by the first mate's order, Ethan nodded to the man and said, "As do I, doctor."

He found Foster at the bow once more, near where the first mate had approached him earlier in the day. The sky had hazed over, muting the light of the sun, which hung low in the West. Much of the day had passed. Foster didn't turn as Ethan took his place beside him along the rail. He rested both arms on the smooth wood and hung his head, weary nearly beyond the capacity for speech.

"That was impressive, what you did down there," the first mate said. "I've seen other conjurers ply their trade, but before tonight I had never seen one heal. I'm grateful to you."

"I was glad to do it, sir," Ethan said, his gaze on the water, following the swirling reflections of sunlight on the dark swells.

"How much more would you be willing to do?" Foster asked, his voice falling to a whisper.

Ethan looked up at the man. A moment later, he straightened, a cool gust of wind chilling the sweat on his neck.

"I'm not sure what you mean."

"Aren't you?"

He opened his mouth to answer, to assure the man that he didn't. Foster stilled him with a raised finger, his eyes darting behind Ethan and then up into the rigging.

"You saw what happened today," the first mate went on. "You are intimately familiar with the severity of the injuries. No one on this ship has a better understanding than you of the captain's brutality—and that of the master gunner."

Ethan didn't have an ounce of spit in his mouth. His heart labored and his limbs trembled, with fear as well as exhaustion. He wanted to retire to the hold, to sleep away the rest of this blood-stained day. He had no desire —none in the least—to stand with this man and speak of mutiny.

For he had no doubt that this was precisely Foster's purpose. He wished to enlist Ethan in his plans to take control of the *Ruby Blade*. And what frightened Ethan most of all was his own sympathy for Foster's cause.

Captain Selker's authority over the men had weakened of late. Their paltry takings from the sloop the morning before—had their raid really taken place only yesterday? —did little to make up for the failures of the past several weeks. And Foster was right: Ethan had seen the savagery and extravagance of the captain's punishment. Despite his best efforts, Billy and the other men he had healed would bear hideous scars for the rest of their lives. All because they dared drink some rum and brandy in celebration of the previous day's triumph. What kind of man would see such punishment as proportional to the offense?

"You have nothing to say? Truly?"

"Forgive me, sir, but I don't know what you expect of me."

"Manhood, Kaille. That's what I expect. You and I are leaders of this crew. They look to us for relief from a man who lacks both competence and compassion. Without the two of us, they are powerless. Together, though, we can prevent a repeat of the horrors we witnessed today. More, we can perhaps salvage from this failed voyage something of value, something we can take home to those we love."

"May I speak freely, sir?"

"Please."

Ethan glanced around to be sure no one could hear. "I don't wish to wind up with a noose around my neck," he whispered.

"And you think I do?"

"I—" He clamped his mouth shut and looked away.

"I said you could speak your mind, sailor. Do so."

Ethan blew out a breath. "I . . . I fear that your animosity for the captain may be clouding your judgment. As poor a master of this ship as he may be, resorting to mutiny would be a grave error."

A part of him hoped the first mate would respond to this with shock and outrage, with shouted denials that he had ever suggested such a drastic course.

Foster did nothing of the sort. He simply stared back at him, an eyebrow raised, his mouth set in a thin, hard line. After several moments, Ethan grew uncomfortable under the man's scrutiny. He glanced away again.

"I'm trying to decide if you're simply young and a naif," Foster said, "or rather a coward."

Ethan's gaze snapped back to his. "I'm no coward," he said, struggling to keep his voice low. "And I'm old enough to know that mutiny is no trifle."

"Quietly, Kaille. Quietly."

"Do you honestly believe you can succeed at this?"

"I know I can. More than half the crew is with us. After the lashings today five more pledged themselves to our side. We have the bosun, the carpenter, and the master rigger. I've already managed to secure most of the weapons, without the master gunner having the least notion. And no one, not even Selker himself, knows this ship as well as I do. She's ripe for the taking, Kaille. The question is, whose side will you be on?"

"If all you say is true, it doesn't matter what side I choose."

"Ah, but we both know it does. You're a conjurer, after all."

"Aye, and how did you know that? You wouldn't tell me before, but you can now. And until you do, I'll not give you an answer."

Foster lifted a shoulder, his indifference maddening. "I told you as much as I needed to."

"Yes, of course. A good first mate knows all."

"You don't agree?"

"My agreement or disagreement is beside the point," he said, frustration mounting. "I'm not asking why you found out. I'm asking how."

"As I've already told you, I know something of your family. I knew of your father, and I heard tales of the witch he married."

Anger flared in Ethan's chest. "She's not—"

"Lower your voice!"

Ethan scanned the deck again. "She's not a witch. Anymore than I am."

"I'm telling you what I heard."

After a few seconds, Ethan gave a grudging nod.

"And so," Foster said, whispering again, "When word reached me of an Ethan Kaille, originally of Bristol and now in Boston, who was seeking employment on a privateering vessel, I let it be known that we'd welcome him aboard. I thought it likely that the son might take after the mother. But I promise you, Kaille, I knew nothing for certain until you were aboard the ship. One morning, not long after we set sail, I happened to glimpse the scars on your forearm. Only then was I sure."

Ethan rubbed a hand on the underside of his wrist. He could almost feel a blade biting into his skin.

"Satisfied?"

"Yes, sir."

"Then, I'll have your answer."

Ethan surveyed the deck one last time, noticing now what he had missed before. Men were watching them, surreptitiously to be sure, but with interest. All who observed them Ethan had thought of as Foster's men, a phrase that took on added meaning in light of what he and the first mate had discussed. Did they know already that he was a conjurer? Did they understand what was at stake in this conversation?

"Did you put them up to it?" Ethan asked, facing Foster again.

"Who?"

"The men who were punished. Did you have them volunteer?"

"What are you talking about?"

Foster's question didn't fool him. The first mate wouldn't meet his gaze. He knew just what Ethan meant. No denials or feigned ignorance could hide the fact. Ethan had been right; those men were chosen for a reason.

"They all had scars already," Ethan said. "Scars from previous lashings. They knew what to expect. To the extent that men can prepare themselves for this sort of beating, the four who took responsibility for breaking into those barrels of rum were prepared. Was this all intended to win me to your cause, or were you casting a wider net?"

Foster considered him with a flinty eye. "Your answer?"

Ethan wasn't sure he had much choice. His refusal wouldn't prevent Foster's mutiny. It would only serve to make him an early target of the men the first mate commanded. It wouldn't take Foster long to realize that killing Ethan presented less risk than allowing him to side with Selker.

At this point, he had little affection for either the captain or his first mate. Neither man deserved to command the *Blade*. But Selker had proven himself a poor master of the ship, and a brutal disciplinarian. Foster might be conniving, but perhaps under his leadership their fortunes would improve, and the beatings would end.

"Sometimes a man has to take risks in order to reap the rewards he seeks," Foster said, filling the silence. "Aye, there's danger here. The captain might find a way to defeat us. But are you willing to let your fear overmaster your judgment?"

"This isn't about fear."

"Then what is it about?"

Trust, he wanted to say. Instead, he shook his head. "It doesn't matter. I'm with you."

The first mate's smile appeared genuine. "Truly?"

"Aye. Tell me what it is you need me to do."

IX

"So he goaded you into it," Sephira said.

"I suppose you could say so."

"It's not supposition, Ethan. He called you a coward and a naif. He played on your fears. Who knew that the great Ethan Kaille could be so easily turned to another man's purposes?"

"Do you ever stop talking?" Kannice asked, glaring at the Empress of the South End.

A grin crinkled the corners of Sephira's eyes. "Only when I choose to, my lovely."

"Speaking of goading . . ." Ethan said.

"I'm just having some fun."

"I'd suggest you keep your fire trained on me. Kannice is more than you can handle."

Sephira looked like she might say more, but Ethan shook his head. "Enough, Sephira. Either listen to my tale or leave."

She eyed him a moment longer before taking another spoonful of chowder.

"How did you do it?" Kelf asked, after a few moments. "Taking the ship. Were you in on the planning?"

"Not really, no. Foster had worked it out to the smallest detail. Once those who took the rum were punished, most of the crew would have done anything to get rid of Captain Selker. To this day, I'm not as convinced as Foster that he needed me on his side. The numbers favored him so—I don't think one conjurer more or less would have made much difference."

"But he disagreed," Sephira said.

"Aye."

"And isn't it true that subsequent events proved him right and you wrong?"

"Things had changed by then."

Her expression turned shrewd.

"Anyway," he said, "you're getting ahead of my tale."

"You're telling it too slowly."

A rumbling sound emanated from the table near the door. It took Ethan a moment to realize that what he'd heard was Afton clearing his throat.

"Yes, what is it," Sephira demanded, acid in her tone as she swiveled to face the two toughs.

"Well, I'm sorry Miss Pryce, but . . . well, me and Nap was wonderin' if we might trouble the mistress for another bowl of that chowder."

Sephira blinked.

The glance Kannice sent the Empress's way came as close to gloating as anything Ethan had ever seen from her. "Of course you can," she said. She stood and crossed to them. "So glad you're enjoying it." She bore the bowls back to the table at which Ethan and Sephira sat, and held out her hand to Sephira.

After a moment's pause, Sephira dug into her purse once more and produced a half sovereign. "I'll take more as well, and an ale."

Ethan thought Kannice would wait for more coin, but she slipped the gold coin into her pocket and carried all three bowls to the kitchen. Kelf followed.

"You really don't tire of it?" Sephira asked Ethan, while she stared after Kannice.

"Of what?"

"This life. You can tell me in all honesty that you would rather be here, working in this ragged tavern, than out on the streets pursuing thieves?"

He met her gaze steadily. "I can. Why is that so hard for you to accept?"

"Because I know you. Loath as I am to admit it, you and I aren't all that dissimilar." She surveyed their surroundings, distaste twisting her lips. "And I couldn't stand to be relegated to such a place."

"And that's your problem. You see a place. I see a life. There's a difference."

"Dear God," she said. "I don't know whether to weep or vomit."

Fortunately, Kelf and Kannice chose that moment to return from the kitchen. Kelf brought Nap and Afton their bowls. Kannice set the chowder and ale before Sephira and reclaimed her chair. Ethan was a little surprised she hadn't poured the contents of both tankard and bowl into Sephira's lap.

"Thus far," Sephira said around a spoonful of chowder, "you've told us a great deal about this Foster character and still almost nothing about Selker. It's almost like you're trying to distract me from my purpose."

"Now it's my turn to urge patience. I'm trying to tell you what happened. All of it. You wouldn't want me to skip over details that might prove relevant to your inquiry, would you?"

She frowned. "Just get on with it."

"Did Selker's daughter tell you anything about the *Ruby Blade*?"

"I'm not prepared to tell you anything about what she has or hasn't told me. Not yet, at least."

Ethan shrugged and sat back in his chair. "Then I believe my tale is done."

She had been lifting another spoonful to her mouth, but she paused, her hand steady, her blue eyes fixed on him. "Don't play games with me, Ethan."

He placed his hand on his knife, which still lay on the table. "Why shouldn't I? I've already told you a good deal, and I'll be happy to relate more of what happened aboard the ship. But I want some answers, too. *Before*, I tell all."

She glanced at the knife, took her mouthful of stew, and dabbed at her lips with her napkin.

"Very well. She told me that the mutiny changed him, or so her mother led her to believe. She was born after the *Blade* mutiny. But according to the mother he had been a doting husband before. After, he grew distant, moody. He spent even less time at home than he had. And he grew secretive as well. Missus Selker became ever more suspicious of him, believing he had a mistress. But in retrospect, Lydia came to suspect that he was hiding something else. Something no less scandalous, but far more perilous."

He sat forward again. "And what would that be?"

She gave an inscrutable smile and sipped her ale.

Ethan didn't bother to hide his amusement. "I wonder sometimes if you enjoy provoking me even more than you do accumulating gold."

"Can't I enjoy both in equal measure?"

"What did Lydia suspect?"

"Finish your tale, and I'll tell you mine."

He drained his cup of Madeira, lifted and dropped a shoulder. "You can probably tell where my story is going. I was a fool, but a predictable fool."

Sephira smirked. "Some things don't change, even after so many years."

X

The mutiny began that very night, with Billy and the four punished men still in a healing sleep induced by a draught from the ship's surgeon, and the balance of the crew restless and watchful. The master gunner, and others who supported Captain Selker, seemed determined not to be caught unawares. Ethan thought they must sense the imminence of a rebellion on the ship: an admission of sorts that the captain had gone too far. In a way, he admired their loyalty. Despite Selker's cruelty, they remained committed to the rule of law. Ethan's father would have been proud to count himself among them. He would have been ashamed of the choice Ethan had made.

Selker's men clustered on the aft deck, near the captain's quarters, pistols and muskets in hand, blades on their belts. Foster's men, who had gathered below, were armed as well, but the first mate swore to Ethan that he wished to avoid bloodshed.

"That's what you're for," he said. "I want you to disarm Pugh and his men before they have the opportunity to open fire. Does that lie within your . . . your talents?"

"All of them at once? I'm not certain. But I can take care of Pugh, which might help you defeat the others."

Foster nodded. "It might at that. Good thinking, Kaille." He clapped Ethan on the back. "With your help, this ship will be ours before dawn, and not a single man need die."

Ethan couldn't say that he shared the man's confidence, but he tried to smile in return.

"I want you out of sight for now. None of the others knows you're a wi— My apologies. A conjurer. And I don't want that discovery to disrupt my planning. You understand."

He did, all too well.

"I can do what you ask," Ethan said, "but I won't do it from a place of hiding. Either I'm with you and your men, or I'm not. I won't skulk about like a cheat."

"Very well," Foster said. "Do you know what kind of spell you'll cast?"

"I've an idea, yes. Do you know so much about conjuring that the name of the spell would mean something to you?"

"No, I was just—"

"Leave it to me, sir. You wanted me as part of your mutiny. Well, you have me now. And you'll have to trust that I know what I'm doing."

Foster flashed another grin, appearing genuinely pleased. "I was worried about you, about your reluctance, and your scruples. I see now that I shouldn't have been."

"Thank you, sir."

A queasy foreboding had settled in his gut, though. The truth was, he didn't like any of this. He was caught between bad choices, between rival factions, neither of which held any appeal for him. And he found himself forced to place his faith in a man he didn't trust.

Within moments, Foster had marshaled his men and crossed to the hatch. Standing on the second stair, he faced the sailors he commanded and raised his hand for silence.

"The *Blade* is ours for the taking, lads. You know it. I know it. Selker knows it."

A cheer greeted this last, and he had to quiet them again.

"Soon enough, we'll be able to earn a proper bounty, and enjoy a suitable share of the harvest, without fear of lashings. Just keep your heads, follow my instructions, and all will go as it's supposed to." He paused, finding Ethan among the faces turned his way. "Mister Kaille is with us now, as I hoped he would be. He has the ability to help us in ways none of you can imagine. Trust him as you would me."

The men around Ethan glanced his way, renewed appraisal in their expressions. Two of the men nodded to him. Despite his misgivings, he felt a rush of excitement and pleasure that took him back to his days aboard the *Stirling Castle*, when he and his shipmates had prepared for battle.

"Up you go, lads," Foster said, motioning the sailors up the stairs. "Don't advance on Selker's men until I give the signal."

The sailors gave another cheer and streamed past him onto the deck. Ethan followed, only to stop on that second stair at a signal from the first mate.

"Where do you want to be?" Foster asked.

"On the rail would be best. Somewhere I can see."

The first mate nodded and waved him on.

Above, Ethan found Foster's men pressing forward, but only so far as the quarterdeck. From the aft deck, Pugh and his small band of men gripped their weapons and regarded the others with grim resolve. Surely the master gunner knew that he stood no chance against so many mutineers. But he gave no sign of faltering. Again, Ethan couldn't deny that he admired the man's courage.

The ship's sails hung slack on the three masts. The night was calm, the seas gentle. The *Blade* floundered, but she seemed to be in do immediate danger.

Ethan swung himself up onto the rail, clinging to the nearest line for balance. A moment later, Foster emerged from the hatch and walked forward, his men parting for him. He carried no weapon. His head was bare and his wheaten hair, unbound, shone with torchlight. Reaching the fore of his company, he halted.

"Mister Pugh," he said, voice ringing.

"Foster."

"I'd a word with the captain, if you'd be so kind as to summon him."

"I'm afraid I can't," Pugh said, his voice strong, steady. "If it's words you want, you can speak with me. Anything you tell me in good faith, Captain Selker will hear, without bias."

Foster gave a small shake of his head. "Not good enough, I fear."

"It's all I can offer. Speak your mind, or return to the hold, your men with you."

Foster's laugh was as dry as white sand. "We both know those are not my only choices. Do you truly think you and your men can withstand our assault?"

Pugh raised his musket to shoulder level and sighted. Even from his distant perch, Ethan could see that the weapon's barrel was trained on Foster's heart.

"I think," Pugh said, "that with their leader dead, your men will be a good deal less bold."

To his credit, the first mate didn't flinch or pale. But he did say, "Kaille!" the name carrying like the peal of a church bell.

Ethan's cue.

He didn't dare cut himself in plain sight. Instead he bit down hard on the inside of his cheek, tasting blood.

Conflare ex cruore evocatum. Heat conjured from blood.

Again, magick hummed in the wood of the *Ruby Blade*, resonating like thunder. The russet ghost winked into view beside him on the rail, a scowl on his glowing lips. For a moment that was all that happened. Others glanced about, appearing nervous, expectant. Even Pugh had straightened, the weapon still at his shoulder, but his gaze wandering the ship.

An instant later, he cried out, releasing his hold on the musket, which clattered to the deck and discharged with a flash of flame, a flat, loud report, and a billow of gray smoke. One of his own men grunted and dropped to his knees, clutching at his shoulder, blood running through his fingers.

"Now!" Foster shouted.

His sailors gave a yell and surged forward, weapons raised. Pugh's other men fell back, most of them too confused and afraid to fight or fire. Within moments, they had been overwhelmed and disarmed by Foster's force. One did manage to squeeze the trigger of his pistol. The weapon belched fire and smoke, the report startling the rest into silence. A young sailor in Foster's company fell, a bloody wound in his belly. Several others jumped the man who had fired and beat him with the butts of their pistols until he collapsed under the onslaught, bruised and bleeding. Ethan didn't expect either the young sailor or the shooter to survive.

Several men clamored to strike at the master gunner, but Foster rescued him before long. The first mate dragged the man into open view, the barrel of his pistol pressed against Pugh's temple. Pugh's shirt had been torn, his nose bloodied. A welt darkened high on his cheek.

"Our first prize, lads!"

More cheers.

"He should swing!" came a voice from within the throng. "For Rob and James, Peter and Jonathan! And Billy most of all!"

Many shouted their approval. But Foster shook his head.

"No one's to be hanged without my say-so. For now, he lives." He shoved Pugh to his knees, keeping a firm grip on the man's collar. "Tie him, but that's all. He's still an officer."

Several others descended on Pugh, binding his wrists none too gently.

Foster strode to the captain's door and tried the handle, only to find it locked. He glanced back at the rest of them, shook his head in disapproval, and pounded a fist on the wood.

"Captain Selker, sir. We've some matters we wish to discuss, if you'd be so kind as to open your door."

The crew laughed. A few echoed, "Captain Selker, Captain Selker," in a sing-song.

Ethan heard no reply from within.

Foster waited the span of a few breaths, then gestured several men toward the door. Two in particular were nearly as large as the men who had been lashed earlier that day—it felt like years ago.

The first mate stepped back, nodded once. Men standing in line with the door scurried to one side of the ship or the other. The only two who remained were the man who had been shot, and the man who shot him. Both lay utterly still.

The two behemoths set themselves before the door, shared a quick look, and in unison kicked the door in. Two shots thundered from inside the quarters, but by this time, both men had jumped back out of the way. Selker's bullets did no harm.

Foster motioned again and the men stalked into the captain's quarters. When they appeared again, they held Selker between them, his arms pinned to his side. He appeared small and fragile beside the sailors, like a child brought to discipline by grown men. He wore no wig, and his auburn hair fell about his face in lank strands. He was dressed, but carelessly so, as if he had thrown on his clothes in haste. His boots were unlaced, his captain's coat unbuttoned, part of the collar bent inward at his neck.

The men led the captain to Foster, and, at a sign from the first mate, released him. Selker's knees gave way and he sank to the deck at Foster's feet, his arms limp.

"Now, Captain," Foster said with a faint smile, "as I was saying: We have matters we wish to discuss with you."

Selker canted his head, and glared up at him, a sneer on his lips. "No, you don't. Gentlemen discuss their differences. They don't resort to barbarism. They don't rely on a rabble to help them get their way. You're not interested in airing grievances. You want my ship, plain and simple."

"Actually, Captain, I believe I have your ship. Unless you've been hiding a small army in your quarters."

The men behind Foster chuckled at this. Selker continued to glower.

"If you intend to kill me, get it over with."

"No," Foster said with a shake of his head. "I've no intention of killing you." He bent down, forcing Selker to look him in the eye. "A quick death is more than you deserve."

"You can have my shares," Selker said, shrinking back from him, the words coming out in a jumble.

"Aye, I intend to take them. And the shares of the ship's owners as well. Not for myself, mind you, but for all. We'll also be enjoying your wine and your rations, not to mention the rest of your brandy. And I intend to take your quarters for my own."

"Y-yes, all right. That's—I understand."

Foster laughed cruelly. "I'm so glad." He faced the two men who had pulled Selker from his quarters. "Strip off his coat and shirt. Tie him to the aft mast."

"No!"

The men grabbed for Selker, but the captain scrabbled away like a crab, drawing jeers and laughs from the rest of the crew. The men caught him a moment later, and bore him to the mast as he writhed and flailed and yowled for help. There they stripped off his clothes as Foster had instructed, bound his hands on the far side of the mast, and shoved him down so that he knelt with his head leaning against the rounded wood.

Foster joined them at the mast a few seconds after, having retrieved the cat-o'-nine-tails from wherever it had been stowed.

The captain whimpered, his skin appearing pasty and soft in the flicker of the torches.

"It was thirteen lashes, wasn't it?" Foster asked, looming over the man. "Or fifteen. That's what you gave the lad."

"Please don't do this." Selker sobbed the words, straining against the bonds that held him. "I was wrong. I know that now. I beg your mercy."

"You showed none," Foster said. "You shall have none."

More sobs wracked the captain's form.

"You are unmanned, Captain. For the sake of this crew that was once yours, pull yourself together."

Selker offered no reply save more pathetic cries. Foster frowned, but the captain's display did nothing to dissuade him. He dipped the lash in a bucket of water, set his feet, and struck his first blow.

The captain's scream spiraled high, sounding more like that of a young boy than a grown man. Blood ran from the wound opened on his back by this first lash, staining the back of his white trousers. At the same time, dampness spread from his crotch and a trickle of yellow liquid flowed over the aft deck.

"He's pissed himself!" one of the men said.

This elicited more laughter.

At Foster's second blow, the captain screamed again, then sagged, lolling onto his side as far as his bound wrists would allow.

The first mate raised the cat-o'-nine-tails to hit him a third time, but then lowered it.

"Out already," he said, sounding disgusted. "We'll have to continue this tomorrow lads. Don't worry, though. He can pass out again, and again, and again. But he'll have his fifteen lashes. You've my word on it." He turned to where two men held Mister Pugh. "In the meantime . . ."

It didn't take Foster's men long to untie the captain and bind the master gunner in his place. Unlike Selker, Pugh took his punishment with the same stoicism shown earlier by Foster's men. He never begged to be spared. Aside from a stifled grunt, he hardly reacted to the blows rained down upon him by the first mate.

With each strike of the cat-o'-nine-tails, Foster appeared to grow increasingly frustrated, as if he had hoped to draw more response. When he finished, and his men started forward to release the gunner, Foster waved them back.

"No one touch him," he said.

He pivoted on his heel and hurried below, only to reemerge from the hold moments later with a small wooden box in hand. He opened it, dumped the contents into his open palm and dashed them across the raw wounds on the gunner's back.

Pugh howled, back arching, the tendons and veins in his neck bulging.

Salt from the kitchen, Ethan realized belatedly.

Many of the men cheered this, as well. But not all, he saw. Some looked to be as disturbed by what Foster had done as he. Foster's grin returned, as if he was mollified for the moment. He ordered the man untied and taken below.

Ethan had seen enough. He jumped down off the rail and strode toward the hatch, reaching it just a stride behind the men who bore Mister Pugh.

"Where are you going?" Foster called from the aft deck.

Ethan halted at the top of the stairs and glared back at him. "To tend his wounds," he said, voice raised.

He thought Foster might order him not to, but after glancing at the faces of those around him, the first mate nodded once.

Ethan started down the stairs.

"Not the captain, Kaille," Foster said. "Just Pugh."

He faltered on the second step, nodded in turn, and continued down into the stale, warm air of the hold. Candles burned in the center of the hold where several men had gathered.

The ship's surgeon had already directed the sailors to lay Pugh on a blanket, and he knelt next to the gunner, *tsking* over the wounds. The gunner moaned; blood glistened on his back and shoulders. Captain Selker lay nearby, poultices on his injuries, his eyes open. He followed Ethan's every step.

"You'll need water first," Ethan said, his voice overloud in the closed space.

All turned to him.

"To wash away the salt."

"Salt?" the surgeon said, scowling.

The men who had borne the gunner below looked away rather than meet his gaze.

Apparently this was all the confirmation the surgeon needed.

"You heard him," he said. "I want water. As fresh as you can find and plenty of it. Now!"

Still the men hesitated.

"Foster sent me down to help with his wounds," Ethan told them. "I can't do that without water. Now, do as he says."

"Aye, sir."

They hurried away. The surgeon eyed Ethan. Even Pugh had turned his head to look his way.

"Why are you down here?" Pugh asked, in a voice scraped from stone. "Really?"

"As I told them—"

"Yes, yes. You want to tend to my wounds. What can you possibly . . ." He narrowed his gaze. "What happened to my musket? That was you, wasn't it?"

"What are you talking about?" Selker demanded from his blanket. "What did he do?"

"Please give me a moment, Captain," Pugh said with deference. "As soon as I understand, I'll tell you what I can."

Ethan didn't expect that this would satisfy Selker, but though the captain continued to regard Ethan, he said nothing more.

"Tell me what you did," Pugh said after a moment.

He considered denying that he had done anything. But the surgeon already knew he was a conjurer and Ethan sensed that the doctor remained loyal to the captain. Clearly the master gunner already suspected. The only other man in the hold just then was Selker, who no longer had any power over him.

"It was a heat spell," he said. "Directed at your weapon."

The way Pugh stared back at him one might have thought he had spoken in a foreign tongue.

It was the captain who said in a whisper, "Dear Lord, he's a witch."

"A conjurer, actually. Witches are the stuff of nightmare and false sermons."

The master gunner managed to raise himself a few inches, his arms trembling. "You used magick on me?"

"I did. And I would use more, if you'll allow it. I can heal your wounds."

"I wouldn't—"

Ethan's raised hand stopped him. "Think before you refuse me. We're in the tropics. And despite that salt, you risk infection so long as the wounds remain open. That could be days. I can heal them in a matter of minutes."

"And mine?" Selker asked.

Ethan turned. "Forgive me, Captain, but I've been ordered not to heal your wounds."

Pugh lowered himself to the blanket again. "Then you won't heal mine either."

"Don't be a fool, Pugh," the captain said. "Kaille's right. Your wounds are worse than mine, and you're of no use to me dead. Understand?"

Ethan hadn't expected this from the man. He couldn't tell if the master gunner was surprised. Pugh merely closed his eyes and said, "Aye, Captain."

The two sailors returned a short time later, each carrying a bucket of water.

"It's sea water," one of them said. "Mister Foster said he wouldn't waste our store of fresh water on the gunner."

"That's unacceptable," the surgeon said. "You go back and tell him that we must have fresh water."

Before either man could answer, Pugh said, "It's all right, doctor. Any water at all will be a balm."

"I'm not so sure."

"Leave the buckets," Ethan said. "Return to the deck."

The men did as he told them. When they were gone, he addressed Pugh. "If you allow me to heal you, the kind of water won't matter at all."

Pugh shifted his gaze to Ethan again. After a moment, he tucked his chin.

"This is why Foster wanted you."

Ethan hesitated, then faced the captain. "I don't know why he wanted me, sir."

"Of course you do. You've got a brain, sailor. Use it. He's probably been planning this for months. Maybe longer. But he needed to be certain that he would succeed. A failed mutineer is a dead man. Something you should keep in mind."

"I'm not here to argue with you, sir. I came down to heal Mister Pugh. If I hadn't been given a direct order, I would offer to do the same for you."

"Really," the captain said, his tone dry. "It seems you've come late to your sense of duty."

The surgeon poured water over Pugh's back. The master gunner stiffened at the first touch of the water, hissing a breath through gritted teeth. After a few seconds, though, the tension drained from his form. When the surgeon had washed away the salt thrown onto Pugh's back by Foster, he set the buckets aside and reached for his herbs and bandages.

"Doctor," Ethan said, stopping him.

The surgeon frowned, but leaned closer to the gunner. "I can place poultices on your back. Or . . . or you can allow this man to heal you. What is your preference?"

"Let him work his witchery, Mister Pugh," Selker said. "That's an order."

"Aye, Captain." Pugh's eyes found Ethan's. "You heard him."

Ethan nodded and knelt beside him, opposite the surgeon.

"But understand this, Kaille," the gunner added. "Whatever you do to mend these wounds only hastens the moment of your reckoning. I detest a traitor, and I won't rest until every one of you who aided Foster is dead."

I detest a traitor . . .

He wanted to protest, to tell them all that he despised treachery every bit as much as they did. He knew, though, that they wouldn't believe him. By his own actions, he had earned their contempt, and the threats that came with it.

Still, pride made him meet the man's gaze. "I understand," he said. "Perhaps if the captain had been more merciful earlier this day, none of this would have happened."

Selker laughed. "A naif, Pugh. The lad is a naif."

Foster had said much the same about him. He didn't like it coming from either man. He might have been young, but he had never thought of himself in such terms, nor did he care to now.

He pulled his blade from its sheath, drawing a gasp from Selker. Pausing, he held it up for the captain to see. Then he rolled up his sleeve and cut his own arm. Another gasp.

Ignoring the captain now, he placed his hands on Pugh's back and cast the healing spell. As with the other men, he had to repeat the conjuring several times to complete his task. When all the wounds were closed, he cut himself once more and put Pugh to sleep with one final conjuring. He didn't doubt that the master gunner meant what he said: He wanted Ethan dead, along with every other mutineer. Even wounded, Pugh was a formidable man. And expending so much of his strength on magick had left Ethan weary. He was in no condition to fight the gunner tonight.

"I'm not certain what to say."

Ethan glanced over his shoulder. At some point as he worked, the captain had raised himself into a sitting position.

"Sir?"

"I've always thought of witchery as evil. The black arts and all that. But this . . ." He lifted his chin in Pugh's direction. "I can see nothing evil in what you've just done."

Again, the man had surprised him.

"Thank you, sir."

Selker looked past him to the surgeon. "Please leave us, doctor. I assure you, I'll come to no harm. No more harm, that is."

"You have my word on that as well," Ethan said.

The surgeon faltered, his reluctance no doubt fueled by his mistrust of Ethan. But the captain had ordered him away, and at last he left them, returning to the deck, where an uncertain fate awaited him.

"Foster will kill me," Selker said, when they were alone. "You know this."

Ethan didn't answer.

"He'll subject me to the balance of my lashes, and then he'll slit my throat, or have me hanged, or simply run me through and throw my body overboard. Whatever mercy he might show the others, he has to rid himself of me."

Try as he might, Ethan couldn't fault the man's logic.

"Are you willing to be party to murder as well as mutiny?"

"They're both hanging offenses. I can only die once."

"A clever dodge, Mister Kaille."

"Why did you have to punish the lad and those men so cruelly? If you hadn't done that—"

"If you think Foster mutinied because of the lashings, you're mad."

Ethan shook his head. "I'm not that much a fool. He wanted the ship, and was willing to go to great lengths to get it. But the extravagance of your punishments convinced others to follow him. Your treatment of Billy convinced me."

Selker blew out a breath, but he didn't argue further, as Ethan expected he would. "I value discipline. I make no apology for that. Those men defied an order. The boy stole from me. I was angry."

Ethan nodded, looked away. He could almost feel sorry for the man. Almost. But Selker didn't make it easy for a person to like him.

"You'll let Foster take my life?"

"What would you have me say, Captain? I've cast my lot with the first mate and his men. The master gunner has vowed to kill me when he wakes. Do you honestly believe I can change course now?"

"I do. The question is, have you the courage to do so?"

Ethan slanted a glance his way. "I grow tired of having my courage questioned, of being called a naif, of being treated like some callow fool. I chose my path, and I had reasons for doing so."

"And then you came down here to heal Pugh. Foster couldn't have liked that."

"Your point?"

"That you're right: I shouldn't have questioned your mettle. I'll even grant that I might have given you cause to side with Foster."

Ethan frowned. "You'd say anything to turn me, to win me over."

"Maybe. That doesn't mean I can't be in earnest."

The creak of old wood and the scrape of boots on the stairs announced an arrival.

"What are you about there, Kaille?"

Foster.

Ethan surged to his feet.

"I ordered you not to heal him."

"He didn't," Selker said. "You'll see as much, if you care to inspect my wounds."

"Are you trying to steal my conjurer?"

The captain forced a smile that wouldn't have convinced anyone. "Yes. Can you blame me?"

Foster sauntered to where Ethan stood, eyeing both of them with suspicion. "And have you succeeded?"

"No. Congratulations, Allen. He's your creature, through and through."

"I believe that remains to be seen." Foster cast a glance Ethan's way. "Leave us."

Ethan and the captain shared a look. Ethan dared do no more. Was he Foster's creature, as Selker said? He wasn't sure he believed it. He felt certain Foster didn't.

With a nod to the first mate, he crossed to the hatch and climbed to the deck. Foster and his men had been busy while Ethan was below.

The surgeon and several other men loyal to the captain had been herded onto the quarterdeck, their hands bound behind their backs, a rope looped around each of their necks. They knelt in a tight cluster, the rope keeping them from moving independently of one another. Foster's men surrounded them, speaking and laughing among themselves, all but ignoring their helpless prisoners. Ethan wondered what Foster had in mind for the men. He shuddered at the possibilities.

Ethan walked to the bow and leaned on the rail, staring out at the ebon ocean and the glittering stars overhead. He had lost track of the time, but he thought dawn couldn't be far off. This night had lasted an eternity.

A scream made him straighten and spin. Others stared at the hatch. A second wail pulled his gaze there as well. The only men below were Foster, the captain, and Pugh. And with Ethan's spell in place, the gunner wouldn't be awake for hours.

"What's he doing to him?" the surgeon demanded over a third scream.

"Nothin' that matters to you," said one of the sailors.

The doctor pressed his lips into a hard line, and he shot an angry scowl at Ethan, as if this were his fault.

Isn't it?

Selker's screams continued intermittently for some time. Even Foster's men began to look uneasy. In time, though, the cries ceased, and Foster returned to the deck, brandishing a brass key for all to see.

"His riches are ours, lads," he said to loud cheers. "It just took a bit of persuasion."

Ethan leaned on the rail once more, his back to Foster and the others. When he heard approaching steps, he knew who had come.

"You don't approve," Foster said.

"My approval or disapproval is irrelevant."

"Aye, it is. But still I want an answer."

Ethan straightened again, faced him. "You command the ship. I'll follow your orders. Does it really matter what I think of your actions?" He spoke the words with as much conviction as he could muster, but within his mind, a question echoed like thunder. *What have I done?*

"Not if you can keep your thoughts to yourself. But your expression gives you away, Kaille. I imagine you must be terrible at cards."

He smiled. Ethan didn't.

Sobering, he said, "I'm captain now. By all rights, you should be my first mate, and I'll gladly designate you as such. But I have to be certain that you can serve me as circumstances require. I can't have you questioning my methods or my orders. And I can't have you sulking like a school boy here at the rails."

Ethan's anger flared. "I'm not sulking. But don't ask me to condone torture."

"I needed information, and I extracted it. I make no apologies for that."

Ethan grinned, hearing in this an echo of Selker's words.

Foster's cheeks reddened. "You find something amusing?"

"Just that you and Selker are more alike than either of you would care to admit."

"Meaning what?"

"What did the captain do to you? Why do you hate him and his men so much?"

"That's not your concern."

"But it is." Ethan swept his hand in a wide gesture. "It's the reason for all of this. I want to understand it."

"This ship should have been mine a long time ago. And now it is. That's all you need to know."

"So this is about greed? Vengeance?"

Foster glared. "It's about justice."

"If you've borne this grudge for so long, why has Selker kept you aboard as first mate?"

"He had no choice. It was a condition of his commission."

Ethan narrowed his eyes. "I don't understand."

"And I have no intention of explaining myself further. I need to know if I can trust you to carry out my orders. I want you to swear loyalty to me, right now."

"Loyalty is earned. You can't just demand it."

Foster stepped closer to him. "Oh, but I can. Do you doubt that any of these other men will do as I ask? Do you doubt that they'll kill you if I order them to?"

"I don't doubt that they would try," Ethan said, with bravado he didn't quite feel.

Foster blinked at this. After a moment, he bobbed his head. "You have some backbone after all. I like that. But keep in mind, I'm not a man you want as an enemy."

"Yes, sir," Ethan said. It occurred to him, though, that Foster wouldn't want him as an enemy either. For now, he kept this to himself.

"Come along then," Foster said, half turning back toward his men. "We have a ship to run."

Ethan followed.

XI

As silver dawn crept into the eastern sky, Foster had several sailors construct in the back of the hold a crude gaol. Those same sailors then led the bound men down into the hold and to the enclosure.

They built a separate space adjacent to the larger pen, this one for Selker and Pugh, both of whom were also bound with ropes around their necks. Foster had yet to administer more lashings to the captain, but dried blood from a lattice of cuts now covered one side of the captain's face, tokens of the torture that had yielded that brass key.

Ethan busied himself with mundane matters—the lines, the sails, the tidiness of the decks—as if he might convince himself that all was as it should be aboard the *Blade*.

Foster, though, had liberated the remaining barrels of rum, perhaps assuming that an inebriated crew would be more pliable. Men drank and laughed and sang. Some slept. Only a few paid attention to the maintenance of the ship, making Ethan's work that much more difficult. The most competent of Foster's men had been ordered below to keep watch on the prisoners. Ethan wasn't yet sure what Foster intended to do with them.

Late in the morning, while Ethan checked the lines again, more for something to do than because of any real concern for their integrity, several sailors climbed through the hatch from below, like ants emerging from a nest. They appeared excited—whispering, chortling, peering over their shoulders at something or someone behind them. Ethan stopped what he was doing to watch, knowing this couldn't herald anything good.

Foster followed them, pulling Selker along with him. Dark, dried blood still masked one side of his face. The flesh around the cuts from Foster's blade had grown swollen and red, further distorting his features. His hands were tied before him, his upper torso still bare. The wounds on his back looked even worse than those on his face.

Foster carried the cat-o'-nine-tails. Several men hurried ahead of him to the aft deck. Two others scrambled down the rat lines bearing empty buckets.

Seeing Foster and the captain, anticipating what must be about to unfold, men from all over the ship converged on the ship's stern. They watched, some shouting their approval, as Foster pushed Selker to the deck and ordered men to tie him to the mast.

The two sailors climbed back over the rails with their buckets full and brought them to the first mate.

Foster dipped the lash in one of the buckets, but then paused, scanning the ship until he spotted Ethan.

"Kaille, come here."

Every man on deck turned his way and stared as he waded through the crowd of men to the aft deck. He didn't know what Foster had in mind for him, but again, he was certain that nothing promising could come of it.

"Don't look so unnerved, Kaille," Foster said, as Ethan joined him by the mast. "I'm not about to ask you to whip the man."

He spoke too loudly. Anyone in the rear half of the *Blade* could hear him. Ethan wanted to tell him to lower his voice, but he didn't dare. He kept silent and waited for whatever was coming.

"I think I know how you'd respond if I did," the first mate went on, in that same carrying voice. "And neither of us wants that." His grin could have rimed the ship's sails. "Quite the opposite. I'm offering you a reprieve of sorts. You don't want to watch this. We both know it. But there are several men below, tasked with watching our prisoners, who do want to see. So you go below and relieve them of that duty." He opened his hands, as if this were the most simple and natural solution to a vexing problem. "Let them come up here, and then you don't have to watch. And we both know that with your . . . your skills, you have little to fear even if those prisoners do get loose."

Ethan glanced around. Men continued to watch him, many now appearing confused, others wary. None of the expressions turned his way bespoke much fellowship or sympathy.

"Aye, sir," he said, the words thick on his tongue. He strode to the hatch, shouldering past sailors with nary a glance backward. He tried to keep his mien neutral, but he seethed.

He understood Foster well enough by now to know that the man did nothing without forethought. The first mate sought to isolate him, to alienate him from those men who had taken the ship, knowing that the others, those still loyal to the captain, already thought him a villain. Clearly, Foster didn't trust him. More than likely, the first mate feared him and the powers he wielded. But he would wish to keep Ethan on a leash, so that he might use him again should the need arise. What better way to do so than to render him friendless and thus utterly dependent on Foster?

And while Ethan was not so desperate as to consider pledging his unqualified loyalty to the first mate, he could not help but admire the shrewdness of Foster's tactic. Alone, without allies in either quarter, he was at the man's mercy, despite his conjuring abilities.

As he made his way to the hatch, he heard Foster say, "Time to continue the lashings, lads!"

Cheers.

"And this time, if he blacks out on us, we'll wake him with a dousing and start again!"

Ethan went below, the hot, stale air hitting him like a fist in the throat. The hold stank of urine and shit, of sweat and the sweet, sick fetor of putrefaction. His arrival prompted stares from the captives and their guards alike.

Friendless. Isolated.

"You're free to go up on deck," he told the three men Foster had assigned to watch the prisoners.

They didn't question the order or hesitate to leave the hold, nor did they say more than, "Aye, sir," as they filed past him. Ethan sensed they had been expecting him. Foster might have prepared them. They left him a pair of pistols, loaded and full-cocked. Of course, if the captain's men managed to get free, two bullets wouldn't be enough to save Ethan's life. He would need a spell or two for that, which was probably the point.

The men in the enclosure considered him with manifest hostility. In the smaller pen to the side, Pugh sat on the floor, his shirt off, his broad frame shining with sweat, the rope at his neck tied to a beam outside the enclosure

"You come to curse us, witch?" asked one of the men.

Pugh bared his teeth, so that he resembled a ghoul. "Everyone knows now," he said.

"There were bound to be questions after I healed you."

The gunner's smile slipped. Some of the men in the other enclosure looked his way, frowns creasing their brows.

"It wasn't me," he said, clearly discomfited. "Foster's made sure we all know."

Ethan nodded. Of course he would.

"But you didn't tell them that I ministered to your wounds," Ethan said, indicating the other prisoners. "That would have made me something less than evil in their eyes."

"You're a traitor. What more do they need to know?"

"Nothing, of course. Telling them everything might complicate matters, make it seem like I'm something more than a devil."

A high scream from above kept Pugh and the others from answering. The master gunner looked up at the ceiling, as if he might see through it to the captain.

"You couldn't stop him?" he asked. "Did you even try?"

"He sent me away," Ethan said. "He doesn't trust me much more than you do."

"You're a witch," said another man. "What do you expect?"

Ethan sat on a barrel and picked up one of the pistols. "Nothing," he said. "I expect nothing."

A second scream pierced the wood overhead. It was followed by laughter and a splash of water, which ran through seams in the deck down into the hold a few feet from where Ethan sat.

"They'll kill him," Pugh said, gazing upward again.

"I know." Ethan breathed the words.

Pugh looked his way. "You can stop them."

"No, I can't. I was able to defeat you last night because I had all those men with me. What I did was meant as a distraction and no more. This would be . . . I can't overcome so many men. They'd kill me, and then they'd turn their attention back to killing him."

Another of the prisoners said, "At least you'd be dead," eliciting laughs from his companions.

Pugh turned to glower at them. "Quiet."

A rustle of discontent went through the enclosure, but the men fell silent.

"Foster cares only for himself," the master gunner said to Ethan.

He had already worked this out for himself. He didn't say as much, though.

"You think he'll give you more gold—"

"I didn't do it for gold."

Pugh arched an eyebrow.

"All right, some of my discontent was sourced in the captain's timorous approach to privateering. But Foster didn't promise me riches."

"No. He made the captain out to be a brute."

Above them, Selker screamed again, weakness and terror in the sound.

"The captain made it all too easy for him. So did you, for that matter."

Pugh's gaze slid away, his mouth twisting.

"Did those men really deserve the lashings you gave them? Did the boy?

"They disobeyed an order. Billy stole the captain's brandy."

"Aye. But thirteen lashes? Fifteen? Is that what you would have done, had you been captain?"

"I'm not," the gunner said. "Selker is, and he commanded me to administer a punishment, as is his prerogative."

"How convenient for you."

"To hell with you!"

"Aye, that seems to be the path I'm on. But I have a feeling I'll see you there."

Pugh opened his mouth to say more, but Ethan stopped him with a sharp wave of the pistol.

"Neither of us has acquitted himself well, Mister Pugh. Indeed, I'd go so far as to say that no one on this bloody ship has any right to be proud of his actions. I judge myself more harshly than you ever could judge me, and I sense that you're as hard on yourself. So let's dispense with the self-righteousness and recriminations. If that's all you have to offer, I'd suggest you hold your tongue."

Several of the sailors looked from Ethan to Pugh, clearly expecting the gunner to respond with equal heat. He didn't. Rather, he stared at the ceiling, waiting for the next scream, wincing when it came.

"Foster won't kill him straight away," Ethan said, giving voice to his thoughts as they came. "He'll want the captain to steep in his humiliation for a time. It may be that in the interval, I can convince him to spare all of your lives."

"Why would you?"

Ethan scowled. "Have you heard nothing of what I've said?"

He didn't wait for a response. He stood, claimed the other pistol, crossed back to the stairs, and sat there. He steadfastly avoided looking in Pugh's direction. Positioned under the hatch, he could hear the vicious crack of the cat-o'-nine-tails, and so was prepared for the cries that followed. He heard as well the laughter, the shouts of "Douse him again!"

As on the day before, fifteen lashes seemed to last an aeon.

When finally the punishment ended—at least for the time being—two men bore the unconscious captain into the hold, Foster following, the cat-o'-nine-tails still in hand. The flayed flesh on Selker's back wept blood, and dark drops fell from the strands of the whip, staining the floor.

The men didn't bother placing Selker in the crude gaol, but instead lay him on the bloodstained blankets that still covered the floor.

"Heal him, Kaille."

Ethan narrowed his eyes. "I thought you didn't want me healing him."

"That was before. I'm not ready for him to die. And I've given you a direct order. Now do it."

Ethan didn't move. "You can't just give him a lashing, allow me to heal him, and then show him the whip again. That's not how conjurings work. Even if I mend his wounds he'll need days to recover, perhaps more. I can't be certain whether he'll survive a second beating on the heels of this first one."

"Then perhaps an experiment is in order." Foster pointed at Pugh. "Bring him onto the deck," he said to the men who had carried Selker.

"That's not—" Ethan stopped himself. He hadn't meant to endanger Pugh, but his intentions wouldn't matter to the first mate, or to the gunner, for that matter.

"Don't do this," he said.

"You're too soft-hearted for your own good." Foster uttered the words with contempt.

Ethan shook his head. "No, I'm not. But we have the ship. So let's put it to use. Let's put them off on the nearest isle, find another vessel to board, and start earning the gold we've been after since we left Boston. That's what this is all about, isn't it? Claiming the gold that Selker was too weak to find for us?"

Foster canted his head and stared, another vague smile on his lips. "You almost convinced me that you mean it."

"I do mean it. This mutiny of yours could well end with nooses around our necks. Unless as a result of it we start sending to the Crown and to our sponsors all the gold they've been expecting. That's the only way we're going to come through this alive. So let's get to it."

"No."

"But—"

"I said no!" Foster's voice echoed in the tight, sour air. "We'll get to that eventually. Because you're right in some of what you say. But this wasn't about gold. Not entirely. Not even mostly." He indicated the prone form of the captain with a jerk of his chin. "This is about him, and about me. And that's all I'm going to say on the matter."

"If it's about you and Selker, then leave Pugh out of it."

Foster had started to turn his back, but he rounded on Ethan again, drawing his pistol from his belt as he did. He aimed the weapon at Ethan's brow, cocked it.

Ethan went still, his gaze fixed on the barrel.

"I swear, Kaille. Another word and I'll splatter your brains through the hold."

"It's all right, lad," Pugh said. "Do as your . . . your captain asks, and heal Mister Selker. I'll be fine."

Foster laughed. "Fine is it? We'll see, Pugh. We'll see." He eyed Ethan for a moment longer, then eased the hammer on his pistol forward, and slipped the flintlock back into his belt. He gestured for the men to follow and returned to the hatch, swinging the cat-o'-nine-tails as he walked. "Bring the gunner."

The two sailors opened Pugh's cage, untied one end of the rope from the wood beam, and led the master gunner out of the hold.

Ethan's hands shook. He had been sure the man would follow through on his threat. And though Foster didn't in this instance, Ethan felt more and more certain that it was only a matter of time before the first mate killed him, or had someone else do it.

He lowered himself to the floor beside the captain. He trembled still, and he let out a breath, his shoulders slumping. But after sitting thus for a few seconds, he shifted onto his knees and placed his hands on Selker's back. Using the blood that covered the man's body, he healed his wounds. These newest lashes, coupled with those from the day before, couldn't help but leave a crosshatch of scars. But he did what he could, and then, because Foster hadn't told him not to, he cut his own forearm and turned his magick to the cuts on Selker's face. Again, his ministrations wouldn't keep the captain from bearing scars for the rest of his days, but he did manage to ease the fever and swelling in those wounds.

All the while, the crack of the cat-o'-nine-tails and grunts of pain from

Pugh reached them through the wood of the deck. Blood dripped through spaces between the planks.

The captive men watched Ethan work his healing spells, some no doubt thinking him a villain, others likely convinced he was a monster, possessed of black talents. None of them spoke a word as he worked, but they did flinch at every impact of the lash. All the while, the glowing ghost who allowed Ethan to access his magick hovered at his shoulder.

The gunner's beating ended before Ethan finished, but no one returned to the hold with Pugh. Ethan feared the gunner might be dead. He heard laughter from above, conversations, even a song or two. He didn't hear the splash of a body hitting water though he listened for it, even as he continued to heal Selker's wounds.

When he'd finished, spent and sweaty, one of the men, whose name Ethan remembered as Josiah Feld, said, "He looks better."

Ethan wiped his brow and nodded to the man.

"Pugh's right. You can help us. With that magick of yours, we could retake the ship."

"There's too many. We'd be killed."

"We're going to die anyway. At the very least we'll be tortured until we wish we was dead. Is that what you want for us?"

"Or are you willin' to throw us to the sharks," another man asked, "if it means savin' your own neck?"

Ethan didn't know this sailor's name.

"I ain't ready to throw in with a witch no matter what he says." That from a third man, with a surname of McCall. Ethan couldn't remember his given name. He should have been better with all these names by now. His inability to recall them didn't speak well of his work as second mate.

"All of you, shut your mouths," Feld said. "He nearly got his head blowed off talking to Foster a minute ago, and it's being a witch that might let him save us."

"I'm not a witch," he muttered, the denial reflexive.

"Then what was that you just did, if it wasn't witchery?"

"A conjuring." He shook his head. "It doesn't matter. What's important is what I told you before. I can't overcome so many men. And since you're vastly outnumbered, we can't prevail in direct combat."

Feld started to object, but Ethan raised a hand, quieting him.

"I'm not saying there's nothing to be done. But . . . but I need you to think. All of you have been aboard longer than I have; you know this ship and her crew in ways I don't. What might we do to even those numbers a bit? How can we win back the support of some of Foster's men?"

They eyed him, some appearing surprised by the question, others clearly wary.

"So you're switching sides, just like that?" asked the man whose name he couldn't remember. "And you expect us to trust you?"

"I'm not—" He bit back what he had intended to say. Was he switching sides? He wasn't certain he had a side anymore. "I'm trying to save lives," he said. "Yours, mine, Pugh's, if he's still alive. And the captain's as well. I never wanted to see anyone killed, or even beaten."

"So you thought your mutiny would be bloodless?" Feld asked. "Were you really that foolish? All mutinies are bloody affairs, but you thought yours would be clean and polite?" He shook his head, laughing bitterly. "You're an idiot."

Ethan didn't bother to argue. He *was* a naif, and a fool, and an idiot, and more. "You're right." He dropped his voice to a whisper. "But now I'm trying to make amends. And I've good reason for wanting to. You said it yourself: Foster came within a hair's breadth of killing me. Next time, he won't hold back. I've no friends on this ship, and our new captain is afraid of me." He eyed the second man. "That may not be the best reason to trust me, but it will have to do for now."

The sailor gave as much of a shrug as the rope around his neck would allow. "Actually, as reasons go, it ain't too bad."

Ethan grinned, and so did the sailor.

"All right, then," Ethan said. "How do we win back Foster's men?"

XII

It didn't take Ethan long to realize that he had asked the wrong question. They didn't need to win back Foster's men. And probably they couldn't. But they could give the sailors cause to doubt the first mate, and to wonder if perhaps they had erred in backing him.

Foster himself proved helpful in this regard.

Mere moments after Ethan and the sailor finished their conversation, the two men who had carried Selker into the hold descended the stairway again, this time carrying the limp form of Mister Pugh. As before, Foster followed them, the ever-present lash still in his hands.

"Thought we'd lost this one," he said, his tone too jaunty. "Would have thrown him overboard if the surgeon hadn't insisted he was still alive." Seeing that Selker remained unconscious, Foster halted, a frown darkening his expression. "Put Pugh on the blanket. And wake him up."

"No," Ethan said. He placed himself between the first mate and the captain. "Wake him now, and subject him to another beating, and you'll kill him."

Foster's expression turned icy. "Not this again, Kaille."

"Take me instead." The man who had been most suspicious of Ethan moved to the front of their unrefined prison. His gaze flicked toward Ethan, but then settled on the first mate. "I'm one of his men. Take me. You can have the captain when he's awake."

"I'm your captain," Foster said.

"Then for all I care, they can lash you, you bloody bastard."

Foster narrowed his gaze. After a moment he flashed a smile Ethan didn't believe. "Fine. Bring him then. He's right, after all. We've plenty of time." To Ethan he said, "This man saved your neck. You should be grateful."

"I am," Ethan said, sharing another glance with the sailor.

"I want Pugh healed. One of them—Selker or the gunner—is next under the lash. I don't care if it kills them."

Foster retreated from the hold, leaving it to the two men he'd followed down to extricate the bold sailor from the rope and gaol.

"What's your name?" Ethan asked, as they led the man past.

"Benjamin Green. Ben."

"I'm sorry, Ben. I didn't mean for this to happen."

"I chose this. Don't forget it. Don't forget us."

Ethan nodded and watched them usher the man up onto the deck. When they were gone, he turned to healing the master gunner, working as quickly as his magick and the man's wounds would allow. Again the glowing ghost watched him, as did the other sailors. Ethan heard the lash falling above, Ben crying out again and again. He knew Foster would keep beating these men as long as he kept healing them, but he couldn't bring himself to withhold his magick, to make these men suffer in the vain hope of thwarting the first mate's designs.

The problem was, though, so long as he was healing them, he couldn't commence his attempt to sway Foster's men. Perhaps this was part of the first mate's plan: to keep him occupied, to use his compassion against him.

At some point he would have to leave a man wounded, at least for a time. But not this one. Not Pugh. Not after the lashing Foster had administered. He could barely bring himself to look at the man's ravaged skin. At the feel of it under his hands, his stomach gave a nasty lurch. Pugh breathed still and Ethan felt certain that he could revive the man. But he was also sure that another beating like this one would end his life.

An idea came to him as he cast his spells. He looked over his shoulder, checking the stairway to the hatch. Seeing no one there, he eyed the men in the gaol.

"If I can keep the captain from waking up for a time," he said, his voice low, "will one of you risk going up in his stead?"

Five of them lifted a hand. Their courage humbled him, and forced him to consider that he had formed his opinion of the captain too quickly. Any man who could inspire such loyalty from his sailors deserved some respect.

He paused in his healing, cut himself, and cast a sleeping spell on Selker. After a moment's thought he did the same to Pugh. It would be hours before Foster could rouse either of them.

By the time Foster and his men returned to the hold with a bloody, dazed Ben, Ethan had mended Pugh's wounds, at least to the extent that he could.

"Wake Selker," Foster said, glowering at Ethan.

"I doubt I can. I've told you, healing magick only does so much. You need to—"

"Yes, I heard you before. Do it."

Ethan shrugged, jostled the captain, called his name, pushed him and pulled him ever more vigorously, shouted for him. To no avail. Selker remained insensate.

Foster scowled. "I take it the same will be true of Pugh."

"I would think."

"Very well." The first mate stepped to the gaol, and scanned the sweaty, begrimed faces before him. "Him," he said at last, pointing to Josiah Feld.

Feld paled, but nodded. He managed to avoid even a glance at Ethan.

Green appeared to be in a good deal of pain, but Ethan didn't think he would suffer too greatly waiting for healing magick. He watched as Foster's men freed Feld from the prison and the common rope. And as they led the sailor past him and toward the hatch, Ethan followed.

"What are you doing?" Foster demanded.

Ethan halted just in front of him, refusing to flinch from his glare. "Joining you on the deck. Is that a problem?"

"I thought you'd want to heal the man we brought down."

"I will, eventually. But you've others to lash in the meantime, and I need a breath of clean air." His pause was brief. "Unless you intend to make a prisoner of me. Or at least try."

Ethan discerned a flicker of apprehension in the man's gray eyes.

"No," Foster said. "I'm surprised is all." A smile stretched his features, his discomfort already gone. "I figured you were too tender-hearted to let the poor man suffer."

"Perhaps you don't know me as well as you thought."

The first mate's smile remained, but doubt clouded his gaze again. He turned, falling in step behind his men. Ethan trailed them. As he neared the stairway, he removed his knife from its sheath and slipped it into his sleeve, where it was concealed but within easy reach.

Stepping onto the deck, Ethan had to squint and shield his eyes against the glare. But he watched Foster and his men, waiting while they stripped Feld and bound him to the mast. The men on deck had cheered earlier in the day, when Selker and Pugh were brought up for their lashings. Few of them cheered now. Many appeared uneasy, darting gazes from Foster's newest victim to those standing around them, and shifting their feet with restless uncertainty.

When at last Feld was on his knees, his back exposed to the sun and that bloodstained cat-o'-nine-tails, Foster took his stance over him and dipped the lash in a nearby bucket.

"What have you done with that brass key?" Ethan asked, stepping forward and pitching his voice to carry over the surf and wind.

Foster had raised the cat, but he lowered it now and faced him.

"What?"

"You found that brass key, and you spoke of the riches in Captain Selker's cabin. What have you done with it? With them?"

Foster eyed the men around him. It seemed their curiosity had been piqued by Ethan's questions.

"They're safe, Kaille."

"From whom, Captain? Or should I say, 'For whom?'"

"I don't like what you're implying."

"No, I don't imagine. Tell me this: We took this ship because we want more gold, because we want to engage more ships." He gestured with an open hand, indicating the mast and its furled sails, the cat-o'-nine-tails, and the watching sailors. "Instead, we're floundering, and you're lashing sailors. How does this further that aim? How does this bring us profit?"

"This is not a matter of profit!" Foster said. "It's a matter of justice."

"No, sir," Ethan said. "Your first beating of the captain might have been a matter of justice. Same with your first punishment of Mister Pugh. But there is no justice in harming that man before you. Or in beating Benjamin Green bloody."

The men around them had gone silent. They might not have been swayed completely by what Ethan had said, but neither were they quick to side with the first mate. Ethan saw their irresolution, and he pounced on it.

"We're long past justice now, Mister Foster. You seek vengeance, for what I don't know. But that man at your feet has done nothing to deserve what you're about to do to him. And when you're done, I'll still be no closer to earning the gold I sought when I came on board."

A few men actually nodded at this.

Contempt twisted Foster's features. "You don't know—"

"I don't care to know," Ethan said, talking over him. "Your feud with Selker means nothing to me. This is a privateering vessel. And I want my gold."

Murmurs of agreement.

"Someone seize him!" Foster said, pointing a rigid finger at Ethan. "We'll see how he endures a beating."

Ethan had anticipated this. The men around him hesitated, Foster's order undone by his own decision to allow rumor of Ethan's powers to spread through the ship.

As the nearest men considered him, he let his blade slide into his grip and slashed it across the underside of his other forearm. As blood welled, he whispered, "*Ignis ex cruore evocatus.*" Fire conjured from blood. The glowing ghost appeared at his side, feet planted, fists on his hips, sunlight streaming through his form.

Ethan made certain not to aim the spell at any man. Rather, he directed it toward a nearby barrel, which burst into flames, the wood crackling and popping. Sailors fell back from it, wide-eyed.

"I can do the same to any man on this ship," he said. "Including you, Foster."

"Then why don't you?"

"Because I don't wish to hurt anyone. As I said, I want my gold. That's all."

He cut himself again, even as the first mate raised the lash to strike. "*Incide ex cruore evocatum.*" A slicing spell. The nine strands of the cat fell to the deck, severed from the plaited thong.

Foster stared at the useless piece of leather he held in his hand. Then he tossed it aside and drew his pistol.

A third gash on Ethan's forearm, a third whispered spell, and Foster dropped his weapon and shook his hand. The pistol discharged when it struck the deck, but the bullet only gouged the wood.

The pistol's barrel glowed red, and smoke rose from its blackened stock.

"I can do this all day," Ethan said. A lie, but he didn't imagine anyone would challenge him. "You wanted me on the *Blade* because I'm a conjurer. We all know it to be true. Now you can live with the consequences of that choice."

"All of you, seize him! He can't use his witchery against every one of us!"

"All of you keep your distance! Or be the first to die."

Even Foster's most trusted followers hesitated.

The first mate's face had gone red with rage, but after several moments he began to laugh. "Good luck sleeping at night, Kaille. You can't stay awake forever. Eventually your vigilance will slacken, and then you'll be ours."

Ethan used another slicing spell to cut the ropes that bound Feld. The man scrambled to his feet, backed away from Foster until he had reached Ethan.

"My thanks," he muttered.

"Can you free the others?"

Feld eyed him, nodded.

"You're outnumbered, Kaille. You're about to begin a war you can't possibly win. Do you honestly believe any of these men would willingly follow Selker again?"

"No, sir, I don't." He cut his hand one last time, and said, *"Dormite ex cruore evocatum."*

Foster staggered, braced a hand against the mast.

"I intend to take the ship for myself," Ethan said, striding forward onto the aft deck. The ghost walked with him.

Foster slipped to his knees, looked up at Ethan, his head lolling. At last, he toppled sideways and moved no more.

"What did you do to him?" one of the men asked.

"I put him to sleep. That's all, you have my word. I'm taking this vessel. No more lashings. No more blood." To Feld he said, "Go below. Release the others, but make it clear to them that there's to be no retribution, no violence."

"What about the captain and Mister Pugh?"

"Let them sleep."

Feld dipped his chin, regarded the sailors around him, and went below. None of Foster's men made any attempt to stop him.

"I won't take orders from a witch," said one sailor.

Ethan didn't see which man spoke the words. But several others nodded their agreement.

"Do you care to fight me, then?"

"Foster was right. You can't stay awake forever."

"I'm a light sleeper. You're welcome to try sneaking up on me, but I'll turn you into a torch before you get near enough to do anything."

Ethan glared at the men, daring any of them to challenge him. But after a few moments he blew out a breath and shook his head. "I'm not looking for a fight," he said. "I'm trying to end the lashings before someone dies. I'm looking for some way to keep all of you from winding up with nooses around your necks."

"Why?"

"Because I was one of you. Because Selker was a poor captain, and Foster is worse. The rest of us deserve better."

The response seemed to take the man by surprise.

"If all of you can agree on someone to captain the ship—someone other than Selker and Foster—I'll relinquish command in his favor. I give you my word."

"Your word as a witch?"

He lifted his chin. "My word as a loyal subject of His Majesty King George II, and as the son of Captain Ellis Kaille of His Majesty's Royal Navy."

XIII

"And that was enough?" Sephira asked, eyebrows arched. "Your word?"

"Aye," he said, refusing to take the bait. "It was enough. They settled on the bosun, Mister Holme, as the ship's newest captain, and I immediately surrendered myself to his custody."

"Wasn't the bosun one of Foster's men?" Kelf asked.

"He was."

"And you trusted him anyway?"

He opened his hands. "It wasn't my choice to make. The men trusted him, and I had vowed to honor their choice. As it turned out, he was the perfect man for this. Foster's men trusted him, and so were willing to follow his orders, even though the first mate had been imprisoned. And though Selker's men were slower to come around, they were so relieved to see Foster imprisoned in the hold, that they were willing to give the bosun a chance. The following day, despite his wounds, Mister Pugh returned to his post as master gunner, which further appeased the captain's men."

"And Selker himself?"

"Yes," Sephira said with her usual purr, her gaze finding Ethan's once more. "Do tell us about the good captain."

"Selker seemed content to grant command of the *Ruby Blade* to Holme. Perhaps he feared that if he reassumed the captaincy, the men would mutiny again. Or maybe his wounds left him craving nothing more than rest." Ethan faltered, remembering a detail that meant little to him at the time, but now caught his attention. He knew it would catch Sephira's as well. "He did insist, though," he finally said, "that he be returned to his cabin."

She acknowledged this with the faintest of smiles.

"And the men agreed to that, too?" the barkeep asked, frowning.

"Holme did. You have to remember, Kelf, the captain had done nothing wrong. He had broken no laws. His punishments, while extreme, were by no means beyond his prerogative as commander of the ship. He was the victim in all of this. And more to your question, his word, and his accusations, would determine the fate of every man who took part in the mutiny. Including Holme."

"And you, Ethan." Again, Sephira made no effort to conceal her amusement.

"Aye. And me."

XIV

After relinquishing command to Holme and surrendering himself to the new captain's authority, Ethan went below. Foster had been placed in the same make-shift gaol he himself had ordered the men to build. Alone in the prison, he sat against a wooden post, a rope around his neck, his wrists and ankles bound as well.

Ben Green and Josiah Feld guarded him, both men armed with blades and pistols.

"Come to join me, Kaille?" Foster asked, eyes shining in the dim, rank hold.

"Aye."

Foster's face fell. Green and Feld shared a glance.

"You're to be put in there?" Feld asked.

"I don't know, honestly. I surrendered to our captain. I'm not certain what I'm supposed to do. But I don't deserve to be up on deck with the rest."

He didn't enter Foster's cell, but he removed his coat and sat on the floor, as if held there by shackles.

Not long after, Holme joined them in the hold.

"What the hell are you doing?" he demanded of Ethan.

"I surrendered mys—"

"I know it. But you're no more guilty of anything than I am, or any of the others for that matter."

"Is that what you're telling yourself, Holme?" Foster asked, sounding smug.

"You shut your mouth. And you," the bosun said, facing Ethan again. "I want you back on deck. You're no different from the rest of us, no more deserving of chains and gaol."

"But I am. I conjured, remember?"

"It doesn't matter. You've—" Holme stopped, eyeing the two guards in turn, and then Foster. "Come with me."

He stalked back to the hatch. When Ethan didn't follow immediately, the bosun waved him over. Ethan stood and crossed to the stairway. Holme led him back onto the deck, and to the larboard rails.

"Look, Kaille," he said, his voice low, "what you did and what I did ain't that different. For that matter, the same can be said of the master rigger and more than fifty men."

"And Foster."

Holme shook his head. "Foster was different, and you know it. He led us, and then he resorted to those lashings. He's going to hang." His voice fell further to a whisper. "There's nothing that can save him. But the rest of us—and you and me in particular—we might be all right. You took the ship back for Selker, and I'm sailing us home to Boston. That should keep them from putting ropes around our necks." He jabbed Ethan's chest with a finger. "But only if you play along. You can't treat yourself as a convict and expect the rest to see you any other way."

Ethan shook his head.

"I'm not asking, Kaille. I'm ordering. You're my first mate now, and you're to comport yourself as such, understand? It's our only hope."

He couldn't defy the man without worsening his own circumstance, and so he agreed and resumed his duties on deck.

But later that day, Selker summoned him to the captain's cabin. It was dark within, the quarters lit only by a pair of candles. The air was warm and still, and it smelled of sweat and the bitter residue of burnt spermaceti. Selker reclined on his bed in a white shirt and breeches.

"Mister Kaille," he said as Ethan entered. He indicated the desk chair.

"Please sit."

"My thanks, Captain. How are you feeling?"

Selker shrugged. "Sore, tired. But I'm alive, and we both know that I have you to thank for that."

"You're kind to say so."

A gossamer smile touched his lips and vanished. "I think we both know better, don't we?"

Ethan lowered his gaze.

"I understand that Holme has made you his first mate."

"Aye, sir."

"And Foster did the same when he took the ship."

He stiffened.

"It's all right. There's no shame in that. Indeed, I wonder if I had been graced with the opportunity to do the same, would we have avoided all this unpleasantness."

"You didn't know me, sir."

"True. I also didn't have that choice. Representatives of the Crown made it clear to me long ago that Foster was to be my first mate. It wasn't my appointment to make."

"Do you know why?" Ethan asked.

"Not in any detail. I know he served aboard a naval vessel, and that by necessity he assumed her captaincy for some time. I never learned why, or why he was never offered another ship. But he was guaranteed this posting for as long as he wanted it. I was stuck with him."

Ethan pondered this, wondering what might have occurred on that other ship.

Selker folded his hands on his belly, and stared at them for several seconds. At last he said, "Holme seems to believe that he can avoid a court-martial simply by piloting the *Blade* back to port. You and I know better."

"Aye, sir."

"You can't avoid one, either."

"I understand."

"The same is true of the master rigger, and a few of Foster's most ardent followers among the crew. I want you to know this, because I feel I owe you candor and time to prepare yourself, perhaps to draft missives to your father and anyone else you should care to tell."

"Thank you, sir."

"I also wish to tell you that I intend to argue for leniency in all cases except that of Allen Foster. He must hang. But I hope to spare you and the others."

"Again, sir, my thanks. That's probably more than we deserve."

"What we deserve and what befalls us are seldom one and the same."

Ethan said nothing, and after a moment Selker looked his way. "That's all, Mister Kaille. You may go."

He stood and stepped to the door. But before he could open it, Selker spoke his name again. Ethan turned.

"For what it might be worth, I'm ashamed of some of my actions. I won't go so far as to say that I brought the mutiny on myself, but I did not acquit myself well. I—I want you to know that I'm aware of this."

"Yes, sir. Thank you, Captain."

XV

"That was the last time we spoke in private," Ethan said, sipping his wine. "But he remained true to his word. He attended my court-martial, and he spoke on my behalf. I would have been executed had he not. As it was, I imagine it was a near thing. A mutineer *and* a witch? To this day, I'm not certain why they didn't put me to death."

"And deny us the pleasure of your wit and charm?" Sephira's voice dripped with irony. "The Admiralty Court's mercy was a gift to us all."

"You saved Selker's life," Kannice said, casting a quick, blazing glower at the empress. "Pugh's as well. And you took back the ship from Foster. You deserved mercy. You deserved better than you got."

"I don't know about that." Ethan rubbed his bad leg, the one he'd nearly lost during his fourteen years as a laboring prisoner on a sugar plantation in Barbados. "I'd say I got just about exactly what I deserved."

Even Kannice wouldn't recognize the phrase. She might not even have known where his thoughts wandered in that moment. For he had paid a price beyond his court-martial, one that pained him at the time more than any other. A slow death that nearly overwhelmed him. Elli.

As Selker suggested that day in his cabin, Ethan sent letters. Two, to be precise. One went to his parents. His mother responded with a missive of her own, the pages filled with sympathy and love and a promise that even his father, angry as he might have been at the moment, would forgive him eventually.

The other letter he mailed to Elli. A confession. He was a conjurer as well as a mutineer. He begged her forgiveness, assured her that he would never cast again, professed his eternal love.

To this day, he could still recall, word for word, passages from her response.

"You do not love me. You never did. There can be no love where there is deception, where faith in a merciful God is sacrificed before the wickedness of black magick. Whatever we shared—what I, in my innocence, believed to be love—was founded on deception, lies layered upon lies. There was no love, and so there can never be again. I want nothing to do with you, ever. You are to write to me no more. Should you ever return to Boston, a fate better than you deserve, you are to stay away from me, from my family, from my home . . .

"Even if I were to believe your professions of love, even if I were to allow that these tears, this ache in my breast, were products of the love I might once have felt for you, I cannot abide lies and evil. God punishes those who sin, as He is punishing you now. I take no pleasure in imagining you today, a wretch, brought low by your fellowship with the Devil. But I am reassured in the righteousness of my own faith. And I am certain that you have got exactly what you deserve."

His love for Elli had long since died, and yet the memory of her words still stung. He wasn't sure why. Perhaps they hewed too closely to his opinion of himself at the time of his incarceration.

"Ethan?" Kannice said, taking his hand, peering into his face.

He brought her hand to his lips. He had found love again, more deeply this time than before. His life was full in ways he never would have thought possible. He'd done well for himself, infinitely better than he deserved. "I'm fine. Really."

"So you say." She kissed his hand in turn.

"Yes, this is all very interesting," Sephira said, sounding anything but interested. "But what about Selker? What more do you know about his fate?"

Ethan shook his head. "Nothing. Not really." Sephira watched him, silent, seeming to know he would say more.

"It was about eight years into my sentence," he went on at last. "We had harvested the cane, but an outbreak of influenza struck the laborers and several of our overseers before the harvest could be taken to port. Usually prisoners weren't permitted to leave the plantation, but the owners were desperate, and by that time I had earned a reputation for being . . . reliable."

"Of course you had," Sephira said. He knew she didn't mean it kindly.

"We made our way to the Town of Saint Michael the following day and met the ship that was to transport the cane. It was there I saw him. Or rather, he saw me, and somehow recognized me through my tattered clothes and gaunt, sunburned features and the limp I'd acquired a few years earlier."

XVI

"Mister Kaille?"

Ethan froze, but didn't turn. He felt the overseers scrutinizing him, no doubt wondering why one of their charges would be known by a free man in this port. They were new to the plantation, as yet unversed in the tales of mutiny and witchery that had accompanied Ethan to this hell of heat and disease and tortuous labor.

"Ethan Kaille, that is you, isn't it?"

By then, Ethan had recognized the voice. He didn't want to turn. He didn't want this encounter. For the first time in his years here—and probably the last—he wished he were back in the prisoner hut on the plantation. He never dreamed that ramshackle, vermin-infested pit could be a haven. But from this man, from this conversation, it would be.

"Gentleman's talkin' to you," said one of the overseers, grinning now, reveling in Ethan's discomposure. "You'll face him, or you'll suffer the consequences."

"There's no need for that," came the voice again. "If he doesn't wish—"

Ethan turned. "It's all right, Captain. Thank you though."

Selker appeared much as he remembered. His face had thinned somewhat, making the scars he still bore from Foster's torture that much more pronounced. He had also developed a paunch. And he no longer wore a powdered wig. His dark hair, pulled back in a loose plait, elongated his features, made him look older, harder. But the dark eyes remained much the same. He wore breeches and a white, sweat-stained shirt. No coat.

He eyed Ethan with concern that bordered on pity. Ethan averted his gaze. He neither desired nor deserved the man's sympathy.

Selker opened his mouth to speak, but hesitated, glancing at the overseers.

"Gentlemen, please give us a moment. I promise you, he won't run off."

The man who had threatened Ethan frowned and drew his flintlock, but he and the other overseer backed off a short distance. They continued to watch Ethan's every movement.

"I didn't want this for you," Selker said. "I argued for leniency."

"I know you did, sir," Ethan said, still not looking him in the eye. "The sentence was fair. It fit the crime."

"The crime perhaps, but not the circumstance."

Ethan lifted a shoulder, watched a sailor struggle to maneuver a barrel of rum off a ship.

"You would prefer that I left you alone, wouldn't you?"

He forced himself to regard the man. There was nothing Selker could do to him, no power he might still wield over Ethan's fate. The worst that could happen to him had become his daily routine, and his misery brought with it a certain bleak freedom.

"Aye, sir, I do."

Selker answered with a grim smile and a nod. "I understand."

Still looking the captain's way, Ethan noticed what he had missed before. Selker held in his hand a small parcel, wrapped in dirty cloth. It could have been a purse, or an object. It appeared to have some heft to it.

Noting the direction of his gaze, Selker gave a self-conscious laugh, and shifted his hand to conceal the parcel behind his back.

"A trifle," he said. "Something I found here in Town of Saint Michael for my daughter."

"I didn't know you had a child."

Selker's expression brightened. "Yes. Just the one for now. She was born . . . well, after you and I knew each other."

"And you've found her a gift."

"That's right."

Ethan didn't think the captain was lying about having a daughter; his joy in speaking of her, even in this limited manner, could not have been feigned. But he knew beyond question that the item Selker held had nothing to do with her. There was value here, and danger.

Envy flared in his chest. Not that he coveted whatever lay beneath that soiled scrap of cloth. But despite his belief that he deserved his fate, he dearly wished he was free to pursue adventure, to live a life of consequence and peril and intrigue. He doubted he ever would again. Even if he survived this place, he felt certain that his years of exploit and excitement were behind him.

"I should leave you," Selker said.

"You should conceal what you're carrying. Even if it is only a trifle for a child, this is not a place to flaunt valued items. Someone is likely to rob you."

Color leeched from Selker's cheeks, and his gaze darted over the lane, alighting at last on the overseers.

"Aye, they might be a threat to you. They're men without conscience or mercy."

"Yes. Yes, of course. Thank you, Mister Kaille." He turned back to Ethan, though this seemed to take some effort. "I wish you well. I—I hope this place doesn't break you."

Ethan straightened, strove for an expression of resolve. "It won't. I had a life before this; I'll have a life after."

"That's the spirit, Kaille. Good for you." He glanced again at the overseers, clutched his parcel a shade closer, and cast a weak smile Ethan's way. "Farewell."

He hurried away, leaving Ethan in the lane. The overseers strode forward and flanked him, the one man still holding his pistol.

"So, who was he?" the man asked.

"A sea captain I once knew."

"Sea captain? Didn't look like much, did he? Had more the look of a customs man, if you ask me."

"There's more to him than his appearance suggests."

"What was that he was carrying?" asked the other man, staring after him with interest.

Ethan shook his head. "Nothing. A trifle for his child."

XVII

Sephira eyed him in the candlelight, irony in the hard gaze. "You truly said that? A trifle for his child?"

"I did."

"Well, loath as I am to admit it, I believe you were right. It did wind up with his child, though I doubt very much that it was a trifle. I think that . . . thing in his hand, whatever it might have been, is what was stolen from the Fowls's home."

"You think, but you don't know."

She acknowledged this with an impatient shrug. "You never heard from him again?"

"No. He died only a few years later. 1758, I believe. He was in the Indies and contracted dysentery . . ." He trailed off.

Sephira was shaking her head, smug as ever. "Selker is alive," she said. "That, at least, is what I've been told."

"By whom?"

"Come now, Ethan, you know better than to ask that. I have sources— on the wharves, among the royals, and—" She waved a hand—"elsewhere."

He leaned back, a chill running through him. "Please tell me he's not in Boston."

"Sadly, he's not. That would be a reunion I'd pay to see. No, the venerable Captain Selker lives far from here, in the Indies, as last reported. I gather he leads a life that even I would find quite comfortable. It would seem he eventually overcame his reluctance to board enemy ships. Or he found some other path to riches."

"And you believe he provided for Lydia as well."

"Why else would she change her name? Why else would she be so reluctant to tell me what was in that chest, even after her husband engaged me to recover their lost property. Rayne Selker has made her a rich woman, and, I would wager, he has done so with ill-gotten wealth."

Ethan could hardly fault her logic. But his thoughts had taken a different turn. "I wonder how his men felt about that."

"She's his daughter. Surely—"

"She's married to a customs man. Privateers wouldn't like that. And who else would have known precisely what to steal?"

He and Sephira stared at each other across the table. After a few seconds a smile crept over her features. Wicked though she was, she could be quite fetching at moments like these.

She stood abruptly. "Thank you, Ethan. I've an idea of where to go from here."

She whirled, took a step toward Nap and Afton.

"Wait," he said, stopping her.

She regarded him over her shoulder, dark curls framing her face.

"I want to come with you."

She raised an eyebrow. "Are you allowed out so late?"

He ignored the question. "You came for my help."

"And you've given it. I have names now."

"You don't know which ones are responsible."

"A small matter."

"You don't know what they look like, nor do you know how to conjure."

Sephira appeared unmoved. "I've overcome such hinderances in the past, and I've done so without you."

"I want my fifty per cent," Ethan said, "and I don't trust you to calculate the share."

He'd hoped to rile her, but her mien remained placid. "I would have thought it was way past your bedtime."

Ethan didn't react any more than she had.

"You're all right with this, Missus Kaille?" Sephira asked, facing Kannice. "Your husband venturing into the lanes at this hour with another woman?"

Kannice crossed her arms over her chest, and raised her chin. "He'll not be with a woman; he'll be with you."

Sephira narrowed her eyes.

"You don't mind?" Ethan asked Kannice, before the Empress could speak again. "Truly?"

"Go," Kannice said. "Find Pugh and whomever else you suspect, and come back to me. It's cold, and I've no intention of sleeping alone."

They shared a smile. Ethan retrieved his flintlock from the upstairs room he and Kannice shared, grabbed his coat from near the door, and shrugged it on. He pulled the door open and waved Sephira out into the night. He followed her directly, stepping in front of her toughs. Light snow still fell from a velvet sky, flakes gleaming with candlelight from nearby windows. A blanket of white covered the city. The wind had stilled. Smoke rose in thin columns from every chimney in sight, the scent of burning wood tinging the frigid air.

"It's a vast waterfront," Sephira said, as they trudged through the snow toward Cornhill. She held her hands in the pockets of her cloak. Already her cheeks had turned pink. "Where shall we begin?"

"Long Wharf," Ethan said. "Or Hancock's. The harbor has started to freeze over. They're among the few that still reach to open water."

She nodded, and they walked on. It didn't take long for Ethan's bad leg to start to ache. The cold was bad enough; fighting through eight inches of snow pained him even more.

"You don't miss this?" Sephira asked.

"The snow, you mean?"

She scowled his way. He grinned.

"Aye," he said after a brief silence. "I miss it. And Kannice has already said that she doesn't mind me working a few inquiries now and then."

"But now and then—"

"That's all I want, Sephira. I'm older than you are, not by a lot, but enough. And those years as a prisoner took a toll. I'm not done in the streets, but as hard as this may be for you to credit, I enjoy my life with Kannice. I enjoy being married, working in the tavern, avoiding beatings from Afton and Gordon and Nap."

The smaller man chuckled behind him.

Ethan lifted a shoulder. "I'm happy. And you should be, too. I'm not competing with you for clients anymore."

"You were never much competition." The words were typical, but she spoke them without enthusiasm, as if reciting lines she knew were expected of her.

In time, they reached Long Wharf and halted at the edge of the lane. A few ships were tied to bollards close in, their hulls trapped by the pale ice that ringed the harbor. Farther out, several other ships bobbed on gentle swells beside the dock. But Ethan saw no one on the wharf itself.

"This would be easier in the morning," he said.

"Come morning they'll be gone. The storm kept them in the city, but with its passing, they can set sail. We have to do this tonight."

"All right. Then what do you suggest?"

She shrugged, as if the answer were obvious. "I'm Sephira Pryce. If I wish to search a ship, there isn't a man in Boston who can stop me."

It must have been nice to carry such confidence, and to know beyond doubt that it was justified.

But he had a better idea.

He whispered. "*Veni ad me.*" Come to me.

"What did you say?"

He shook his head, watched as the glowing form of his spectral guide appeared on the snowy lane, glowing like a newly risen moon. In recent years, Ethan had come to think of the wraith as Uncle Reg, named after the temperamental uncle of whom the ancient figure reminded him.

"Do you remember the men I healed on the *Ruby Blade* all those years ago?"

"Who are you talking to?" Sephira asked, glancing about, a crease in her brow.

"A ghost."

The specter frowned at this. So did she.

"Do you remember them?" he asked again.

Reg nodded.

"Good. One or more of them might be on one of these ships. I'd like you to search for them."

Another nod, and Reg vanished.

"You honestly expect this creature—whom I can't even see—to find the men we're after?"

"I do. And you're not the only one who can't see him. Neither can

Pugh or any of the others."

"And what if there's another conjurer aboard one of these vessels. They would be able to see him, wouldn't they?"

He hadn't considered this. "An interesting thought. A companion for Mariz and me."

Her scowl grew more pronounced.

Moments later, Reg winked into view again just in front of him and shook his head.

"None of them, eh?"

No.

"They're not here," Ethan said, turning from the wharf and starting toward Hancock's in the North End.

"He's certain?" Sephira asked, hurrying after him.

"He seems to be, yes."

She seemed increasingly unhappy with every step they took. She didn't like to rely on magick, he knew. Nor did she like to rely on him.

When they came to Hancock's Wharf, Ethan sent Reg to search again.

Sephira swiped a hand at a snowflake that had alighted on her eyelash. "What if he's wrong? What if he doesn't know them after all these years?"

"If he doesn't, chances are I won't either."

"Well, that's reassuring. I shouldn't have gone to that shabby tavern in the—"

He held up a hand, silencing her. Reg had appeared again. Not where they stood, but out on the wharf. Beside a ship. Ethan pointed.

"He's found someone," he said. "Come along." He looked back at Nap. "Have your pistol ready. Pugh was reputed to be as good with a flintlock as he was with cannon."

Reg waited for them by the vessel, clearly pleased with himself. The ship was a brigantine, not unlike the vessel Rayne Selker had refused to engage so many years ago.

"How many?" Ethan asked him in a whisper.

The specter held up two fingers.

"Pugh?"

He nodded.

"And Green?"

A puzzled look.

"Or Feld, maybe?"

The wraith shrugged.

Even in the darkness, Ethan sensed Sephira's growing impatience with the conversation, which, unable to see the wraith, she couldn't possibly follow.

"McCall, perhaps."

"It doesn't matter!" she said at last. "Based on what you told us in the tavern, I'd wager that the second man will follow Pugh, no matter who he is. You sailors are so respectful of rank. Except when you mutiny, of course."

She was right, notwithstanding the sarcasm.

"Very well," he said. "How do we lure them out?"

"Like this." She glanced at the escutcheon. "Ahoy the *August Star*," she called, in a voice like a pealing bell.

After a few seconds, came the reply, muffled from within the hull. "Ahoy! That the wench I prayed for?"

Laughter.

"This is Sephira Pryce, Empress of the South End. And the man who addressed me so had better hope I never learn his name."

Silence met this.

"I'm looking for a gentleman named Trevor Pugh. I await him here on the dock."

She turned, signaled to Nap and Afton that they should conceal themselves. "You, too," she whispered to Ethan. "He's as likely to recognize you as you are to know him."

He nodded, stepped farther out on the wharf, placing his feet with the care of a house-breaker. Once he was deep enough in the shadow of the next vessel, he drew his knife, pushed up his sleeve, and waited.

It was several minutes before a dark figure finally appeared on the ship's deck. Broad, tall, somewhat rounder in the middle than Pugh had been when aboard the *Ruby Blade*. He appeared to be wearing a coat, which would have increased his bulk, and Ethan thought he wore a Monmouth cap as well.

The man descended the ratlines to the wharf, took a step in Sephira's direction, and halted there. He considered Sephira for a moment, then looked past her, and over his shoulder in Ethan's direction. Ethan kept still, hoping the darkness would conceal him.

"What can I do for you?"

Even at some distance, the sound of that voice, the Welsh tinge in his words, carried Ethan back twenty-five years.

"You know who I am?" Sephira asked, sounding anything but intimidated, despite Pugh's size.

"You gave your name as Pryce. And claimed to be royalty, I believe."

"Sephira Pryce. Empress of the South End is a title bestowed upon me by the generous denizens of our fair city. I'm the most renowned thieftaker in Boston, the only one who has ever really mattered."

Ethan laughed silently in the shadows. That last had been meant for him.

"What would a thieftaker want with me?"

She *tsked*, and shook her head. "I expected more from you, Trevor. I thought for certain you would at least take pride in a theft well-executed. There's no shame in being caught, at least not by me."

He glanced around again before turning back to the rat lines. "You're wasting my time, and unless you care to warm my hammock, I've nothin' to say to you."

"Stay where you are."

He froze.

Ethan assumed she had produced her flintlock, though he couldn't see past Pugh. He cut his forearm. Reg, still standing nearby, watched him, eagerness in the glowing eyes.

"You stole a chest of gold from Missus Lydia Fowls, formerly Miss Lydia Sheed, and before that Lydia Selker. She'd like it back, please."

"Green!"

Ethan saw movement above them, on the *August Star*, and he spoke the first spell that came to mind. "*Pugnus ex cruore evocatus.*" A fist spell to the gut of the man on the ship.

Ethan heard a grunt. He cut himself again and cast a second time, acting on intuition. Moments later, the man on the ship—Ben Green—cried out. Something clattered to the ship's deck, and the report of a pistol echoed across the harbor.

Pugh lunged for Sephira. She fired—a flash of light and another thunderous report. Pugh spun and collapsed to the wharf, clutching his arm. Nap and Afton raced forward. Afton loomed over Pugh. Nap scrambled up the lines to the ship's deck. Ethan heard a muffled crack and another grunt. Green wouldn't be reloading anytime soon.

Ethan walked to where Pugh writhed in the bloodstained snow. Sephira joined him there, pistol hand lowered.

"I might be able to heal that," Ethan said.

Pugh went still, opened his eyes. "Kaille?" he whispered.

Sephira rolled her eyes. "How lovely. A reunion."

"What the hell are you doing here?"

"Ethan used to be a thieftaker as well. Not a very good one, mind you. But competent at least. And he still has his uses."

Again, Ethan had to laugh.

She looked his way. "You don't heal him until we have the chest and its contents in hand. Understood?"

"Of course."

To Pugh, she said, "Where is it?"

"I didn't steal anything," he said, his voice a rasp.

She stepped around him until she reached his bloodied arm. And she kicked the wound with the toe of her boot. Pugh yowled.

"These are new boots, and I hate to see them stained. But I'll keep doing that until you tell me the truth. So shall we try again? Where is the chest you stole from Missus Fowls?"

He glared up at her, saying nothing. After a few moments, she reared back to kick him again.

"No! It's—" He pressed his lips thin, looked away for an instant. "It's on the ship, in the back corner of the hold, in a compartment we use to hide goods from the Customs boys."

"Do you believe him?" Sephira asked Ethan. "Or should I kick him again?"

"It's the truth, damnit!"

"Nap and I will have Green take us to it," Ethan said. "If it's not there, you can always put another bullet in him."

A smile brightened Sephira's face. "Why, Ethan! I'm surprised. Perhaps domestication hasn't softened you so much after all."

He didn't bother to respond, but stepped to the ratlines.

"Thank you, by the way," Sephira called after him. "I believe you saved me from being shot."

He glanced back at her. "A moment of weakness. Not one I'm likely to repeat."

She was still laughing as he swung himself over the rails and onto the deck.

Nap stood with Green, a pistol pressed to the man's back. Blood ran from Green's lip, and he stood slightly hunched, perhaps still feeling the effects of Ethan's fist spell. He remained thin, wiry. His face had aged, and wisps of hair poked out from beneath his cap.

Perhaps fifteen other men had joined them on the deck, drawn, no doubt, by the pistol fire. They stood in a broad arc facing Nap and Green. Several brandished knives, others held loops of rope. Nap appeared alert, though not particularly alarmed.

"What the hell is all this?" one of the men demanded as Ethan halted beside Nap. "Who are you? And who fired those shots?"

"My name's Ethan Kaille. I'm a thieftaker, as is Miss Pryce, who currently has her pistol trained on Trevor Pugh's heart. She's already shot him once; she'll gladly do so again. Pugh and Green are guilty of a crime, and we're here to retrieve what they've stolen."

"And what if we don't let you?"

Ethan shrugged, cut himself again, and whispered a sleep spell. The man before him staggered, reached for the nearest rail. Missing it, he dropped to the deck, fast asleep.

"Anyone else?" Ethan asked. "I don't have to put you to sleep. I can light you on fire instead."

"You're a witch," said another sailor.

"I'm a conjurer."

None of the other men seemed inclined to challenge him.

Ethan cast a quick look at Nap. "We're to take him below." To Green, he said, "You're to retrieve the chest of gold you stole from Captain Selker's daughter and hand it over to us."

Green gaped at him. "It really is you."

"That's right."

"But how—"

"It doesn't matter. You've been caught. Sephira Pryce is Boston's finest thieftaker, and she's tracked you down."

Nap grinned.

They escorted Green below, Nap with his pistol now pressed to the side of the sailor's head, Ethan with his knife in one hand and his own flintlock in the other. There must have been ten more men in the hold, not a full ship's complement, but enough to create problems for Ethan and Nap if they chose to.

Ethan put two more of them to sleep, which dissuaded the others from interfering. In short order, Green had pulled from within the compartment in the hull an oak chest that might have been a foot long, eight inches wide and another eight inches deep. Ethan took it from him, surprised by its heft.

"Should we open it?" Nap asked, eagerness in his gaze.

Ethan looked back at the men. After a moment's hesitation, he unlatched the clasp that held the top of the chest in place, and opened it. Gold and silver gleamed within. Coins, jewelry, cut gems.

"Damn," Nap whispered.

"Aye. Do you think Sephira will return all of it to Missus Fowls, or keep some for herself?"

Nap's cheeks warmed, but he didn't answer.

They left the hold, still dragging Green with them. The men on the ship's deck eyed them with hostility, but let them pass. The man Ethan had hit with his spell remained asleep, curled up in the snow on deck, as peaceful as a child.

Ethan descended to the wharf first, carrying the chest. Green followed. Nap kept his pistol aimed at the sailor as he climbed down. Once Green was on deck, under Ethan's guard, Nap came down as well. Pugh, Afton, and Sephira hadn't moved, though Sephira watched Ethan, clearly interested in the chest.

"Did you look inside?" she asked, sauntering to him.

"Aye. It's a quite a little treasure she has. I have a feeling you'll want a few baubles for yourself."

She smiled. "Maybe. Not much. I do want my fee, after all."

"Our fee."

"Yes, of course. Our fee. Would you care to pick out a trinket for Missus Kaille?"

Ethan handed her the chest. "No, thank you. My half will be plenty. How much is she paying you, by the way?"

Sephira paused, then shrugged. "Twelve pounds."

"Really?"

"I thought about lying to you, but decided against it. You did save my life."

"Yes, let's not speak of that again."

She grinned.

"What about these two?" he asked.

"The sheriff might be interested in them."

"He might. Or we could simply let them go."

Green looked his way, his mouth open in a small "o." Pugh gazed up at him as well.

Sephira regarded them all in turn. "I think I'll leave this to you, Ethan. I'll return this to Mister and Missus Fowls in the morning, and will have your share of the fee brought to the tavern immediately. You have my word."

This once, he said nothing about the reliability of her assurances. He didn't doubt that she would pay him as promised.

She led her toughs away, leaving Ethan alone with Pugh and Green.

Ethan knelt in the snow next to Pugh and bent lower to scrutinize the wound. It bled profusely. Two wounds rather than one. The bullet, it seemed, had passed through the arm.

"I can heal this if you want me to," Ethan said.

Pugh nodded. "Yes, all right." His voice sounded thin, weak.

Ethan placed his hands over the man's bloody arm and muttered a healing spell. At the first touch of magic, Pugh went rigid. But a moment later he exhaled and closed his eyes briefly.

"You're going to let us go?" he asked, as Ethan worked his magick.

"Aye. I've no desire to see you in gaol. But I would like to know why you did it. I thought you would have done anything for Rayne Selker."

"I would have. *We* would have. Once." He shook his head. "Not anymore."

Ethan looked at both men. "What happened?"

"You've met the man," Green said. "What do you think happened?"

He didn't have to ponder the question for long. "He owed you shares."

Green's laugh was bitter. "Owed us implies he meant to pay at some point. He trimmed us, is what he did. We sailed with him for a bunch of years more after the *Blade*. We was even in the know about his 'death,' such as it was, and we worked his new ship for several years more, when he went by Dobbin Crane. He fobbed some other men, but he paid us, so what'd we care?"

"Serves us right," Pugh said.

"Aye, I suppose it does. In any case, one night, about four years ago, we put in to port in Kingston, and some of us, including Trevor and me, we leave the ship for a time, looking for rum and women. When we come back to the wharf, the ship is gone, with nary a word from the captain. We ain't seen him since."

"But you found his daughter," Ethan said.

"That's right. We wasn't gonna do a thing to her. That's not our way. But then we start hearin' tales about all this money she has, and no one knows where it comes from. Except we know, don't we?"

"So you figured that chest was filled with the shares he owed you."

"Stands to reason, don't it?"

Ethan saw a certain logic in what they'd done, and he couldn't say with any certainty that Lydia Fowls deserved that gold more than did these men. By the same token, he couldn't bring himself to justify a house-breaking.

"I didn't know," he said after a lengthy silence.

Pugh frowned up at him. "Of course you didn't."

"No, I mean when I told Sephira I'd help her. I didn't know I was pitting myself against the two of you."

"Would you have done different?" Green asked.

"Maybe. Probably. We sailed together." Which was really all he needed to tell them.

"It's all right, Kaille," Pugh said. "This could have ended worse for us. For me in particular. You've done all right, lad."

Ethan raised an eyebrow. "Lad?"

Pugh laughed, winced, his free hand straying toward his wounded arm.

Ethan completed the healing, and he and Green helped Pugh to his feet.

"If there were a bit more justice in the world, you'd have taken some of that gold from the chest before you hid it."

Green and Pugh exchanged glances, and Pugh smiled again.

"Who's to say we didn't?"

"Well, all right then," Ethan said. "In that case, I won't feel too guilty about taking my share of Sephira's fee."

He shook hands with both men and started away, back to the lane.

"You get that limp while you were a prisoner?" Pugh called after him.

Ethan halted, looked back. "Aye."

The man nodded. "Otherwise it seems you've done all right for yourself."

He considered this for all of a second. "I have. Better than all right, really."

"I'm glad. Take care of yourself, Kaille."

"I will. And you."

Ethan continued on into the North End and toward the Dowsing Rod, navigating the streets by the silver glow of starlight on fresh snow. After a night of hard memories, of poor choices re-examined, and consequences relived, he couldn't help but be grateful to be a free man in Boston, breathing in the clean air of a winter night, and returning to the warmth of his home.

Kannice would be waiting for him, he knew. For reasons surpassing understanding, she loved him, saw him as more than a mutineer and a convict. He was a husband now, a tavern worker as well as a thieftaker. And yes, for ill or good, a conjurer as well.

About the Author

D.B. Jackson/David B. Coe is an award-winning author of historical fiction, epic fantasy, contemporary fantasy, and the occasional media tie-in. His books have been translated into more than a dozen languages. He has a Masters degree and Ph.D. in U.S. history, which have come in handy as he has written the Thieftaker novels and short stories. He and his family live in the mountains of Appalachia.

Visit him at http://www.dbjackson-author.com and http://www.davidbcoe.com.

CPSIA information can be obtained
at www.ICGtesting.com
Printed in the USA
LVOW11s0846010418
571865LV00001B/92/P